D0106046

"Caz Frear has fashioned her second terrific crime thriller . . . a sumptuously unsettling mystery that lives up to all the hype. . . . This is the kind of mystery Agatha Christie would have penned these days if she were still alive. . . . And Kinsella is the best female detective from across the pond since Detective Chief Inspector Jane Tennison of the brilliant Prime Suspect series."

—Jon Land, *Providence Journal*

"Terrific writing and self-deprecating wit."

—*Jersey's Best*, "What Fran's Reading: The 10 Best Books of 2019"

"Caz Frear has done it again. The author of the critically acclaimed bestseller *Sweet Little Lies*, has created another can't miss summer hit. . . . Like its predecessor, this novel is spellbinding from start to finish. Frear effectively combines a family drama with a captivating psychological mystery, while incorporating effective descriptions of police procedurals. Blend all of that with an unpredictable and intelligently witty storyline and you've got a winner."

—*New York Journal of Books*

"Frear has created one of the most engaging characters in the mystery/ thriller genre, and this series is already drawing comparisons to the works of Tana French, who may very well be the best in the business."

—*Book Reporter*

"The second police procedural by this young Brit. Praising her first one, *Sweet Little Lies*, the column dared to predict that this one would be as good or better. Good call, column!"

—*Sullivan County Democrat* (New York)

"The plotting is excellent, and the twisty ending reveals a very surprising murderer. . . . And the ending promises another entry in this very fine series." —*Criminal Element*

"Frear once again excels at creating memorable characters and realistic dialog. . . . Highly recommended for fans of police procedurals with compelling detectives." —*Library Journal*

"The story, characters, and language here immerse readers in a twisty case that involves more than one dysfunctional family." —*Booklist*

PRAISE FOR *SWEET LITTLE LIES*

"A gripping mystery." —*People*

"A dark and smart page-turner." —*New York Times*

"A remarkable debut." —*Minneapolis Star Tribune*

"Frear keeps the reader riveted both to the progression of the case and the complicated truths the investigation exposes. In Cat, she has created a protagonist who is edgy and defensive yet wry and incisive." —*Newark Star-Ledger*

"A gripping mystery starring a fascinating female detective, *Sweet Little Lies* is an exciting debut procedural that will leave readers wanting more from Caz Frear." —*Bustle*

STONE
COLD
HEART

ALSO BY CAZ FREAR

Sweet Little Lies

STONE COLD HEART

A NOVEL

CAZ FREAR

HARPER

NEW YORK • LONDON • TORONTO • SYDNEY

HARPER

Originally published in Great Britain in 2019 by Zaffre.

A hardcover edition of this book was published in 2019 by HarperCollins Publishers.

FIRST HARPER PAPERBACKS EDITION PUBLISHED 2020.

Library of Congress Cataloging-in-Publication Data has been applied for.

ISBN 978-0-06-284990-8 (pbk.)

20 21 22 23 24 LSC 10 9 8 7 6 5 4 3 2 1

For Thomas, Katie & Charlie

*@**MadLou** wishes I'd been choked with my own placenta at birth.*

*@**daveholby2** wonders how I can live with myself.*

I won't dignify Mad Lou with a response, but Dave makes a fair point. You see, I always knew I had it in me to kill someone. Whether I could live with it afterward, now there was the real question.

Because you can kid yourself that you know who you are. You can declare yourself to be a strong person, a weak person, or maybe one of life's middle-grounders, ricocheting between warrior and wimp depending on which side of the bed you got out of. But trust me, until you've seen the light fade from someone's eyes, knowing it was you who flicked the switch, you who crushed their last seconds of hope, then you've got no clue about what strength or weakness means. You've got no idea about the horrors you can learn to live with.

See, ultimately, *life* makes you live with it. Its routines. Its regimes. Its way of pulling you on to the next thing before you've properly evaluated the last.

And fundamentally, nothing changes anyway. The world still turns. Night still follows day. You still stand in supermarket queues, wondering how you always manage to pick the slowest one. You still whine about train fares, phone bills, non-dispensing cash machines.

You still *live.*

And she'd have lived too, if only she'd calmed the fuck down.

1

AUGUST 2017

"Cat, wait . . ."

He knows my name. *How the hell does he know my name?*

I keep moving forward, pretending I haven't heard him over the incessant gurgle of the coffee machines and the insipid soft jazz. I'm nearly at the door now. Just a few more strides and I'll be safely outside, away from Casanova's attention and basking in the scents of a grimy London summer.

Warm beer. Bus diesel. Raindrops hitting hot pavements.

Bliss.

"Hey, Cat, wait a second . . ."

This moment's been looming and I could kick myself for not listening to my gut and taking my custom elsewhere. Actually, I could kick DC Ben Swaines. Swaines has become the worst kind of coffee snob since he started dating a barista from Sydney, and now it's all "earthy" this and "resinous" that, because why use one adjective when you can use three or four?

I don't even drink the damn stuff.

Casanova, owner of The Grindhouse, has been using this as a ruse to flirt with me over the past few weeks, suggesting he whisk me off to Vienna—first class, of course—where the traditional *Fiaker* is bound to convert me, and declaring that "Only sex and a round of golf at Gleneagles" can match the thrill of finding a new single-source coffee bean.

It takes all sorts to make a world, as my mum used to say.

"Please . . . hang on . . ."

He's louder this time. Insistent. It doesn't help that it's late afternoon and The Grindhouse is in the dead zone. There's only me and one end-of-tether granny shoveling goo into a squirming toddler's mouth, so there's no way I can ignore him again without appearing rude or stone deaf. With no other option, I put my game face on and swing around, smiling. He's already walked out from behind the counter and I'm momentarily thrown by the full length of him, as he's been half a human the entire time I've been coming here. Just a floating buff torso in a Ralph Lauren shirt, doling out la-di-da come-ons and caffè macchiatos.

"Oh God, don't tell me." I slap my hand to my forehead. "I've left my card in the machine again, haven't I?"

Could this be my fault? Maybe I've led him on? Maybe he's mistaken forgetfulness for a convoluted form of foreplay?

"No, no, you're fine," he stutters, which in itself is a bit odd. "I just wanted to ask you something. It's rather delicate, really. Can we sit down?"

It's an instruction rather than an invitation and I should absolutely say no. I should have said it weeks ago, in fact. I should have said, "No, I don't want to go to Vienna. I don't want to go anywhere with you. I have a boyfriend who makes my insides flutter" instead of laughing it off with some crack about having lost my passport. But then, I've never been good at out-and-out rejection. It's the people-pleaser in me. It's the same reason I do the coffee run when I don't even drink coffee.

And for that same reason, I reluctantly sit down, giving him a quick aesthetic sweep as I do. I don't know why, but from the other side of the counter I'd never quite appreciated just how striking he is. Coal-black hair. Eyes the color of aged whiskey. Lashes I'd gladly swap mine for. Around early forties, I'd say, with that killer combination of boyish good looks and older-guy knowingness. I doubt he sleeps alone too often. I'd say he's rejected even less.

"So, what can I do for you?" I sound like an overgrown Girl Guide. "Although you'll have to be quick. I can't have the troops' coffee going cold. I've seen people fired for less."

He pauses, clearing his throat. "Well, it's all a bit awkward, and honestly, I'm so sorry to trouble you with it, but it's about my wife, you see. She's been acting rather . . . well, *odd*, I suppose, saying really quite disturbing things. It's completely out of character and, truthfully, I'm starting to worry."

His wife?

The toddler screams and I quickly feign interest, buying myself a few seconds to recalibrate where we're headed now it appears I'm not about to be hit on. Unfortunately, though, there's only so long you can feign interest in the confiscation of a stuffed giraffe and so, reluctantly, I turn back, pasting on a sympathetic smile.

"I'm sorry to hear that. Not sure how I can help, though."

"Well, I'd have thought that's obvious," he says, looking perplexed. "You're the police."

"And how do you know that?"

"Know what?"

"That I'm a police officer." I can wave bye-bye to any future undercover work if my institutionalization's *that* obvious.

"You walk by with that fat chap most days—and he's definitely one. Believe me, if you work near a police station for the best part of ten years, you get to know the signs. The badly fitting suits, the air of importance. They're dead giveaways." His face softens. "Not you, though."

Moving on. "I still don't understand—how does me being a police officer help you with your wife?"

"I need advice, of course."

Instantly I relax, knowing I'll be laughing about this in ten minutes' time. Cracking jokes with the team about the guy who mistook the Metropolitan Police for Marriage Guidance. It's on a par with the fool who asked Parnell—said "fat chap"—to arrest his neighbors because their tree was blocking his Sky dish and he couldn't watch the wrestling.

Still, I'm a professional and so I rustle up an appropriately solemn tone. "Look, I'm sorry you're having problems, I really am, but this isn't a police matter. Surely there's a friend or a family member you can talk to? Or if you're genuinely worried about her mental health, maybe a doctor might . . ."

"A doctor! Worried about *her*?" His laugh is hale and hearty and shot through with malice. "You don't understand. It's not *her* I'm worried about. It's me. She's unstable. She's made threats against me, several times."

This changes things. I won't be dining out on this anytime soon.

"OK, well, threats *are* a police matter. Has she physically threatened you? Because if she has, we take that kind of thing *very* seriously. But you need to go to your local station and make an official complaint. That's my advice."

He circles his thumbs, agitated. "They aren't physical threats. She's too clever for that. She's subtle, you see. Sly. People underestimate her."

"Can you be more specific?"

"Specific?"

I'm cautious of putting words in his mouth but time's ticking on and I've got a tower of witness statements to slog through—a chip shop stabbing on the Caledonian Road where, would you believe it, everyone was too busy buying haddock to notice a murder happening two feet in front of them.

"Well, has she blackmailed you? Damaged your belongings?"

"No, no, nothing like that." His tone says he's frustrated with me. Christ, *I'm* frustrated with me. I feel like I'm missing the subtext here. "It's more that . . . well, she keeps saying she's going to make me suffer, she's going to make me pay. And it's almost every day now. The mood swings. The threats. Is that specific enough for you?"

Specific, yes. Criminal, no—although it's a gray area and it's getting grayer. Words still aren't quite weapons in the eyes of the law, but with new legislation coming through, making someone's life intolerable isn't as tolerated as it once was, and amen to that.

"So what have you got to pay for? Sorry to ask, but context is really important with these kinds of complaints."

He suppresses a smirk that says *take a good guess*. "What can I say? None of us is perfect, Cat. I never claimed to be the world's most honorable husband."

A statement only ever made by the bottom 10 percent.

In that moment, I make a decision: throw him a bone and get the hell out of here. Back to the chaotic safety of Murder Investigation

Team 4's (MIT4) squad room. I'll even buy Swaines one of those fancy-pants coffee machines if it means never having to set foot in here again.

"Look, all I can say is that if it's becoming a daily thing, you might—and I stress *might*—have a case for Controlling and Coercive Behavior." He leans in closer, enthralled—a bit too close and enthralled for my liking; this guy isn't big on personal space. "It's a fairly new offense that addresses emotional abuse within relationships. There isn't much precedent, though, and I'll warn you now, it's very, *very* hard to prove."

"Controlling and Coercive Behavior," he repeats, eyes glinting as he tries the term out for size. "Thank you."

I stand, picking up the now lukewarm coffees. "As I say, I'm not even sure it applies here without knowing more, and it's not my area of expertise, I'm afraid. But speak to someone at your local station, see what they think."

He shakes his head. "No. No, I don't need to speak to anyone else. You've been more than helpful." I'm not sure I have. I'm even less sure I want to be. "And besides, I'm not actually going to make a complaint. I'm not even going to tell her that I've spoken to you. That isn't what this is about." His grin makes my organs shiver. "I'm just safeguarding my position, that's all. Working out what I can threaten her with further down the line if her behavior gets worse."

·This is madness. I only came in for three Café Cubanos and an apricot flapjack.

He walks me to the door, positioning himself in front of the handle. "So what is your area, Cat? Let me guess—I'm thinking murder?"

"Got it in one."

This amuses him. "Really? I was joking. You look far too . . . too sweet to be dealing with murder. It must be the curls—and those freckles, of course." He taps the bridge of my nose, a movement so quick and light that I barely have time to flinch, never mind knee him in the bollocks. "So tell me, how long have you been a police officer?"

"It was my five-year anniversary last week." I tip my head toward the door. "And if I want to make it to six, I really need to get back."

"Wow, five years and you're still doing the coffee run?" He smiles knowingly, although I'm damned if I know what he thinks he knows. "You must be very keen."

And there it is. That posh-bloke entitlement. That ego-driven reflex that assumes I do it because of him.

"You should take this then. In fact, I insist you do, as a thank-you." He reaches behind me to a carved wooden ornament—a black-and-red devil mask, wizened and grotesque. "Wood's the traditional five-year anniversary gift, and I've been meaning to get rid of it anyway. It scares the customers, especially the children. It's antique, though, worth plenty." He holds it in front of his face, amber eyes twinkling through the narrow, jagged slits. "I picked it up on a work trip to Huehuetenango—that's in Guatemala, if you're not familiar. It's supposed to be El Conductor, otherwise known as Lucifer's principal assistant."

I offer a tight smile, dredging my manners up from somewhere. "Thanks, that's really kind of you but I can't take it, I'm afraid. It's against the rules to accept gifts from the public and I'm a real stickler for the rules."

Which is a statement beyond parody, given the lies I've told. The lines I've crossed.

But hey, I never claimed to be the world's most honorable police officer.

Another statement only ever made by the bottom 10 percent.

2

NOVEMBER 2017

Tuesday

It's not until the last ambulance pulls away and the graffiti comes into full view that I realize I've been to Coronation Gardens before. Several times before, in fact. Almost twenty years must have passed since I sat in the living room of number thirty-nine, bashing out "Incy Wincy Spider" on Mrs. Flint's grand piano, and yet still the bleak slogan looms large above the wheelie bins, barely weathered by time at all.

I SEE HUMANS BUT NO HUMANITY

Mrs. Flint must be well-weathered by now. Eighty at least, maybe more. In fact, given she never seemed in the best of health, even back then—pale to the point of translucence with the kind of cough that could strip wallpaper—I think it's fair to assume she's probably dead.

Whereas Naomi Lockhart is definitely dead. And she was only twenty-two.

"Cheery statement, that," says Parnell, zipping up his forensic suit. "Fancy seeing that every time you left the house. Wouldn't exactly put a spring in your step." He tosses me a pair of shoe covers. "Although rather fitting today, I'd say, wouldn't you?"

I grunt in agreement but honestly, I'm not sure. I see humanity running along the entire length of the outer cordon. It's in the sounds of the pensioners, the ones gawping and griping and reminiscing about the days you could leave your front door open and the coppers didn't look like babies. It's in the frowns of the parents, the ones clutching their kids that little bit tighter, promising them extra playtime tonight—a reward they've earned for the simple virtue of being alive. It's in the shrieks of the schoolkids, the little ones laughing at the dog cocking its leg against the wheel of Steele's Audi and the slightly older group shouting, *"Look out, it's the Teletubbies"* as Parnell and I rustle by in our billowing paper suits.

Humanity is everywhere. It shows its face in the very best and the very worst of situations. It's actually quite rare that the sinkhole opens up, sucking away everything that's pure and light and hopeful in its wake.

And when it does, that's when the likes of Murder Investigation Team 4 come in.

Coronation Gardens is a maze of flat-roofed gray bungalows, each one identical and each flanked by a set of high concrete walls that offer much in the way of privacy but little in the way of light, metaphorical or otherwise. Just a dreary little estate on a dreary north London side street about a five-minute walk from the bustle of Turnpike Lane—an area rich with multicultural vibrancy if you listen to estate agents. An area rich in crime and crap shops if you listen to Parnell.

In other words, the type of place you wind up living when your budget is tight and your options are few, which just about sums up most Londoners under thirty.

Although better to have lived here than died here, of course.

"Twenty-two. This is my youngest," I tell Parnell as we idle outside number fifty, waiting to get the nod from the uniform standing sentry. Technically, we should be good to go, but he's under strict instructions from Mo Vickery, our ray-of-sunshine pathologist, to *"let no other bugger in, I don't care if it's the Commissioner or the Archbishop of Canterbury"* and judging from his smacked-arse expression, I'd say he's already experienced Vickery's bark or maybe her bite. There's actually very little to distinguish them. They're both equally spine-chilling.

Parnell's surprised. "Youngest? Twenty-two? Well, aren't you the lucky one. My second case was a six-year-old dumped on a seesaw in

Violet Hill Park. I'll spare you the details, but let's just say I hardly ate for a month. I lost a ton of weight."

He invited the question.

"So how much is it now, then?"

Parnell slides his hands down his noticeably trimmer stomach. "Ten kilos. Not quite Slimmer of the Year, but not bad, eh?"

"Kilos? Only fitness fanatics talk in kilos. Layman's terms, please."

"About a stone and a half then. And I'm not a fitness fanatic, Kinsella, I'm just adopting a healthier lifestyle."

"I know what it's about," I say, trying and failing to keep a straight face. "You failed the fitness test, didn't you?"

"Wrong."

I give him a nudge. "Ah, come on, you can tell me."

"And I'm telling you—I didn't."

I shake my head. "Nah, don't believe you. There's no way you'd be swapping KFC for chia seeds unless *she'd* put you on a health kick."

She. DCI Kate Steele. The woman we happily run through brick walls for and the yardstick I'll never measure up to. Parnell doesn't put her on quite the same pedestal because they go way back; back to when she made the odd cock-up herself, apparently.

Except what I did wasn't a cock-up, it was a deep-dyed cover-up.

"Kate-bloody-Steele had nothing to do with it," insists Parnell. "If you must know, Maggie forced me to go to this Well Man thing at the doctor's. It's like a health check for old farts."

"And what did they say?"

"That I wasn't a well man. Cholesterol through the roof, at risk of diabetes, gout, the works."

"I thought only the upper classes got gout?"

"It's not the gout that worries me, it's the heart failure." He's deadly serious. "I can't be keeling over anytime soon. I've still got kids in short trousers."

"Well you're looking good on it," I say genuinely, although what I mean is he looks better. I'm not sure if Luigi Parnell's ever looked good. Even in his wedding photos, he looks in a mild state of disrepair. "I like the new suit as well. Navy's your color."

"Glad to hear it. It cost nearly six hundred quid."

"Hey, big spender. That's outrageous. I kitted my flat out for less."

"You know what I always say, Kinsella—buy cheap, buy twice."

Buy cheap, buy twice. The dog who chases two rabbits catches neither. Parnell has a saying for everything, and I'd missed them when I'd been seconded to the mayor's office earlier in the year. Admittedly, the hours had been good and the vending machines more reliable, but apart from that it'd been pretty mundane. Just meetings and memos and spreadsheets and blame.

Although no dead twenty-two year olds. Be careful what you wish for.

Vickery appears in the doorway. "Oh, good, it's you pair." I'm tempted to check there isn't someone else behind us—DC Renée Akwa perhaps, because everyone likes Renée, or DS Seth Wakeman, who's generally spared the worst of Vickery's scorn on account of the fact that they both studied at Oxford.

"Nice to be wanted, Mo." Parnell gingerly steps forward. "Can we?"

"You can." Vickery edges aside. "I was worried it would be that Flowers chap again. Nothing against him per se, but he's the size of a small continent and our crime scene, as you can see, is not."

The door leads us straight into a drab pocket-kitchen, less than a hundred square feet and cluttered with cupboards and various electrical appliances that look like they'd need a good kick to get them started.

It's further cluttered, of course, by the body of Naomi Lockhart.

Long, lilac hair, glittery eye makeup, pretty; the type of body that trash-mags insist on calling "curvy," meaning she looks nourished and normal and probably north of a size ten. She's lying on her back with her silver smock dress bunched high around her thighs. Her left arm is twisted upward while the other lolls heavy by her side, and around her wrist there's a charm bracelet—ten pink beads spell out the word *DISCOBUNNY.* Her toenails are painted spearmint. Her hands are bagged, tagged and sealed.

Vickery stares down at her dead charge. "Nasty business."

"Aren't they all?" says Parnell. "So what've we got?"

We drop to our haunches with varying degrees of ease—Parnell's stiff joints are a crime-scene staple.

"Cause of death is *almost* certain to be craniocerebral trauma—a sharp-force trauma to the back of the skull which is *almost* certain to have been caused by this." She points to the bloodied, blade-sharp corner of a small glass cabinet. "You can call in the blood pattern experts if you wish—that's Steele's call, her budget—but I'm sure even DC Kinsella here is capable of reconstructing what's *almost* certainly happened." I give her my most vacant look, happy for her to spell it out. "Your victim's head was slammed into this sharp edge at considerable force, which caused her to slump to the floor and eventually bleed out. I can't say how quickly just yet, although I will say that the smell of alcohol is still quite prevalent around the body and, as you may or may not know, alcohol thins the blood, which increases blood loss, so we must take that into account."

There's a knife block by the microwave and a pair of scissors by the sink. Easier weapons of choice, it strikes me. "No chance it was an accident? She slipped and fell backward?"

I have to ask. Parnell once had a case where it turned out the victim had been doing squat jumps in front of a YouTube video when she slipped and bashed her head off the fireplace. Life declared extinct, and all in the pursuit of a thigh-gap. Tragic doesn't even come close.

"No, no, of course not," says Vickery. *Of course.* "The sheer force shown by the amount of damage to the skull suggests foul play, as do the faint marks around her throat and under her chin, suggestive of it being held and pushed back." She prods Naomi's face with her penlight—dispassionate, like every good pathologist should be. "Additionally, this mild bruising to her right cheek suggests she was involved in some sort of altercation shortly prior to death. Slapped, I'd say, as the bruises are parallel and linear, which is typical of an open hand, rather than a fist or an object."

I catch Parnell's eye. We're both thinking the same. One: a woman's more likely to slap—it's not scientific gospel but it's a fairly sound bet. Two: a slap is usually a knee-jerk expression of anger rather than any real attempt to cause harm, meaning that if it was a man, it's probably someone who knew Naomi—and liked her—in their own cretinous, fucked-up way.

Put another way, this was personal. Or that's how it feels, anyway, and "feels" are all we have in the earliest stages of a case.

"Sexual assault?" asks Parnell.

"Nothing to suggest that, *at the moment*." Meaning *wait for the postmortem, you tedious little man*. "Obviously her dress is hitched up but that could just be the way she fell. Her underwear looks intact and there's no external bruising."

"Anything under her fingernails?"

"Nothing of note, at first glance. There's certainly no superficial damage to her nails or hands."

Which means it wasn't a fair fight, and we enter a whole new level of depressing.

"Time of death?" I ask.

Vickery stands up. "I understand from DCI Steele that she was last seen at a party on Saturday evening, exact time yet to be established. Given there's some slight softening of the muscles, post-rigor, I'd estimate she died within roughly twelve hours of leaving that party— Sunday morning at the very latest." Something catches her eye. "Ah, DCI Steele, just the woman. I've brought them up to speed, after a fashion, and now I'll take my leave."

Steele's joined by the Crime Scene Manager, who's introduced as "The Mighty Bal Sangha," despite being somewhat un-mighty in stature. Only a forehead taller than Steele, who's practically pint-sized in her crime-scene flats. Sangha nods at Parnell, who seems to know him, and gives me a tiny salute. We wait a few minutes, making *isn't it awful?* small talk while Vickery packs up and ships out without so much as a goodbye.

When I'm sure she's out of earshot, I say to Steele, "Permission to ask a question without feeling like a half-wit."

"Permission more or less granted."

"Who found her?"

"Her housemate. Name's Kieran Drake, thirty-four. He's a personal trainer—looks the type. Renée's getting a full statement now but, in a nutshell, he's been away since Saturday lunchtime, 'partying' with mates over Hounslow way. He got back around one thirty p.m.

today. He had to come back as he takes a HIIT class on a Tuesday evening, whatever that is."

"High-intensity interval training," interjects Parnell, all pleased with himself. "It's really popular. The kids think it's a new thing but Sebastian Coe swore by it."

"Yeah, thanks for that, Lu, very informative." Steele's face says it all and she's not alone in struggling with this new version of Parnell. Thing is, while we all accept that what he's doing is a Good Thing, most of us were pretty fond of the old version, the ten-kilos-heavier version who ate pork pies for breakfast and bought doughnuts *"because it's Tuesday."* "Anyway, Drake says the last time he saw Naomi—who's Australian, by the way—was Saturday morning. They didn't speak much because she was doing chores, vacuuming, changing sheets, what have you. I'm not quite sure what the story is between them; he's a fair bit older, which is weird for your average houseshare, right? He seems genuine, though. Shaken up, shocked—puking, according to Renée."

"But?" I'm hardwired to Steele's tone by now.

"*But* there's no signs of a break-in. So she either knew her killer and let them in, they let themselves in, *or* they were already inside. A housemate fits every scenario."

"Well, yeah, but if he was 'partying in Hounslow' there'll be witnesses galore, surely?"

Steele shifts out of the way as a trio of CSIs troop past carrying lighting equipment. "I take your point. But unless there's a credible witness who was glued to him for the whole of Saturday night and Sunday morning, Drake's still a potential suspect. He has to be given the lack of a break-in, and more importantly, given—"

I know what's coming. It's Class 101 at Hendon. The police training equivalent of learning to count to ten. "Yeah, yeah, given the fact that the most obvious suspect is usually the right one."

Parnell turns to me. "Listen, I know you turn your nose up at anything beyond Zone 3, but Hounslow's not exactly Timbuktu. A couple of hours to slip away unnoticed, that's all he'd have needed."

"No decent prints off the doorbell," says The Mighty Bal Sangha, giving more credence to the idea of someone with a key. "It could have been a wipe-down job but it's not unusual for them to smudge, so there's no way of telling. I doubt we'll get a lot from outside either. It rained on Sunday, remember."

"Rained" is putting it mildly. It had lashed ferociously, like a vengeance from the gods. Aiden and I had been walking off a Sunday roast around Victoria Park, and we'd taken shelter in the bandstand. It might have been romantic if it hadn't been for the twenty other people with the exact same idea.

"Anything off her body?" I ask Sangha.

"We've lifted a few foreign hairs. A couple from the bed too."

"Her phone?"

Steele shakes her head. "We'll search properly once these folk finish up, but . . ."

"Forget it," says Parnell. "A twenty-two-year-old girl? She'd never be more than three feet from her phone. It'd be somewhere obvious if we were going to find it."

"If it's gone, at least it implies there's something on there that links her to her killer," I suggest. "Phone records should shed some light."

"Loving the positive mental attitude," says Steele. "That fella of yours is certainly doing the trick."

I roll my eyes, a teenage *whatever*. "Here, Vickery mentioned she was at a party on Saturday evening. How do we know this? Drake?"

"Mmm, I was coming to that. When they ran her name through the system"—*they* probably being Ben Swaines, who rarely ventures far from the office, poor lad—"they discovered a 101 call had been made by a colleague who was concerned when Naomi didn't turn up for work for the second day in a row. She's the one who mentioned there'd been some sort of employee bash at their boss's house." She taps at her phone. "The boss's name is Kirstie Connor. She runs a recruitment firm in town."

"So no one followed up the call?" asks Parnell.

Steele winces. "Apparently not."

Not that it'd have made any difference; Naomi was long dead by then. All it would have done was bring us to this exact same point about three hours earlier, but it's this kind of detail that gets the tabloids twitching. *Concerned colleague palmed off amid further police cuts.* I can see the headlines now.

Steele sees them too. "Look, that's someone else's shitstorm, thank God, but for what it's worth, things were done by the book. Naomi was only a temp. She was paid weekly. She had no strong ties to the firm and there were no red flags. No depression the colleague was aware of. She'd have been deemed fairly low risk. I know it's not great but, well, we are where we are."

Corporate-speak for "we're just going to have to suck it up."

With the arrival of yet another CSI in the kitchen, the room's starting to resemble a teenage house party and the urge to move somewhere, anywhere, kicks in. "OK if we look around Naomi's room?" I ask Sangha, meaning me and Parnell. "Just to get a feel for her?"

Sangha hesitates, then nods.

I chivy Parnell out of the room and down a short, Artexed hallway where the walls are stained with nicotine and the carpet's the color of slush. There's only two rooms off the hall—his and hers bedrooms, it turns out—which means the bathroom must be off the kitchen and there's no living room or communal space at all. A one-bedroomed property reconfigured into two.

Welcome to the London rental market in 2017.

Naomi's room is the larger of the two, probably the old living room as there's a three-bar fire still mounted to the wall and a dent in the carpet where the sofa used to be. My first thought is that whatever she was paying, it was definitely too much, because while it's spotless and tidy and furnished with all the basics you'd expect to see—a wardrobe, a bed, a bedside table, and a desk—the bed's a lousy single, the wardrobe's missing one door, and there's a thick wedge of cardboard propping up the not-quite-level desk.

The bedside table's pretty, though. Cheap but ornate. Odds on, she bought that herself.

So she'd tried to make it homey, habitable at least, and I'm not sure if it's the sparkly sunshine-print duvet or the Mickey Mouse ears pinned high above the bed that gets me, but there's a lump in my throat that's proving hard to dissolve.

Not so long ago it was the blood that floored me: the wounds, the mess, the indignity of picking over someone's body when you can still smell their perfume, but increasingly now it's the victim's *stuff* that really stings. Their tickets and trinkets and clothes strewn across the floor. After all, it's their stuff that holds the essence of who they were and what they loved. Their body, by the time we're acquainted with it, just holds their organs.

"She liked her music," says Parnell, staring at a sea of ticket stubs tacked to a corkboard.

Rihanna, Little Mix, Ariana Grande, Adele.

A girl's girl.

"This is heartbreaking," I say. "She was so bloody young."

"Jesus, Kinsella, you might be a bit of an old soul but you aren't exactly ancient yourself."

"Yeah, but this job ages you. It's like dog years—I reckon I'm about ninety-seven in cop years. And anyway, there's young and there's *young*." I point to the giant poster dominating the back wall. "For a start, I don't think *The greater the storm, the bigger the rainbow*."

"Don't care, twenty-six is still an infant."

"Twenty-seven next week. That's proper late twenties."

"Oooh, dicey age. Didn't a load of famous people die at twenty-seven? Hendrix, Joplin, Morrison, Cobain, Winehouse. All the greats."

"Kinsella'll be all right then." Steele's standing in the doorway.

"Too right I will. They all died from wild excess. I'm as boring as they come, these days."

"That'll be Mr. X," says Parnell, winking at Steele. "He's a calming influence, whoever he is."

Mr. X. Aiden Doyle. That my lovely, open book of a boyfriend should be shrouded in so much mystery would be laughable if it wasn't so vital.

I stare at Naomi's messy bed, finding a reason to change the subject. "Hey, Boss, didn't the housemate say she changed her sheets on Saturday morning? You'd think if she'd changed them she'd have made the bed. It's a good guess anyway, the rest of the room suggests someone fairly tidy."

"Your point?"

"I'm just saying that even though she obviously wound up back in the kitchen, she must have got into bed on Saturday night at some point."

"She's not dressed for bed," counters Parnell. "I'm no expert on women's fashion, but that silver thing she's wearing isn't a nightdress, is it?"

I pull a face. "Do me a favor, Sarge. I'm always falling into bed fully clothed when I've had a few."

"You do surprise me." Parnell's in peak work-dad mode, naggy and disapproving.

Which reminds me, it's my turn to call my *actual* dad this Sunday. Five to ten minutes of banal, awkward chitchat and toxic codependency.

Still, it keeps my sister, Jacqui, happy, and that makes both our lives easier.

Not that we deserve an easy life. Not after what we did.

Steele cuts across my thoughts. "OK, so she went to bed when she got home—what does that tell us?"

"Not sure." I gave up trying to bluff Steele a long time ago. "The clean sheets tell us something, though."

"Go on."

"If they were fresh on Saturday morning, there's a good chance the hairs they've lifted were shed Saturday night."

Steele nods, cautiously. "Mmm, possibly, but at the risk of sounding like a devil from the dark side . . ." The defense, she means—Steele's thinking about a conviction before we've even interviewed a suspect. "There's always the dreaded transference to contend with, and juries don't convict on the basis of a 'good chance.'"

"I know, I know. But a lover boy works as a theory, though—she changed the sheets on Saturday morning because she was expecting a special someone Saturday night?"

Steele smirks. "Is that the only time you change your sheets? When you're expecting a night of passion?"

"Every other week, actually. And anyone who says they do it more often is either a liar or a germ freak."

"Or has a cleaner." Parnell grins at me, although the barb's aimed at Steele.

She takes it in good humor. "Yeah, OK, I've betrayed my working-class roots. Shoot me for working seventy hours a week and not having time to wipe my arse, never mind mop my floors." She rolls up her sleeve to check her watch—a rose gold TAG that I've fantasized about stealing. "Talking of time, we need to get going with the real work, folks. I've got The Feast and The Famine on fast-track house-to-house." Aka burly DS Flowers and bony DC Cooke. "I want you pair to get over to this boss-lady, Kirstie Connor. See what went on at this party. Who Naomi was mingling with, anything else she thinks we should know . . ."

In other words, forget "transference" and "sharp-force trauma" and all the other things every good detective needs to understand but not obsess over, and instead concentrate on what we do best. On what gets us up in the morning. Or, more truthfully, what keeps us awake at night.

People. Suspects. Witnesses.

Lies.

Or in the words of *our* boss-lady—"*Real* work."

3

Money. Politics. Sex. Religion. Four topics it's generally wise to steer well clear of, but if you're talking to a Londoner, add another to the mix.

Postcodes.

I admit I'm on my soapbox.

"This place always seems just that little bit *too* pleased with itself," I say as we inch along Muswell Hill Broadway, battling the last of the school pickups in their 4x4s and family estates. "Like it's looking down its nose at the rest of north London. You know what I mean, right? I *know* you know what I mean."

In fairness, Muswell Hill, the perfect urban enclave just a ten-minute drive from its less-than-perfect cousin, Turnpike Lane, can't do anything but look down. Despite being miles from the bright lights and the bedlam of Zone 1, its location on top of one of London's highest peaks makes it the perfect viewing platform for everything the capital has to offer. The bridges, the spires, the skyscrapers, the filth. Muswell Hill surveys all the madness without ever having to join in. It doesn't even have a tube station, which only adds to the air of exclusivity.

"Ah, you're only jealous," says Parnell, glaring at the traffic lights as if iron will alone might make them turn green. "We've got friends here and they love the villagey feel, the sense of community. They reckon it's nigh on impossible to pop out for a pint of milk without bumping into at least five people you know. Don't you think that's nice? Christ, the only time I speak to anyone on our street is when they've signed for a parcel or there's a car alarm going off." The lights finally change and we trickle through slowly. "Yep, I think we could all learn a lesson from the good folk of Muswell Hill. People should say hello. They should look out for each other more."

I know he's right, but his pitch is wasted on me. I love the anonymity of London, the idea that you can drop off the radar and the city doesn't shed one tear.

"I bet your friends aren't coppers. You couldn't rent a garage around here on our salary."

"A garage! We'd struggle to rent an allotment, kiddo."

I smile. "Ah well, that's the price you pay for good schools and artisan bakeries."

"That's the price you pay for safety, you mean." He lifts his hand off the gearstick, holding up four pudgy fingers. "That's how many stabbings around my way last month. All kids as well, one of them only fourteen. I'm telling you, if I won the lottery . . . It's a £14 million rollover tomorrow, by the way."

"Hey, half of that's mine, remember." Parnell insists on us having our own micro-syndicate. He claims it's not worth hitting the jackpot if we have to split it across the whole squad. "Anyway, who said Muswell Hill's safe? What about Dennis Nilsen? Didn't he live around here?"

We turn left. Parnell squints through the driver's window, trying to make out the house numbers. "Christ, that was nearly forty years ago, Kinsella. I think they've managed to stay serial-killer-free since then." He nudges the brake. "Righto, here we are."

"Ah, but how do we know that, Sarge? They walk among us, isn't that what the profilers say about serial killers?" I jerk a thumb toward 22 West Pool Avenue. "You never know, we could be about to meet one."

Parnell digs a pair of tweezers from the side pocket of the door. "In that case, I better do something about my nose hair. They're notoriously fastidious, serial killers . . ."

While Muswell Hill is undeniably snazzy with its bars and its pop-ups and its urban art gallery spaces, 22 West Pool Avenue categorically is not. Like many others, the Connors seem to have followed the age-old adage that it's better to buy the worst house in the best area, because there's certainly nothing snazzy about loose guttering and disintegrating front walls. Shabby, would be the better word. Shabby without the chic. A blight on an otherwise tidy terrace of Edwardian redbrick houses.

"Bloody hell, that's awful. You'd better come in."

Standing on his porch, wearing yellow Lycra cycling gear and a knocked-sideways expression, it's a wiry Marcus Connor who rides the first wave of bemused shock. We follow him down the hall into a half-finished kitchen extension that smells of baked potatoes and melting cheese, a heady blend when you haven't eaten since breakfast, and then only a Snickers. A teenage girl and her elder doppelgänger, presumably her mum, are perched on stools next to a breakfast bar. Both have the kind of surfy-blond hair that instantly reminds me of my sister, Jacqui, and the girl's got Jacqui's manner too—all hoppy and curious, nose stuck high, as though sniffing out how she benefits from our arrival before she even knows who we are or why we're here.

The woman's the exact opposite. She turns to face us but barely reacts, simply waiting to be introduced with a stillness that borders on freaky.

"Um, this is my sister, Rachel, and my niece, Clara. Guys, this is the police." Marcus rubs a hand over his scalp. "Jesus this is terrible. I'll go and get Kirstie. She's outside with Danny."

It's dark now but through the window I can just about catch the blur of a small child running in aimless circles on a trampoline.

Parnell gives a solemn nod to the women. "DS Luigi Parnell, and this is DC Cat Kinsella."

"What's happened?" asks the sister, concerned but still calm as a millpond.

"We'll explain in a minute, Mrs? Miss?"

"Mrs. Madden, but Rachel's fine."

The niece, Clara, aims a cocksure grin at Parnell. "Hey, not being funny, but you don't look like a Luigi."

Parnell offers a small smile. "I was born the night Italy won the Eurovision Song Contest. My mum had them in a two-pound sweepstake, so she thought it was a good omen. Two pounds was a lot of money back then."

I've heard a few variations on this. There's one about an opera singer, another about an ice cream man. Steele once told me he was born plain old Lewis Parnell but he changed it for a dare, although she might have been winding me up.

The back door opens and Kirstie Connor flies in, a hurtling mass of corkscrew curls and artfully mismatched prints. For a split second I think she might attack us. It's not entirely unheard of. "Don't shoot the messenger" often goes out the window when a sudden death's involved. Mercifully, she pulls up with about a foot to go, her voice shaky but strident.

"Marcus said Naomi's dead! That can't be right, surely?"

Marcus rolls his eyes at the suggestion he might have picked it up wrong.

"Someone's dead!" says Rachel, eyebrows hitting the skylight.

"Who's Naomi?" asks Clara.

Kirstie rails over the top of them. "How can she be dead? I mean, when . . . What the fuck happened?"

Parnell takes the lead. "We can't say too much at the moment but we believe she was murdered, Mrs. Connor. And as you were among the last people to have seen her, we need to—"

"I haven't seen her since Saturday," she says, instantly prickly.

"We think she's been dead a few days."

"Oh my God." She grabs the edge of the sink to steady herself. "Oh my fucking God."

"I'll make some sweet tea." The sister, Rachel, heads for the kettle, stopping momentarily to turn the oven down, clearly at home in her brother's half kitchen. She's tall, model-tall, and yet there's such a slightness about her, such a timidity to her movements, you could almost forget she was there. A mere incidental presence.

"Fuck tea, Rach." Nothing timid about Kirstie Connor. "Have we got any brandy? Jesus! *Murdered?*"

Marcus Connor rummages in a cupboard, emerging empty-handed and, to my mind, disproportionately angry given the circumstances. "There was a fifty-quid bottle of brandy in here on Saturday, Kirst. Those thieving little shits!"

Tea it is, then.

Parnell leans against the fridge. The words D-O-G and E-G-G are spelled out on either side of his head in alphabet magnets. "We understand Naomi attended a party here on Saturday?"

"It wasn't a party," says Kirstie, all defensive. "I made a big pot of chili and we let off a few fireworks, that was all. We're not at the fancy work-do stage yet, but it's been a tough few months and I wanted to do something."

I jump in. "So when did you last see Naomi?"

It's a simple enough question, but she looks ready for combat; arms crossed, chin high. "Look, I don't remember. I was a bit pissed, if you must know. It's all a bit of a haze."

"A haze?" scoffs Marcus. "A black hole, more like. You were out of it."

"I wasn't *that* bad."

"Oh no? So you remember getting in the shower with your jeans on? You remember calling Rachel and comparing Joseph to Hitler?"

I normally can't stand drunk-shamers, but Kirstie Connor's abrasive enough sober—she must be a nightmare after a skinful. "So is your memory any clearer, Mr. Connor?"

"If you're asking when I last saw her, no idea. Kirstie's crowd bailed at around tenish—you better believe I was watching the clock. I assume Naomi left with them."

"How did she seem that day?" asks Parnell.

"Well, I don't know how she usually is, but she seemed nice enough, polite, you know? She'd brought a potato salad, which was more than the other leeches had." I glance over at Kirstie, who's quietly seething. "That's all I can tell you, though. I didn't really speak to her, other than 'hello.' Kirstie's crowd were mainly in here, or smoking in the garden, and I was in the living room with Rachel and Joseph—that's my brother-in-law."

"And me," adds Clara, keen to stamp her place in history. "For an hour or so, anyway."

"Look, she seemed fine, completely normal," Kirstie insists. "Not that I talked to her much either. I was flitting between everyone, keeping the drinks flowing, and she was . . . I don't know how to put it . . . quite aloof, I suppose. If you didn't talk to her, she didn't talk to you, that type of girl."

I give her a thin smile. "So maybe shy, rather than aloof?"

"Maybe." She looks at me, puzzled, as though she's never considered the difference. "If I'm honest, she didn't fit the team culture very well. But I couldn't exactly invite everyone else and not her, could I?"

"Were there problems with anyone at work?" asks Parnell.

"God, no. She was a bit boring, but I wouldn't say anyone disliked her."

"How long had she worked for you?"

She drags her hand across her forehead. Her pointed nails are bright coral. "Oh hell, I'm terrible with dates, but it can't have been more than nine, ten weeks. She was just a temp. She had a one-year visa, I think."

I pick things up again. "What was her job? Actually, what's *your* job?"

"I run a recruitment firm—Elite Fashion. We partner with elite brands to find them the best talent in the marketplace, for a fee, of course. Naomi's kind of a PA—*was*, I mean. Jesus! She did a bit of finance, diary management, invoicing. Everything I'm bad at, basically."

"Do you know where she worked before? Or the names of any friends? We need to build as broad a picture as possible."

"No idea about friends." She pauses briefly. "I'm sure she mentioned seeing someone, although I've no idea who. As for places of work, check with the agency but I think this was her first job in the UK. Fresh off the boat, as they say. I've hired her type before—they're hungry, hard-working."

"Cheaper, more compliant," adds Marcus.

Kirstie stalks to the kitchen door, flinging it open theatrically. "Oh, just get lost, Marcus. We all know you didn't want the party in the first place, but you can hardly blame me for *this*, so why don't you take your snide comments and piss off out on your precious bike again. Or here's a novel idea: Why don't you do something useful for a change, like taking Danny for a haircut? He looks like a tramp."

Marcus hightails it for the door, delighted to have an out.

Parnell isn't finished, though. "Not yet, I'm afraid, Mr. Connor. Why didn't you want the party?"

Marcus pauses in the doorway, the top of his head nearly brushing the frame. Judging by him and his sister, the Connor parents must have been giants.

"Call me Marcus, please." True to form, most people under sixty offer their Christian names within minutes. Kirstie Connor hasn't—although this isn't significant, just irritating. "I'll tell you why I didn't want it. A fortnight ago, our son had his fourth birthday party. We had his whole nursery class around—party poppers, Nerf guns, e-numbers, the lot. And the house was *still* left in a better state than when Kirstie's lot trooped out." Parnell nods his understanding, which only encourages him. "Look, I'm not usually quick to judge, but they're just a load of gobby toffs who can survive on the pittance Kirstie pays them because Mummy and Daddy wire them more in a week than most people earn in a month. Honestly, it's terrible about that Naomi girl. She seemed the nicest of the lot, certainly the most down-to-earth."

All because of a potato salad? And he thinks he's not quick to judge.

Kirstie's close to boiling point. "Oh, here we go, Marcus the great socialist. You weren't so power-to-the-people when you were accepting your MBE, were you?"

He's embarrassed. I'm not sure whether it's the vehemence of his wife's outburst or the truth in what she's saying, but either way, he feels the need to explain. "I got it for my charity, Be a Good Sport—or BAGS, as we call it. It's a sport-for-social-change enterprise. We work with ex-offenders, get them running sports projects with disadvantaged kids. It gives the guys a sense of purpose and it keeps the kids off the streets for a few hours, if nothing else."

"And it's supposedly me who works with reprobates," snipes Kirstie.

You can't help but wonder how these two ever got together. Or is this how all long-term relationships are destined to play out? Trading insults across the kitchen that you can't afford to finish because you've overstretched your finances chasing the dream of a snazzy life.

Parnell nips the bickering in the bud like the seasoned parent he is.

"Mrs. Connor, weren't you concerned when Naomi didn't turn up for work on Monday?"

The kettle whistles and Rachel wafts into life again, giving Kirstie's arm a supportive squeeze as she passes.

"I worked from home on Monday. I wasn't feeling too great." Direct to me. "Trust me, give it another ten years and you'll know all about the two-day hangover." Turning back to Parnell, she says, "Anyway, I emailed Naomi saying not to disturb me unless it was urgent and when I heard nothing back, I assumed she'd taken me literally and didn't think much of it. I was glad of the peace, to be honest. One of my team did text me later to say she hadn't shown up, but what can I say? It wouldn't be the first time a temp's left me in the lurch for a better offer." She throws her husband a chilly smile. "As Marcus kindly pointed out, I don't pay the best. It's the brands we work with that attract people—Hellys, Jo Sebastian, Cutler Couture."

No? Me neither.

She goes on. "And then I half wondered if she'd told me she was off on Monday and I'd forgotten. I'm not very good at holiday records, HR stuff. Relationships are more my thing."

The irony's not lost on Marcus Connor, who risks a wry glance at his sister.

I look around the room, addressing everyone. "Did any of you take photos? We'll need to see those."

Clara and Marcus shake their heads.

"I think I've got a few." Rachel halts the tea-making to take her phone out of her bag—a crappy old Nokia even Parnell would balk at.

Another wry look from Marcus, although there's a coating of warmth this time. "Seriously, Rach, I've got a drawer full of old handsets. Will you just take one, please." He shoots a grin at his niece. "I mean, the shame, right?"

"Mum doesn't do shame, Uncle M. You should know that by now. Anyone who writes thank-you letters to your teachers after parents' evening doesn't know the meaning of the word 'shame.'"

Rachel doesn't look up. "Oh, so politeness is shameful, now? And I don't want a new handset, Marcus. What if I lose all my numbers?"

"What, all five of them?"

She doesn't take the bait, letting Marcus crack on with his annoying brother piss-take thing. At a guess, I'd say it's a little brother piss-take thing, but it's hard to tell exactly. The bare strip-lighting in here isn't doing any of us any favors.

Rachel eventually puts her phone down. "Nothing much, I'm afraid. Just a couple of Clara and Danny playing swingball, and that was early on in the day."

"I'll have to check later," adds Kirstie. "Danny dropped my phone down the toilet this morning and it's still drying out in the airing cupboard. Who'd have kids?"

"Don't say that, Kirst," Rachel chides softly, handing Kirstie a mug of tea. "They grow up so fast, you know. Soon they're applying to university and you wish they were four years old again, dropping your phone down the loo."

Clara makes a vomit gesture. "Yeah, OK Mum, enough of the soppy stuff." She turns her dove-gray eyes on me, the same color as her soppy mum's. "I'm hoping to study Criminal Law or Criminology at university, so I've gotta say, this is all *sooo* fascinating."

"I think you mean horrifying, Clara." Rachel throws her daughter a stern look—or as stern as I imagine she gets. "Sorry about that. My daughter tends to come top of the class at everything except tact."

Clara tries to look sorry but penitence really doesn't suit her. "So which one was she, Auntie Kirst?"

"The Australian."

"Don't remember an Aussie. I must have gone by then." She sounds almost disappointed.

Rachel's voice is soft. "Do you mean the one with the hair? Like Parma Violets?"

Parnell's full of encouragement. "That's the one. Did you speak to her?"

She thinks about it. More out of an eagerness to please, I sense, than anything hopeful. "No, I don't think so. I was mainly in the living room with 'The Olds.'" Kirstie Connor's not impressed with the description. "Oh, not that Kirstie sees herself as an 'Old,' but her employees aren't much older than Clara. They make me feel ancient."

Far from ancient. Her long, delicate features give her an almost timeless quality, like a countess in an eighteenth-century portrait. Her accent is pure working-class London, though. Earthy, nasal, and melodic—like mine before private school sanitized it. "So you didn't see Naomi interacting with anyone in particular? Arguing with anyone?"

She gives a half smile. "The only arguments I heard were between Marcus and Joseph—that's my husband. One of them opened the Brexit can of worms and that was it."

She hands me a mug of tea that there's no chance I'll drink. Too much milk and too little time make it a bad combination and Steele's already vibrating in both our pockets, wanting an update. "We'll need to speak to your husband."

Kirstie scoffs. "I wouldn't waste your time talking to Joseph. Joseph doesn't talk to anyone unless they've got a Mensa IQ or a Coutts bank account. I doubt Naomi had either."

"It's a murder inquiry. Everyone's worth speaking to," says Parnell. "We'll need a list of everyone who was here, actually. Names, contact numbers, addresses, if you have them."

This spurs Kirstie into a kind of frenzied action, running her hands along shelves, opening drawers and muttering *"pen, pen, pen,"* as if she barely remembers what a pen is, much less where she can find one. Calmly, Rachel locates a Biro on the windowsill and passes it over. Kirstie leans over the breakfast bar and starts scribbling furiously. A poster girl for the left-handed—energetic, creative, impulsive.

"My husband's in Barcelona at the moment," says Rachel, watching her. "He's back tomorrow, I think. Shall I ask him to call you?"

"He's back tonight," corrects Clara. "Whoop-de-do, Daddy's home."

"If we can have your address, we'll send an officer over tonight to take a statement," says Parnell.

Rachel half smiles again. "Lucky officer. Joseph's not at his best after work trips. Thirteen meetings in two days, though, it's too much."

Marcus is still in the doorway, frowning and knuckling his scalp, absently. "Look, are you sure it wasn't a burglary gone wrong or something? Not that it makes it any less hideous—but Kieran's got some expensive DJ'ing kit, or he certainly used to have. If someone saw him carrying it in . . ."

It's a race between me and Parnell—Parnell narrowly wins. "Woah, woah, woah. Are you saying you know Kieran Drake, Naomi's housemate?"

Marcus's frown intensifies. "Well, yeah, but not well. He worked on a couple of BAGS projects a while back and I'm friends with him on Facebook. I haven't actually seen him in a long time, though. I'm talking years."

"So he's an ex-offender?" I try to make it sound like it's not a hugely loaded question but I fail abysmally. Marcus sees where this is heading.

"Hey, hang on. He's not a violent ex-offender. Not *murder* kind of violence, anyway."

It's a fair enough distinction. There's petty tit-for-tat violence and then there's the skull-smashed-in kind. It's possible to be a master of the former and incapable of the latter. Still, I'm duty-bound to look skeptical. "So how did Naomi end up living with Kieran?"

"It was a totally random thing. Kieran posted on Facebook that he needed a new lodger and I mentioned it in passing to Kirstie, just as an example of one of our guys who seemed to be still doing OK. And then she says she's got this new temp who's looking for cheap digs."

Kirstie picks it up. "She was staying in this hostel all the way out near the airport, always having problems with the trains, late at least once a week. Well, that's no good to me, so I put her in touch with Kieran through Facebook. I didn't think anything would come of it, to be honest, but next thing, she'd moved in."

"To be clear, I played no part in it," says Marcus, hands aloft, as if to say *don't blame me.*

Kirstie's tone is nasty. "Marcus didn't approve, because despite all the stuff he spouts to the journalists and the council bigwigs, he knows that most leopards *don't* change their spots, and Drake's got a criminal record as long as your arm."

Marcus shakes his head emphatically. "It wasn't a case of not approving, but from what Kirstie told me, I just thought they'd make strange housemates. He's more than ten years older, for one thing, and he's . . . well . . ." I hold his gaze, determined he's going to say what he's desperately trying not to. "They just sounded like different people, that's all."

I turn my attention back to Kirstie. "So if you think a leopard can't change its spots, why did you facilitate Naomi moving in with him?"

She bristles. "Let's get one thing straight, I didn't *facilitate* anything. I put them in touch, end of. I wasn't responsible for her housing arrangements, or any other arrangements for that matter. I was her boss for a few months, not her mother." If her words sound cold, the tremor in her voice gives her away. Guilt underpinning the aggression.

I know it only too well.

The word "mother" seems to trigger a plaintive "Muuummmaaay" from outside the house and as soon as Marcus opens the back door, the child rushes in, brandishing a pack of sparklers that he wants *"opened now!"* A catalog-cute child with the face of an angel and, as his mother pointed out, the hair of a rough sleeper.

"Hey, baby boy." Kirstie hefts him onto her right hip and pretends to buckle under the weight. "We won't be able to do this for much longer. You'll be too heavy for special mummy cuddles soon, won't you, Danny?"

I think we're supposed to coo at this. I probably would too, if it weren't for the fact that there's a mother in Australia who won't be getting any cuddles from her daughter ever again, and *possibly* because this boy's mother saw fit to put her daughter—*her* baby girl—in touch with a convicted criminal.

"Mummy, come and play," demands Danny, hitting Kirstie on the head with the pack of sparklers.

"Mummy's speaking to this man and this lady. You were fine playing by yourself." She puts him down and opens the back door. "Go on, I'll be out again soon."

Danny bolts but Marcus catches his hand just in time. "Come on, mate, enough playing." He ruffles his scraggy mop. "Let's go and get this cut, eh? You've got too much hair and Daddy's not got enough, according to Mummy. Mummy doesn't know what she likes, does she?" He grabs a little blue parka from the back of a kitchen chair and shoos Danny down the hall, before delivering one final barb.

"And for the record, Kirst, it's too late for him to be playing outside on his own. Someone could easily get over the fence. There's weirdos in Muswell Hill too, you know. It's not all coffee-shop freelancers and media tycoons."

I raise an eyebrow at Parnell.

"See, that's the problem with Marcus," says Kirstie, looking to her sister-in-law for backup but getting nothing except the perma-half smile. "He can't make up his mind about human nature. He bangs on about always seeing the good in people—mainly his precious ex-cons—but he can't help looking for the bad. And you can't have it both ways, can you?"

With that kind of black-or-white thinking, Kirstie Connor would make a lousy police officer. Then again, with my lousy black-or-white wardrobe, I'm sure I'd make a dreadful fashion recruiter.

Honestly, though, you can't see good *and* bad in people?

Oh, if only it were that simple.

4

Ten minutes later, after politely fending off Clara Madden's requests to interview us for her criminology coursework, we're sitting outside the Connors' place, marveling at the blaze of green and gold stars lighting up the sky—and marveling rather less at the predictability of Kieran Drake's record. Squinting at his emails, Parnell reels off the contents in a flat, mechanical tone, the sort adopted by every battle-worn officer who's encountered one too many scumbags over a long and arduous career.

"Possession of a controlled substance.

"Three counts of affray.

"Possession with intent to supply.

"Actual bodily harm."

And so it goes on.

Standard Offender Bingo.

He's a bit more animated on the subject of parenting, though. "I'm with the husband, hands down. No way are my boys playing outside after dark. We used to let the older two, but not now, not in this day and age. And it's not just weirdos you have to worry about. It's gangs, dealers. It's bloody Kieran Drakes."

I suppose he's right. I'm not sure I'm qualified to comment. My only point of reference is my nephew, Finn, who at the tender age of seven is sadly more interested in shooting zombies on his Xbox than running wild in the back garden, which means the only thing we've got to fear is repetitive strain injury.

Or predatory grown men trying to chat to him offline.

"OK, so Drake's got a record," I say. "It doesn't actually mean anything."

That gets me a flat stare. "Lovely sentiment, Kinsella, but we aren't charity workers, we're coppers, and we live in the real world."

The real world, where over 50 percent of offenders reoffend.

Still, I'm not feeling it. "Come on, Sarge, even actual bodily harm is a far cry from murder. Kirstie Connor reckons she was seeing someone. I'd be inclined to lean that way."

"*Everything's* a far cry from murder." He leaves that nugget hanging while he dials his voicemail. In the silence of the car, I can just about make out it's Steele. After a minute he hangs up, tossing his phone in the cupholder. "Parents have been informed," he says, miserably. "It's not even four a.m. over there—God, what an alarm call to wake up to. At least they know now, though, that's something."

It is something. It's a woeful sense of relief, but a relief nonetheless. The thought that we know a life is finished, that a victim's organs are breaking down and rigor's starting to set in, when their family assumes they're still out in the world, living their life, doing their thing, is always a heavy load to bear.

"Anyway, Her Majesty wants us back there putting more pressure on Drake, now we know what we know." He puts the key in the ignition. "He's got alibis, apparently, but they're breakable."

Meaning we aren't exactly talking the local vicar.

My phone rings. A flashing "*A.*" Aiden's always stayed an initial, just to be on the safe side. I am nothing if not paranoid.

"Sorry, I've got to take this." I'm halfway out of the car before I turn and shoot Parnell my best pleading glance. "Two minutes, I promise."

The corner of his mouth twitches. "You know, you can whisper sweet nothings in here. It won't be anything I haven't heard before. You kids didn't invent romance."

"Yeah, yeah."

I slam the car door.

"Hey you." I'm smiling as I answer. It's been less than a year and we're still in the involuntary smiling stage. The Connors must have gone through it too, back before kids and kitchen extensions made them involuntarily scowly.

"*Dobré ráno!*" The accent could be anything, but I'm going to assume the language is Czech as we're off to Prague in a few week-ends' time and Aiden's not a man who does anything by halves. He'll know the language, the history, the per capita income and their all-time record goal-scorer by the time we touch down. "Actually shite, *'dobré ráno'* is 'good morning,' not 'good evening.' I don't think I'll ever get the hang of this. Christ, you'd think if I can speak fluent Irish, I can speak fecking Czech."

I watch Parnell watching me, sucking on his vape. "One—you can't speak fluent Irish. I swear you make half those words up. It's not like I'd have a clue. And two—I keep telling you, we won't have to speak Czech. They'll speak English in all the tourist places."

"Well, fair play to them and shame on us." Another explosion fills the sky, a scatter of pink and blue this time. "Jesus, what is it with fucking fireworks in this country? It's called Fireworks Night, not Fireworks Week. Is it ever going to let up?"

"Ah, don't be such a misery guts." I gaze up again, eyes wide, mouth open, like a five-year-old seeing Santa. "I think they're pretty."

"And I think *you're* pretty, but I don't want you keeping me awake every night for a week . . . Ah now, hold on, that's not exactly true, is it?" I laugh, turning my back to Parnell. "Seriously, though, they were still banging at three in the morning. Bastards woke me up. I nearly died—thought it was a gun going off."

"Could have been, around your way."

There's a smile in his voice. "Oh, I forgot, there's no crime south of the river, is there? Tooting's like Walton's Mountain, sure it is."

"One hundred and seventy-six crimes reported in Tooting last month compared with two hundred eighty-nine in Mile End—that's all I'm saying."

"Jesus, I've no chance against Little Miss Statistics, have I? Anyway, I like life on the edge and the pubs are *definitely* better over east. You can't get a decent pint around your way. It's all gin bars and craft beer."

Aiden's embraced the rules of his adopted home well: whether it be north, south, east, or west, you pick a part of London to lay your head and then you defend its honor with your very last breath. Its pubs, its parks, its tube network, even its pigeons.

Parnell toots the horn. I give him the finger over my shoulder.

"Anyway, listen, I'm busy, East End Boy. What do you want?"

"Er, how about a girlfriend who doesn't say *'What do you want?'* when I call her for a chat, that'd be a start." It's fine. This is how we roll. Aiden making out I'm the worst girlfriend in the world while consistently treating me like I'm the best. Me lapping it up and falling harder every day. "Failing that, an ETA would be grand. I'm coming to yours, right?"

"You are."

"Remember, I'm not staying, though. I'm away to the motherland in the morning."

"I remember. I do listen occasionally."

"You do? Well, you never answered my question—ETA?"

"Ah, sorry—um, seven thirty? Well, seven thirtyish."

A tut. Probably a roll of those ocean-blue eyes, the same as his dead sister's. "Always an 'ish' with you, isn't there? I tell you, you'd fit right in back home. No sense of punctuality there either. D'ya know when someone from Mulderrin says *I'll be there now in a minute* they could actually mean anything from an hour to three whole days. That's scientific fact."

"Is it really? I've another fact for you—men from Mulderrin—"

"Are hung like horses? I've heard that, right enough."

"You heard wrong—it's hamsters, not horses. No, men from Mulderrin talk more shite per hour than the rest of the entire global male population combined."

"That so, hmm? And what if I say I love you and I can't wait to see you later? Is that me talking shite?"

"Depends how you say it."

"Meaning?"

My smile spreads wider. "Say it in Czech and I might believe you."

"No problem—*Jdi do prdele!*"

I'm impressed. "Seriously, that means 'I love you'?"

"Nah, it means 'Fuck off.'"

I'm still laughing as I get back in the car—a car that now smells of banana custard, Parnell's latest vape.

"Well, that was more than two minutes," he says. "Mr. X must have had lots of sweet nothings to whisper."

"Jesus, Sarge, that stinks." I wind down the window, choosing to freeze rather than suffocate. "And he doesn't do sweet nothings. He just whinges, like you."

"We'd get on a treat then. Shame you're hiding him away." I ignore him, making heavy work of finding a lip balm in my handbag. "So what's eating him?"

I keep fumbling, unzipping pockets. "The Czech language. My timekeeping. Fireworks. Happy now?"

"Fireworks? Don't blame him. Nearly thirty quid for us to watch the display in Byron Park on Saturday night. I said to Maggie and the boys, we could sit in the car park and watch them for free, but oh no, overruled as usual. Is Mr. X as big a pushover as me?"

I turn to him with a look that says I'm not answering anymore questions. I fully expect him to tut and give up like he usually does, but for the first time he holds my stare, his face etched with something meaningful. Sensing things are about to turn awkward, I try to cut him off at the pass.

"Byron Park? Is that in Harrow? My auntie Carmel used to live over there, but—"

"Is he married, Cat?"

It's so unexpected and so *completely* off base that I don't do anything but blink for a few seconds, riding out the impact. Briefly, I consider saying he is, because it might close down all the questions. But even then I can't bring myself to lie about *that*. To become that type of person in Parnell's faithful eyes.

"Because, you know, all this secrecy," he goes on, not glancing away once. "All this not wanting to talk about him *at all*. I've been thinking, and him being married is the only thing that makes sense. Well, either that or it's someone at work and you're scared Steele will flip her lid."

"It's not anyone at work." I'm so weirded out by the idea of Parnell imagining me and Swaines, or Seth, or, God help me, Pete Flowers, in some sort of clandestine tryst, that I forget the all-important *and he's not married either.*

"Well, as long as you know I wouldn't judge, OK? I'd probably give you some wise old man advice that you wouldn't take a blind bit of notice of, but I wouldn't judge." His cheeks flush pink. "What I'm trying to say, kiddo, is that I care about you and you can trust me. You can tell me anything."

All credit to this lovely, lovely man; he genuinely believes he means this. And all it would take is one weak, obscenely naive moment for me to believe it too and my career would be over. My relationship would be finished.

Me and Dad would be in prison.

It all started last December. A woman's body dumped in a picturesque London square. Horrific, but nothing strange, sadly. A run-of-the-mill case with a car caught on camera and a shifty spouse looking our best bet. However, what had followed had been a journey into hell, more specifically, a journey into my past. A past where I'd always suspected my dad knew *something* about the disappearance of Maryanne Doyle, a teenager from the west coast of Ireland who went missing around the exact same time my family—*my dad*—were visiting.

A teenager who'd grown into the exact same woman who now lay dead in a picturesque London square, spitting distance from Dad's beloved pub.

I've often fantasized about telling Parnell the whole wretched story. It used to cross my mind, in fact, every time we found ourselves alone. In the car. In the pub. On our weekly pilgrimage to buy salt beef bagels on Brick Lane. *What if I just told him?* I'd think. After all, a problem shared is a problem halved.

Thing is, there is no problem to share, not anymore. Not since I pissed on my police oath and sorted it all out. Now all that's left is poisonous, wearying guilt and if a problem shared is a problem halved, then a guilt shared is a guilt doubled. And I wouldn't wish that on anyone, least of all Parnell.

And anyway, where would I even start?

With how my dad has always lurked on the fringes of criminality? With how I was *almost* sure he was a killer for a large chunk of my life? Or would I just get straight to the point and confess that I knew all about Dad's links to Maryanne from the start of our investigation and I never once saw fit to disclose them; not to Steele, not to him, not to anyone? Would I go the whole hog and tell him that Dad knew who killed Maryanne all along, and how I dragged every last detail out of him before letting him walk away scot-free while I arrested the *real* guilty party?

Or at least, that's how I comfort myself.

And would I admit that Mr. X is Maryanne's brother, Aiden? Would I confide that, even after nearly a year, he knows nothing worth knowing about the chirpy, helpful copper he fell for?

About who I am and what I did.

"He isn't married," I say eventually, probably too late to sound believable. "It's just going really well and I don't want to jinx it. I know that probably sounds odd to you, but it's the Irish in me. We're a superstitious breed." I lean across and turn the key in the ignition. "Anyway, can we forget about me? Let's go play *'Who's a naughty boy then?'* with this Kieran Drake fella." Parnell gives me one last look— one last shake of the head—and then pulls away. I feel myself relax a little. "So if we've got Drake, who's interviewing the gobby toffs?"

"Seth and Emily. Steele reckons they'll get more out of them than you and me."

I fold my arms, pretend to be offended. "She forgets I have a touch of the toff myself. Private school educated, remember."

He flashes a grin. "Ah, but you're not the real deal, are you?"

"And what's that supposed to mean?"

"The way you slurp your tea? A proper toff would spot you a mile off."

I laugh, even though I know they wouldn't. I've become so adept at fooling people that sometimes I even fool myself. Sometimes I still believe I'm a good person at heart. Not a liar, or a coward, or, if I'm really swallowing the truth serum, a corrupt police officer.

But then we all mask our true selves. Look at Parnell with all this low-fat, high-intensity business. I clock him eyeing my pain au chocolat every morning. I see the stoop of his shoulders as he trudges to another reluctant session at the gym. And then there's DS Seth Wakeman. Seth's always playing down his blue blood with tales of trips to the darts and weekly food shops at Aldi. But I know his great-grandfather was an earl. The Tenth Earl of Ramsay—I googled it.

There's little point in trying to be something you're not these days, not with the internet being an all-knowing, all-powerful snitch.

But what I am can't be found on the internet. It's not in the stoop of my shoulders or the lines on my face. Shame is too private an emotion to ever make it to the surface, to the top layer that you let people see. Shame is buried so deep that eventually the false you becomes the real you and no one ever comes close to knowing who you really are.

What you're capable of.

How far you'd go to protect yourself.

5

Kieran Drake doesn't want a solicitor. He doesn't want a glass of water either. He could murder another Diet Coke if there's one going, though—his words, not mine—and ideally he'd like this to be over quickly. He's teaching an early spin class tomorrow and he can't function without a full eight hours.

"Not enough sleep's a major factor in weight gain, did you know that?" His face is solemn, as though he's just shared the cure for cancer. "My guess is you work mental hours, yeah?"

The cheeky bastard.

But is he a guilty bastard? Twenty minutes in and I'm not convinced. He's stressed, that much is obvious. His breathing's shallow and the constant zipping and unzipping of his U-Gym fleece isn't just annoying, it's a dead giveaway. But then, why wouldn't he be stressed? He found his housemate dead less than six hours ago and, judging by the number of cans on the table, he's wired to the eyeballs on caffeine. And, of course, he knows his way around the system. He must have an inkling of what's coming, of what we might be thinking. He must know that to a lot of people, police officers included, the notion of rehabilitation is at best a lofty goal and at worst, a token farce.

Not to me, though. I have to believe in some sort of redemption. It's the only way I can stomach my own reflection in the mirror.

"Look, can you just answer the question, Kieran? When did you last see Naomi?" I shouldn't be showing my irritation but it's late and I'm flagging and all we've got so far is a load of wide-boy front and a weight-loss tip.

Drake flops back—legs spread wide, thighs like tree trunks. "What, again? I went through it all with that black copper. Don't you trust her to do her job, is that it? That's racist, that is."

"Actually, I'd trust DC Akwa to do the prime minister's job, but things have changed a bit since then, Kieran. A lot gets found out in the first few hours of an investigation."

Parnell jumps in, not wanting to play our hand just yet. "Tell us *again* about this cozy little domestic scene on Saturday morning. You and Naomi playing house."

"I said all this. I only saw her for twenty minutes." He's playing with his zip again, up-down, up-down, over the same inch of fabric. "She was cleaning the place, putting her washing on. Making a fucking racket, if you must know. I hadn't got in until four and like I said, I need my sleep."

"So you argued?" says Parnell, reasonably, like there's no shame in admitting it.

He jerks forward, angry, affronted. "That's a fucking lie, man. Who told you that?"

"No one, Kieran. It's called hypothesizing." Parnell leans back, stretching his legs—a pointed contrast to Drake's posture. "Come on, though, are you sure you didn't have words? 'Cos I know what it's like, mate. I work five night shifts in a row and then my missus starts with the vacuum when I'm trying to have a lie-in."

Maggie Parnell, mother of four and owner of a successful marquee rental company, is no one's "missus," and Parnell's as familiar with the vacuum as she is. However, he's also a great believer in getting on your suspect's level and with Kieran Drake, that means going low. Basement-level.

Drake sighs. "I'm telling you, we didn't argue and she weren't my missus."

"You fancied her, though, fancied your chances."

"Fuck that. Who said I did?" It takes a few seconds before he flops back again, grinning. "Ah right, hypothesizing. I get ya now."

"You've got to admit, it's a strong hypothesis," I say, tucking my foot under my thigh, getting nice and comfy. "I mean, you're a good-looking guy—why wouldn't you fancy your chances?" I'm not being devious, he *is* good-looking. A bit too beefed-up and bull-necked for my personal taste, and I bet he's got less body hair than I have, but looking at him objectively, I can see the appeal. "What happened, though, Kieran? Didn't she fancy it this time?"

He rubs his bleary eyes, the Hounslow three-day bender starting to take its toll. "You ain't listening. I didn't fancy her."

Naomi's sister emailed a few photos earlier. It always astounds me how people manage to function, to be productive and helpful, when the pain is so raw that it skins them alive. I spread the photos on the table and push the biggest heart-melter toward Drake—a honey-blond Naomi, mid–star jump, full of spark and vitality, wearing faded denim cutoffs and an I Heart New York vest.

"See, I find that very hard to believe, Kieran." I edge the photo closer. "Look at her, she's an attractive young woman. Aren't attractive young women your thing?"

He doesn't like this, his red-bloodedness being called into question. "*She* wasn't my thing, OK? We didn't have anything in common. I didn't know what to talk to her about half the time."

Parnell's still stretched out like a cat, one more slump and he'll be horizontal. "Oh right, so you need an intellectual connection to fancy a girl, is that what you're saying?"

"She was a kid, is what I'm saying. Into pop concerts and all that. And anyway, she was seeing someone."

Parnell laughs. "Very honorable of you, Kieran."

"You saw him?" I say, my skin prickling with hope.

"Nah, she just mentioned him a couple of times. Some rich dude. Runs his own business, flat in town, swanky car, you know the type of lucky git . . ." I pick up my pen. "And no, I don't have no details. I don't know the guy's name."

Parnell sits up and scrapes his chair forward. "I must say, you're very good at predicting our questions, Kieran. But then you're well versed in police interviews, aren't you?"

I swear he looks disappointed with us. At our narrow-mindedness. Our tendency to view everything through shit-smeared glasses.

"Oh *right*, I get it. Just 'cos I got form, you think I'm good for *this*." He jabs at his temple. "Fuck's sake, are you lot mental? Like I'd kill someone. Fuck!" He seems genuinely sickened, puce with indignation. If he's lying, he's a fine actor. "Come on, give me a break, OK? I ain't done nothing wrong for years. I'm like a monk these days."

Parnell weighs him up but I can tell he's on the verge of believing him. Sure enough, he beckons Drake forward, like he's got a secret to share, a code that needs cracking. "Listen to me, Kieran, if the person who killed Naomi didn't let themselves in, she must have, as there's no signs of a break-in." Drake's no codebreaker; his face is totally blank. "Who do you know that Naomi might have allowed in?"

He blinks slowly, apparently stumped by the question. I fight the urge not to slap him around his huge, dopey head. "Your friends, Kieran," I shout, exasperated. "Had Naomi met any of your friends? Anyone who might have dropped by on Saturday night or Sunday morning?"

"What, you want me to give names? Grass people up? No way, man."

Monk or not, some principles die hard.

"It's only grassing if they've done something." I hold up another photo. Naomi's around eighteen in this one, sun-kissed and smiling and seemingly laughing at a choc ice—a senseless, happy moment captured in time. "And yes, we do expect you to grass people up if you suspect they've done this." I put the happy shot down and pluck a crime-scene photo out of a folder, a brutal close-up of the red, fleshy head wound. Drake's face drains of all color.

Does the trick, though.

"Look, she met my cousin, Rocco, OK, when he was home on leave, but he's been back in Kabul for the past month. And she met my girlfriend—well, my sort-of girlfriend—but that's it. No one else as far as I know."

"And what did your sort-of girlfriend think of you housesharing with Naomi?"

"Well, she weren't exactly delighted but I needed the cash and she—Naomi, I mean—could move in quickly. Anyway, it's none of her business. I told her that an' all." He looks to Parnell for an *"atta-boy"* but gets nothing.

"Is she the possessive type, then?"

He smiles. "Hey, it's a cross I bear, you know—possessive women."

Tragedy is, I don't doubt it. There's only one thing a certain type of woman loves more than a bad boy and that's a reformed bad boy.

"So was your sort-of girlfriend with you last Saturday?"

"Nah, strictly a boys' weekend. No nagging, no shopping, no wanting attention all the time."

No twenty-first-century thinking.

"How many times did she meet Naomi?"

"A few, not many. We mainly go to her place. She's got a kid."

"And did she ever talk about her?"

"Not really. We don't do much talking. A little less conversation, a little more action, you know what I'm saying?"

"A little more conversation, a little less bullshit might get you out of here quicker, Kieran."

I regret the word instantly. While Parnell's all for getting on the suspect's level, he insists on keeping things clean. Swearing lessens your authority, he tells me. It blurs the clear and sacred barrier that should always exist between "us" and "them."

"Your girlfriend's name, please?" asks Parnell, all blunt and official.

The penny suddenly drops for Kieran. "Fuck me, you think *she* might have done this? Gone bunny boiler on Naomi?" He laughs and finger-snaps like it's the best gag he's heard all year. "You know, now you mention it, she *is* a bit crazy. Mad jealous, like. I mean, that's a good thing between the sheets but hard work out of it, you get me?"

Parnell doesn't flinch. "Her name, Kieran. And then you can go, for now."

"Kelly Gillette—as in the razors, yeah? She's been at her mate's in Cardiff since last Friday, though, so you're barking up the wrong tree there, mate, funny as it'd be to see her arrested."

"Nothing funny about this, Kieran." Parnell sounds out of gas, physically and emotionally. I'm not far behind. "You think about this, OK, when you're lying in bed tonight, or doing your spin class tomorrow morning. Think about Naomi's family. Think about *her*, how she died. And then if you've got something more you want to tell us, you come right back in here, son. Because we will find out who did this, that's a promise."

Except it isn't. It's a thing we say to suspects but *never* to the victim's family. It's a hollow battle cry, nothing more, given that a quarter of murders remain unsolved.

But hey, it sounds good. And it seems to have made an impression on Kieran Drake, who shuffles to the door far less confidently than he swaggered in.

"When can I get back into my place?" he asks, pausing in the corridor. "I'll have to stay with Kelly, I suppose, but it's not ideal. Not with the kid and that."

I'm deliberately vague just to annoy him. "I'm not sure, sorry. We'll let you know. Although look on the bright side: at least Kelly'll have you all to herself now. Jealous woman like that, she'll think it's Christmas."

I'm getting proper snarky now. Time I went home.

6

I had two stipulations when I was looking for a new place. Firstly, it had to be on a busy main road. Trust me, when you're often rambling home late, after a day of witnessing man's inhumanity to man, the last place you want to find yourself is on an eerie London backstreet, battling pin-drop silence and insufficient lighting at two in the morning.

Secondly, and more importantly, it had to be south of the river.

Had to be.

My usual shtick, my prevailing party line, is that I need a split between where I live and work. Literally speaking, I need the Thames. I need the wide, bendy demarcation line of the city to separate the business of crime from the business of pleasure, or at least the business of eating toast in front of Netflix in bed.

Truth is, it's never been about that. I crossed the Rubicon to the south for one reason and one reason only—a geographical "fuck you" to Dad. A rejection of where I grew up and a revolt against the man who raised me there. The man who equates south London with the Gobi Desert. Who claims, whichever way you cut it, north London is bigger, better, less dangerous, and more fun.

But then, I've always loved an underdog and I love the edgy, tetchy south.

Can't say I love the commute, though. It's seven fifteen when I leave the office. Seven thirty by the time I'm vacuum-packed on the Northern Line for the thirteen standing stops home. By a quarter to eight, I'm starting to question *again* why I put myself through this every day.

By eight fifteen, I'm crossing the threshold of my lovely, minuscule new home.

Not that it's really new, anymore. It's over three months since Parnell and I lugged my belongings up the unforgiving stone staircase; long enough to be on nodding terms with the ragbag of residents, my favorite being Jerry, who claims to have toured the world with the Rolling Stones despite having never owned a passport. *"Jagger had a word, got that all sorted out."*

I love listening to his lies as much as he loves telling them. And anyway, they're only lies if they're hurting someone; otherwise, they're just regrets.

I'm on the top floor, six stories up. Penthouse living at its worst, when you're battling a cantankerous lift and a leaking roof that the landlord's been promising to fix since the Magna Carta, according to Jerry. That said, there's a peace to be found living among the church spires and the treetops. A certain therapy in watching the clouds race each other on a cool, windy morning or staring into the midnight-blue void when I'm awake late at night.

Parnell hates it. Parnell thinks a rowdy houseshare would be better for me; people my own age to cook dinner and bicker over gas bills with. He's not convinced it's healthy for "a youngster" to spend every night cloistered on the top floor of a gloomy Victorian conversion, or drinking stout with a seventy-year-old fantasist who claims he wrote the lyrics to "Jumpin' Jack Flash."

But then it isn't every night. It isn't tonight, for instance. Tonight, Aiden's coming around and I need to get ready. And by ready, I don't mean shaving legs and lighting candles, I mean mentally ready. I mean steeling myself to become the person Aiden thinks I am for just one more night before I do the decent thing and let him go.

This never happens, of course. Aiden Doyle's an excruciatingly hard man to let go of. The way he laughs, the mole on his left eyelid, his insistence on walking on the outside of the pavement to protect me from traffic, have all played their part in one more night morphing into nearly one whole year—and now I'm running out of ways to kid myself that I can walk away.

Will it end tonight? It'd be as good a time as any. It'd probably be a better time than most, given he's off to Ireland tomorrow for a wedding, which means he could drink me out of his system for four days straight. Or shag me out of his system, although the thought of him with someone else makes me want to sandpaper my brain.

So maybe not.

I think about a quick wash, but I do my worst brooding in the shower. There's something about running water that sends my stress neurons into orbit. Instead, I opt for dumbing down and so lurk on social media, scrolling through my newsfeed with my brain switched to standby.

Dog pics. Holiday pics. Bigotry. Food.

Naomi Lockhart's life may be over but the world rumbles on.

I find Naomi quickly. She's blond in her profile picture and so heavily filtered she resembles a cartoon. I don't get much time to delve, though, before there's a knock at the door. An Aiden knock, jaunty and self-assured. A knock that says, "I just know you'll be pleased to see me." I spritz myself with deodorant and check I haven't left any crime-scene photos lying around.

He knocks again. "Have you another man in there, Kinsella? Send him out here and I'll fight him to the death."

I open the door and yank him in. "Keep the noise down, you idiot. This is a respectable household."

"'Tis, yeah. If you ignore yer one's meth lab downstairs."

"How many times? It's not a meth lab." I throw his satchel and damp coat on my nice clean bed. "She's a hairdresser who works from home. The smell's perming solution."

"And the fierce stench of weed coming out of number four's flat? What kind of hair product is that?"

It's weed. Not the easiest thing to ignore when you're a police officer, especially when you're a police officer who used to like a toke of the green stuff yourself.

"Ah, live and let live." I walk over to the kitchenette—essentially an alcove that houses a fridge, a hob, a microwave, and a sink. "I've been keeping an eye on him. He's not dealing, from what I can see."

"Very liberal of you. Hey, any danger of you buying two chairs?" He plonks himself down on the coffee table, looking rightly nervous about its sturdiness. "And Christ, any danger of some heat? I was hoping to get naked at some point."

"The heat's on. You have to rub yourself against the radiator to feel the benefit, though." I waft a hand toward the wardrobe, an IKEA job I'd bribed Parnell into assembling. The bribe being my eternal gratitude and a fried-egg sandwich. "Or grab one of my hoodies. My Irish rugby one's massive, it'll fit you, no probs."

"You've got some serious body dysmorphia going on there. Look at me, I'm twice the size of you. Anyway, don't worry about it, I'll cope. I'm from the west coast of Ireland, they build us hardy over there."

"Suit yourself." I open the fridge door. "Ah shit, I forgot to get wine."

"Good job I remembered then. It's not that white shite, though." He picks up his satchel and pulls out a bottle of expensive-looking Chilean red. "And I ordered fettuccine Alfredo from yer man over the road, is that OK?"

"Yer man" is Leonardo, who doesn't usually do takeaway but makes an exception for me following an "incident" with a stag party where a flash of my warrant card got him paid.

"It's more than OK. Although how d'you know I hadn't cooked something?"

"Because Mercury hasn't aligned with Saturn, as far as I'm aware."

I lob the wine cork at his head. "Yeah, well, last time I cooked you said I couldn't cook. A girl takes offense at that sort of thing." I open the freezer compartment. "Hey, I've got Magnums for afters. I'm not a complete failure of a hostess."

He wraps himself around me, smelling of rainwater and booze—although not his usual lagery scent; something neater, less processed. "Only one afters I'm interested in."

"After! You must be joking. No one has sex *after* pasta. Waaay too stodgy."

His mouth meets mine. "OK, so what are we waiting for?"

"What, now?" I wriggle away. "The food'll be here in ten minutes."

He pulls me back. "Great, we can do it twice."

I laugh away the day while Aiden works his way down my shirt but then the main door buzzes and we break apart reluctantly, exchanging just-you-wait glances. Aiden flies down to get the goodies while I cobble together cutlery and clear crap off the table. The smell wafts all the way up the stairs and I virtually rip the food out of his hands as he walks back in.

"Sorry, I'm starving." I sit on the floor with my back against the armchair. "I was in this house earlier, and they had jacket potatoes in the oven. I swear I was actually drooling."

"Whose house?" He joins me on the floor and I throw my legs across his.

"Oh, just witnesses on a new case. You want black pepper?"

"No. I'll have a kiss, though." I duly oblige. "So you're on a new case? Good job you weren't coming to Ireland then. I bet you'd have had to cancel."

"Probably. Well, I'd have had to choose between Ireland and Prague, that's for sure." I swirl a heap of fettuccine around my fork. "We're too lean, that's the problem. Craig Cooke—you know the one we call The Famine, the one with the new baby—well, he looks like the walking dead at the moment and Emily's still next to useless." I chew my food, reconsider that last statement. "Actually, not useless, that's unfair. But she doesn't show much initiative. You have to spoon-feed her every instruction."

"Jesus, send her to me. I could do with a few people who just do what they're fucking told." I give him a look that says I hope that doesn't include me. "I'm not joking. I'm up to my ears in graduates-with-initiative. They're liabilities—well, some of them."

Aiden works in risk management for a sports trading firm. To quote the man himself, "I use predictive algorithms, human analysis, and real-time insights to create the best betting opportunities for my clients."

Essentially, it's about making money—not something I'm expert in.

Unlike managing risk, which I understand only too well.

"You're coming next time, though? For my cousin's thirtieth?" I thought I'd managed to sidestep the Ireland issue, but it appears not. "Actually, I'll rephrase that—you *are* coming next time." He doesn't get the look he's hoping for. "Ah, come on, Cat—you are, aren't you?"

"I dunno, maybe." I shove in more pasta, as if muffling the words might lessen their impact. "If I can, I will. It's just . . . work, you know how it is."

"Must be tough being that important. Being that bloody indispensable." His tone's waspish but it's borne out of hurt, not malice. He was looking forward to showing me off at the wedding, I know he was.

I sigh. "Not tonight, babe. I've had a really long day and I've got an eight a.m. start tomorrow."

"I start at seven a.m. every day."

These moments are sticky. The moments where you want to say, *"Yes, but you don't have to hold your nerve with a murderer, or watch a face being peeled back during a cranial postmortem."* But of course you can't say those things because they sound patronizing. Let's be honest, they *are* patronizing. For every murder that needs solving, an algorithm needs building or an elite fashion type needs recruiting. Life can't all be about death. I know that.

"What time's your flight tomorrow?" I ask, trying to head off the argument.

"I've to be at the airport for six." He checks his watch, then pours more wine. "Shit, less than nine hours and I haven't packed a thing yet. I haven't written my speech either. What do you reckon, am I officially the worst best man ever?"

"I don't know what you're panicking for. The wedding's not until Friday and you've nothing else to be doing."

He shoots me the side-eye. "Christ, you don't know me auntie Bridie. She'll be giving out shite the minute I get there. *'Give this one a lift here. Drop these sandwiches off there. Oh, and there's a fence down over the back field, if you've a minute. And sure, if you're doing that, you might as well bring the cows up' . . ."*

"Good, you won't have time to be charming any ex-girlfriends, then." I give him a quick shove with my foot. "How many women at this wedding have you slept with exactly?"

"Four." He takes a slug of wine. "Ah well, no, three really." I don't ask. "Anyways, I've no intention of charming anyone. I just want to get plastered with me cousins, raise a toast to me mam . . ." No mention of his dad, who's every bit as dead but much less mourned on account of being *"a bollix of the first order."* "And then on Saturday morning, if I'm not as sick as a small hospital after the wedding, I'm gonna plant a tree for Maryanne. Do you think that's daft?" My stomach drops, but I just about manage to shake my head and form a smile. "She might be buried in fecking Surrey because of that gobshite of a husband, but she was born in Mulderrin and that counts for something, right?"

Maryanne. Just the sound of her name and I shape-shift from good ol' Cat Kinsella into a twisting, coiling serpent.

"Well, that's me stuffed," I announce abruptly. I stand up and take my plate to the sink, letting my body take the lead while my mind tries to flatline.

Keep active. Keep busy. Keep moving. Keep calm.

By the time I've rinsed my plate, my pulse has slowed to something less fatal. Erring on the side of caution, I look around for something else to do and end up wiping the inside of the microwave.

Aiden's not fooled.

"You don't like it when I mention Maryanne, do you?"

My heart freezes, but my hands keep working away. "Why do you say that?"

Suddenly he's behind me, hands on my shoulders, turning me to face him. "Because I've got eyes and you get jumpy every time I mention her."

The lie comes quickly. I'm repulsed at how quick. "Look, I'm sorry. She just reminds me of how we met and the line I crossed when I started seeing you." He shrugs, completely unbothered. "Ah, come on, Aiden. You were Maryanne's brother—my *victim*'s brother. We shouldn't have got involved while the case was still running. It breaks every single code and, I'm sorry, it still makes me feel awkward." I force myself to look at him. "And it makes me sad, you know, that I can't introduce you to my workmates. Well, some of them, anyway. Parnell would love you."

His face hardens and I know what's coming. More fool me; I walked straight into it. "Oh, so Parnell would love me, but your precious family wouldn't?"

"Aiden, no." I shake him off, aggressively. "I'm not going there tonight."

"Because now you've brought it up, Cat, I've got to say that I *kind of* understand why you won't introduce me to your colleagues—although why you can't just lie and say we got together later, I don't know. But there's absolutely no reason not to introduce me to your family, other than the fact you don't want to. And that hurts, you know. That's a really shitty feeling."

Absolutely no reason.

Other than the fact that my dad knew your sister and played a part in her downfall.

"Please." I can't think of anything else to say other than that one simple word. "We're not going to see each other for days, *please* can we not fight about this. Just talk to me about Gaelic football or quantitative risk, or *anything* you like. Talk to me about bloody cows. Just not this again, *please.*"

"Yes, this again, Cat. Because *my* family, me aunts and me uncles and me two hundred cousins, are going to be asking about you this weekend and I don't want to make us out to be something we're not. I don't want to be laughing at all the *'It'll be you next'* jokes if you're just killing time here."

Suddenly, I'm hot with fury. But not with Aiden, with myself. And with my dad and my job and the world and with Cupid himself, but unfortunately there's only Aiden here to use as target practice.

"Oh, for fuck's sake! You're being ridiculous now. Why would you even think that?"

"Because the only thing I can *think* is that you must be ashamed of me. I mean, you know everything about me. You know I'm not exactly from the finest stock, so maybe you think I'm not good enough for the long-term? Maybe I'll do for a shag and a takeaway a couple of nights a week but—"

"Have you lost your mind?" I feel panicked, under attack. And when you feel like that you attack back and attack harder. "Seriously, are you drunk? Were you caning the grappa with Leonardo before I got back? I bloody knew it. I could smell it off you."

His jaw clenches. "Yeah, I had a couple, what of it? You said seven thirty, so I assumed you'd be back by eight. What was I supposed to do? Sit on the doorstep until the big-shot detective got back from the mean streets?"

"A couple too many, clearly." I brace myself to hit the nerve square on. "You know, maybe you're not so different from your dad, Aiden. Isn't this what he used to do after one too many? Spout all this pity-and-paranoia bollocks?"

Head cocked, he drinks me in for the longest moment and there's nothing I can do but hope he hates me more than he hates himself right now. Downstairs, the door slams and someone rambles up the stairs singing. It's such a carefree, happy sound that I can't quite believe it's real.

"I'm going to forget you said that." A pained smile crosses his lips. "See, the thing is, you're not a very convincing bitch, Cat Kinsella. I know you only said that to make me fuck off so you don't have to deal with the conversation." I stare at him, trying to style it out, but he's well and truly got the measure of me. "Well, your plan's worked. I *will* fuck off." He picks up his bag and coat, shaking his head. "I just wish you'd admit who you're ashamed of, them or me. Although if you're ashamed of them after what you know about my crowd . . ."

He opens the door but stays standing just inside, probably waiting for me to smooth things over. To lure him back with an explanation, if not an apology.

But I've lied enough for one night.

I've lied enough for one lifetime.

"I'm not ashamed of anyone, Aiden." I edge forward, backing him into the hallway. "I just don't get on with my family and I think you should respect that."

He kisses me on the cheek, barely, though. "No. No, that's not good enough, Cat. You can't just say 'we don't get on' and leave it at that. I want to understand why. I want to understand *you*."

"You sound like bloody Oprah." I add a pitiful little laugh.

"And you sound like someone who's desperately afraid of something." He glances back at me from the top of the stairs. "I just can't figure out for the life of me what it could be."

7

Wednesday

And so we convene.

There isn't a soul in this room who hasn't learned the hard way that eight a.m. means seven forty-five a.m. To be on the safe side, seven thirty a.m.

You see, Kate Steele doesn't have a lot of time for excuses. Hit traffic, did you? You should have left earlier. Train delayed, was it? Have you never heard of the bus?

Occasionally, she cuts the parents some slack, the parents of little ones, anyway. It's hard to rip someone a new hole when they've been up half the night singing "You Are My Sunshine" to a teething baby. But for the rest of us, the rules are steadfast and simple: by the time Steele takes the floor, your breakfast should be eaten, your bladder should be empty and all discussions about last night's game/row/ spaghetti Bolognese should be concluded.

Not that the rules apply to her, of course. She's currently hovering at the front of the room with a pecan Danish in one hand and her mobile in the other, tapping out a text which, judging by the leer on her face, isn't strictly business-related. They don't seem to apply to Parnell much either—twenty-odd years of working with Steele has seen to that—and he's greeted with a breezy *"Hey, Lu"* as he flies in at seven fifty-nine a.m., into a barrage of wolf whistles at yet another shiny new suit.

"Righto, shall we kick off?" Steele puts her phone down on one of our several empty desks—our monuments to police cuts, a reminder that we *never* have enough people. "I'm trusting you're all up to speed on the whos and the hows, so I'm going to skip the warm-up act and just update on where we are, OK? Prints—forget it, nothing so far. Bal says it's likely our guy was wearing gloves, smooth ones as opposed to woolly ones as they'd have most likely shed fibers. As for all other forensics, it's a case of watch this space. What else? I had a chat with a very nice chap, an Officer Wilson—or it might have been Wilton—with the South Australia Police a bit earlier. Naomi's parents are on their way. They should be touching down at Heathrow around five a.m. tomorrow." She tears off a corner of Danish, waving it around as she speaks. "Thing is, much as it pains me, we need that PM done today, so we can't wait for the family to ID her. The house-mate's going to have to do it."

Which means that despite all the tender care no doubt applied by Vickery and her team, Naomi will look even worse, if such a thing's possible, by the time they arrive. Cut then restitched. Reassembled like Frankenstein's monster. Her long hair shaved off. Her skin a mottled canvas, branded with Y-shaped incisions.

No longer a girl but a cadaver.

"What part of Oz was she from?" asks Flowers. "Sydney, I bet."

"That's the east coast, Einstein. She said *South* Australia." I correct him even though I haven't a clue what constitutes the south. I dropped geography in favor of Latin at school.

AURIBUS TENEO LUPUM.

To "hold a wolf by the ear." An unsustainable situation in which doing nothing and doing something are equally risky.

Aiden.

"Adelaide," says Steele, slicing through my thoughts. "A smallish suburb called Golden Grove. Lots of green space, young families, low crime rate."

So a middle-class idyll, although it sounds a bit *Stepford Wives* to me. My livelihood depends on a high crime rate and I've never been one for the great outdoors.

And as for families . . .

Parnell's looking wistful though, mooning out the window at another drizzly November morning. "Makes you wonder why she left there to come to *this*."

"Well, wonder no more." Steele parks a buttock against my desk, smelling amazing as always; today it's something nuzzling and soft, like sandalwood. "I got the lowdown from Officer Wilson, Wilton, whatever his name is. She had a relationship end pretty badly and her ex was 'a bit intense,' so her parents suggested she get away, make a clean break of it. It was actually they who suggested the UK trip, massively encouraged it by all accounts, funded the whole thing." Parnell closes his eyes and Renée lets out a quiet mewl. Even Flowers shows a shard of sympathy with his whispered, *"Poor fuckers."* "I know, heartbreaking, isn't it? That's them blaming themselves for the rest of their miserable lives, not that it's logical, but you know . . ."

We know.

And we know that unless we catch the person who did this, they'll never have a hook to hang their misery on, someone else to shoulder the blame.

I broach the obvious. "So this 'intense' ex-boyfriend then?"

"Sketchy. He's been a bit of a hermit since Naomi gave him the heave-ho and the only alibi witness he could give last saw him Friday lunchtime, so *technically* it's just about possible. I don't know, though. Trekking to the other side of the world to have it out with your ex isn't 'a bit intense,' it's obsession." I open my mouth but Steele's got it covered. "Of course, we'll check with the airlines, get hold of passenger lists and what have you, but it'll be a waste of time, I'd put the house on it." She rubs her hands together comically, choosing her victim, while we all try to avoid eye contact. "Ems, can you take care of that, please."

I wonder what Emily's done to deserve that? Or what hasn't she done, more likely. Emily's not one to rock the boat, generally; she'd rather sit in the boat with her perfect eyebrows, waiting for instruction.

She doesn't like this instruction, though. No one likes a surefire dead end.

"Ah, dry your eyes, Ems," says Steele. The "Ems" is new. "If anyone should be pissed off, it's me. I should be halfway to Calcot Manor for two days of massages and me time with my sister by now, and you lot stuck here bowing and scraping to DCI Tosspot."

"Terry Bostock's all right," says Parnell, grinning.

"He is to you, Lu. You've got a penis. The three amigos wouldn't fare so well." I assume that's me, "Ems," and Renée. "He'd spend his whole time trying to get them either fired or pregnant."

"Aw, so you stayed to protect us from the big bad man, Boss. I'm touched." My tone's jokey, but genuinely, I am. Although the scrapper in me might have enjoyed going toe to toe with DCI Bostock, the famed moron.

"Yeah, well, don't be too touched. Fact is, I'd rather stare death in the face all day long than spend five minutes in a hot tub discussing HRT with my sister, but she got me at a weak moment, bullied me into saying yes. A new case was the perfect cop-out."

I can't picture Steele being bullied into anything—fist bumps to the sister—but I totally sympathize with the need to cop out. In recent months, I've used "the job" to cancel a shopping trip, a Sunday lunch, an aqua-aerobics class, and an invitation to help build a shed with my sister. In fairness, the shed would have been fun. Jacqui and I get on better when we're being productive, focusing on a task rather than raking over the past. And yet, no matter how much fun we're having, whether it's balking at the price of bags in Selfridges or banging nails into bits of plywood, I know everything will end up coming back to Dad—how we've been getting on, when we're seeing each other next—and I don't have the energy to keep lying. To keep feeding her the apple-pie answers she craves.

"So we're checking out recent burglaries on and around the estate." Steele's voice brings me back. "There's been two in the past fortnight. One was interrupted and they fled pretty quickly, but the home-owner's a big scary-looking bastard, apparently, so it's not surprising they panicked. A bit different from our Naomi."

Our Naomi. The baton passed from her parents to us. Their responsibility in life and now our responsibility in death.

"This isn't feeling like a burglary gone wrong, though. Her phone is gone but her purse was still there, along with a few expensive gadgets and Kieran Drake's DJ equipment." She twists to look at me. "Cat, is everyone up to speed on the Drake interview?" I nod. "And the other interviews, the boss lady, Kirstie Connor?" I nod again. "Great. Well, I'm going to button it then and actually eat this bloody pastry. Who's up next?"

She'll assume Parnell will take the lead, so I surprise them both by jumping up. "OK, so the big question has got to be, who's the boyfriend? Both her boss and her housemate say she mentioned seeing someone and yet we don't have a name, a sighting, or any evidence of this mystery man, bar a few hairs in her bed that may or may not be his—and they're no use to us anyway unless he's on the DNA database."

"First the family had heard of a boyfriend," says Steele, unable to button it for more than a minute. "Her older sister's particularly gobsmacked. They were close—told each other everything, or so she thought."

"Is the sister coming over?"

"Hopefully, in a few days. She's a single mum, it's tricky. She's trying to sort out childcare."

Swaines raises a weary hand. By the look of him, he's either been out on the lash or chained to his desk all night. Either's possible. "We checked with her mates back in Oz too. They all said she seemed to be enjoying herself, taking in the sights, embracing the 'London experience,' whatever that is."

"Everyone ignoring each other and paying a fiver for a pint?" says arch-northerner Flowers, who should probably just move back to Barnsley.

Perhaps somewhat validating Flowers's point, Swaines ignores him. "But they'd heard diddly-squat about a fella. There's no sign of a boyfriend on social media either, although according to one mate, she was wary of posting too many *'Yay, I'm having a blast!'* selfies to avoid hurting her ex's feelings, so she kept it all fairly boring. Snaps of Marble Arch at dawn, black cabs, jellied eels. I'm not joking about that last one either."

I take a second to process all this. "So she told people she wasn't close to—her boss and her housemate—that she was seeing someone, but she didn't breathe a word to her nearest and dearest."

Parnell sits forward, wriggling out of his suit jacket. "You'd think I'd know you well enough by now, but is that an observation or a question?"

"It's a thinking-out-loud." I risk a glance at Steele. Steele's not a fan of conjecture, especially in first briefings. She wants updates, facts, or at the very least, probabilities. Luckily for me, she's got a mouthful of Danish. "I mean, from what we can gather, the boss and the house-mate wouldn't have been all that interested—she wasn't exactly on overly chatty terms with either of them—but if you tell your family or your oldest mates that you're seeing someone, they're going to want chapter and verse. The fact that she didn't suggests she didn't want people asking too much about him."

Seth Wakeman pipes up. "So why not?"

Why indeed? I swallow down the bile that's been bubbling since Aiden left last night.

"Because not everyone's as eligible as you, Lord Wakeman. Or because he's married?" I flash a look toward Parnell—I'm still not convinced he believes me about Mr. X. "Or maybe because he's a wrong'un of some sort?"

Parnell's putting his suit jacket back on; his thermostat's all over the place since he turned health-conscious. "Kieran Drake's a wrong'un."

"An *ex*-wrong'un," I correct.

"You're getting very charitable in your old age, Kinsella. My apologies—an 'ex'-wrong'un. Still not the sort you'd bring home to Mother, though, so maybe he and Naomi *were* involved and he's deflecting attention away from himself?"

"He's still a suspect then?" asks Emily. "I thought we'd alibied him five times over."

Parnell arches an eyebrow. "His alibis are his mates—and what a lovely, fine, upstanding bunch they are."

A thought occurs to me. "Hey, didn't Kirstie Connor say Naomi stayed in a hostel for a while? She could have met the mystery man there, although it doesn't really tally with Kieran Drake's *'swanky car, flat in town'* guy."

"I'm heading over there after this," says Renée. "Leave it with me." A wicked grin spreads across her face. "Oh, by the way, while we're talking alibis, Drake's so-called 'crazy' girlfriend checks out. Except she wasn't at a mate's in Cardiff." Renée's positively glowing; this is going to be good. "She was in Paris with a fitness model called Johan.

Huge guy, looks like he could wrestle a bull. So not quite the needy woman, eh? Serves him right, the arrogant git."

It's the little things that make the job worthwhile.

"Right, CCTV. Who's on that?" Steele's back again, pastry eaten.

Craig Cooke sleepwalks to the incident board, clutching a bunch of CCTV stills and a bucket of coffee—the only antidote to the night-feeds-and-colic carousel he's been riding for the past few months. "OK, so we don't have Naomi leaving the Connors' house. There's surprisingly few cameras around there, wouldn't you know it. And the only time we pick her up is nine twenty-five on Saturday night, coming out of Nazar's News 'N' Wine, near Turnpike Lane station, about a five-minute walk from home. We've had a chat with Mr. Nazar and he's certain she seemed fine. Maybe a bit pissed because she was chattier than usual—she called him 'hon' when he gave her the change. But apart from that, pretty normal. As you can see, we lose her when she turns right onto Langham Road."

"What was she buying?" I ask.

"Bottle of Lilt."

OK, so no condoms. No nibbles for two. No decent bottle of wine to impress "rich dude" with when he turned up later for a roll in the clean sheets.

Cooke sticks another still to the board. "We're also interested in this guy walking down Downhills Way, less than a mile away from Naomi's, at eleven forty-nine. You'll have to watch the footage to get exactly what I mean, but he's walking pretty fast, like he's in a hurry. He could be completely innocent, of course, but . . ."

But it's something.

Steele's attention turns again. "Ben, phone records?"

"I've only just had them, so nothing to share at the moment, Boss. I do have something, though." A smart move by Swaines—never leave Steele empty-handed if you can help it. "The sister forwarded me a text that Naomi sent Saturday lunchtime—*Work do later. Really can't be bothered but should make the effort. Call u tmrw, around 11? Xxx.*" The sister insists she'd have meant eleven a.m. *their* time, which would have been twelve thirty a.m. Saturday night here." He sits back in his chair, pausing for effect. "She never did make that call and you could normally set your watch by her, apparently."

Steele likes this. "Which could suggest she was already dead or at least incapacitated by twelve thirty. Good work, Benny-boy."

"What about her neighbors?" asks Parnell. "Did anyone see anything, hear anything?"

"No such luck," says Flowers. "It's mainly old people on that estate. Bungalows are popular with old folk and most of them were in bed by half ten, out for the count. I did speak to one guy who was rolling home from the pub around half twelve, walking down the path at the back of Naomi's. He *thinks* he saw a light on in what would be Naomi's bedroom. He could just about make it out over the wall. Problem is, he happily admitted he was—close your ears, ladies—'absolutely cunted' so he can't be sure. And it's not like he saw anything anyway, just the light."

I join Cooke at the incident board. "OK, so if she was back near home by nine twenty-five, that means she didn't leave the Connors with the gobby toffs. They didn't leave until tenish—Marcus Connor was clear about that. He was dying for them to leave so he was conscious of the time." I look at Seth. "You and Emily interviewed the gobby toffs, right? Did Naomi mention where she was off to, why she was leaving the party?"

"If you mean to her colleagues—no. She didn't even say goodbye."

"Ah, play the game, Seth—call them the gobby toffs."

Seth straightens his Hermes tie, hamming it up big-style. "They are gobby, I grant you. But toffs? *Puh-lease.* Upper middle class at a push, darling." Smiles all around. "Look, Emily and I took statements from them all. They were patchy on a lot of details—lots of sniggering about being worse for wear, a whole load of puerile nonsense, to be honest—but the one thing they were all clear on is that one moment Naomi was there, the next she was gone. Not that they seemed to mind. I got the impression she wasn't that well-liked. Nothing sinister, I should say, just that her being Kirstie's PA made her a bit separate from the pack."

"Do we think it's odd she left early and without saying a word?" asks Parnell.

"What are you thinking, Lu?"

Since Seth became a sergeant, it's all "Lu" this, and "Lu" that. Parnell wouldn't care if I used his first name too but I generally stick with "Sarge." He might be my work-dad and a good mate rolled into one but, surprisingly, I like the deference. It makes me feel safe.

"I don't think it's *necessarily* odd," I say. "I always sneak out of parties if I'm bored or knackered. Otherwise, by the time you've said your goodbyes, another half an hour's gone." There's a general murmur of agreement, antisocial bunch that we are. "Of course, it could also mean she was upset about something."

"Or summoned by someone," adds Renée.

"Yep, or that. What about the girl who called 101 to report her missing? What did she have to say?"

Emily eyes me cautiously. "Evie Whitlock? Not a lot. Why?"

"I just thought that since she was the only one who seemed to care that Naomi had gone AWOL, maybe they were close?"

"Well, that's certainly not the impression she gave, but you know, there were a lot of them to interview. Seth and I did well to get statements in the time we did. *And* I had to go back to interview Joseph Madden." The name's familiar but my face says *Who?* "The Connors' brother-in-law. He'd just got back from Barcelona. That was a waste of time too. He could hardly remember who I was talking about."

Parnell smiles kindly. "Hey, no one's implying you didn't ask the right questions, Emily, but Cat's got a point. If no one else seemed that bothered, what made Evie Whitlock take it upon herself to call 101? Maybe she saw something at the party but she needs more coaxing?"

"She wasn't at the party, *actually*," replies Emily in a slightly "duh" tone that Parnell will have her for later. "She had flu."

Which sounds fishy to me. "If she had flu on Saturday, she wouldn't have been at work on Monday. It wipes you out for days."

"Longer if you're a man." Steele smirks at poor Seth, who rather unfairly has the moniker Sicknote because he *once* had four days off with tonsillitis. "What's your point?"

"Maybe there's another reason she didn't go? I could be completely wrong, but I'd like to interview her again." That's me on Emily's shit-list. "Me and Parnell are going over to Naomi's workplace in a while so I'll grab her for five minutes then. It's no biggie." I aim this at Emily, who I feel a bit bad about now.

"Yeah, whatever, fine. It'll do no harm." Steele leans over to check her phone. "Right my lovelies, is there anything else? I need to be upstairs for nine."

Upstairs. That mythical land where decisions are made, budgets are slashed, and balls of shit are prepared to be rolled downhill.

"Yeah, I've got one more thing, actually." Heads swivel in unison. Flowers usually can't stand a long briefing. He's always tutting at people for supposedly dragging things out. "Me and Cookey did house-to-house on the Connors' road, just to see if anyone saw Naomi leaving. Well, no one did, but some bloke who lives just across the way, a Mr. Eddie Gallon, reckons he saw a guy hanging around on the street and then walking up the alley that runs alongside the Connors' place, around fiveish. He's sure of the time as he was listening to the football scores coming in on Radio 5 Live. Anyway, he doesn't know exactly what happened then because his wife called him into the kitchen, but he saw him back out on the street a few minutes later—"

Steele interrupts. "Well, who was it?"

"Marcus Connor doesn't know. He can't remember anyone coming to the door after about three. That's when Kirstie Connor's sister arrived to take Danny—the son—to her house for a sleepover. However, Kirstie said a window cleaner knocked on the door at some point, touting for business. She's not certain of the time, though—she just knows it was nearly, but not quite, dark."

"Funny time for a window cleaner to start knocking," says Parnell. "Saturday, late afternoon?"

Flowers nods. "That's what I thought, so I checked with some of the neighbors and they didn't have any window cleaners calling. Could be nothing, but it's strange that he'd knock on their door and not others."

"Maybe the Connors have particularly filthy windows." She may sound flippant but Steele leaves nothing to chance. "Check the surrounding streets. Bang on every single door if you have to. Like you say, it could be nothing but it needs closing off."

And who knows, it could open things up. The "could be nothings" crack more cases than the plucky-cop hunches or the lucky-cop breaks ever do.

8

We decide against driving. Well, Parnell does, I don't get a say. Parnell wants to put a dent in his ten thousand steps and to be fair, it's a pleasant enough day, kind of wishy-washy, typical of late autumn in London, and our office is less than a mile from the eastern end of Oxford Street—although in the lunch-hour scrum it can easily feel like ten.

Calling it the "eastern end" is an act of kindness. The "shit end" is actually the more commonly used term; the seventh circle of tourist hell, where souvenir shops peddle cannabis-leaf snow globes next to teapots commemorating the marriage of Kate and Wills, and where the £1-a-slice pizza stands should come with a public health warning, or a side of Imodium, at least. You'd be hard-pushed to use the word "adequate" to describe anything down this end, never mind the word "elite," and yet it's here we find Elite Fashion, two floors above a musty-smelling internet café with a sideline in unlocking **ANY!!!** mobile phone.

We aren't exactly expecting a show of black armbands or an open book of condolence as we walk into the main office, but a slightly subdued atmosphere might be nice, a general veneer of sadness permeating the place. What we find is business as usual. Kiss FM blaring out old-school Ibiza classics across an open-plan workspace. Laughter. Swearing. The words *HUMP DAY!* chalked on a blackboard next to the obligatory artist's impression of an ejaculating cock and balls.

Aside from the music and the cock-and-balls masterpiece, the office isn't that different from ours, in that it's gray, cramped, and functional. They do have a fancy juicing machine, though, the kind you need a PhD in engineering to switch on, and you can't move for rolled-up yoga mats, no doubt the product of some shoot-me-now training course: *"Stretching While Selling!"*

Parnell's face is a picture as we wait by the reception desk, attracting stares and corner-of-the-mouth comments from the snappily dressed workforce. "Jesus, don't tell me they're the latest trend again?" he mutters as a redhead whips past in blue velvet flares. "I had a pair of those back in the late seventies and they were out of fashion then."

"No idea, Sarge. Anyway, a true fashionista doesn't follow trends. She's all about originality."

"Or *he*," he corrects.

"Or he." Although the men—three by my head count—aren't looking in any way original. In their starched white shirts and slim-fit suits, they could be tax accountants, albeit dapper tax accountants.

Parnell frowns. "And Hump Day? Dare I ask?"

"Wednesday. By Wednesday you're over the hump of the week. You're nearer to the next weekend than the last, get it?"

"I get it." He walks over to the blackboard, raising his voice to drown out the radio. "There'll be no next weekend for Naomi Lockhart. Have any of you considered that?"

A few look ashamed, although I'm not sure if it's of themselves or of him. Parnell may be rocking sharper suits these days but he's still as uncool as they come.

Kirstie Connor, looking stunning in a simple white tee and black taffeta skirt, has the grace, or at least the sense, to seem mortified.

"Get that crap off the board," she growls at the nearest bank of desks. A girl in a tartan pinafore physically jumps. "It's supposed to be for leads, top candidate lists, *work* stuff. And turn that radio down while you're at it—or better still, *off.* Haven't you got client calls to make?" Tartan Pinafore's caught between a laugh and a cry, and going by the amused horror on everyone else's face, I'd say Kirstie Connor doesn't pull rank too often. "I'm sorry about that," she says, turning back to us. "Anyway, come through."

She steers us toward her office, which is essentially just another desk sectioned off by a glass partition embossed with the Elite Fashion logo. Naomi's desk sits adjacent to Kirstie's, but due to the L-shape layout, Kirstie's view is of her empire and the BT Tower just beyond, while Naomi spent her days staring straight at a gray stone wall, bare but for a laminated list of dos and don'ts in the event of a fire. No wonder she covered her bedroom in sunshine and rainbows.

"It's not as glamorous as I thought it'd be."

It's a knee-jerk observation but Kirstie takes it as a dig, looking me up and down in a way that suggests I'm not so glamorous myself.

"Well, I'm sorry to disappoint, Detective . . . Sorry, I've forgotten your name."

"Cat's fine, and apologies, I didn't mean any offense. A W1 postcode is pretty glamorous, full stop. You must be doing well."

She gestures for us to sit—I think I'm back onside, just. "Ups and downs like any business. I just don't see the point in fancy artwork and £500 swivel chairs, not when this"—she circles her fingers, meaning the office—"is only where the admin gets done or the occasional meeting happens. If my guys are doing their jobs right, they should be out and about most of the time, meeting clients, earning trust."

I turn back toward the main hub. "There's a lot of people here today. I guess they don't feel like meeting clients, putting on a professional face."

"I certainly don't." She drops heavily onto her chair. "Look, I think I was in shock when you were at the house yesterday. I probably seemed a bit . . . well, a bit cold, I suppose. I just couldn't take it in, and then with Marcus having a go at me . . ." We nod along, oozing sympathy. "Well, I just wanted to say I'm sorry, that's all." I wave her apology away but she's stuck in contrite mode. "And now I just wish I could say sorry to Naomi too. I wish I'd been kinder to her. Not that I was cruel or anything, but I found her a bit irritating, if I'm honest. I'm not very good with meek people. I walk all over them, I know I do. But I feel terrible now. She probably thought I was a cow."

I'm a sucker for good self-awareness and I feel myself softening slightly. "We still need your photos from the party, Mrs. Connor. I take it your phone dried out?"

"Kirstie, please." She gives a quick laugh. "Yeah, eventually. Until next time, anyway. That's the third time it's ended up in the toilet."

I pick up an Elite Fashion pencil—*who uses pencils?*—and scrawl my email address on a random scrap of paper. "You can send the photos straight to me. It'll save the upheaval of another visit from our forensics team."

Naomi's PC is gone already. There's no flies on those guys.

Parnell jerks his head toward Naomi's desk. "We should get on, really. We'll be as quick as we can—well, as quick as it takes."

"Actually, I was hoping to have a word with Evie Whitlock," I say. "Is she here?"

"Evie?" Kirstie laughs again but her face is pure vinegar. "She's here—but she won't be for much longer."

I follow her glare to a girl in the corner who's shoving all manner of stuff into small plastic crates—stationery, cereals, moldy ballerina pumps. Kirstie makes a "be my guest" gesture, and with Parnell already settled at Naomi's desk, I walk across to Evie Whitlock and point out the bloody obvious.

"So you're off then?"

"I resigned this morning," she says, mulling over a pair of gold-rimmed sunglasses before tossing them in the bin. "She told me to go straightaway. It's not unusual in this industry. They don't want you stealing contacts from the system."

She's older than the rest of the team—not by much, maybe late twenties, but enough to make a difference, and from the sense I'm getting, a negative one.

"Can you stop for a moment, Evie? Is there somewhere we can talk?"

Another pair of sunglasses bites the dust. "I already spoke to someone about Naomi."

"I know, but I've got a few more questions. It'll only take a few minutes."

She nods but keeps packing. "Fine. But I need to get this done and there's no privacy in this office anyway, apart from the so-called boardroom and there's someone in there already. Just ask what you need to ask here." A quick glance toward her soon-to-be ex-colleagues. "Like *they'd* be interested anyway. There's a big pitch for Liberty coming up and *obviously* that's far more important than someone dying."

"So how's the flu?" I say, not even trying to sound genuine.

She knows what I'm driving at. "Look, I didn't go on Saturday because I knew I was resigning on Monday. It would have felt weird."

"Today's Wednesday."

"I didn't realize Kirstie would be 'working from home' on Monday." The bitchiness is good. Bitchiness implies bitterness and bitter people make better witnesses. More forthcoming witnesses, anyway. "I didn't care at first. I was set on doing it over the phone, just to get it over with, but then with Naomi not turning up things were hectic. And then yesterday . . . well, yesterday was obviously difficult. It didn't seem the right time."

And the day after is?

"So why are you leaving? Better offer?"

"No," she says defiantly, actually meeting my eyes for the first time. "I just figured life's too short to be unhappy. I don't like the culture here anymore, the values."

"So has the culture changed or have you changed?"

"Oh, the culture, 100 percent. There used to be two directors, Kirstie and Anna—Anna Nugent. She and Kirstie had some sort of falling-out a while back and it ended with Kirstie buying Anna out. Ridiculous, if you ask me. Anna was the brains of the outfit, the proper businesswoman. She wasn't all about short-term profit, she wanted to build something."

"And Kirstie?"

She gives a disapproving sniff. "She'd do anything to make a quick buck."

"Such as."

She counts them off. "One, placing people in jobs before we've got the correct documentation—that's bad practice, for a start. Two, advertising jobs that don't exist just to get business in." She leans in, lowering her voice. "And the PA before Naomi told me she sometimes invoices clients using her own personal bank details. That's got to be dodgy, right?"

See, aggrieved people tell you everything. Pure investigative gold.

"And it's all so vacuous here these days." Her sadness seems genuine and I'm inclined to believe that *most* of what she's saying is the truth, even if there's a little spice added. "Anna used to hire experienced recruiters and teach them about the fashion industry. Kirstie hires fashion-obsessed babies and tries to teach them about recruitment, but it doesn't work. They aren't interested in working with a broad range of clients, they just want the brand with the best handbag."

I steer the conversation back. "Naomi didn't really fit the culture either—Kirstie admitted that. Does that mean you two were close?"

"Close? No way." She's on the move again now, flinging self-help book after self-help book into the final crate. *The Power of Now*, *The Road Less Traveled*, *How to Stop Worrying and Start Living*—I've read and reread them all, sad fool that I am. "We were friendly but not friends, that's probably the best way to put it. I'd moan about Kirstie and she'd moan about her housemate or the cost of living in London, but that was about it."

I try to sound casual. "Oh yeah? What was her problem with her housemate?"

"Usual stuff. He's messy, she's tidy. He seemed to be under the impression that girls enjoy cleaning. And, well, she found him sort of . . . not creepy exactly, that wouldn't be fair, but a bit overfamiliar. I mean, it didn't sound like much to me. He'd say she looked nice if she was going out, that sort of thing, but she wasn't comfortable with it." She shrugs. "Take the compliments where you find them, I say."

"Did she ever mention a boyfriend?"

"Mmm, did she or didn't she?" She cocks her head back and forth, repeating her own question while searching for the answer. "No," she says finally. "She didn't mention anyone specifically but I think there was someone. She got flowers a few weeks ago, a massive bouquet with ribbons and allsorts. A bit tacky, if you ask me. I asked who they were from and she laughed and said, '*Ah, wouldn't you like to know,*' which was ridiculous as I wasn't the slightest bit interested. I was only being polite."

Urgh, flower deliveries. A florist in central London makes the proverbial needle in a haystack seem easy. Hopefully that search has got Swaines written all over it.

"So what made you call 101?" I ask, changing tack. "I mean, it was absolutely the right thing to do but no one else seemed that worried."

"My mum told me to." She grins as if to say "*yeah, I know, at my age."* "She'd called to see if I'd resigned and I said I still hadn't because our temp had gone missing and she said I should . . ."

She stops mid-sentence as something catches her eye behind me. Suddenly, I'm aware of voices—Kirstie Connor's, distressed, *"No, no, it doesn't make sense"* and then Parnell overlapping, *"Kirstie, can I ask that you don't touch it."*

Naomi's phone?

Surely we couldn't be that lucky?

I leave Evie to her packing and stride toward Parnell, praying to the god of murder investigations that I'm about to behold the holy grail of evidence.

Only it isn't a phone. It isn't any type of device, or a diary, or any object that looks like it'll make our jobs significantly easier. It's just a perfectly square gift box. Shiny and silver and about to be bagged by Parnell.

"What? What is it?" I say, sensing something seismic. Kirstie's hand is over her mouth and she's shaking her head, murmuring *"no"* on repeat.

Parnell seals the clear bag and hands it to me, pointing at the plain white gift card tucked under a black ribbon. The message on the card is clear. Neat to the point of weird. Almost calligraphic.

All my love, J xx

"Houston, we have a boyfriend," he says.

I'm puzzled. Parnell's usually the last to jump to conclusions. Even the bouquet of flowers could have come from a girlfriend, a relative, an Elite Fashion client.

"Hold on a minute, Sarge, we don't know that for sure. This could be from anyone. What was in it? Where'd you find it?"

"It was in her bottom drawer, it's empty. And we know it's from a boy—well, a man, at least. Kirstie thinks she knows who 'J' is."

"I don't *think* I know, I do know. It's Joseph, my brother-in-law. You met Rachel yesterday, remember? Joseph's her husband."

Joseph Madden. Barcelona Man. The guy who told Emily he could barely place Naomi.

His first lie.

Something to build on.

Kirstie zips back to her desk and makes a grab for her phone. Surprisingly Parnell's just as quick and their hands jostle for ownership before Parnell backs off, warning her, "Do not contact anyone, Kirstie. Not yet. Not until I say so." He softens his tone. "Now just calm down for a minute. How can you be so sure this is your brother-in-law's writing?"

"It's fairly bloody distinctive, isn't it? I've seen it enough times over the years." Her voice rises with each word, attracting the interest of her team, who start to drift down the office under the guise of needing to shred, photocopy, fill water bottles, anything. A few don't even bother with props. "Joseph's a very particular kind of person. He takes pride in everything, even his writing. It's definitely his."

Parnell issues another warning. "OK, well, we'll need to speak to him *first*. That's imperative. You can't call anyone who might—"

"I wasn't calling anyone," she snaps. "I needed to show you something." She scrolls through her phone, whispering *"Fuck, fuck, fuck."* "I was about to send my photos to you and I saw this. I didn't think too much of it at first, but now . . ." She stares at the gift box, as if fearful of its powers, its ability to throw her life into unutterable chaos. "Look. Look at this." She hands me her phone.

The scene is harmless enough. Several of life's beautiful people leaning over the breakfast bar in the Connors' kitchen. A daisy chain of privilege and perfect white teeth.

"What am I looking at?" I say, trying to spot a blemish between them.

"Give it here." She snatches it back, making the picture bigger until several figures in the background loom larger, if a little bit blurred. Two of them are chatting, nothing more, but when one of them is Naomi, chatting takes on a whole new level of significance.

"That's Joseph!" Kirstie prods the photo with her fingernail— electric blue today, not coral, which means she repainted them last night after hearing about Naomi. I try not to judge. "I was there last night when that other detective took a statement from him. I'd dropped Rachel and Clara back after dinner because Rachel's car was out of petrol and they'd had to get the bus down to ours and . . ." She stops to catch a breath. "Joseph was there, talking to that detective, and he definitely said he didn't remember Naomi. And yeah, sometimes he can be flippant about people, but he's not forgetful, far from it." She scrolls through her phone again, stopping on a handsome guy in his forties, holding a wineglass and smoldering at the camera like an aging pop star who knows he's still got it. "See, that's Joseph earlier in the day. You can see the shirt's the same. It's definitely him talking to Naomi."

My first thought is, are my cheeks burning?

My second thought is, should I have recognized his name?

My third thought is that the answer to the second is almost certainly no. I'm pretty sure he never told me and it's not like I ever asked. I mean, why would I? He was just the guy in The Grindhouse who served me coffees and chat-up lines.

Until that day he freaked me out with his crazy wife woes.

"Sarge," I say loudly, over the static in my head. "You're not going to believe this but I know this guy. I've met Joseph Madden."

9

"For God's sake, I don't *know him*, know him."

Two hours later and I'm backpedaling like crazy in Steele's office. The door is closed and the blinds are down, which is known around these parts as a "B or B."

Someone's getting a bollocking or having a breakdown.

Steele's on her throne, fashioning her bangs into a cool retro quiff. I'm standing with my eyes lowered, memories of the one time I ended up in the head's office flooding back. An oversight with a Bunsen burner that could have decimated the school.

"Right, this is how I see it," she says, liberally spraying the quiff. "You've got one simple question to answer, whereas I've got a hundred difficult decisions to make—so tell me, who's got more right to be standing there looking like they've stepped in dog shit? Is it you or me?"

"You."

"Correct. So I'll ask you again: Do you know our suspect or don't you? You need to start getting your story straight, lady."

I look up. "My story straight? You make it sound like I've done something wrong."

She plucks a compact from her makeup bag and checks her handiwork in the mirror. "It's not about right or wrong. It's about the fact that Madden's brief is going to be here any minute and I could really do without a conflict-of-interest issue. We're understaffed as it is."

"Conflict of interest? No way. Look, he runs The Grindhouse, OK. That poncey coffee place Swaines used to wank over. I haven't seen him in months, though, because—"

"Fine. He served you a few lattes, we can live with that." She snaps the compact shut, subject closed. "Send Benny-boy in, would you? He can start checking out florists."

"Wait a minute, Boss." I sit down, uninvited. This alone triggers Steele's *"oh shit"* sensor. "What I was about to say is, I haven't been in there for months because the last time I was he asked if he could have a word and then he . . . well, he said some pretty weird things about his wife. I gave the shop a wide berth after that, told Swaines to buy his own coffee."

"Christ, if *you're* saying it was weird, that worries me. Define 'weird.' "

"He said she'd threatened him—nothing physical, just that she was going to make him pay for being a crap husband, essentially. 'Make him suffer' was the term he used, I think."

"And you didn't mention this to anyone?"

"I did, actually. I mentioned it to Seth, and I think Emily was there too. We had a laugh about it and then we got back to whatever we were doing—you know, solving murders, not sorting out beefs between coffee snobs and their loopy wives."

"You met her yesterday, did she seem loopy?"

I picture Rachel Madden, calmly making tea and finding Biros while the Connor house pulsed under the specter of bad news. "No, not at all. She seemed quiet. A bit drippy, if anything."

She lets out a long, weary breath. "So I suppose you didn't log it then? This deep and meaningful with our suspect?"

I look her straight in the eye. "No, I didn't log it. There was nothing to log. It wasn't an official complaint. He just had a weird vibe about him, that's all, and last I checked that wasn't a criminal offense." I'm aiming for defiant but it's coming out all defensive. I pause for a second, dialing down the outrage. "Look, it was a bit bizarre, granted, but have you never had someone bore the arse off you at a dinner party about illegal parking on their street? Well, it was kind of like that, just more awkward."

She swoops straightaway. "Why awkward?"

"Well, 'cos he'd been a bit flirty, and then here he was, talking about his wife . . ."

Steele's hands fly up. "Stop right there. He flirted with you? That puts a different spin on things."

"It was nothing, just some stupid tea-versus-coffee banter." And an invite to Vienna, but I leave that bit out. "Honestly, Boss, it went from him teasing me about being a tea pleb to him asking if threatening to make someone 'suffer' was a criminal offense."

"And you said?"

"As little as possible. I said he might—*might*—have a case for Controlling and Coercive Behavior but that he should go to his local station, see what they advised. That's when he said he didn't want to make an official complaint. He just wanted to know what his options were. What he could threaten his wife with if things got worse."

"Christ on a cracker! And that's what passes for marriage these days, is it?" She takes another deep sigh, swiveling right, then left, on her throne-on-wheels, weighing up her options. "OK, given we're on a skeletal staff already, I really can't afford to lose you. But you're not to go anywhere near Joseph Madden, OK? Renée's already had a quick chat with him so she and Parnell can do the interview when his brief gets here." She pauses. "Now is there anything *else* I need to know?" I shake my head. "Wonderful. Right answer. Now let's get out there, shall we? Much as I love our girly chats, there's work to be done." She opens the door. "After you."

Just days ago, there was a different feel to this room. We hadn't had anything new for weeks, and if you'd watched us with the sound down, you could have mistaken us for any other office. Insurance brokers. Corporate travel agents, maybe? Just a bunch of drones in business-casual, sharing biscuits and filling out forms. Right now, though, there's a zip in the air, the inimitable bounce of not just having a new case, but a possible suspect too. Everyone looks sharper and more focused. Like dieters on New Year's Day—full of promise and unshakable belief.

"Boss." Emily practically rugby-tackles Steele. "I've checked his statement word for word. He said, '*I never spoke to her. I barely recall even seeing her.*'"

"OK, good, Ems. We've got the photo to disprove that. Renée, has he said anything yet?"

Renée, typing something at frenetic speed, recites their conversation. "Once he got home from the party, he had a minor marital hoo-ha with his wife and went for a stroll to cool off. He's not sure of the time but it must have been around eleven forty-five as he was only thirty minutes or so and he remembers looking at the clock when he got back and it was twelve fifteen. He doesn't know Naomi or anything about what happened to her, but he'll do everything he can to help. He's being quite cooperative, really. Quite charming."

Charming? I didn't find him charming. But then I don't do intensity. Give me easygoing and even-tempered any day of the week.

Aiden.

"That's good too," says Steele. "The gift box proves—or *suggests*—some sort of prior relationship, so that's two lies we've caught him in already."

Swaines comes bounding over. He's had a spruce-up since earlier and looks less like he slept on a park bench. "We've blown up the CCTV and, well, it's a bit grainy, but Madden's a strong match for the person seen walking in the direction of Naomi's house not long before midnight."

"OK, well, that's another thing to throw at him, although 'in the direction of' isn't exactly a smoking gun, is it?"

"Nothing we have is," says Parnell, killing the mood slightly. "Lying about knowing her doesn't prove he killed her."

Flowers slams his phone down. "That was the front desk, Boss. Madden's brief's here. Are you going down?"

"No, I'm due at the postmortem in an hour." She walks to the center of the room, pivoting on her four-inch heels, making sure everyone hears clearly. "Listen, Lu's right about us having nothing conclusive. Between the photo, the gift box, and the CCTV, I can just about make a case for 'reasonable grounds' but make no mistake, *mes amis*, we're on thin ice. If I have to take my begging bowl to Chief Superintendent Blake for an extension, I'm going to need a juicier pitch than 'A liar went on a midnight stroll nearish to the victim's house.'"

"This isn't going to help your pitch much either, sorry." It's a cute quirk of Swaines's—his need to apologize when he can't make the evidence fit, like it's his personal responsibility to lighten Steele's load. "Thing is, Joseph Madden's number isn't showing up at all on Naomi's phone records. There's still a few pay-as-you-go numbers we need to look into, but they only appear a couple of times and they're fairly short calls."

"Social media?" asks Emily.

A no from Swaines. "We're still trying to get access to her Facebook account and he doesn't use it—we've checked. I suppose there's a chance he's got an account under another name, and Digital Forensics are on it, but at the moment there's nothing that suggests regular contact between them. Nothing that suggests a relationship."

"Maybe they weren't having a relationship," says Parnell. "Maybe it was completely one-sided and he was stalking Naomi, sending her flowers and gifts. It'd explain why he's trying to distance himself now." He pauses, spotting a flaw. "Only issue is they seem to be chatting amicably in that photo, and would she really chat away to someone who'd been making a nuisance of himself?"

I channel Naomi as best I can. "OK, so you're young, fairly new to the country, pretty 'meek,' to use Kirstie Connor's description, and you're at your boss's house, trying to make friends, when in walks the guy who's been giving you the creeps, and it's only your boss's brother-in-law. Are you going to start causing a scene if he talks to you? Probably not." There's a few nods but none of us is sure about this, least of all me. "For the record, though, my money's still on an affair. We know she was seeing someone."

"You'd expect *some* phone contact between them," insists Swaines.

I shrug. "First rule of dating a married man . . ." I can feel Parnell staring. "Well, the first rule is don't do it, it's a trashy thing to do, but second rule—keep contact to a bare minimum."

"Listen to the woman." Steele heads back toward her office, taking a quick pit stop by my desk. "Kinsella, get over to the Maddens' place—I'll get you the address now. Seth's gone ahead to do the hard yards, so I want you to get the measure of the wife, and you're to call me as soon as you're done. *As soon as*. Don't make me have to call you."

The "hard yards" means the search: Madden's clothes, his car, all the family devices, anything at all that might link him to Naomi. Something sodden with her blood would be great, in the most depressing sense of the word.

It very rarely happens but we can but dream.

10

Built in the 1960s, and looking every last day of it, the Pendown Estate is a sprawling concrete kingdom stretching out over half a mile long. A grim monument to the failure of Britain's social housing experiment and one of the roughest estates in north London. The ninth worst estate in the UK, according to a recent pointless poll. The kind of place where *"even the dogs think twice about walks"* if you're to believe a certain newspaper.

And definitely not where I imagined Joseph Madden to live.

I don't know why—lazy stereotyping, I guess—but when Steele had told me to get over to the Maddens' place, I'd assumed I'd be heading back to Muswell Hill—to the Village of the Damn Privileged, or at least one of its nearly-as-nice surrounds. You see, I've no idea how much coffee-shop owners earn, or whether those first-class tickets to Vienna were a first-class windup, but from what I recall, there was something about Joseph Madden—his poise, his confidence, and, less figuratively, his designer shirts—that screamed money. Or at least comfort, which in London these days should be considered a high enough prize.

However, the Pendown screams of hardship and despair. Of boarded-up windows and blocked-up rubbish chutes. Of a clear lack of investment, although evidently not a lack of humor—some joker's sprayed *Abandon Hope All Ye Who Enter Here* across the welcome map by the entrance.

Tonight, it's cold enough to crack the pavement as I march toward Cranford House—the Pendown's magnum opus, the largest and most notorious of its concrete slabs. The wind swirls viciously around the tower block, whipping up mini-cyclones of litter and dog shit; and by the look of the deserted courtyard, it's chased even the hardiest of residents indoors—the gangs, the dealers, the lookouts, the thieves.

Amazing how a blast of wild weather can deliver what years of community policing never managed: a peaceful night on the Pendown for once.

Chief Superintendent Blake will be pleased.

Kirstie Connor, on the other hand, is not.

"She's providing moral support, apparently," says Seth, rifling through a hallway cabinet, elbow-deep in utility bills and pizza flyers. "Which appears to mean stamping her feet and shouting at me. The husband's with her, though—Rachel's brother. He seems a bit more amenable, although frankly it wouldn't be hard."

"What's with Fort Knox?" There's a complicated system of bolts, locks and latches on the back of the front door. "Bit excessive, don't you think? Even around here."

He stops rifling. "No idea. I didn't speak to them for long. I just told them to stay put in the sitting room until I'm finished."

I walk into the living room—"sitting rooms" are for the great-grandsons of earls—to find Rachel Madden standing by the window, staring out on to the oppressive gray horizon, and Kirstie Connor penciling her eyebrows in a wall mirror, watched by her husband. The room's spotlessly clean. Recently cleaned, if the choking scent of pine is anything to go by. But as the old saying goes, you might as well put rouge on a corpse, because from the lumpy brown sofa to the blotchy damp walls, the whole place smacks of neglect. Of a landlord who won't decorate and lives that haven't quite panned out.

"Oh, it's you."

Last night, at the Connor house, Rachel Madden had simply been a floating blond wisp serving really bad tea. Today, in her own surroundings, she couldn't be more of a flesh-and-blood woman. Shell-shocked and barefoot in £5 blue sweats. Although I'm not sure who's more shocked: Rachel, at the sight of her home being dismantled, or me, at the fact that Joseph Madden—smooth, posh, erudite Joseph Madden—lives *here*. In this joyless, grotty duplex, a world away from posh coffee and rounds of golf at Gleneagles.

And crucially, a galaxy away from Kieran Drake's *"rich dude . . . lucky git."*

Kirstie Connor spins around, appointing herself chief spokesperson. "Finally! Someone who knows what they're doing." I nearly laugh, imagining Steele's face. "Look, we understand why you've taken Joseph in for questioning. We understand why you're taking his things. But Rachel's phone? Clara's laptop?"

"Please," whispers Rachel, her voice fractured and dry. "Clara needs it for her coursework, for her uni applications. It's a critical time. She can't fall behind."

Which seems an odd thing to stress about when your husband's at the cop shop.

"I mean, are you even allowed to take their things?" demands Kirstie. "Well, are they, Marcus? Are they? Can they take Clara's laptop if it's got school stuff on it?"

Marcus looks bewildered by the question, by the very fact of being here. While Rachel had looked at home in the Connors' kitchen last night, Kirstie and Marcus look lost here. Not quite sure where to put themselves. I doubt they're regular visitors, despite Muswell Hill being less than three miles away.

"I wouldn't have a clue," Marcus says, gesturing helplessly. "I might work with ex-cons, but this is new territory for me too, you know."

He stands, pushing his shirtsleeves up. On his forearm, there's a faded tattoo of a skull in a top hat smoking a cigar. *1982* inked on a scroll just below. A reference to his birth year, perhaps? I guess if you look past the frowns and the premature hair loss, thirty-five seems about right. There's still a real boyishness to his sporty, springy gait and he has the kind of baby-blue eyes destined to stay bright, even in old age. Not classically handsome, but with his height, definitely striking.

As if stirring awake, Rachel rounds on her sister-in-law. "Oh, get a grip, Kirst. How the hell would Marcus know? He's not a fucking lawyer. He's not the fucking oracle on everything."

If I'm stunned by Rachel's outburst, I'm even more stunned by Kirstie's reaction, or lack of it. Head bowed, she shrinks into herself. "I'm sorry, Rach. I'm sorry . . . I just . . ."

"No, no, I'm sorry." Rachel vaults over to Kirstie and they collapse into a bear hug, leaving Marcus standing there like a six-foot-something spare part. "I shouldn't have snapped like that. I just can't think straight. This is an actual living nightmare."

"To answer your question," I say to Kirstie, crashing their love-in, "we are allowed to take them. It's standard procedure to seize any devices a suspect may have access to." The word "suspect" acts as a muscle spasm, jolting all three of them. "We'll give them back as soon as we can—once we're satisfied there's nothing relevant on them."

Kirstie can't help herself. "It's ridiculous. As if Joseph would use Rachel's phone to conduct his sleazy little affairs. Or his daughter's laptop!"

I ignore her, mentally bookmarking his "sleazy little affairs" for later. "So is that everything, Rachel? We obviously have Joseph's phone, but does he have any other devices?"

A look passes between the two women. I stare expectantly, giving them approximately ten seconds before I start getting stroppy.

Marcus gives them two seconds. "For God's sake, you two—this is serious. You need to tell her, Rach." He guides his sister to the sofa, delicately, like a young man helping an old lady across the road.

Rachel collapses down. "It's, well . . . I don't know if he's got another one now, I certainly haven't seen it but . . . well, he's had two phones before." She puts her head in her hands, unable to carry on.

Kirstie picks up the baton. "He's got form for it, basically."

Rachel's head snaps up, eyes pleading. "Joseph is weak, I know that. But he isn't capable of this. Of *murder*." She leaps up and starts pacing, hands fluttering by her sides. "Is he coming home tonight? Is he? Because I'll need to get everything straight again if he is. He'll be furious that you've been through his things." She sounds almost concerned for me before quickly reassessing. "Actually, it's *me* he'll be furious with for letting you do it. I need you to go. I need to get things ordered."

I step in front of her, halting her gallop, trying to bring her out of her jittery trance. "Listen to me, Rachel." I shake her gently by the shoulder. "Listen to me. I need to ask you some questions. I don't know when Joseph will be home, but what I do know is that if you don't lie to me, if you answer my questions truthfully, this will all get sorted a lot sooner, OK?" I'm aware I'm speaking to her as you'd speak to a child witness—slowly, clearly, and in kind, reassuring tones. Next I'll be asking if she understands the difference between a truth and a lie and sending out for her favorite pizza. "So to be clear, why has Joseph had two phones in the past?"

She sits down again, drawing a knee up to her chest, hands clamped around her pale bare foot. "I'm sure you can guess why. You don't have to embarrass me."

My patience wears thin. "I'm not trying to embarrass you, Rachel, I just want to—"

"For his girlfriends, of course. His *lovers*." She spits the word salaciously, as if excited and appalled by the concept at the same time.

"So was Naomi Lockhart his lover?"

No emotion. "I've no idea."

"Did you get the sense he was seeing someone?"

"I *always* have that sense." She glares at me—contempt for me or contempt for Joseph, I'm not sure.

I scale down the question. "OK, but did he ever mention Naomi? We know he spoke to her at the party and we have CCTV that puts him near Naomi's house late on Saturday night. We also found a gift from Joseph among Naomi's things. I'm guessing Kirstie's filled you in on that?"

None of this seems to move her in any way. Her manic energy has been replaced by something different, something resigned. "He's hardly likely to have mentioned her if she was who you're saying she was. And as for Saturday night, we had a row when we got back and he stormed out. It was nothing. He was angry with me for smoking, that's all. He says it makes me look ugly and he's right." Kirstie mumbles something—I only catch the word "tosser." "I assumed he'd gone to the Cocked Hat, the pub on the corner. They have a lock-in after hours at the weekend." Her hand flies to her mouth. "Oh God, I shouldn't have told you that, should I? Will they get in trouble? The landlord's ever such a nice bloke and he's had cancer, *twelve* rounds of chemo. Forget I said anything. Joseph's always saying I never think before opening my stupid fat gob. He's right about that too."

Marcus and Kirstie share a weary look.

"So what time did Joseph get back?" I ask, trying to center her again.

"I don't know. I was awake until gone one and he wasn't back by then."

"You didn't wake up when he got into bed?"

"He never comes to bed after a row. He stays up watching science programs or documentaries about painters—he's really clever like that—and then he usually ends up falling asleep on the sofa. Especially if he's been drinking and he's taken a Tammie."

A Tammie. A jellie. A Tem-Tem. An egg. Temazepam—the drug of choice for the perpetually sleepless. I considered taking it once—a year ago, when the Maryanne bomb first dropped.

"So when did you next see him? Was he on the sofa the next morning?"

"Well, yes." She hesitates, resting her chin on her knee. "But I didn't come downstairs until around eleven. I needed a lie-in and, well, if I'm honest, I was nervous of the row starting up again."

"And did it?" I want to gauge Joseph's frame of mind that Sunday morning. Was he somber? Jumpy? Uncharacteristically cheerful?

"No, it was fine." She sounds upbeat, as though she's living the relief again. "He didn't even mention it. We just got on with our day. Joseph made roast lamb for lunch with proper roasties. He's a brilliant cook."

Cultured. Clever. Makes a mean Sunday roast. He'd be pretty much the perfect catch if he didn't sound like such an insufferable, philandering arsehole.

Seth appears in the doorway, his face reddened from lifting mattresses and shifting furniture. I probably should have helped, but then Steele did say she wanted me to get the measure of Rachel Madden and I haven't even got the half measure yet. She's not so much an enigma as plain baffling. Hardly a person in her own right, just a construct of her husband's cruel opinions.

Seth says, "Mrs. Madden, where's your husband's car? And I'll need his car keys, please."

"I don't know where it is, you'll have to ask him. I haven't seen it for a while, though. He was talking about renting a garage, so perhaps he did that. He gets worried about people stealing his expensive gear."

I glance around the room, struggling to spot one expensive item. Even the TV's an old-school portable—small in size but a ton in weight.

Marcus scoffs. "He's got a fifteen-year-old Mazda convertible, not a bloody Aston Martin. He's paranoid, if you ask me."

"Is that why there's all the bolts on the door?" I ask Rachel. "Joseph's paranoia?"

She doesn't get a chance to answer. Kirstie's straight in there. "My God, as if! Joseph wouldn't spend money protecting his family, only on himself. How much did that last set cost you, Rach? About £500?"

"He's away so much for work," explains Rachel. "And it's scary when it's just me and Clara." She flicks her head toward her brother. "Marcus gave me the money."

Which is clearly news to his wife.

"What the actual fuck, Marcus? So we cripple ourselves buying that house so Danny can get into Muswell Hill Primary and you're giving money away?"

Marcus shakes his head at Rachel—*yeah, well done blabbermouth.*

Although she should count herself lucky. My deadbeat brother, Noel, once stole that much off me.

"Look, it was £500, Kirst. It was hardly going to sink us."

She snorts. "Oh well, that's reassuring. Do you realize, most MHP kids get private tutors from Year 2 if they want to even *think* about Latymer Grammar? Have you any idea how much tutors cost? Trust me, £500 will come in damn handy then." She sits down beside Rachel, taking her hand. "By the way, I'm not having a go at you, Rach. Marcus just doesn't think. He always has to be the good guy . . ."

Rachel snatches her hand away. "You and your MHP and Latymer." She gives good snarl, more than I'd have given her credit for. "There was no waiting list or selection criteria for any of Clara's schools and she's doing OK. More than OK. And without the help of any rip-off tutors as well." She looks to me. "I think if you've got the brains, you've got the brains."

The dynamic's not unusual. In-laws tussling over bragging rights.

Whose kid walked first, talked first, got the lead part in the school play. It's the timing that's really off. The weight of importance being given to something that surely shouldn't matter right now.

A girl has been murdered, for Christ's sake.

Someone close to you is in the frame.

Seth brings things back in line. "Mrs. Madden, we need the clothes Joseph was wearing over the weekend. Can you show me where they are, please?"

"Sure, sure. Anything if it'll help." She springs up, glad of a mundane task to focus on. "They should still be in the basket. I'm a bit behind this week. I've been so focused on Clara's uni applications and, what with Joseph being in Barcelona, I thought I might as well wait until he got back to do a big wash." She looks at me for validation. Little does she know she's looking at someone who still hasn't bought a washing machine. "OK, so I think it was the Hugo Boss shirt and his Paul Smith jeans . . ."

No £5 sweats for Joseph Madden.

Marcus waits until she's out of earshot. "Those locks on the front door—do you know why she got them? Joseph was going away for work and he told her there'd been a spate of violent break-ins on the estate. Several people—*women*—beaten to a pulp. Of course, I was worried so I looked into it. I've got a few police contacts because of my charity." He lowers his voice. "There'd been no violent break-ins. Not one. Not for months and months. Joseph likes Rachel terrified— that's why he said it."

I nod, taking this in, although I'm not sure what it tells us, other than the fact that Joseph Madden could do with being beaten to a pulp himself.

Kirstie grabs my arm like we're old friends gossiping about another friend's love life while they're in the toilet. "Seriously, no messing now." *Messing?* "You don't honestly think Joseph could have done this?"

I retrieve my arm. "Do you?" The question's aimed at them both.

Kirstie pauses, pressing her glossed lips together. "No. No, of course not." It doesn't matter what she says now; that pause tells me everything. It tells me there's a chink in her armor, a doubt in her mind, no matter how microscopic. "I mean, there's certainly no love lost between us. Joseph's a pig of a husband and a bully of a father as far as I'm concerned—but a killer?"

"He wouldn't want to get his hands dirty, for a start," adds Marcus.

"But he's denied knowing Naomi," I tell them. "And that's what we call a provable lie. In the absence of a confession, it's the next best thing."

It's another good sound bite but alas, not strictly true. Clara Madden, with her law and criminology leanings, would undoubtedly call me out on it, reciting all the reasons people lie that don't necessarily point to guilt. But hey, Clara Madden's not here, and as Rachel pointed out, the Connors aren't "fucking lawyers." They'll accept what I say as fact.

Kirstie shakes her head, gobsmacked. "I just find it so bizarre, the idea of Joseph with *Naomi*? She was *so* not his thing. Joseph goes for more of a refined type. *Women*, not girls, like Naomi. He likes them older, more cultured."

Marcus cuts in. "What my wife means is: he likes them richer."

"Well, you saw the photo, Kirstie. You saw the gift box." I let that settle. "So did you ever see Joseph hanging around your office? Or did he ever pop in unexpectedly, since Naomi's been working for you?"

"No, he's definitely never been to the office." She walks to the door, pushing it not quite closed. "But he occasionally drinks in the same place as us—Scarfes Bar at The Rosewood. You know, the Covent Garden end of High Holborn." I haven't got the faintest. The idea of dragging my lot to a hotel bar for £20 cocktails is farcical—fantastical, even. "Well, it's popular with the Friday after-work crowd and as The Grindhouse isn't far, it's not unusual to see him in there. Not that we really mix. He's with his colleagues and I'm with mine. We don't really get on."

No shit.

"But he could have met Naomi there, is that what you're saying?"

"He *could* have, I suppose . . ."

"Spit it out, Kirstie."

"Well, it's just that Joseph doesn't usually get there until later. The Grindhouse doesn't close until seven and Naomi only ever came out for a couple, so the chances are she was probably gone by the time he'd arrive."

"Probably?"

"Yes, probably." Firm, bordering on arsey. "I don't take a register."

The door opens and Kirstie shuts up immediately, painting the broadest, falsest smile across her face. Only an imbecile wouldn't realize they were being talked about, but by the looks of her, Rachel's got bigger things to worry about. Seth's signaling something over the top of her head, but as we don't have the telepathic link that Parnell and I seem to enjoy, I haven't a clue what he's trying to tell me. He might just be about to sneeze.

"I can't find his clothes." Rachel races over to Marcus, tugging at his hand, breathless with angst. "I've looked everywhere. In the washing basket, in the machine, in his wardrobe—you know, just in case he washed them himself and hung them back up." Kirstie can't resist a *"yeah, right."* "Can you check, Marcus? Or you, Kirst? Maybe I can't see for looking. My head's all over the place." She swings around to face me, eyes wide with terror. "You don't understand. He'll go mad if I can't find them. He always says I'm rubbish at looking for things. I'll get the blame for this. I always get the blame."

I take her gently by the shoulders again and she softens like a newborn, soothed by physical contact. "Look, stop panicking." I enunciate each word slowly. "No one's going to blame you. Sergeant Wakeman will have a proper look around and while we're doing that, can one of you make us all a nice hot drink?" Marcus nods but Kirstie's already out the door. "So just relax, OK? If Joseph's clothes are here, we'll find them, I promise."

Her head jerks. Utter confusion. "What do you mean, if they're here? Where else would they be?"

Where else indeed?

On a bonfire?

In the Thames?

In a skip on the other side of Blackfriars Bridge?

If there's one thing this city's good for, it's the keeping of dirty secrets.

———

By the time I leave the Pendown, London's at its most glorious peak: noisy and grubby and frothing with road rage. Cars belching out fumes. Drivers hollering *"fuck you, mate"* at anyone who dares to want to get home, same as they do. Pedestrians scuttling along pavements, running for buses, many running on empty after another hard day's graft in this ant colony we call home. While part of me yearns to stand for a minute, dizzied by the tempo and reveling in the rush-hour symphony of car horns and cuss words, my first priority—my master's orders, in fact—is to put a call in to Steele, and for that, I need quiet.

A wooden bench in the park opposite provides some brief sanctuary. Behind me, a row of crumbling gravestones overlooks a deserted netball court like a line of ghoulish spectators, and while I'm not usually one to spook easily, I'm relieved to see I'm not alone. I've got a woman and a toddler and a yappy brown dog for company.

Steele answers immediately, getting straight to business.

"He's a queer fish, isn't he? I only caught the tail end but he's *way* too calm for my liking. Sitting there with this stupid smirk on his face, like it's all a bit of a novelty, just something to pass the time. Well, Blake's approved the twelve-hour extension so Madden can pass the time in a cell tonight—see if that's enough of a novelty for him. I know giving him bed and board is eating up the custody clock, but hopefully by the morning we'll have more forensics."

"His alibi's iffy," I tell her. "His wife agrees they rowed and he stormed out, but she's got no idea when he came home. It was definitely after one, though, 'cos she was awake until then." Steele gives a low whistle then announces, *"Bye-bye alibi"* to whoever's in the incident room. "There's more—the clothes he was wearing on Saturday are missing. It's not looking good."

"It is for us." I picture her punching the air. "So how does the wife seem?"

"She's a bit of a queer fish herself but she's convinced he's innocent. She knows about his affairs, but she seems pretty resigned to them, to be honest. She's hard to recognize from his loopy-psycho-bitch description, that's for sure. If anything, I'd say she's scared of him.

He's emotionally abusive, that's without doubt." The toddler runs up to me, babbling heatedly about sausages and something else I can't quite decipher. "Anything interesting from the PM?" I ask, smiling at the mad little human.

"Not much we didn't already know. Cause of death as expected. No signs of sexual assault or recent sexual activity. Oh, and she was in fine physical health until some bastard caved her skull in."

In fine physical health and once a mad little human too, babbling about sausages or whatever else took her fancy. It's terrifying really, how we're all just running the gauntlet. How there's no rhyme or reason to who meets a violent death in their twenties and who trundles contentedly toward old age.

I park the existential angst. "So what's he saying?"

"Madden? What, apart from kicking off at having his Rolex confiscated?"

"A Rollie? Are you serious? That's worth more than the entire contents of their flat." I make a mental note to check the property store first thing. "Anyway, yeah, apart from that."

"Take a guess."

"A full confession and a promise to plead guilty?"

"Not quite. Try again."

"Er, let me see . . . no comment?"

"You got it, more or less. So much for saying he'll do everything he can to help. 'No comment' to where his car is. 'No comment' to every piece of evidence. Honestly, it's worse than tinnitus . . ."

"Nothing new there."

"True enough. But do you know what is new? Suspects requesting specific officers to interview them." My stomach flutters, and not in a good way—my body prepping my brain for the arrival of bad news. "Oh yeah, I kid ye not. There's only two people he's prepared to talk to, apparently. One is his wife, and clearly that isn't going to happen, and the other one's you, m'dear."

"Me?" I swap the phone to my other ear. "Why? What's that all about?"

"Who knows? He thinks you'll be a more sympathetic ear? You're nicer to look at than Parnell?"

I should be pleased. Normally I'm clawing at the interview-room door, desperate to get involved and feeling childishly aggrieved when I'm not allowed. But the fact that he's asked for me makes me anxious. Hell, it makes me cautious. An unfamiliar feeling for a lemming like me.

"I assume you told him to get real." The line's silent except for the distant shout of *"mine's a large Hawaiian"* in the background. Cooke, I think. "I thought you didn't want me anywhere near him?"

She sighs, obviously torn. "I don't. But we need him talking. We can only trip him up if he's talking."

There's a beep on the line, someone else calling. My heart says it's Aiden—we haven't spoken all day and that's unheard of—but my head says it's Jacqui, blowing a gasket about some drama at school pickup.

"OK, so it's on my shoulders to heal the mute, then?"

Another sigh. "Is that one of your biblical references, Kinsella? God, you can take the girl out of Catholic school—" She breaks off to bark *"no green peppers"* at someone, then in a flash she's back with me. "Anyway, it's not all down to you. He's not getting a private audience. Parnell'll be with you. And actually, since you mention it, he hasn't been *completely* mute. He has admitted one thing."

"Oh yeah?"

"Barcelona was a load of bull. He wasn't there at the beginning of the week."

"So where was he?"

"Croydon."

"Croydon?" A laugh escapes, a much-needed exhale. "Well, there are similarities. They both have tram systems."

"He has a 'friend' there, apparently. He was shacked up with her on Monday and Tuesday, then going in to work as normal during the day."

I never claimed to be the world's most honorable husband.

"Jesus, that's a bit risky. What if someone saw him? Told his wife?"

"From what you said, he wouldn't care. And anyway, he's arrogant. Arrogance breeds risky behavior."

Does that make me arrogant? Right now, my whole world's built on risk. On a fault line that could erupt at any time.

My phone beeps again. "Look, Boss, I've got someone trying to get through. Do you want me to come back to the office?"

"No, no need. Get an early night and get ready for mind games, that's the best thing you can do. I mean it, Cat—you're going to need your full eight hours for this guy. He's a sly one." Which is exactly what he said about his wife in The Grindhouse that day. "*And* he's got Lucas Stein on board. How he's affording his fees is anyone's guess. We need to look into that, actually . . ."

We say rushed goodbyes and then it's just me, staring at my phone screen with a sense of dread so acute I daren't risk standing up.

Missed call: The number "Dad" called at 6:15 p.m. on 8th Nov but left no message.
Missed call: The number "Dad" called at 6:16 p.m. on 8th Nov but left no message.

Two alerts.

Two cracks in the fault line.

Anyone else's dad, it'd be nothing. A DIY anecdote that doesn't warrant a voicemail, or a rant about the fuckwit who cut him up on the M25.

Not my dad.

My dad calls me, or I call him, at a set time every week—Sunday noon, for about ten minutes, never more. We rarely speak outside that scheduled time. It's a courtesy call, simple as that. And more of a courtesy to Jacqui than to each other. If it wasn't for Jacqui, we might never speak at all.

So two missed calls from my dad on a Wednesday evening can only mean one thing.

Trouble.

11

Thursday

Heeding Steele's advice about being match fit for the morning, I'd climbed into bed early last night—"climbed" being the operative word, given I sleep on a six-foot-high sky bed. A common feature of "bijou living," according to the prepubescent rental agent.

It's grown on me, the sky bed. I feel whimsical, like Heidi climbing into the hay bales, every time I turn in for the night, and there's no denying I sleep better in it than I've slept anywhere in a long time. Parnell jokes that's because of all the action it's getting. I joke it's because I sleep closer to God.

Last night was no joke. Eight restless hours agonizing over why Dad wants to speak to me, and why Aiden patently does not.

Although, trust Steele to teach me the real meaning of agony before I've even had my Weetabix.

"Right, folks, we've done a lot of talking about Naomi Lockhart's death, so just for a minute I want to talk about her life. I met her mum and dad first thing and trust me, you're going to want to headbutt the wall."

A tension descends. Glances are exchanged. When Steele's visibly upset, you know to assume the brace position.

"So . . . Naomi was born with a congenital diaphragmatic hernia, a serious condition I can barely pronounce never mind explain, but basically it's something a baby should never have to go through. Happy days, she made a full recovery, but it was touch and go for a while and she needed breathing support until she was two. She raised money for the hospital that looked after her ever since: cake sales, fun runs, she even threw herself out of a plane the minute she turned eighteen—raised nearly $2,000 that time."

Point being, we've lost a good one. And it doesn't matter what blah-blah we churn out about all victims being equal, some slice you more than others. Fact.

And there's more.

"She was also in a nasty car accident a few years back. Some idiot texting while driving landed her back in that same hospital for the best part of three weeks. She made another full recovery and passed her accountancy exams a couple of months later." Steele's voice remains steady but her hands are balled into fists. "And then, after battling through all that, she comes to the UK to have some fun and see a bit of the world, and a couple of months later she's dead. On *our* patch. I, for one, am taking that very personally, folks." She scours the room, locking eyes with each and every one of us. "So someone, *anyone*, give me good news, please."

Problem is, no one has any. And no one's brave enough to try polishing the proverbial turd.

"The Rolex is fake," I offer, even though I'm not sure how that's good or even particularly newsworthy. "I had a quick check on my way up. It's not a good fake either."

"Oh, you're an expert, are you?" At least Steele's smiling now.

"Actually, I am a bit. It's all in the second hand. A real Rollie has a smooth second hand but the cheap fakes are stuttery. My dad's into watches," I add by way of explanation. "Expensive watches and cheap women."

I shouldn't have said that. Dad might have managed to fly under the criminal radar just enough to get me through the police vetting process, but uttering his name in this office feels wrong and pollutive.

I must call him back.

What the hell did he want?

Renée raises a hand. "I've got a few updates. His girlfriend's place in Croydon is clear. His missing clothes definitely aren't there and she—name's Sadie Paulson—kind of balked at the suggestion she'd have washed them for him. Laundry's not in her job description, if you get me. I'd say she's one of those . . . well, whatever the female equivalent of a sugar daddy is? She's not massively older than him, about my age I'd say, fifty at a push, but she's married and minted. Runs her own PR firm. Oh, and she's paying for his brief."

"Married?" repeats Steele, as confused as I am. "He was at her flat for two nights. Where's the husband while Madden's warming the bed?"

"Edinburgh. She works down south during the week, goes home at weekends."

"Are we sure of that?" I ask. "Does she have a firm alibi? If she thought hers was the only bed being warmed, that could get nasty. Especially with Naomi being half her age."

Renée nods. "She's got a hundred-plus alibis, including two politicians and a Queen's Counsel. It was her husband's fiftieth birthday party—he's a big cheese in something or other."

"So she's paying his legal fees?" Parnell's intrigued. "Most cheaters run a mile at the first sign of inconvenience. He must be quite the Romeo."

Casanova.

"Or she's paying to make it go away?" I suggest. "If this goes to court, she'll have to testify and she's not going to want that if she's married." I turn to Renée. "I'm assuming he was never violent toward her? Nothing we can throw at him?"

"Oh, you're going to love this, Cat." Renée flicks through her notes. "Ah, here we are. *Joseph is not a violent man, although he's certainly a vigorous lover. But then I'd hardly risk my reputation and a very expensive prenup for five minutes of missionary, would I?'*"

"Bloody hell, I would," says Cooke, miserably. "I haven't got near my Karen since the second trimester. I'm getting the snip this time, I'm telling you."

The men squirm in unison. Steele gets things back on track with one booming word. "Phones!"

Swaines jumps to life. "Oh, OK, well, Forensics are working on the deleted stuff, but at first glance it all looks fairly boring. Rachel Madden's phone is pretty shit, so it's not gonna tell us as much as a smartphone. She doesn't seem to use it a lot anyway. At the moment, the only things I'd highlight are the lack of recent contact between the Maddens—there's virtually nothing for the past few months, just the occasional message asking if he's coming home so she can bolt the door. The daughter's laptop is the other slightly weird thing; well, her search history, I mean. It's a bit on the dark side."

"Dark?" bawls Steele. "What does 'dark' mean? A bit dodgy? Full-on deviant? Listen, Ben, Joseph Madden could have had access to that laptop, so if there's anything relevant—*anything* at all—we need to know now. Those two . . ."—a point to me and Parnell followed by a shoo of the hand telling us to get going—"are about two minutes off going head-to-head with Smarmy and Smarmier and we need every fleck of dirt to fling at them."

Swaines reddens but, fair play, he holds his own. "Well, I don't mean there's a load of *'How to get away with murder'* searches, Boss. The daughter's interested in criminal activity, that's all." He picks up a printout. "www.crimespree.com, www.release.org.uk. Research into various cases—and I'm talking *lots* of research. Oh yeah, and she googled *'naomi australian murder north london'* at nine fifty-two on Tuesday night."

"I wouldn't read too much into that," I say, scraping my hair back into an austere ponytail, ironing out the curls that Joseph Madden thought were so "sweet." "She wants to study criminology, so it's natural she'd be interested in a crime this close to home."

But how close to home?

With any luck, we're about to find out.

Expensive briefs fall into two distinct categories—the Show Ponies, who ply their trade using bombast, bluster, and out-and-out trickery, and the Calm Assurers, who breeze by—and succeed often—using nothing more than a dollop of self-confidence and a sunny disposition.

Lucas Stein isn't nicknamed Cool Hand Luke for nothing.

Charming and quietly calculating, very little fazes Lucas Stein. He possesses the wiliness of a fox and the heart rate of a hibernating tortoise, and it rubs off on his clients—none more so than Joseph Madden, it seems. As we enter the room, Stein and Madden are standing over the bolted-down table, chatting amiably, with all the laid-back ease of two men manning a BBQ with cold beers in their hands.

Our suspect looks well, even more striking than I remember. Most people are dulled against the backdrop of a gloomy gray interview room. Joseph Madden does the opposite. He brightens the place up.

Stein extends a hand. "Lu, good to see you again. Detective Kinsella."

I don't get a handshake, just a smile that could melt carbon.

Parnell sits down with a word of warning. "I hope you're feeling chattier this morning, Joseph. Last night wasn't fun for anyone."

Madden doesn't hear him. He doesn't hear him, doesn't see him, doesn't acknowledge any other presence except mine, and without a hint of false modesty, I'm looking the ropy side of average today—broken sleep and an old jumper dress that first lost its shape back in 2015 will do that to a person. Madden doesn't care, though. He's gazing at me with the kind of tender fervor usually reserved for firstborns.

It's like being drowned in oil.

"I'm so glad you're here, Cat," he says, radiating gratitude. "I wasn't sure you'd come—well, I wasn't sure you'd be allowed. I was chancing my arm, really." He smiles at me, making me part of a conspiracy I don't understand. "Honestly, thank you. We can get this business cleared up now that you're here. You were so helpful last time."

Parnell starts the recording, bringing a blessed end to Madden's fawning.

"For the tape, it is Thursday the 9th of November 2017, and the time is 9:14 a.m. Present are DS Luigi Parnell, DC Cat Kinsella, Joseph Madden, and his solicitor, Lucas Stein. In accordance with the Home Office Circular 50/1995, I am obliged to inform you that this interview is being remotely monitored and the custody record has been endorsed with the names of the officers monitoring."

Just one officer—Detective Chief Inspector Kate Steele, who was so eager to get a front-row seat for this one, she practically brought popcorn. Madden locates the camera in the far right corner and offers a regal wave.

I picture Steele waving back, her middle finger circling the air.

"So, Sergeant Parnell, I was wondering . . ." Madden grins at me like I'm *sooo* going to love this. "Are you any relation to Charles?"

Parnell thumbs a file, disinterested. "Who?"

Madden reacts with faux surprise. "*Surely* you've heard of Charles Stewart Parnell? The Irish nationalist? Leader of the struggle for home rule in the late nineteenth century."

Parnell looks up. "Never heard of the bloke. I'm a relation of Roger Parnell, though. Captain of the Hog and Hen's bar billiards team, if that's of any interest."

Madden turns his gaze back on me. "I bet you've heard of him, Cat. You seem very smart, and you must be Irish with a name like Kinsella."

Lucas Stein chimes in, gently tugging his client's reins. "So, just to explain about yesterday. Joseph was suffering from a mild migraine and didn't feel up to answering many questions, hence why he may have seemed uncooperative. However, you heard what the man said. He's keen to get things cleared up now, so ask whatever you need. He's got nothing to hide."

I assess Madden coolly, adding a few drops of scathing. Parnell always says I should copyright that expression. I've tried to teach him how to do it but his scathing comes off as sulky. "You should have told us you had a migraine, Joseph. We'd have arranged for you to see a doctor."

He shrugs. "I don't see doctors. I don't have much respect for what they do. I've lived in this body for forty-three years so I think that makes *me* the expert in how it functions, don't you? And anyway, I have an unusually high pain threshold." He leans in, making me wish I were in Parnell's seat—a 45-degree angle feels less intimate than head-on. "Once, when I was a child, I sliced my foot open on a Stanley knife—and let's just say, my mother didn't believe in doctors either. So do you know what I did, Cat? I mixed some salt water to sanitize the wound, then I stole the thinnest fishing line I could find out of my neighbor's garage and I stitched myself up in silence while my mother was downstairs giving her boyfriend a blow job in front of *Dallas*. I was only seven at the time. Doctors have to train for seven years, did you know that?" He sits back again, satisfied his point's been made.

"You take Temazepam," I say. "Your wife told us that. They must come from a doctor because you wouldn't be stupid enough to buy drugs off the internet, am I right?"

"They are from a doctor," he concedes. "But she's a very, *very* good friend of mine who I trust implicitly. Therein lies the difference."

Parnell's pen's primed. "Name, please."

"Her name? OK, as you wish—it's Dr. Siobhan Casey. S-I-O-B-H-A-N C-A-S-E-Y. She works on Harley Street. She's a consultant in musculoskeletal medicine, the second youngest in the country, I believe. There aren't many women who understand the body like Siobhan does." He smiles. "I'm an exceptionally lucky man."

Moving things on before I hurl or hit him, I snatch the photo from the file and shove it under his nose. Enlarged, it's a bit more blurry than we'd like. Not enough for Stein to start acting the fool, though.

"What can you tell us about this then? If you really want to get things cleared up, you're going to have to explain why you're pictured interacting with a woman who, you claim in your witness statement, you barely recall seeing."

"And I stand by that statement." He stretches his arms out, cracking his knuckles. "All that photo does is capture a fleeting moment where I said '*hello*' to someone who'd said '*hello*' to me. *That's* all you have evidence of—a millisecond of 'interaction,' as you call it."

Stein's impressed as he watches Joseph Madden do his £750 per hour job for him. I look away, trying to give off an air of disdain, but actually, what he's said is right. Photos capture color, they capture climate, they can even capture emotion. What they can't capture is context—and context is everything.

Parnell keeps the pressure up. "Let me get this straight: Naomi said hello to you first? So did you think she was coming on to you, was that it?"

Stein shifts, ready to earn his keep if required, but Madden's happy to answer. "Not at all. I thought she was making her way to the bread rolls and, as she had to squeeze past me to get to them, and because we live in a civilized society and most people have manners, she said hello as she did so. The story really does end there."

Stein chips in, tapping the photo. "As you can see, the bread rolls are pictured to the right of Joseph."

It sounds ludicrous, but this is what so many cases come down to—the mundane, almost farcical, "facts." Madden won't be flouncing out of here anytime soon based on a basket of brioche, but there's a certain weight in the detail, a plausibility to what's being said. There'll be even more if it gets to court and it's made a "thing" by some barrister with booming patrician tones and a sideline in stand-up. Seriously, I've met barristers who could make bread rolls sound as pivotal as DNA.

Still, we persist.

"You're admitting now that you spoke to Naomi," I state. "So why did you initially claim you couldn't recall her?"

"I'd forgotten, simple as that." He angles the photo toward himself. "She's hardly what you'd call memorable."

"She's got long lilac hair," I counter. "I'd say that's pretty memorable."

"They all have unusual hair these days. They all have unusual everything. Everyone's so desperate to be different that they've all become the same. Individuality is dead and uniformity is king."

"You're quite the philosopher, Joseph, but that doesn't really answer the question."

"Look, I work in retail. I must say hello to over a hundred people a day. I rarely take note of them."

"Do you send gifts to a hundred people a day?" asks Parnell, completely deadpan. "You're aware we found a gift box in Naomi's desk, and you haven't denied it's your handwriting on the tag."

"Yes, I'm aware, but I've been pondering this and I think I can explain what's happened." He draws his chair in, eager to share his conclusions but not half as eager as we are to hear them. "I've sent Kirstie a few gifts over the years, usually to her workplace as there's rarely anyone in to sign for them at home. That gift box could be an old one of Kirstie's. It could have sat in this girl's desk for years."

"You sent Kirstie Connor gifts?" Kirstie, who called him a tosser? Not to mention a pig and a bully. "That seems a bit . . . unusual?"

I'm no expert in family dynamics, but still.

Madden suppresses a yawn. "I buy all my own gifts. I think there's a real art in choosing the perfect something for someone—and, well, I wouldn't leave it to Rachel. She doesn't exactly have good taste."

Evidently.

"Blimey," says Parnell, pretending to be impressed. "I haven't got a clue what I got my wife last Christmas. I know how much it cost because I saw it on the credit card statement, but I couldn't tell you what it was. Same as a lot of men, I reckon."

"Oh, but I'm not like other men, Sergeant. I'm not like them at all."

And the chilling thing is, it doesn't come across as a brag. Just an icy statement of fact that blankets the room like an arctic frost.

"Kirstie Connor had never seen it before, but hey, nice try," I say, trying to thaw the air. I lay the CCTV image on the table. "Can you confirm this is you, please, Joseph?"

For the first time, Madden seems happy to play understudy to Stein, who says, "Whether or not this is Joseph is rather a moot point, given it's taken 0.46 miles from Naomi Lockhart's house. Not on her street. Not on any of the adjoining streets. 0.46 miles away."

Someone's been busy.

"Ah, but it's this that makes it of interest." Parnell plants a finger on the time stamp. "Look—eleven forty-seven p.m. We have reason to believe Naomi came to harm within an hour of that."

Stein puts both hands behind his head, classic holiday pose. "And I wouldn't dream of challenging that, Lu. Not yet, anyway. But listen, I took Brandy—that's my red setter, by the way—for walks around Hoxton Square last night, and I'd say there were a fair few crimes committed within 0.46 miles of there, wouldn't you?" He offers up his wrists. "So do you want to slap the cuffs on me now? You see what I'm getting at?"

Parnell stares Stein down while speaking to Madden. "Tell us about the argument you had with your wife on Saturday night."

Madden sighs, as if any discussion about Rachel is wasted airtime. "She was supposed to have given up smoking—*again*." Another sigh. "It's honestly so sad. She was a beacon of health when we met—a professional dancer, actually. I really don't know what happened . . .

Anyway, I'd caught her outside at the party, in the alley beside the house, sucking on a cancer stick like her sad little life depended on it, and when we got home I reminded her *again* that it's a filthy habit that only the very weakest people indulge in. That was it. That was the argument."

Bar the odd joint, I've never been what you'd call a proper smoker, but Joseph Madden makes me want to chain-smoke forty Marlboro Reds so I can cough repeatedly in his face.

I pick up Renée's notes, the ones she made when Madden first came in, solicitor-free and, would you believe it, migraine-free as well. "Joseph, you told DC Akwa that you went for a walk to cool off after this row, but that you were no longer than thirty minutes, returning home around twelve fifteen. Do you still stand by that?"

"Yes, of course I do."

I land our best punch. "You see, the problem we have is that your wife's statement contradicts this. Your wife was still awake at one a.m. and she says you hadn't returned by then. Is she mistaken?"

He laughs. "What? Mistaken about me going into the bedroom and snatching the duvet off her? Mistaken about her throwing a photo frame at me?" He still looks relaxed, but a slight hysteria has crept into his voice.

Progress.

"So Rachel's lying, is that what you're saying? Listen, I've met her, Joseph, and she's very upset. She doesn't believe for a second that you could have done this, so why would she lie?"

"Because that's what she does. She's unstable. Impossible to live with. I told *you* that months ago."

I'm ready for this. Inside I'm fizzing but on the outside I'm an android—cool, calm, and completely impassive. "For the tape, Joseph, can you explain what you're referring to?"

He's thrown by this. He didn't expect me to mount the elephant in the room quite so easily. "You know what I'm referring to. I told you my wife was out to get me."

Which is true, but we need more detail. I clear my throat and focus on speaking slowly and clearly. "For the benefit of the tape: sometime in August 2017, I can't be precise about the date but toward the end of that month, Joseph Madden asked me for some informal advice regarding a situation with his wife. While not convinced it was a police matter, I suggested he speak with an officer at his local station who would be able to assess it in more detail and decide on the correct course of action. Joseph, would you agree this is a fair representation of our very brief conversation?"

Because it *is*. When you take out the flirting and that weird moment with the devil mask, what I've stated—for the tape—*is* all it boiled down to.

"Yes, I suppose that's a fair representation." *And relax.* "But to be clear, the 'situation with my wife' was a series of threats she'd made to make me suffer, and this is *exactly* what she's doing now—lying about what time I came home to make me look guilty."

Parnell looks like he's giving this due consideration, then, "Where's your car, Joseph?"

The swerve in questioning throws him. "My car?"

"Yes, we know you have a Mazda convertible, registration SB52 VDX. Traffic-monitoring cameras put it in the Arnos Grove area, so we will find it. It's only a matter of time."

"I'm surprised you haven't found it already. You only had to ask Rachel."

"We did. She didn't know."

His head tilts. "She didn't know? She didn't know it's been at the garage for the past few weeks and that's why I've been using her shit heap to get to the driving range?" He breaks into a broad smile, nodding slowly, as if he's finally grasped the rules of the game. "See, I think I get it now. This is Rachel's idea of fun—stringing things out, trying to wind me up." He laughs. "You know, she's grown quite the pair of balls over the past few months. If it wasn't so tedious, it'd be sexy."

"We'll need the name of that garage, please," I say, blankly, not giving him the reaction he wants. "We've also been unable to locate the clothes you were wearing on Saturday evening. Can you shed some light on this too, perhaps?"

"In the washing basket or in my wardrobe if they've been washed already, which they probably have. When it comes to housework and Clara's homework, Rachel runs a very tight ship."

"Rachel checked both of those places—along with an officer from our team, I should add. Your clothes weren't there."

Another laugh, stone cold this time. "Can't you see what this is about? I told you she was threatening to punish me and now she's got the perfect opportunity. She's lying about what time I came home and she's lying about my clothes. They were in the washing basket—I put them there myself. She's obviously hidden them, destroyed them, maybe."

Parnell doesn't react. "A team is continuing to search your house, Joseph, taking away any items that might be of interest to this investigation. If your clothes are there, we'll find them, don't worry. And if we find any proof that your wife has concealed them, she'll be dealt with accordingly, you can be sure of that."

Madden leans diagonally across to Parnell, arms folded on the table, man to man.

"Look, just let me speak to Rachel, OK? She's had her fun, played her little game, and now it's kiss-and-make-up time. It'll be fine. I'll make her see sense."

"That won't be possible, I'm afraid."

He slams a fist down. "I'm allowed to make a phone call and I demand to speak to my wife!"

He's chosen the wrong man to demand this of. Parnell *loves* correcting this common misconception. "I'm afraid you've been watching too much telly, Joseph. You don't have the right to speak to anyone, however, we can get a message to your wife."

Madden looks to Stein who confirms the bad news.

"Look, believe it or not, we're trying to help you." I say it even though I know he's far too smart to believe it. "Have you ever heard the phrase 'every contact leaves a trace'? Well, we have hairs, fibers. It won't take us long to match them."

"As my client has admitted, Naomi Lockhart brushed past him briefly at the Connors' house. You're going to have to do better than that."

"Don't worry, Lucas, I've got this." Madden lays a hand on Stein's arm, effectively shushing him while looking straight at me—straight into me. "You and your fat friend here run along and do all the tests you like. And when they come back clear, and I've heard all your apologies, I'll go home and deliver a message to Rachel myself.

"One she won't forget in a hurry."

12

"Well, he's a charmer."

"You're not wrong, my fat friend."

Parnell pinches several inches and pretends to look offended. "Cheek of him! I tell you, back in the eighties, I'd have lamped him. Now all I can do is comfort-eat. I'll have to do a hundred burpees to burn off one of these bad boys."

It's a while later and we're debriefing in Steele's office, chewing over events and chowing down on Thai chicken meatballs. A quick celebratory scoff to mark the news that Chief Superintendent Blake's given us the nod for the ninety-six—the longest detention warrant we can apply for.

"I'm surprised Blake went for it." I plunge a meatball into my pot of curry sauce, earning me a *"heathen"* look from Parnell. "I mean, everything we've got is circumstantial."

"Everything we've got is circumstantial." Steele mimics me using that shrill, whiny tone she uses to mimic anyone who's annoyed her. "You kids. You shit a brick over anything 'circumstantial.' Well, let me tell you something, back before fingerprints and DNA and bloody Shoe-print Image Capture, all you had was 'circumstantial' and the prisons were still full. Coppers still made their collars."

She's right, of course. Many a case is won on circumstantial. It's actually quite rare that things get tied up in a nice neat bow— "Professor Plum in the library with the candlestick."

Urban policing is no game of Clue.

"So how'd they go at The Grindhouse?" I ask. "No shrines to Naomi, by any chance? No locker full of her dirty knickers?"

"No second phone?" adds Parnell. "You know, without any digital contact between them, my money's still on him stalking her, not an affair."

"Ah, shit!" Steele drops a meatball down her peach silk blouse. Not that it's a problem, her office is part investigative epicenter, part walk-in wardrobe. "No, no, nothing that concrete, sadly." She dabs herself with a napkin. "But it wasn't a wasted visit, far from it. Seth and Emily spent a good while with the staff and it seems our Joseph Madden is a bit of a Walter Mitty. That's a Billy Bullshitter to you, Kinsella."

"Hey, I know who Walter Mitty is."

"So what's he been fibbing about?" asks Parnell. "Don't tell me, he's a Formula One driver at weekends?"

"He invented the cappuccino?" I say, joining in.

Steele laughs. "Not quite, but he doesn't own The Grindhouse like you thought. He doesn't even manage the place. He's just a plain old catering assistant. No disrespect to catering assistants, by the way—I earned my silver-service stripes back in the day. Anyway, he's been there the longest and he's the only full-time staff member, so naturally he's got extra responsibilities, but when it comes down to it, he skivvies for some guy called Stu Graham for not much more than the London Living Wage. Graham owns three places and flits between them all, so he relies on Madden to keep him in the loop about stock levels and what have you, but ultimately, he's a glorified pot-washer."

"So Barcelona, Vienna, Guatemala, all the work trips, they're made up?" Steele throws me an odd look. It's the first she's heard of the last two. "Well, it explains a lot," I say, moving quickly on. "Where he lives, the fifteen-year-old car . . ."

"Speaking of the car," says Steele. "We seized it a few hours ago. The paperwork checks out. It's been in Shelby's garage in Arnos Grove since the 25th of October, as he said. Not sure how relevant that makes it to us but we're to 'leave no stone unturned'—orders of Blake." She spears another meatball, more successfully this time. "Like I'm in the business of leading half-arsed investigations, the cheeky devil."

Parnell chews as he ponders, waggling his fork. "So, OK, how do you charm the pants off—*literally* charm the pants off—a Harley Street doctor and what was the other one?"

"A PR guru," I remind him.

"OK, how do you pick up women like that when you haven't got a penny to your name?"

"Easy," says Steele. "You pretend you're some sort of coffee impresario, jetting all over the world sniffing beans, or whatever it is they do. Even if it doesn't pay that much, it's still quite glamorous, isn't it?" She jabs a stack of papers with her fork. "And he's got a load of credit card debt so he's obviously not afraid to spend a bit of money maintaining the illusion. Renée went to see that Dr. Siobhan Casey and she said that, while she realized he wasn't wealthy, she assumed he was comfortable. Her jaw nearly hit the floor when she found out she'd been doing the horizontal fox-trot with a pot-washer. Do you know what he'd actually said to her about the Temazepam? That he needed it because all the caffeine and jet lag played havoc with his sleep. Christ, you almost have to hand it to him . . ."

"*Her* jaw nearly hit the floor," I say, practically frothing. "His own bloody wife thinks he's a coffee impresario. She's turned that flat into a fortress to protect her and her daughter when their Lord and Master's away on business, and all the time he's playing house with his rich lady friends? Wanker."

"You know, I don't think it's just about them being rich. God, I've eaten too much." Steele flops back, tugging on her waistband. "I think it's about status. Take this Siobhan Casey. He couldn't wait to tell us she's a Harley Street doctor, second youngest in the country and all that crap."

"And what status does Kinsella have?" asks Parnell, suppressing a burp—he hasn't had spicy food in months. "'Cos he certainly seemed enamored with her."

Steele casts me an assessing glance, as if she can't work it out either. "Only woman in the room, I suppose," she concludes eventually. "The Grindhouse staff say he's a Grade-A flirt. And Kinsella's in a position of power. Power equals status."

"Am I?" I ask. "Well, I wish someone had told me. I'm sitting here bursting for the toilet because I was scared you'd shout at me if I was late to the meeting."

"God, am I that much of a tyrant?" To her credit, she sounds genuinely surprised. "Although if you could hold it in a bit longer, that'd be great. I'm heading off in ten minutes. I'm sure you can squeeze until then. You're twenty-six, no kids—you should have a pelvic floor like a bear trap."

I cross my legs, exaggerating. "So what else did The Grindhouse staff say? I'm assuming they never saw Naomi hanging around?"

"No, but from the description a couple of them gave, they might have seen his daughter a few times but they assumed she was his girlfriend, wound him up about her age." I pull a grossed-out face. "Yeah, well, it gets worse. He didn't correct them."

"Oh, Jesus, now that is *sick*. The guy's certifiable."

"Never underestimate male vanity, Kinsella. Especially middle-aged male vanity."

Parnell considers defending his gender but settles for snaffling the last meatball. "All in all, I'd say Joseph Madden's a bit of a fantasist."

"Fantasist or con artist?" I say.

"But he's not really conning them out of anything," argues Steele. "The impression Renée got from Siobhan Casey, and the other one, Sadie Paulson, was that they both liked spoiling him, buying him expensive gifts, designer clothes, shagging him in expensive hotels and so on, but it's not like he's ever asked for money. Sadie Paulson *insisted* on paying for his brief, he didn't ask. The only thing he's conning them about is who he really is and that's a bit different. That's more of a fantasist."

"Kieran Drake said the guy Naomi was seeing was rich and had a flat in town. That sounds like the kind of shite Madden would come out with." I bite the bullet and offer a completely unsubstantiated theory. "Maybe he'd sold Naomi that line and then when she saw him at the Connors', she overheard something to suggest he's just a plain old skivvy, and she called him on it and he snapped?"

"It's possible," says Parnell, cautiously. "I don't think he'd take kindly to having his cover blown. His self-image is obviously massively important to him. I'd say he's a bit of a narcissist—borderline, at least. All that Charles Stewart Parnell nonsense—he needs to feel intellectually superior to everyone, even to Lucas Stein, and that man's got the alphabet after his name. *Don't worry, Lucas, I've got this.*'"

Steele chips in, "'*I have an unusually high pain threshold.*'"

"Yeah, and that," says Parnell, laughing at another terrible impression. "Classic narcissistic boasting."

Steele groans. "Fantasist. Narcissist. Any more 'ists' while we're at it?"

"Yeah, sexist," I say. "All that 'housework and homework—Rachel runs a very tight ship' bollocks. The guy's odious."

"Agreed." There's a long pause while Steele rubs her face, seemingly wrestling with something. "But is he *definitely* our guy? I mean, what he said about his wife? Could it be . . . ?"

Parnell lets out a chest-rattling sigh. At first I think it's indigestion, but it's not, it's exasperation. "Kate, no." *Kate*, not "Boss"—an appeal to her common sense. "Please tell me you don't believe that claptrap. Not you, of all people."

The implication being he wouldn't put it past me.

Encouraged by Steele's open mind, I say what's been dancing around mine for the past few hours. "You know, I don't think we can ignore the fact that he said three months ago—a good few weeks before Naomi ever graced the tarmac at Heathrow—that his wife was being weird, threatening to make him suffer. And then, lo and behold, she gets a gold-plated opportunity when we turn up." Parnell shakes his head; he's clearly not for turning. "Look, I'm not saying I think he's innocent. We've got other stuff that *suggests* he's guilty. But I also think she *could* be lying about his alibi to make it worse for him. *Could.* I don't know about destroying his clothes, though—that does seem a bit more calculating."

"That's more or less where I am." Steele smiles. "Here, what are the chances of that, Kinsella? You and me being on the same page?"

And yet it's not as cozy a page as Parnell's. I'm so used to it being us against the bad guys. Us against Steele. I feel sad at the thought of him doubting me, questioning my judgment. I feel a bit orphaned, pitiful as it sounds.

"Look, just hear me out, Lu." Steele's voice is gentle—full-on "Kate" mode. "I don't know what I believe yet, that's the honest answer. All I know is that until we've got stronger forensics—because we don't want a potential jury getting the 'circumstantial' heebie-jeebies like

Kinsella here—Madden's missing clothes and his wife's contradiction of his alibi are the most damning pieces of evidence we've got, so we've *got* to make sure she's whiter than white. We can't risk it biting us on the arse in a few weeks or months when she changes her mind because they've kissed and made up. I think we need to take a closer look at her, definitely." She lays her hands flat on the table, drumming her fingers lightly. "So there, I've said it."

Parnell's still skeptical. "If we pull her in, it tells Stein we're giving credence to Madden's claims. Are you sure you want to do that?"

It takes her all of five seconds to sidestep the problem. "So we do it informally, then. We don't bring her within a mile of this station. We get everything on the QT—everything Stein will go after to prove she's out to get him: phone records, bank records, you know the drill. In the meantime, Cat, you act as a sort of light-touch Family Liaison Officer." The plan rolls off her tongue, she's clearly been strategizing all day. "But I mean light-touch. This isn't a full-time thing. I still need you here, but you're to buddy-up to her a bit, OK? Keep her updated on what's happening. Do the whole, 'you're a victim too' spiel. Right now, Rachel Madden is our best witness—our best piece of evidence—and I'm entrusting her to you, m'dear. Are you up for it?"

It takes me all of two seconds to sidestep my doubts.

Mission accepted.

13

"You are kidding? This is a joke, right?" Rachel forces out a despairing laugh. "I mean, *obviously* I knew it'd be my fault somehow, but he's really lost the plot this time."

Third time lucky tonight, or at least third time less stressy.

This is my third encounter with Rachel Madden but the first without Kirstie Connor, and honestly, it's like breathing at a lower altitude; infinitely more pleasant. Without Kirstie's imposing, twitchy presence, Rachel seems less wound up, more forthcoming.

"So I'm hiding his clothes, then? I'm lying about his alibi?"

We sit facing each other in the Maddens' stiflingly hot living room. Me on a leather pouf, or whatever the uncomfortable thing's called, Rachel in the armchair, wearing a pink fluffy dressing gown that adds a bit of bulk to her slight frame. The air's thick with the scent of cheap, cloying candles, and every other chair, every other surface, is stacked high with piles of neatly folded ironing. It appears that, to quote the man himself, when it comes to housework, Rachel Madden does indeed run a tight ship.

"And *I* made threats against *him*?" She makes it sound like utter lunacy. "Threats to do what, exactly? To have a life of my own? To become less reliant on him? Because that's what he feels threatened by—the idea of Clara leaving home and me striking out a bit more."

"He said you'd threatened to make him suffer," I tell her. "To make him pay for being a bad husband."

She's goggle-eyed, more stunned than furious. "Well, I might have said *something* like that in the heat of an argument once. Probably more than once. But really, he made a complaint about *that*?" She shakes her head, exasperated. "God, I knew he was getting worse, but . . ." Her voice tails off as her head drops low.

"It wasn't a complaint, exactly. He was just concerned about what you might do."

Her head shoots up. "What, like wait for a temporary employee of a relative to be murdered and stitch him up for it? Has he lost his mind? Have you?"

It all seemed so simple in Steele's office, my instructions so clear. Explain the accusations to Rachel Madden. Listen. Assess. Report back. Right now, though, I feel a fool for even being here. For posing these questions. For humoring Joseph Madden's probable tripe.

I keep my voice firm and steady. "Look, I'm here to help you, OK? To keep you updated, to be a friend of sorts, as weird as that sounds. But that means I'm also going to have to ask some difficult questions—and before you answer, I want you to remember two things. One—I *have* to ask them. I'm not accusing you of anything or implying anything, I'm just doing my job, right?" She shrugs, comfortable as she can be with this first part. "Two—a young woman is dead. You're not to think of her as someone Joseph might have been involved with. You're to think of her as a young, impressionable twenty-two-year-old, not that much older than Clara." I let that percolate while I shuffle the pouf a little closer—it's not a strategic move; the gas fire's scorching my back. "We just need to know the truth about what happened to her. Her mum and dad need to know."

I'm not sure if it's the reference to Clara or Naomi's parents, but with a nod of her head, we form an uneasy alliance.

"So, cards on the table—do you know where Joseph's clothes are? The clothes he was wearing Saturday night."

"No."

As consummate as a trained witness addressing a jury. Loud, but not booming. Insistent, but not rude. No theatrics. No backlash. Just "No."

"And did you lie about what time he came home?"

"No," she repeats, warier this time. "But I told you, I don't know *exactly* what time he got back. All I know is that Kirstie called around one—well, you can check that on my phone, can't you?—and there was still no sign of Joseph. Kirstie was worried about me," she adds, second-guessing my next question. "She knew Joseph would go off about me smoking and she just wanted to check I was all right. Anyway, we talked for a few minutes but she was still really drunk and she wasn't making much sense. Afterward, I tried to read a few pages of my book but I was too tipsy and I must have read the same sentence ten times, so I turned the light out and went to sleep. It must have been around one fifteen. Joseph definitely wasn't back."

"So he didn't storm into your bedroom and snatch the duvet off you? You didn't throw a photo frame at him?"

"No! Is that what he's saying?" Initial shock gives way to a brittle laugh. "I mean, it's exactly like something that *would* happen. It probably *has* happened. But on Saturday night, no, definitely not."

Music starts up in the room directly above us. The distant, sulky tones of Drake, boo-hooing over an ex who's had the cheek to move on.

I flick my head toward the ceiling. "What about Clara? Maybe she heard something?"

"She didn't." Rachel shifts slightly, a ripple in an otherwise calm ocean. "She heard us arguing when we first came back so she put her headphones in. Fell asleep like that. It's how she zones out when we get going."

Memories pinball around my skull. Seven years old and soothing myself with crisps and Fanta, nicked from the pub cellar, while Mum and Dad tear strips out of each other in the flat upstairs. Fast-forward another seven years and it wasn't crisps doing the soothing, it was vodka. Vodka and older boys.

Clara's got the right idea—music's a far less malignant crutch.

"We've found Joseph's car," I say, shunting the memories to the back of my brain; the part that bursts alive at three in the morning. "It was booked into Shelby's in Arnos Grove on the 25th of October." She shifts again, not sure where I'm going with this. "Thing is, Joseph claims you knew this because he'd been driving your car while his was in the garage. And if that's true, Rachel, then you've either got a very bad memory, or you deliberately withheld that from us. Which one is it?"

"He put it in Shelby's *again*? I'm not surprised it's been in so long then. He always brags about getting 'mates' rates' from Marc Shelby but he doesn't seem to realize that puts him way down the priority list." I give her a look that says she's rather missing the point. "OK, yeah, now you mention it, he *has* been driving my car recently, but that's not unusual. He often takes mine if he's out of petrol and broke. Honestly, I had no idea it was in the garage. He certainly didn't tell me. Mind you, he doesn't tell me a lot these days." She leans forward, wrapping her arms around herself, an act of self-care rather than a defensive gesture. "It used to be the exact opposite, you know. Phone calls ten, fifteen times a day and God forbid I didn't answer. I always thought it was a bit much, a bit too possessive, but maybe it's better than being ignored."

"He's asked to see you," I say, not sure if I'm trying to provoke or console her. "Not that it's possible, but—"

"No! No way. Not when he's like this." She grips the arms of the chair, like she's terrified I might rip her out of the flat and haul her in front of her husband. "I mean, I want to see him, of course I do. I want him home, for God's sake. But he's going to be so angry with me." Her grip tightens, her knuckles turning pearlescent white. "How long are you keeping him for?"

"We've been granted another three days."

Her face screams outrage but her posture gives her away. Her grip loosens, her shoulders soften. Relief reigns supreme.

Three days of peace.

"Can *I* see him?"

Clara Madden, looking a shadow of the girl who farmed out grins and sparky put-downs in the Connors' kitchen the other night, stands in the doorway wearing a pair of microscopic shorts and a crop top— or, as my gran used to say, *"an outfit that wouldn't dress a crow."*

Rachel glides to her side, taking Clara's face in her hands, eye level. "No, darling, that's really not a good idea. Dad's a bit stressed at the moment and he'll only upset you. You know how easily he upsets you."

"You wouldn't be allowed anyway," I say. "Not while he's being questioned."

Clara explodes, smacking both hands off the doorframe. The thud makes me wince but she barely even flinches. "This is so fucking unfair!" she storms. "You know, it's all over Snapchat already. Well, from what I've heard anyway, given I don't have a fucking phone or laptop."

I offer a thin, neutral smile, a yard short of apologetic. "I'll check on their progress tomorrow. Shouldn't be long now."

"'*Shouldn't be long now,*'" she mimics, taking a few stomps into the room. "Do you have *any* idea how it feels to have people *obviously* talking about you but no idea what they're saying? It's worse than torture."

"Maybe it's better not to know," I say.

"Maybe it's better not to spout pointless platitudes."

Ouch. We've got a live wire here.

Rachel tries to pull her close but Clara pushes her away, evidently in no mood for mummy cuddles. "As if I haven't got enough problems at college, Mum. Why the fuck is this happening?" Before Rachel can answer, Clara flies out of the room, giving the doorframe another thwack and thundering back up the stairs, offering one final thought midway—"Fuck my life and fuck Dad!"

Rachel turns around, weary but less upset than I'm expecting. "Sorry about that. Seventeen-year-old girls, eh? They're explosive at the best of times and now *this.*"

"No need to apologize. She's a victim too. If she's close to her dad, she's bound to act out."

"Close? To Joseph?" An alien concept judging by Rachel's face. "She craves his approval—not that she'd admit it—but I wouldn't say they're close." Her expression shifts. "Listen, do you want a drink?"

Truth? I want several. Although, of course, what I *really* want is for Dad not to have called me and for Aiden not to have stopped. And for Naomi to be alive. But as there's very little I can do about any of those situations, I want enough wine to scuff my edges, enough vodka to convince me I don't care.

Shame then that drinking on the job went out in the seventies, along with brown Ford Cortinas and the Bay City Rollers.

"Well, I'm having one," Rachel says, not waiting for an answer.

I follow her out to a thin galley kitchen which makes the Bay City Rollers seem modern—heavy oak cupboards, terra-cotta tiling, and a boarded-up serving hatch completing the unintentionally retro look.

On the side there's a half-drunk bottle of supermarket gin, which probably explains why she seems more relaxed than usual.

"OK, so I've got gin, beer, cider—pear or normal." She opens the fridge door. "And there's wine, although it's been open a week. Or there's mineral water, but that's Joseph's so we probably shouldn't open that. He won't drink tap water. He says tap water is just toilet water with contraceptive drugs mixed in. He's right when you think about it."

Gotcha, Joseph Madden. I read that *NYT* article. I smiled at that very same quote. Your wife might think you're this witty, worldly sage, but I know you're a leech who passes off other people's opinions as your own. You aren't as clever as you think.

The thought cheers me immensely.

"A glass of toilet water will do me, much as I'd love a proper drink." I'm about to explain that I'm on duty but after getting the awkward questions out of the way, it's time for Operation Buddy-Up, a nice girls'-night-in vibe. "Bloody antibiotics," I add, tutting. "Better not."

Rachel pours herself a drink—three parts gin, one part lime cordial—and leans against the worktop. "It's a myth, you know. There's only a handful you shouldn't mix. Metronidazole, erythromycin, and . . ." She closes her eyes, testing herself. "Damn, I can't remember the others now. It feels like a lifetime ago."

"What does?"

"Life before Joseph. Life before I walked into the Coach and Horses on Greek Street and the most beautiful man I'd ever seen asked if I'd got a light." She swills her drink around, caught in a memory. "He wasn't so anti-smoking back then."

"And the antibiotics?"

"Oh God, yeah, sorry—I was training to be a nurse when I met Joseph. I was a dancer too. Clara came along a year later and put paid to both."

"What kind of dance?" I'm smiling. I think it might be part-genuine. "I was an Irish dancer in my youth. Boys kind of put paid to that too."

She smiles. "Oh, a bit of everything. I was a promising ballet dancer when I was young. The Royal Academy was even mentioned, although

I'd have needed a scholarship because my parents weren't rich. They weren't that interested either, and you need interested parents if you're going to succeed in life, I think. Don't get me wrong, they weren't *bad* parents, they were just . . . passive, a bit cold. They kept us fed and clean and warm and safe and they felt that was enough, I suppose—job done."

"So you didn't stick with it then? The ballet?"

"I filled out a bit too much." I shoot her an arch stare. "Yeah, I know, hard to believe, right? But it's a brutal industry. Any *hint* of a breast or a hip reminds the audience that you're human, and you're not supposed to be human. You're supposed to be art."

I divert the conversation—gin and regret aren't great companions. "You had Clara quite young?" I'd put her around mid- to late thirties but if she's any older, a dose of flattery won't hurt Operation Buddy-Up.

"Twenty-one." Which, if Clara is seventeen, makes Rachel thirty-eight. Definitely the older sibling. "I suppose it was young. My mum and dad weren't best pleased, anyway. Marcus was the headache back then, you see—nothing bad, just a bit wild. I was supposed to be The Good One. The one they could brag about down the British Legion—the one with the nice little nursing career, the solid bloke with a solid trade, the nice house, maybe a couple of kids wearing the latest trainers a bit further down the line." She gives a little sniff. "The nice house! Who in London lives in a nice house, except celebrities and those City types?"

"Marcus and Kirstie do. Well, it'll be nice once it's finished."

"Whenever that is. They can't afford it, you know. You only saw the kitchen. You should go upstairs and see the bathroom—it's a bomb site. And the whole place needs replastering, rewiring as well. Joseph told them they were buying a money pit but they wouldn't listen. It's all about the postcode, the catchment area. They're highfliers now, see."

There's something in that statement I can't quite catch. The meaning flutters past quickly and before I know it, it's my turn to speak again.

I jump back a few topics. "So you never went back to nursing, after Clara?"

"No. Lost my confidence after a few years out. And anyway, I loved being a full-time mum. Still do. I don't know what I'm going to do when Clara goes to uni."

"So you don't work?"

"Bits and bobs. I look after Danny one day a week. Kirstie and Marcus pay me a few quid and I'm a damn sight cheaper than most of the nurseries in Muswell Hill. One of them was asking for £105 a day! I said to Kirstie, *'What are they feeding them? Foie gras?'*" Her drink's almost finished and while she's not exactly slurring, there's a looseness to her speech, a slight sway to her shoulders. "I do around eight hours a week for Marcus too, just admin stuff at BAGS. I'm supposed to be there tomorrow, actually. Don't know if it'll be good to take my mind off things or if I want to hide away from the world. What do you reckon I should do?"

"Your family must be proud of Marcus," I say, not answering.

A shrill laugh. "Dunno. Neither of us have seen them in years. I had a falling-out with them over Joseph, and Marcus kind of took my side—and, well, that meant they fell out with him too. We exchange the odd Christmas card, birthday card, that's about it."

"Are they in London?"

"Uxbridge, if you call that London. That's where me and Marcus grew up. It's a funny old place—you're part of a London borough, but you're not *London* London, do you get me? It's a real locals' place. You might as well be living in a small town somewhere. It's like my mum and dad—the only time they ever went into 'London proper' was to see the Oxford Street Christmas lights every year. The rest of the time, they'd just stick around Uxbridge, shopping in the local supermarkets, drinking in the local pubs. Used to drive Joseph mad. He could never understand it. *He* couldn't wait to leave Sheerness."

I try to place it: fail miserably. "My geography's terrible, sorry."

"No reason you'd have heard of it. It's on the Isle of Sheppey—the north Kent coast, basically."

"When did he move to London?"

"As soon as he could. On his sixteenth birthday, he reckons. It's probably an exaggeration, but you get the point. London was there for the conquering, that's how he saw it. That's how he sees everything.

Although Kirstie's the same—she's from some small town in the Midlands and London was always *it*, you know? The be-all and end-all. I think when you grow up in London—or practically London, like me and Marcus—the city's in your bones but you're less impressed by it. It washes over you."

I get what she's saying but I respectfully disagree. I'm mesmerized, then horrified, then galvanized by this city every day. Sometimes all three within the space of one hour.

"You and Marcus seem close," I say, moving on.

"I suppose. Although I'm probably closer to Kirstie these days. I certainly see more of her."

"Always good to be friends with your in-laws."

"Friends?" she says, surprised. "I'm not sure I'd call us friends, exactly. Neither of us has many friends, that's the problem—Kirstie 'cos she rubs people up the wrong way, me because I keep to myself—and I suppose that means we end up leaning on each other. Does that make us friends? I don't know. She's a good role model for Clara, though, I'll give her that."

"In what sense?"

"Well, like I said, she's a real highflier and I want Clara to be too. I want her to make something of her life." The *"not like me"* hangs heavy, a cloud of self-reproach. "Look, do you mind if I smoke? I'll have to open the front door, though, so Joseph doesn't smell it when he's back."

"Sure, knock yourself out. You should try the vape," I add, all chummy concern. "My boss swears by it. Well, he does now—he used to swear at it."

She smiles, a lazy gin-soaked smile, and goes to open the front door. "I tried vaping once," she calls back. "But Joseph says it's weak. No substitute for willpower. Of course, he gave up just like that." She clicks her fingers as she walks back in. "I think Clara's started now as well. I can smell it on her clothes and she reeks of mints. That'll be my fault too, you wait. Well, it *is* my fault, but I can hardly have a go, can I? And she's been stressed out enough lately."

"She mentioned problems at college?"

The tiger mum rears up. "Other people have problems, *that's* the problem." I wait for her to elaborate, wondering if I'll ever get that tap water she promised or whether to just help myself. I'm bloody parched. "The problem is Clara's bright. *Very* bright. She was going to sit the Cambridge entrance exam before Joseph talked her out of it, and, well, if you're bright *and* beautiful, some girls don't like that."

It's true enough. *Some* girls don't, particularly at that age. But I get the feeling—that gut-deep detective's feeling that's so razor-sharp, it's clairvoyant—there's probably more to it than that. After all, it's possible to be bright, beautiful, *and* eminently likable; it's just that stroppy, sweary Clara Madden is not. And all power to her, I say.

Still, there's nothing like the whitewashing of a mother's love.

"So why did Joseph talk her out of Cambridge?"

Her anger's still raw. "He convinced her she couldn't handle the pressure. I was bloody furious. Seriously, the thought of Cambridge or Oxford would have been ridiculous not so long ago, but now they're really focused on diversity, reaching out to working-class students, trying to up the application rate. And then all it takes is a few supposedly 'helpful,' but actually plain nasty, comments from *him* and she loses her nerve, parks the whole idea."

She takes a drag of her cigarette, calming herself as she watches the smoke rise in a feathery cloud. "Joseph isn't the biggest fan of universities. He says all they do is fill your head with other people's dogma. And he wants her to stay in London, at least. Close to home. But Clara's got her heart set on York, Exeter—I think Leeds is the current fave." All great universities and, interestingly, all two hundred miles away. "I just want her to go where she's happy. She works so hard, and I don't just mean at college. She works four shifts a week, collecting glasses at some grotty little pub in Wood Green, and she does bits and pieces for Kirstie too—mailings, cleaning up the database, all sorts of things. She knows we can't support her through uni so she's trying to get as much money together as possible." She slams her glass down, the full injustice of it all finally hitting. "You know, this is the worst possible time this could happen. She's in the middle of applications—the deadline's January. This can't mess up her future. I mean it, it can't. She's worked too hard. *I've* worked too bloody hard."

I won't have someone else's dead daughter messing up the future of mine. Nice.

"I have to say, Rachel, you seem more concerned about Clara's uni prospects than you do about Joseph. Most people would be fuming."

"Most people aren't married to Joseph. Nothing surprises me anymore."

"And yet you're sure he couldn't have done this?"

She swivels toward me, elbow on hip, cigarette aimed skyward. "Have you got a boyfriend, Cat?" I mouth a "no," partly because I'm not sure if I still do, but mainly because I've sullied Aiden enough just by being with him, and his name sure as hell doesn't belong in this choky, cheerless kitchen. "Well then, you might not understand, but when you love someone—and I mean, *really* love them, warts and all—then you know the core of them. You know every nasty little thing they're capable of, but you also know where they draw the line. Joseph doesn't have murder in him."

"Does he have it in him to pretend to be on work trips when he's really shacked up with other women—in London—right under your nose?" She bites down hard on her lower lip and I feel a slight stab of shittiness. It passes when I think of Naomi and her sunshine-print duvet. "You say you know the core of him, but you don't even know what he does for a living, not really. He's never set foot outside The Grindhouse, Rachel. He's never been to Barcelona or anywhere else."

I expect her to shrink but she expands, squaring her scant shoulders. "He hasn't always worked there, you know. He had a really good job in the City years ago, in IT recruitment. He absolutely loved it— the culture, the prestige. The money was a bit up and down—low base salary, high commission, that's the norm—but he was good at it. There were more good months than bad. We had a nice flat in Tufnell Park for a while—well, nicer than this—but we couldn't keep it on after his job went south. I said we should move out of London to somewhere cheaper, but of course to Joseph, leaving London means admitting failure."

"So why'd he lose his job?" I ask, expecting another credit-crunch sob story.

"Oh, there was some sort of falling-out with a colleague, something to do with client ownership, I think. Joseph walked, anyway. Told them where to stick it." A faint trace of admiration—no one controls *my* husband.

"But if the money was good? Couldn't Kirstie have taken him on?"

"Kirstie was just a skivvy herself back then. And anyway, fashion and IT recruitment are completely different. Joseph gave her a lot of advice when she was setting up her business, though. He's smart like that. Savvy."

The supermarket gin. The cracked tiles. The stack of red-letter bills stuck to the clapped-out fridge-freezer. "Not so savvy walking out on a well-paid job."

She opens her mouth, closes it again quickly, but if she thinks she's getting away with that, she's got another thing coming.

"Rachel?"

"What?" She stands up straight, suddenly full of purpose. "Oh God, I didn't get you that drink, did I? How bloody rude of me! Sorry, my head's all over the place. Are you sure you just want water?"

"Rachel, you were about to say something? About Joseph's job."

"It was nothing." I employ silence and a belligerent stare—the standoff lasts all of ten seconds. "It's just that . . . well, things got a bit physical, I think. I don't know the details. I didn't want to know. I know I got the blame for it, though." I cock my head, genuinely intrigued by how he managed to spin that one. "I wasn't supportive enough at home," explains Rachel, not scathing enough for my liking. "I stressed him out as soon as he walked through the door. That's what made him snap at work, apparently."

"So he obviously has a temper?"

"He has an *anger*." She draws her fist to her stomach. "Right here. He thinks it's him against the world. He gets off on the whole 'lone wolf' thing. A lot of it has to do with his family. He never knew his dad and his mum was a bit of a party girl. I never met her but Joseph says she wasn't fit to feed a rabbit, never mind raise a child. She's dead now."

"So he has an anger toward women?"

"He has an anger toward me, definitely. Kirstie winds him up too, sometimes, but apart from that I don't really see him with other women. I hear he's popular with them, though."

"Oh yeah? Who'd you hear that from?"

"Him, of course." She stubs her cigarette out, grinding it so hard into the ashtray that all that's left is ash and pulp. "In great detail, actually."

Later, settled in my one armchair with what I'm grandly calling a cheese and meat platter—essentially two chicken drumsticks and a Babybel—I scour Rachel Madden's phone records, undeterred by Swaines's scrawl at the top of the page.

Had quick look over past few weeks. Nothing juicy. Boo ☹

Boo indeed. Rachel Madden's recent world is so small, it's tragic. The same four numbers repeated over and over: Clara, Kirstie, an 0345 number that I'm fairly sure is telephone banking, and the occasional call to or from Marcus.

No Joseph Madden since October 3rd, over five weeks ago.

It's further back I'm interested in, though—three months or more. At first, the pattern continues, more or less: Clara. Kirstie. Telephone banking. The odd Marcus. A random London number turns out to be the offices of Elite Fashion. A Caribbean takeaway makes a couple of appearances, here and there. I'm briefly piqued by an unknown mobile number—several calls made to Rachel around the same time Joseph Madden was claiming his wife had gone loopy (my words, not his)—however my intrigue's short-lived when it turns out to be some two-bit claims management firm who've recently been sanctioned for nuisance calling.

But then, as the clock creeps to midnight and the drunks start singing "Bohemian Rhapsody" on the street outside—*something.*

Several calls made *by* Rachel over a three-week period back in July.

It's probably nothing. It's probably less than nothing. But after another internet search, I'm staring at the website of Morgan Cripps LLP, a "leading Portsmouth-based legal firm" whose goals are to **L**isten. **A**dvocate. **A**chieve. At first, I figure they're just another ambulance-chasing parasite and that perhaps Rachel flipped, made a complaint, told them to take her number off their database and never darken her door again—God knows, it takes them long enough to get the message, which would explain the number of calls. Eight in total.

But Morgan Cripps aren't an ambulance chaser, they're a family law specialist, and while the world might be going to hell in a hand-bag, at least according to Parnell, I don't think we've yet reached the depths of actively encouraging break-ups.

"Hi, have you called your spouse 'a loathsome little shit' on more than one occasion? Perhaps you should consider our Fast-track Divorce offer! Get a free carriage clock just for inquiring!"

So was Rachel Madden considering divorce? It'd go some way to explaining her "out of character" behavior—if Joseph Madden's to be believed, anyway. And if she did vow to "make him pay," she could have meant it financially—although, if she did, it proves once and for all that she knows jack shit about her husband. Joseph Madden's current bank balance makes even mine look buoyant.

Still, it's a life buoy the defense could cling to, because if Rachel Madden wanted out of her marriage, *there's* her potential motive to lie. *There's* her reason to enjoy making things sticky for him.

And there's reasonable doubt cast on her contradiction of his alibi.

I drop Renée a note asking if she'd mind calling Morgan Cripps in the morning. There's somewhere else I need to be, and anyway, Renée's better at doing the "client privilege" dance than I am. Renée manages to hit the right note of *"Don't make me throw my weight around,"* whereas I go straight in throwing my weight around. In my defense, it's an age thing. My generation were raised on texts and email and instant messages, and when it comes right down to it, we just aren't that great on the phone.

Another good excuse not to call Dad back.

Dad. Back again, front and center.

What on earth could we need to talk about, outside of Sunday morning? Our safe, allotted time with the safe, routine agenda.

Jacqui's latest home improvement drama.

My brother's whereabouts. (The custody suite of Policía De Almuñé-car, Spain, at last check.)

The pub trade.

My nephew, Finn.

Darling Finn.

With a fierce palpitation, I realize Dad's call could have been about Finn's seizures. They've stabilized over the past six months but we all live in horrific limbo, waiting for the next one to strike. But then, wouldn't Jacqui have called me if that was the case? In fact, if it was anything to do with our family, Jacqui would be bustling at the center of it, making arrangements, barking orders, directing the heavy traffic of our lives.

Which means it's not family business. It's "us" business.

Me and him.

And I really can't deal with that right now.

14

Friday

There's two people kissing on the tube as it crawls into Canary Wharf—London's corporate dystopia, built on the former Docklands. To be fair, I'm nearly joined in holy matrimony to the City boy I've been pressed up against for the past ten minutes, but at least we have the good grace to look mortified about it. Seriously, kissing? On the tube? At eight thirty a.m.? And not Eskimo kissing either, or a light gentle peck before they part ways for the working day. Proper kissing. Tongues. Saliva. Lips tugged between teeth.

As Finn's taken to saying, *"Urgh—Barf City."*

I decide they're *definitely* having an affair and give them a prim, censorious stare as I shuffle out of the carriage onto the stampede of the platform.

I'm being an idiot.

It's been a long week.

And I miss Aiden.

It's the wedding today. The wedding in Mulderrin I should have been at. Aiden's cousin Declan and his soon-to-be-wife, Ava. I've never actually met them but I liked them instantly from the invitation.

No gifts please, donations to St. Brigid's Hospice
Kids and grumpy ol' fellas welcome
Bad dancing compulsory

As I wait for Parnell outside One Canada Square, the tower that stretches so high it comes with its own aircraft warning light, I'd give anything to be in Mulderrin right now, straightening Aiden's tie and bitching about seating plans. I want to be there so badly that instead of thinking about the case, I'm googling flights to Knock from London Stansted, even though the logistics would never work and the idea is pure madness. The wedding starts in five hours and the flight alone would wipe out my food budget for a month.

Although Parnell would make sure I didn't starve. Lashings of Quorn and mounds of quinoa might do me the world of good too.

"Sorry, sorry, sorry." Speak of the devil—a devil who's ten minutes late with the look of the peak-hour commuter about him. "I don't know how people do this every day, I honestly don't." He leans against a pillar, fanning himself with a copy of the *Metro*.

"Bad morning?"

"The worst. Woke up to find the new puppy's chewed nearly every shoe I own, and then to cap that off, some idiot parked his Beamer in front of my drive so I couldn't get the car out. Which meant I had to walk to the station, and then there was signal failure on the Victoria line." He wrestles with his top button, loosens his tie. "Christ, this never happened in *Starsky & Hutch*. You never saw them getting in a flap topping up their Oyster card. They just jumped in the Gran Torino and off they went." He looks up at the forest of skyscrapers surrounding us, then down at the avalanche of people hurtling through their doors. "You know, I remember this place when it was still just a building site. Christ, I just about remember when it was actually a dock, full of ships not falafel restaurants."

This isn't Parnell doing his "old codger" routine—it's not surprising he remembers it. Canary Wharf, at least in its Capitalism HQ reincarnation, is only thirty years old, looking shinier than ever or sterile as fuck, depending on your aesthetic preferences.

I hand over a coffee. "Here, get that down you quickly—and don't panic, it's skinny."

He swigs half, not caring that it's still lava. "God, I'm knackered and the day hasn't even started. And to think this morning started so well."

"Oh yeah? Maggie can't keep her hands off you now that you're all buff, is that it?"

Something like a "Pfft." "Chance would be a fine thing. Puppies are no good for your sex life, Kinsella—there's a life lesson for you right there." He drains the rest of the coffee. "It is about sex, though. Well, 'the suggestion of sex' as our legal friends say. I had a lovely five a.m. text from Her Majesty this morning—the hairs off Naomi's body and her bed? They match Madden."

I mouth a "wow." "The big fat liar."

"Well, hold your horses—they match to the naked eye, at least. They couldn't get a root off any of them, so no DNA extraction, but alongside other evidence we'll be able to make the inference. He was in her bed, 90 percent."

"Nicer if it was 100 percent. The CCTV is about the only irrefutable thing we've got at the moment and Stein's right, it's weak. It only puts him in the area, not even on her street."

"Ah, but I haven't finished yet. I bring more news of the hairy kind." Parnell hands his cup to a passing road sweeper, who's whistling a tune and looking infinitely more in love with life than the sharp-suited desk jockeys coursing past us. "Forensics *also* lifted what initially looked like long gray hairs from Madden's car, but under the microscope they turned out to be—"

I don't let him finish. "Lilac."

He nods. "They still need to be DNA-tested before we start popping the corks, but seriously what are the chances?"

My mind zooms. "And as his car's been at the garage since the 25th of October, that puts him with Naomi weeks before the Connors' party." I pause. "Hey, it's a kick in the nads for your stalker theory, though. If she was in that car, they knew each other."

"Looking that way," agrees Parnell, ecstatic to be wrong if it means simplifying the investigation. "So, anyway, I got your message but remind me, what exactly are we doing here?"

"A bit of background on Mr. Madden."

Specifically, evidence of a bad temper to add to our ammunition.

"Joseph Madden? Jailbait Joe! God, that name takes me back, and not to a good place, I tell ya."

Michael Redfern, CEO of TechMinds, is what you'd call "a character," if you went heavy on the air quotes. A balding, jowly, pension-age barrow boy with the wonky nose of an ex-boxer and the woozy eyes of a fierce drinker, even though he hasn't touched a drop since Christmas Day 2013.

I've no idea why he told us this, or how it even came up. Sitting across from Michael Redfern, as he fiddles with his cuff links on his Bond-villain chair, feels less like a police interview and more like "An Audience With . . ." The man literally never stops.

Still, I like him. He's brash and he's bold and he swears like a navvy with a stubbed toe.

And he's just called Joseph Madden, *"Jailbait Joe."*

Ka-ching.

"What a nickname to give someone, eh?" His laugh is raucous, bouncing off the wood-paneled walls. "Things were rough and ready back then, though. Moneymaking and piss-taking, that's all anyone was interested in."

I'd ask him to elaborate but Michael Redfern doesn't need prompts.

"He was a bit of a charmer, see, was Joseph. A proper flirt, you know. Anyway, one day he gets talking to this young sort on reception, giving it all the chat, typical Joseph. But what he doesn't realize is she's here on work experience." The laugh starts up again. "Now fair's fair, she did look older. Could have passed for nineteen, twenty. But, well, the 'jailbait' thing stuck."

"When did Joseph join the firm?" I ask, conscious of how stuffy I sound across from this cyclone in pinstripes.

"Fucking hell, love, I don't know dates off the top of my head. I'm not Rain Man." He rubs at one eye, trying to work it out. "Be around 2006, I reckon. Business was still good, anyway. Afraid I can't be more specific than that, though. It was a bit like the Wild West back then. Less regulation. We didn't have HR like we do now. People came and went, that's just the way it was. And we hardly ever bothered referencing people. If you had the gift of the gab and you were money hungry, then you were in, basically. Can't say I cared if you told a few porkies on your CV." He smiles to himself. "Although Joseph told more than a few. I checked him out *after* he'd left—Westminster School scholarship, my arse."

"So when did he leave?"

"Now that I *do* remember—2008. Not long after Lehmans collapsed and the party came to an end. I remember thinking to meself—so many bloody losers in this crisis, and yet Jailbait Joe's still benefiting."

I'm confused. "How so?"

He wheels forward, puts his forearms on the desk, Cartier cuff links in full view. "Well, he could blame the credit crunch for losing his job, couldn't he? Before that, if you left a recruitment firm, it was because of two things: one, you couldn't sell hay to a farmer, or two, you were more trouble than you were worth. But with the market in free fall, there's your third reason. Plenty of good recruiters got their P45s that year, I tell ya. I lost some good men." He's wistful for a moment, an ex-captain thinking of the trenches. "So here, what's this about then? What's Jailbait Joe done?"

Parnell does the spiel. "We're investigating a murder, Mr. Redfern. Joseph Madden is someone we're interested in and we believe he was involved in some kind of altercation here with a colleague? That it's the reason he left?"

"Murder? Fuck me!" After spluttering for a moment, Redfern composes himself, offering Parnell a sharp, suspect stare. A glimpse of the shrewd operator behind the boy-done-good act. "Look, we settled all that in-house, mate. I don't know how much I should be saying. I need to talk to HR."

"You need to talk to us, Mr. Redfern. And we need to talk to that colleague. Are they still here?"

"Stacey Nash? Nah, she left years back."

Stacey.

She.

"Went off to have her second kid, didn't she? Didn't come back. We offered her part-time, you know. Said we'd look into a job-share. Oh yeah, no sexism around here. We're all about equality and diversity an' all that." There's a tinkle in his voice that suggests he sees them as harmless fads, something he's good enough to humor.

Although maybe I'm the bigger sexist. I'd assumed the fight was with a man.

This could be the break we need, though, and Parnell knows it too.

His right knee's dancing a jig under Redfern's desk. "So the fight was with a woman?"

Redfern twirls a cuff link. "Well, I'm not sure I'd call it a fight, mate. He assaulted her."

I could cheerfully lean over and kiss his liver-spotted head.

"But it wasn't reported to the police?" says Parnell. There's a strain of *oh-God-please-say-we-didn't-miss-something* threaded through his voice. "Joseph Madden hasn't got a record."

"Stacey didn't want your lot involved, she just wanted him gone."

Sadly, not unusual. "So when you say 'assault'?" Parnell queries.

Palms up. "Listen, Stacey and Joseph never got on. She was a bit older, had a kid, a disabled dad, if I remember rightly, and she was a bit above all his antics. She wasn't impressed by him and it niggled him. Anyway, something kicked off over who'd generated a lead, I think, and according to Stacey, Joseph collared her in the kitchen, pushed her up against the wall and stuck his knee between her legs, aggressively, like." *As opposed to nicely?* "Day after, we gave him his marching orders. Well, we gave him a compromise agreement, actually. Two months' money if he left without a fuss. 'Course, Joseph said he wanted three but I said, 'Yeah, and I want a rubdown off Halle Berry but it ain't happening, sunshine.'"

"Why the compromise agreement?" I ask. "Surely what he did was gross misconduct?"

He puffs out his cheeks. "Look, there were no witnesses, just her word against his. And you're not gonna like me for saying this, but she did have a reputation for being a bit of a handful, a shop steward sort. She'd raise a grievance soon as look at ya, that type."

"So why did you take her side?"

"Truth?" he says, hands wide. "Look, a lot of the lads were pests back then when it came to women. Different times, love." I smile sweetly, though I suspect I look constipated. "Anyway, I thought it was about time I made an example of someone. No way was I having my business slapped with a load of sexual harassment cases, so I thought if I made Joseph the sacrificial lamb, the rest might simmer down. And it worked, an' all. The rest of 'em shat themselves at how speedy I got rid of him. Made them think twice about getting handsy again, I tell ya." He's delighted by his own genius. "And anyway, Joseph wasn't a massive loss. He had the makings of a good recruiter but he got on clients' nerves half the time. Couldn't quite grasp the difference between being confident and being an arsehole, you know? He was steady, but he wasn't a top biller."

Meaning if he was, Stacey Nash would have been the one compromised out.

Parnell shifts forward to the edge of his chair and I follow suit—we have what we came for, no point hanging around. "Don't suppose you know where we can find Stacey Nash?" I ask, standing up. "An address? A next of kin, even?"

Redfern shakes his head. "Nah, sorry love, can't help you. Bit too long ago. We keep records for seven years and then get rid. You could try LinkedIn, although I don't think she's in the industry anymore, not in a long time."

"Thanks. We'll do that." Well, Ben Swaines will.

Redfern leans back, in no hurry to show us out. "You know, for what it's worth, I can't see it meself—murder." We nod our thanks for this searing insight and head for the door. "I'll tell you something, though," he calls after us. "He always was a vindictive little shit. My car was scratched a few months later. It was a 1995 Mercedes-Benz SL, soft-top. My pride and joy. And then a few months after that, my house was broken into."

Now he has our attention.

"They didn't take much, just thirty quid cash we'd left out for the cleaner and a watch on the bedside table. Well, that made me chuckle. It was a shit fake Rolex my daughter had brought back from Thailand the week before. I thought, 'Yeah, good luck shifting that, mate.' Anyone in the know would see it was dodgy." Parnell and I exchange glances but Redfern doesn't notice. "Nah, I was more bothered about my wife's underwear—knickers and bras all over the floor, halfway down the stairs, a right old mess. I always fancied that was Jailbait Joe getting his own back, but 'course, there's no way I could prove it."

However, there might just be now.

15

Another chat with Rachel Madden beckons, but not before a quick dive into HQ to check on a couple of things.

First, the progress of Rachel's and Clara's devices. If I'm delivering bad news, it'd be nice to be the bringer of good gifts. A spoonful of sugar to help the forensics bombshell go down.

Second, I want to know just how much of a "headache" Marcus Connor was back in the day. After all, one person's headache is another person's crimewave and Rachel Madden clearly sets a low bar when it comes to judging bad behavior. Did her brother smoke a few funny fags, smash a few windows, in his youth? Maybe urinate up against the wrong person's garden fence one too many times?

Or does he have a history of violence we need to be acquainted with?

One quick search and the answer's no. Marcus Robert Connor was summoned to attend Highbury Corner Magistrates' Court on the 15th of August 2014 for doing fifty in a thirty zone, but apart from that one, quite frankly, moronic act, he's squeaky clean as far as we're concerned.

I have more luck with the phones and laptop. Both are cleared to return and an hour later I'm back at the Maddens' flat. Clara answers the door in her knickers and last night's crop top, her wispy blond hair matted into loose dreadlocks down her back.

"Mum's gone to work," she says, rubbing her eyes. I've obviously woken her up. "Well, she calls it work. Answering the phone, making the tea, watering plants." I frown, feeling a sharp churn of protection toward Rachel—Clara can wait for her devices a bit longer, the ungrateful little brat. "Sorry, that probably sounded awful," she adds, sensing my disapproval. "It's just that Mum's capable of a lot more, but she's got no confidence so she's terrible at job interviews. Auntie Kirst tried to give her some coaching once but she's a lost cause. It was nice of Uncle M to take her on, I suppose. I mean, he doesn't need her. It just gives her something to do."

As rude as she is, Clara's assessment isn't far wrong. When I reach the offices of Be a Good Sport—which turns out to be a converted shipping container overlooking Regent's Canal, on a site rather charmingly called Containerville—there doesn't appear to be a whole lot going on.

Rachel's drinking coffee with her feet up—literally. Marcus is on his way out, weighed down with sporting equipment; badminton stuff, I think. His face sours at the sight of me hovering at the entrance. An unfortunate part of the job but one you quickly get used to.

"This is cool," I say, and actually mean it. Compared to Canary Wharf, there's color, at least. Each container—and there must be fifty—is secured by a brightly colored safety door: hot pink, lime green, neon yellow to name just a few, and on the decking outside, the picnic benches are painted pastel. One of them lilac, the exact shade of Naomi's hair.

"We like it," says Marcus. "Great location, low overheads, what's not to like? And there's a real community feel among the tenants."

"Good. That's nice." Not so sure the other tenants will be sharing their picnic tables quite so readily once the news about his brother-in-law gets out, but maybe I'm cynical. "Anyway, don't let me keep you, I just wanted a word with Rachel."

He looks back to his sister, who flicks her hand to say she's fine, get going.

"They've got a team event," she says, referring to the emptiness of the office. It's a long, thin space with a bank of desks facing directly on to the wall. A set of patio doors at the far end open out on to a balcony overlooking the canal.

I pull Clara's laptop from my bag, followed by both their phones. "Beware police bearing gifts. Thought you might like these back."

Rachel smiles as she takes them but it's faint and slightly forced.

Without gin reinforcements, she's slipped back into meek mode. A talking doll on low batteries.

She takes her feet off the desk and slides them back inside her knockoff Uggs. "I'm not sure they are gifts, but thank you. It's been nice having Clara not stuck to her phone, to be honest. We actually *talked* this morning. She got into my bed and we talked—she hasn't done that in years." Her voice rallies a bit. "I told her what Joseph's been saying, of course. I'm not keeping anything from her. She's nearly an adult, much as I hate to admit it."

"Is she OK? As OK as she can be?"

"She's angry, but she misses him, even though he's hateful to her sometimes." Her passivity astounds me. *It is what it is.* "Let me show you something." She reaches down for her handbag while I take a seat at the next desk—"Steve's" desk presumably, given it houses "Steve's mug" and "Steve's diary" and a whole load of other "Steve" paraphernalia. "Look at this, this was me at sixteen." She pulls a photo from the back of her purse. "I was in *The Nutcracker* at Sadler's Wells—not a soloist, just part of the corps de ballet. That's where Clara's name comes from, you know? The little girl from *The Nutcracker* who falls asleep and dreams of a prince." A little snort says, *"Didn't we all?"* "Anyway, remind you of anyone?"

I take a look, even though it doesn't take a curling old photo to remind me. Even now, tall, blond, gray-eyed Rachel is Clara's double, only two decades older and more kicked about by life.

"I often think that's why Joseph's so mean to her," she explains. "She's too like me and he can't stand it. Although she's more like him, personality-wise."

Same here. I got Mum's nose, her thick hair and her tendency to turn lobster in mild heat. I got Dad's restlessness, his recklessness, and his tendency to fuck up.

She stares at Clara's laptop on her desk. "'Course, I don't know how I'm going to stop her reading about it now. At least they haven't named him, I suppose that's something. They're still calling him 'a forty-five-year-old man from north London' which is kind of funny as he's only forty-three and he's pretty sensitive about his age. How long will he stay anonymous?"

Time to get real. "They won't name him unless he's charged, but listen, Rachel, it's starting to look more likely. That's what I came to tell you. We've got forensics that put Naomi in Joseph's car *and* Joseph in Naomi's bed."

She doesn't miss a beat. "That only proves he was sleeping with her."

"Well, yes, but that along with him going AWOL on Saturday night, his missing clothes . . . it's not looking good."

She drops her head into her hands, taking a few deep breaths before mustering the strength to lift it again. "Look, he wouldn't have hurt her, I *know* he wouldn't. He wouldn't hurt a stranger."

I leap on this. "And what about you? Has he ever hurt you, physically?"

Silence. A brief interval of hope before she shoots me down. "I can handle it, Cat. I'm hard to hurt, these days." As if to prove her point, she grabs a fistful of pale forearm, her nails gouging into the flesh. "Look, skin of a rhino, me."

"We know he hurt one woman, Rachel. Joseph didn't leave Tech-Minds because of a fight over business. He was asked to leave after he sexually assaulted a colleague."

She's on her feet. "Oh, right, so he's a rapist now, as well as a murderer?"

"He didn't rape her. He pushed her against a wall and forced his knee between her legs."

Rachel's face, astonishingly, suggests this isn't so bad. I'd walk straight out of this shipping container right now if it wasn't for the fact that there's a fair chance it *isn't* that bad compared to what she's endured.

"Look, women are always throwing themselves at Joseph," she says.

"According to Joseph."

"And I know he was sleeping with someone at TechMinds, so maybe it was sour grapes. Maybe this woman asked him to leave me and when he wouldn't, she lied." She looks me right in the eye, a look that says *know this*—"Joseph would never leave me."

It's the rebel yell of many a cheated spouse. A swell of pride. A warning shot fired.

Out of Rachel Madden's mouth, it's the saddest prediction ever made.

I want to shake her.

"Rachel, there's so much you don't know about him—*how* can you be so sure he's innocent? Aren't you wondering where he was Saturday night? Don't you think it's odd his clothes have just vanished?"

She contemplates this. "I—I have to believe in him. I need him."

I might actually shake her.

"Is that why you've never left him? Because you think you wouldn't cope?"

"I've never left because of Clara. I didn't want her coming from a broken home."

But did she ever ask what Clara wanted? God knows, I was never one of those made-for-TV schmaltzy kids, wishing that Mommy and Daddy still loved each other. I prayed that Mum would leave Dad—one Hail Mary followed by two Our Fathers every night between the ages of ten and twelve. My prayers were never answered.

"Clara's older now, what's stopping you?"

"Love, I suppose." She walks out onto the small balcony, lifting her face to the low November sun.

Seeing an in, I join her outside, watching the joggers, the cyclists, and the slightly bewildered tourists making their way along the canal path on the other side.

"Rachel, the truth now: Are you sure you weren't thinking of divorcing Joseph? Because if you were, we need to know. It helps build a picture of what's been going on in Joseph's life and it's much better for you—and for Joseph," I add, though it chokes me, "if we find out these things from you."

"No. No, of course I wasn't." Based on my five years and three months of sitting across from consummate liars, I'm going to say she sounds genuine—*sounds*, not *is*. "But what makes you ask that? Oh, I know—Kirstie, right? She's the one who's always saying I should divorce him, and OK, sometimes I agree, just to shut her up more than anything."

"You called a family law specialist a number of times back in July."

She turns her head, face screwed up in confusion. "Morgan Cripps. They're based in Portsmouth."

"Oh, them." She turns fully this time, facing inward, both elbows propped on the balcony ledge. "Clara was thinking of applying to Portsmouth back then. She's got a few friends in their first year there and they've said good things. And, well, as she'll have to pay her way through uni, I thought that rather than collecting glasses in another grotty pub, she could try to get a part-time job with a local law firm—you know, to link with her studies. I'm always proactive when it comes to Clara's education, so I called a few times to make inquiries. Reception could never seem to put me through to the right person, though, so I gave up in the end."

My phone vibrates in my pocket. I'm going to have to drop this for now, although something's definitely not sitting right. Maybe not so much what she's said but the freedom with which she's said it. It's the most she's said since I've been here and she didn't even ask how I knew.

I go back inside and answer my phone. Parnell.

"Sarge."

"Make your excuses," he says, no preamble. "The guy across the road from the Connors, the one who saw someone hanging around on Saturday evening?"

"Yeah?"

"He came in to look at some photos. Guess who?"

Rachel's come back inside. "No idea. Enlighten me."

"Flowers pulled his photo off the database. It's only Mr. Keep Fit, Kieran Drake."

"OK, great. Thanks for letting me know." I'm assuming Parnell will get the hint that I can't really talk.

He does. "Oh, like that is it? Where are you, location-wise?"

"Regent's Canal, about halfway between Shoreditch and Angel."

"OK, well, I'm driving up to U-Gym now. Meet me there in half an hour—we're bringing him in."

"Uh-huh, will do."

"Oh, and walk it, Kinsella: far quicker *and* healthier. It's only off Old Street so you're virtually down the road."

Parnell rings off and I quickly check my messages. If Renée's managed to speak to someone at Morgan Cripps and Rachel *was* a client, I've just about got time to have it out with her *and* get to Old Street in half an hour.

No Renée, though.

Only Dad.

A missed call and a text this time:

"Don't have yr new home address so if I don't hear back I'll have to come to the only place I know where to find u—work. Neither of us wants that. Call me."   *12:48 p.m.*

16

I *do* call Dad back and I *do* walk to Old Street. Who says I can't follow instructions?

I get a busy signal at Dad's end, which means the ball stays well and truly in my court, and then I'm almost mowed down by some clown crossing City Road, prompting another clown farther up to comment, "Cheer up, love, it might never happen." Needless to say, I'm not in the best of moods as I stomp into U-Gym, and the only small sweetener is the look of "*oh shit*" on Kieran Drake's face when he clocks me and Parnell.

The first and only time I'll ever intimidate anyone in a gym.

Drake's calmed down a bit by the time we're cozied up in Interview Room Three, although he's made it clear, several whiny times, that he'd rather be interviewed by that "black lady copper." He's obviously got fond memories of Renée, who gave him solace and sweet tea, back when he was just the poor guy who'd found Naomi's body. Renée doesn't stay popular, though. Drake goes right off her when we say she's currently out of the office, triple-checking his alibis—which is a lie, she's actually tied up trying The Renée Approach on Joseph Madden—and then, after some wrangling over whether he wants to wait for the duty solicitor, he says no, he can't be bothered. Why would he need a solicitor when he's got nothing to hide?

"Do your worst," are his final words on the matter.

So we do.

Parnell kicks off. "OK, Kieran, can you tell us what you were doing at 22 West Pool Avenue in Muswell Hill at approximately four forty-five to five p.m. last Saturday? Saturday the 4th of November, to be precise."

Dates disconcert people. Numbers make them nervous. Numbers scream, *"I've got my facts straight. How about you?"*

"I wasn't there. Can I go now?" He might not sound nervous but his left eyelid's going mental, twitching like a rabbit's nose.

"We have a witness."

"Oh yeah, who's that?"

I pick up the mantle. "A neighbor."

"Oh right, a nosy neighbor," he says, drumming a beat on the table, trying to play it cool. "Always find them a bit weird, don't you? Net curtains and all that."

I drum a little beat of my own. "I'll tell you what I find weird, Kieran. We give you an address and you just say, *'I wasn't there,'* nothing else, whereas most people would say one of two things. Either *'Who lives there?'* or *'Oh, the Connors' house. I wasn't there.'* Your lack of curiosity—well, it's a bit suspect."

"Sorry if I'm not curious about what some old bag with cataracts *thinks* she saw." The huffy tone really doesn't suit a man the size of a forklift.

"That old bag is a fifty-eight-year-old ex–Air Traffic Controller, Kieran. That means perfect eyesight and *that* means perfect witness." No response. Nothing. I let out a little sigh. The kind of sigh mums make when their kids won't put their shoes on and they're ten seconds from losing their shit. "Listen Kieran, me and my colleague here, we didn't win a competition to become police officers. We didn't enter a raffle. We're trained in this. We've been on courses called 'How to detect bullshit.'" His left eyelid's off the scale now. He rubs at it, trying to bring it under control. "We're doing you a favor here. We're giving you the opportunity to be honest with us when, frankly, we have you, anyway. We've got your phone now and phone towers tell us everything."

He scowls, openly rattled. "Look, what'd you want with me anyway? I heard you got someone for this."

"Oh yeah, who'd you hear that from?"

He shrugs. "Just heard it on the grapevine. You know, like the song—Stevie Wonder."

"Marvin Gaye," corrects Parnell. "Maybe you know your Elvis better than your soul legends. Ever heard 'Jailhouse Rock?'"

Drake takes the point; starts pulling at his lip, making quick decisions.

"Look, OK, I went there. Happy now? I needed to tell Naomi something. I forgot about it the first time you interviewed me, honest . . . my head was still mashed, man, and well, I knew you'd read something into it if I suddenly changed my story so . . ."

"What did you need to tell her?"

"Just something to do with the heating, the timer. I wasn't sure it was working properly."

Parnell does his puzzled face. "So why didn't you just call her or send a text? And remember, Kieran, we have your phone, we can check."

He's growing paler by the second. "It was too tricky to explain by text and I didn't call her because . . . well, I fancied going out on my bike, and I remembered where the Connors lived 'cos I went around there once to pick something up—something for a BAGS football match—so I just thought, why not?"

He's thinking on his feet, I'll give him that. Not as dopey as I first thought.

"So what did you do when you got to the house?" I ask.

"I spoke to her. Told her about the timer."

"No, no, no." I'm all heartfelt disappointment. "Why did no one else see you, then? You're pretty hard to miss."

"Because Naomi answered the door and we talked on the step. It was, like, two minutes, then I was gone."

"Naomi answered the door in someone else's house? Pure luck, that."

He nods along. "Yeah, it was, actually, because I hadn't seen Marcus in years and I couldn't be bothered with all that *'Hey, how's it going?'* crap."

Parnell and I share weary glances. "To be honest, Kieran, we can't be bothered with all this crap. You didn't go to the door. You hung around outside and then you went up the side alley." He looks beaten, like a gambler down to his last chip. "Let me tell you something, me and him"—a nod to Parnell—"we haven't got any plans tonight, so you're our hot date. You're the guy with the dubious alibis who had a tête-à-tête with our victim, in an alleyway, less than twelve hours before she was murdered. I promise you, in our world, dates don't come hotter than that."

He turns his head, staring miserably at the empty chair beside him. It could be a way of avoiding eye contact, or he could be cursing his decision to fly solo without the duty solicitor. I pray it's the former because he can change his mind about the latter at any time.

My prayers are answered.

"Look, it was drugs, OK?" He exhales like he's been holding his breath for centuries. "Nothing major, just a bit of blow. Three grams, that's all. She'd been let down by her usual guy and I was helping her out. That's why I was there."

I sit up straight. "For the tape, you were delivering three grams of cocaine to Naomi Lockhart?"

"Naomi? Fuck, no way. She was proper square. To Kirstie Connor, I mean."

Kirstie Connor. I'll process what this means later. For now, I'm just glad it wasn't Naomi. Because while it shouldn't be the case—and I'm shamefaced that it is—it makes our job a lot easier if we have a nice "perfect" victim to market. A smiley, happy fund-raiser who got manipulated by an older man.

"So how well do you know Kirstie Connor?" asks Parnell, keen to process things now.

"I don't, really. We've been Facebook friends since she sent Naomi my way, but that's all. We'd never actually met. She must have known about my past through Marcus and thought it was worth a try messaging me. She sounded a bit desperate, to be honest, said she was having a shit time and needed a bump but her usual guy was abroad. I said her best bet was this dude in Streatham, but I doubt he'd travel north of the river on a Saturday afternoon for the sake of three grams, so then she says, 'Will you get it for me?' and I'm like, 'Fuck that!' but then she offers me fifty quid for the trouble and fifty quid's fifty quid, innit? And I've got the bike so I don't need to worry about getting stuck in traffic . . ."

And just like that, our "ex-wrong'un" casts off the all-important "ex." I can't pretend I'm not disappointed.

Another one in the eye for the notion of redemption.

"Drugs, hairs, assaults. God, I need a drink."

Steele's standing on her tiptoes, rooting through the top drawer of her filing cabinet while Parnell, Renée, Seth, and I are arranged on various chairs and boxes around her office. I'm sitting on a box marked *"Fragile."* Insert your own joke here.

"I can offer you a slug of Gaviscon—use-by date Feb 2017. Or I could mix up a few cystitis sachets." She slams the drawer shut. "Jesus, what sort of DCI am I? Not a bottle of liquor to my name."

"Anyone fancy a pint of dishwater in the Tavern?" asks Seth. "The hairs are something to celebrate, at least."

"And the fake Rolex," adds Renée, looking at me and Parnell. "Michael Redfern came in while you two were in with Drake. He's almost sure it's his Rolex. It's very similar, anyway."

Steele shoos Seth out of her chair. "Which is about as helpful as tits on a fish."

"It was nine years ago. He'd only had it a week. Best he could do."

"Is it worth getting Forensics on it?" I suggest. "I know it's a long shot, but Redfern's skin cells could be embedded in the links, maybe? And if it *is* his watch, well, it doesn't really help us directly with Naomi, but it's another black mark against Madden."

Steele thinks about it, making a clicking noise with her tongue. "Yeah, why not? Might as well completely decimate the budget altogether, eh? You might have to bring your own tea bags to work at this rate, but we need every bit of dirt on this shitbag. The discovery of the hair is great, but I've had Lucas Stein on the phone already, bleating about transference." She brings up the blurry photo of Naomi and Madden on her laptop. "And I mean, look at them here. There's hardly five inches between them, so it isn't beyond the realms. We're not home and dry."

Parnell's sitting on a pile of crates, manspreading for England. "But Naomi's hair in his car—he can't explain that away?"

"Oh, he can," says Renée. "*We* planted them. Well, actually, it was *you* who planted them, Lu. You took against him on sight. You're past your prime and desperate to show you've still got it, apparently."

To his credit, Parnell laughs. "Only thing I'd like to plant is my fist on his nose."

"Get in the queue," says Steele, then, "Right, folks—Kirstie Connor and this Colombian marching powder. Thoughts?"

Seth takes his tie off—a sure sign he's headed for the Tavern, even if no one else is. "Well, she's clearly not to be trusted."

"Why?" I ask. "Just because you've got a little habit doesn't mean you'd lie about a murder."

"Makes her recollections a whole lot hazier, though."

"She admits they're hazy. Yeah, OK, she said it was because of drink but that's more of an omission than an out-and-out lie."

That distinction is everything to me. It's the plinth my self-esteem rests on. It's the argument I'd make to Steele if Dad's involvement in the Maryanne Doyle case ever came out.

Hell, it's the argument I'd rely on in court if it ever came out.

Steele flaps a hand. "Omission, lie, whatever. You know what it gives us?"

I do. "Leverage." Blackmail, in layman's terms. "Successful businesswoman, husband runs a charity—she isn't going to want a whiff of scandal, is she? So we hold it over her, tell her she gives us the real lowdown on Joseph Madden and that marriage, or else. I'm pretty sure he's been violent to Rachel, for a start, and that goes to pattern of behavior."

"How's it leverage?" Renée asks. "We only know about the drugs after the fact. It's not like we caught her with it. There's not a lot we can do, legally."

"Yeah, well, I'm banking on her not realizing that, but at the very least we can threaten to make things sticky for her. Her record's clean, she's never been in trouble, so one vague threat and she'll cack herself, I reckon."

"You're forgetting something else," says Parnell. "The phantom window cleaner, remember? Kirstie Connor made that up to throw us off Drake's scent. There were a good few man-hours wasted following that up. Perverting the course of justice—that's not a vague threat."

He's right, as ever. I let him bask in the glory briefly before throwing a hand grenade. "What about Drake? This throws a whole new spotlight on him too. He might be desperately trying to come across as Mr. Three-Gram Small-Fry, but if he *is* still dealing, it's likely he keeps a stash or money at the house."

"A house that's been searched from top to bottom," warns Steele.

"He took it with him then?" I say, 100 percent riffing. "Maybe he was supplying in Hounslow? It'd explain why his alibis are so keen to back him. But a thief wouldn't know that, would they? A thief—an associate or a rival—might have heard that Kieran was away, thought he'd help himself to the goods and came across Naomi and pow!"

"No obvious signs of a break-in," Parnell reminds me. "Which *could* bring us back to Drake. Naomi comes across him dealing and there's an argument? We know she was a so-called square, so she wouldn't have been too happy. I think we turn the heat up on his alibis, see if we can get any evidence to back this up."

Steele nods.

"Do we know for sure she was a square?" asks Seth. "Is her tox screen back?"

"Clear," confirms Steele, suddenly tapping away on her laptop. We wait for her to finish but she makes a gesture with her finger—*chat among yourselves.*

"What about Madden?" asks Parnell.

"We're getting a bit late for blood, urine, saliva," says Steele, looking at us, touch-typing as she goes. "It'd be out of his system by now. We'll run tests on the hairs, of course, but as you know, we're looking at a ninety-day detection window so it'll tell us bugger all, really. We don't care if he put Pablo Escobar to shame at a party two months ago, we want to know his state of mind on Saturday night."

I turn to Renée. "Talking of Mr. Madden—what's he saying about the sexual assault at TechMinds?"

Steele stops typing, offers a note of caution. "You might want to be careful using that term, m'dear. At the moment, it's an *alleged* sexual assault at best, and we haven't a hope of using it anyway until we find this Stacey Nash—Swaines is on the case, by the way. Even then we'd have to prove the sexual element and you all know how hard that is."

"Really? He forced his knee between her legs."

"Yes, and he should be strung up by the knackers as far as I'm concerned, but we'd have to prove his motive was gratification, not intimidation. It's definitely assault, but throw in the word 'sexual' and the CPS gets jumpy."

Technically, *depressingly*, she's right about the Crown Prosecution Service.

"Naomi wasn't sexually assaulted," Parnell points out. "So plain old assault would do. We just need a pattern of physical aggression toward women."

"Well, look, whatever we're calling it, he claims it never happened," says Renée. "It was all a conspiracy to get rid of him."

"People were jealous of his talent, apparently," adds Seth, who's also had the privilege of Madden's company today.

"God, he's some specimen." I shake my head, reeling at the guy's front, wondering if he actually believes his own hype or if he cries into his pillow every night, stricken by the weight of his own worthlessness.

"He's one brazen motherfucker," says Steele. "So where are we on the wife, Kinsella?"

Where indeed?

I look at my four seniors—Renée isn't senior in terms of rank but she is in everything that matters—and I feel a weight of expectation. The pressure to say something concrete, even though every conversation with Rachel feels like standing on shifting sand.

"She's, um, a tricky one."

"Well, that's very insightful, thank you. Is she lying to make things worse for him? That's all I want to know."

"Gut feel?"

"In the absence of a crystal ball, yep."

I take a quick deep breath. "No, I don't think she is—with a very heavy emphasis on the word 'think.'"

"Emphasis noted. And what makes you *think* this?"

"She's devoted to her daughter. Clara's in a crucial year at college and I can't see Rachel creating all this drama just to spite Joseph. It's too harmful to Clara. Having your dad arrested for murder isn't exactly going to help your concentration, is it?"

There, it's out. I *think* I believe Rachel. I feel a slight sense of relief at having tentatively picked a team.

"I do think she's lying about something, though. She was considering divorce earlier in the year, I'm sure of it. She made several calls to a family law specialist in Portsmouth—Lucas Stein will be all over that as a way of discrediting her—"

Renée stops me. "Oh sorry, that happened while you were in with Drake too. They came back to me—Rachel wasn't, *isn't*, a client of Morgan Cripps."

This throws me for all of two seconds. "She could have used a false name if she was just having provisional conversations over the phone. It's only if she went in for a face-to-face that she'd have to bring ID, their marriage certificate, and all that bumf."

"Why use a false name?" says Steele. "And why bloody Portsmouth?"

It's hard to explain, but I try. "You'd need to meet her, Boss—*'Joseph says this,' 'Joseph thinks that,' 'Joseph will be so angry.'* It's like he's this all-seeing, all-knowing omnipotent being. I think she'd have been nervous of using her own name, worried about it getting back to him, which I know sounds ridiculous, but if you met her, you'd know what I mean. It's probably why she didn't want to use a London firm either. Although I've no idea why she picked Morgan Cripps."

"Did you ask her about it?"

"Of course. She denies it. Gave me this bluff about Clara considering Portsmouth Uni and wanting to help her find paid work experience, something related to her studies."

Steele shrugs. "I've heard taller tales. What makes you think she's lying?"

I air the thought that's been niggling away all afternoon. "Look, it does sound plausible, but the thing is, Clara's applying to Leeds, Exeter, York—Russell Group universities. There was talk of Cambridge at one point. No disrespect, but Portsmouth isn't in the same league. It doesn't sit right."

A silence falls again as everyone chews it over.

"Why lie?" asks Parnell. "We know the marriage isn't great. Why not just admit she'd made inquiries?"

"Frightened of him finding out?" offers Renée. "I don't think Joseph Madden would take kindly to being divorced. Or being threatened with divorce."

"There's that," I agree. "But also because, for all his bad points— and she's not shy of pointing them out—she's adamant he didn't do this. She's adamant she loves him and she's standing by her man. Admitting she considered divorce muddies that narrative a bit."

And, you know, I get it. I'm a slave to a similar narrative myself. I've had thoughts about my dad that are blacker than ink and colder than stone, yet I'd defend him to the hilt.

I *have* defended him to the hilt.

There's a knock at the door and Ben Swaines pokes his head around.

Steele's face brightens—there's no denying she's got a soft spot for Swaines. An old cynic might say it's his passing resemblance to a young Clint Eastwood that puts him in favor. Anyone who knows Steele knows it's his utter devotion to her and the job.

"Benny-boy, come in, come in. Pull up a—" She looks around at the lack of seating options. "Here, sit in my chair. I've been sitting down all day. It's not good at my age. Not good for the varicose veins."

Swaines laughs nervously and says he's fine standing. "I've got to get back to my desk anyway. I want to crack the rest of that florist list before I head home. I just thought you'd want to know—Stacey Nash, she's dead."

He barely pauses but it's just long enough for us all to race to the same twisted conclusion. "Oh God no, nothing like that," he says, cottoning on. "Suicide. In 2010. Jumped off the balcony of her own flat, nine floors up. Terrible."

I look over at Parnell. "God, didn't Redfern say she'd left Tech-Minds to have her second kid? Poor little things."

"Postnatal depression?" Seth and Renée echo each other.

Swaines interrupts. "Actually hold on, sorry, I should have said, '*suspected* suicide.' Coroner gave an open verdict. There was no note, no history of depression or self-harm. Her family said she seemed fine in the days leading up. I suppose an open verdict was the only way to go."

"No foul play?" I'm sure he'd have mentioned it, but still, I've got to ask.

Swaines shakes his head. "She had a 0.06 blood alcohol level, so she was mildly tipsy, we'll assume. That slightly ups the possibility of an accident, or misadventure, whatever you want to call it. In all likelihood, though, it was suicide. No evidence of foul play."

I nod my head and say nothing. I've got nothing to say. No evidence. Case closed.

Steele's not fooled. "What, Cat, you think *two years* after she makes a complaint against him and he loses his job, Joseph Madden wreaks revenge by chucking her over her own balcony?"

I pause. "Probably not, no."

And that's exactly where I am. I think it's *probably* unlikely. Probably isn't definitely, though, and I can still hear Michael Redfern's words, as clear as if he were in the room.

"He always was a vindictive little shit."

17

I've had more exciting Friday nights. I've had more exciting Monday nights, truth be told. Just one hour in to a bit of domestic catchy-uppy and I'm already wishing I'd gone to the Tavern with whoever Seth managed to round up. Briefly, I consider heading back out or calling to see if they've staggered on to some other over-crammed hellhole, but it's pelting now and it probably isn't worth the drenching. Not for a few hours' bitching about cutbacks and arguing over the jukebox selection.

And I shouldn't drink anyway, not in my current mood. Not after Stacey Nash. Not when I'm being simultaneously phone-stalked by Dad and ignored by Aiden. Add one too many house whites to that dubious mix and it's got ugly-crying written all over it.

So instead, I clean. I pull on scraggy tracksuit bottoms and a gray T-shirt that used to be white, and I scrub and sponge and scour the past few days away. And when there's literally nothing else to buff or shine—and seriously, there is nothing else, I've even dusted the ceiling fan—I collapse into a shattered but satisfied heap, surprised to realize I haven't thought about Aiden once.

Except now I have thought about him, of course, and the lure of Facebook proves too strong. Within seconds, I'm on his page, wobbling over a photo he's been tagged in by somebody called Michelle Neary (*542 friends, born 8th March, studied at the Teresian College, Donnybrook*). In it, he's about to down a shot of something headache-inducing, flanked by two women—one of whom is Michelle Neary—neither of whom will be troubling the cover of *Vogue* anytime soon, although they're both nice-looking. Nice enough to make me want to get the hell out of Facebook and seek solace in numbers—namely, Rachel Madden's bank records.

Food shops. Petrol fill-ups. A £20 cash withdrawal here and there. That's more or less the sum of Rachel Madden's existence. Interestingly, there's no regular wage coming in from Be a Good Sport, which gives us piss-poor leverage, if required, as I doubt Rachel or Marcus have declared this small cash-in-hand arrangement to Mr. Taxman. Infuriatingly, the odd payment to AMERICAN GOLF (TRADING) LIMITED suggests Joseph Madden uses Rachel's meager income to fund his hobby.

Although a few pages in, I'm wondering if Rachel's got a little hobby of her own.

10 July POS Highcliff Hotel, PORTSMOUTH £9.90
14 July POS Highcliff Hotel, PORTSMOUTH £9.90
19 July POS Highcliff Hotel, PORTSMOUTH £4.45
25 July POS Highcliff Hotel, PORTSMOUTH £13.75

Mind whirring, I stare out at the rain, running scenarios through my head but always coming back to the same one.

A woman. A hotel.

A woman I'm fairly sure is lying about something.

A woman who admits she was striking out, building more of a life for herself.

And a husband who claimed his wife was acting "odd."

An affair? It's a possibility, surely? Google Maps puts the hotel on the same street as Morgan Cripps, so could Rachel have been involved with someone working there? Last I checked, legal advice wasn't usually dispensed over G&Ts on velvet bar stools.

Clearly, on a professional level, I know this isn't great. I know that *possibly* having an affair casts the same doubt on Rachel's credibility as the idea she wanted a divorce. Personally, though, I can't help thinking, *nice work, Rachel Madden.* What's good for the goose is good for the gander and all that. I also can't resist clicking on the Meet the Team section of Morgan Cripps's website for a quick game of "Guess Who?"

Morgan Cripps have nine employees in total: seven earnest, clean-cut men wearing seven different shades of gray, who I instinctively dismiss as too old, too young, too new to the firm for Rachel to have been visiting in July and, God forgive me, too ugly.

There's no accounting for taste, but still.

The firm's two women sit at opposite ends of the career spectrum. Twentysomething Grace Hollis radiates zeal and optimism, fresh from her double first from Bristol, while Lydia Coe is a handsome woman in her fifties wearing a tribal-print poncho and dangly jade beads. I click on Lydia's profile for no other reason than her poncho stands out and it stops me from thinking about Aiden downing shots with Michelle-bloody-Neary.

> *Lydia Coe is a senior family law practitioner, providing advice and court representation to a wide range of clients on issues including care proceedings, domestic violence injunctions, divorce and financial settlements, and all aspects arising from separation.*
>
> *Lydia has a particular interest in cases that protect and promote the rights of women and she works closely with the End Violence Against Women Coalition and Women's Aid, while providing training to many domestic abuse organizations and Citizens Advice Bureaus.*
>
> *Lydia is Morgan Cripps's pro bono champion and is passionate about supporting those less fortunate in a climate of relentless legal aid cuts.*

When I grow up, I want to be Lydia Coe.

A knock at the door and I'm straight back in Aiden-Land, aching to see him standing there on the doormat, even though the certainty of a Facebook time stamp puts him five hundred miles away. Slightly confused, I open the door cautiously. Only Aiden, Parnell, the Met's HR department, and a smattering of utility companies know my new address, although Dad has a way of finding things out.

As does Frank Hickey evidently.

My "uncle" Frank once told me you could track any "fucker" down if you were in possession of one of two things: enough money or enough rage.

I was nine years old when he shared that particularly touching pearl of wisdom.

"Catrina, Catrina, as I live and breathe," he says, beaming with false affection. "You haven't changed a bit. Well, maybe a bit of weight, but sure, where's the harm, says I."

I stare for a few seconds, practically concussed. I haven't seen Frank Hickey in six years, not since he shook my hand at Mum's funeral then whispered in my ear that she'd always held Dad back. The memory sparks a fury that makes me want to shunt him down the stone staircase, and I'd probably get away with it too. There's rarely anyone in these flats on a Friday night, only Rolling Stone Jerry, and he's the type to help you hide a body, no doubt about it.

"Well, aren't you going to invite me in?" He's halfway through the door already, taking advantage of my temporary stupor. "It's a shit of a night, right enough. I could do with a hot toddy."

I might not have changed, but Frank Hickey sure has. The Marbella tan has turned sallow and he's dropped the "gangster central casting" look in favor of something more suburban: an Aran sweater that covers the paunch he always fought tirelessly against and the kind of beige slacks that old men wear to weed the garden. Before I know it, he's standing in the center of the room, jiggling his keys while appraising my life choices.

"God Almighty, you turned your nose up at *Claremont* for this dump?" A hand goes up in placation. "Don't get me wrong, darling, I've the greatest of respect for anyone who wants to make their own way in life, but even you deserve better than *this*."

Claremont. Claremont Heights. A high-rise new-build off the Clerkenwell Road, offering "designer interiors, cutting-edge technology, and 360-degree viewing terraces," not to mention a fifteen-minute walk to work for me. Just say the word and the keys were mine, Dad had said. *"Frank's investing, going straight in his dotage."*

I signed the lease on *this* "dump" the very next day.

"What do you want, Frank?" I leave the door wide open.

He ignores the question, staring idly at a note I've Blu-Tacked to the fridge door: "RECYCLING—EVERY FRIDAY!" "By the way, Cynth says hello. She's not been well, God love her. The big C, o' course. They're managing it, mind, shrinking it." He turns back to face me. "Ah sure, it'll get her in the end, I dare say."

Common decency nearly forces *"I'm sorry to hear that"* from me but I bite down hard, resisting the natural urge to offer sympathy. "I said, what do you want, Frank? You know, I just spent two hours scrubbing the dirt out of my flat and in you come. I'll have to bleach the place now."

He laughs but it's all snarl, no smile. "Your manners haven't changed much either, I see. Always were a little weapon. Too much to say for yourself, that's your problem. Same as your mother, God rest her soul."

I could take the bait. I could clamp my jaws around it, let him feel the full throttle of my rage, but then that's what he wants. In fact, until he answers my question, it's the only thing I'm certain he wants.

"How'd you find me?"

He answers this one. "Ah, nothing much to it. I had someone wait outside the cop shop and follow you home one evening. You should be flattered I take an interest, Catrina. It's more than your dad does. He could have done the same if he was that bothered about seeing you." He waits to see if that stings as much as he hopes. Truth is, it does, but his acid tongue is no match for my poker face. "Problem with your old fella, he's never been what you'd call 'proactive.' He's not a problem-solver, not like me. Who knows, maybe if he'd let me handle that Doyle lass, things could have worked out different." He laughs. "I mean, she'd still be cold in the ground, but it'd be on my conscience, not his, and, well . . ."

He doesn't need to finish. Frank Hickey lost his conscience with his baby teeth.

"Dad's got nothing on his conscience. He did nothing to Maryanne except try to help her." My tone is blithe but my words are treason. A betrayal of Aiden. A betrayal of myself, even, as this is absolutely not what I believe. "See, you think Dad's just like you, but he isn't, Frank. He despises you, deep down."

Smiling, completely unaffected, he reaches into his inside pocket, and for one fevered second I think maybe he's come to kill me, because if not for *that*, what in God's name is he here for?

He clocks my fear and his smile breaks wider, an ugly great slash across his ugly lined face. "Jesus Christ, darling, I may be bad but I'm not that bad! I haven't killed a family member yet and there'd be a few ahead of you in the queue, trust me." He hands me an envelope, pink and ominously weighty. "Just wanted to give you this, that's all. From me and Cynth. For your birthday."

"You're not my family. As far as I'm concerned, you're just a waste of human tissue."

"Ah now, that hurts," he says, pretending to stagger backward. "Especially when I think so highly of you." He nods at the card. "It says so in there. Go on, open it."

Sure enough, there's a treacly rhyme inside stating how special I am to everyone and a thick wedge of fifties giving credence to the claim. I've no idea how much exactly, but enough to buy a washing machine and to hire a plumber to fix the heaters.

Shame I'd rather die of cold wearing clothes that could walk off me.

"Take it," I say, holding it out to him. "I don't want your card *or* your money."

"Are you sure, now?" He takes in the room again. "You're not exactly drowning in good wishes, are you? Although there's still a few days to go—thirteenth, isn't it?" I don't answer. "You were actually due on the tenth, did you know that? Me and your dad were beside ourselves as it was the West Ham/Millwall derby the same day. You held out, though, fair play to yer. T'was only after you were born you became a proper pain in the hole."

"Fuck you."

He roars with laughter as I toss the card back at him. "So you're not going to offer me a drink then, after I came all this way? Christ, south of the river on a Friday night—you'd think you'd be a bit more grateful."

"Thanks for coming." I walk to the door. "Now fuck off."

He hesitates, then finally moves. "Jesus, how are you and Jacqui sisters, hey?" he says, reaching the door. "Sure, Jacqui'd nearly kill you with kindness. It's all *'Have another drink, Uncle Frank'* and *'No, you have the last rasher, Uncle Frank.'* Great little hostess, that one. Great little figure too, kept herself nice." He looks at me, sadly. "Shame, really, you were always the runt of the litter. The little piggy runt who grew up to be an actual pig."

"Goodnight, Frank." I'm bored now.

"Still, you must have something going for you." There's a glint of victory in his eyes. "I mean, that Aiden's a nice fella. A good-looking fella too. But then his sister was a fine-looking woman."

My heart stops as my head explodes. My vision zigzags, nothing but a vista of fizzing black lines. Frank keeps talking but I can't make any sense of it; something about Dad's pub, about whiskey chasers, about glory-hunting Man United fans and trust me to take up with one.

"You bastard!" I lash out wildly, shoving him hard out the door. Slowly, my surroundings come back into focus, but even then I can only see one thing—the look of *game, set, match* on Frank Hickey's face.

"I'm warning you, Frank, stay away from Aiden."

"Stay away from him!" Eyes twinkling, he's in his element. "Did you not hear what I said? He came to the pub, darling. *He* came to *us*. Said he was a friend of yours, that he was just passing. *'A friend?'* I says to your dad. *'Tell me another!'* Looks like I was right, n'all."

I slam the door but Frank's not finished. "Yeah, lovely fella," he taunts from the other side. "Glad I got to meet him. What were the chances, eh?"

The chances? No doubt Aiden would have an algorithm that could work this one out. What were the chances of him going to Dad's pub on the very same night Frank Hickey was there? Frank Hickey—the man who takes silent partnering to its invisible extremes.

Very fucking low. I'd say that's what the chances were.

About the same as the chance of me and Aiden ever working out.

"The greater the storm, the bigger the rainbow." That's what the poster declared on Naomi Lockhart's wall. I'd told Parnell I didn't believe it, but I could do with believing it now. I'd be only too happy to kid

myself that even though Frank knows about Aiden, it'll all be OK in the end.

It won't, though. Because do you know what often follows great storms?

Howling, destructive tornadoes.

18

When I was a child, I got lost at a funfair. A scrawny little one, the type that pops up overnight then vanishes just as quick. But at the goofy age of six, and with a social life consisting of Mass every Sunday and the odd trip to Brent Cross for school shoes, it was the highlight of my year. Jacqui's and Noel's too. Jacqui would get to thrust her B-cups at all the greasy, handsome Waltzer lads while Noel would get to pickpocket little old ladies in the crowd, maybe even start a mass brawl. For me, though, the draw was always Dad. The chance to spend time with him. To watch him knock coconuts off tin cans. To share foot-long jumbo hot dogs with him, giddy with the knowledge that if Mum knew, she'd go mad.

Happy, happy days.

Until the day I wandered off, that is.

Without Dad's brick-wall presence beside me, everything seemed sinister, every sight and every sound a new form of attack. Suddenly, the screams from the rides rang with menace, not glee. The goldfish looked anguished in their clear plastic bags. Even the helter-skelter— by far my favorite ride—morphed into a looming metal monster, without the rock-solid safety of Dad there.

It could only have been a few minutes, but when his face finally emerged through the rippling sea of strangers, I nearly died with relief. I certainly cried with relief.

And, as I watch him from the doorway of McAuley's Old Ale House, broad and robust and busying himself with till rolls, I'm not far off crying now.

"You could have fucking warned me," I say, stamping down my neediness.

He looks up, his face flushing with twenty different emotions.

"That's quite an entrance, Catrina. Do you want to try again with '*Hi Dad, good to see you*'?"

Our voices peel out around the midnight quiet. Back in the old days there'd be lock-ins, stragglers, dodgy geezers playing poker. These days, there's just Dad and whichever employee drew the late-shift short straw.

Tonight it's a brunette whose bar towel matches the color of her dress. Dad says, "Lex, this is my baby girl. You'll have to excuse her, she's normally got better manners."

I step forward. "Funny, Frank Hickey said the exact same thing when he came to my flat."

Dad gives "Lex" a tiny nod of dismissal which could mean anything from "get yourself home" to "get yourself upstairs and get the bed warmed." There's no reason to think the latter, but with Dad, you can never rule it out. "Lex" saunters out the back and he strides toward me. "Frank came to your flat? When? I mean, how did he . . . ? What the hell did he want?"

"You tell me!" He's close enough to hug now, close enough to slap. There's a shaving nick along his right jawbone and the smell of mints on his breath. "Jesus, Dad! Why didn't you warn me Frank knew about Ai—" I pull up, can't say his name. Can't work out whether I want to hug or slap *him* either. "You know, normal people leave messages. They don't plague you with missed calls or send cryptic texts."

Normal people. Maybe next time around we'll come back as normal people. Just normal folk with normal problems. No twisted "uncles" or dead sisters of secret boyfriends to disrupt the steady treadmill of our lives.

"I didn't want to leave a voicemail. I didn't want to scare you. I wanted to talk to you properly, face-to-face."

"Well, I'm here now. Talk to me properly." I widen my stance, meaning business. "I need to know everything that was said, Dad. Everything Aiden knows."

The back door slams. No bed-warming duties for Lex, then.

"There's not a lot I can tell you, sweetheart. Frank talked to him more than me." He slumps against the quiz machine that used to be the fag machine, bone-tired. "We had a big crowd in, see, a thirtieth, and they were kicking off about the bill and I was ages dealing with that. I was just glad Frank was distracted, if I'm honest. Bloody typical, he doesn't come in for months and then when he does, World War Three breaks out over a few bloody side dishes. It doesn't look great, you know, it looks sloppy, bad management. Anyway, by the time I got back over to him, he's made a new friend, hasn't he? *Your* friend, apparently." He gives me a look he's got no right to give. "Name's Aiden Doyle. Comes from a little town called Mulderrin . . ."

"And?" I say, tetchy.

"And what? I shook his hand. Told him to put his tenner away— none of my kids' friends pay for drinks in my pub. Then I slagged off Man United for a bit and bolted upstairs, said I had to make a few phone calls. I couldn't sit there chatting with him. I just couldn't . . ."

"So you left him with Frank? You thought that was a better move?"

"Yeah, I know, but remember, Frank knew Maryanne. He was involved too. So he's hardly going to say, *'Well you'll never guess who your "friend" is, mate. She's the daughter of the guy who—'*" He stops, can't bring himself to put a name to it.

I can, though. Dad's the guy who set Maryanne on the path that led to her death and he's the guy who tried to steer her off it. The guy who didn't realize that kindness would ultimately get her killed.

I sell myself both versions, depending on my mood. When my anger needs fueling, Dad's an out-and-out sinner. When my soul needs soothing, he's certainly not a saint, but he's just a fuck-up. Just another weak schmuck with a knight-in-shining-armor complex.

"You know, you should have told me about this Aiden fella. How long has it been going on?" I say nothing—he doesn't get to ask about my love life. "Come on, sweetheart, you've got to see that this—*he*— is a really bad idea? If you can't see that then you haven't got half the smarts I thought you had."

"Oh, I've got the smarts, Dad. I've also got a heart and feelings. I must get those from Mum's side, eh?"

His face contorts, anger battling a fatherly sense of pride. "Oh my God, it's serious, isn't it? My baby's in love."

A red mist descends. "Yeah, sure, Dad, it's *really* serious. We're going to have babies and everything. Hey, maybe if it's a girl she'll get the Doyle genes and then your granddaughter will look *just* like the girl whose life you royally fucked over. A nice walking, talking reminder to visit you in your care home. That'll be nice, eh?"

I *know* I've gone too far. I'll say sorry in a bit, no doubt, in that roundabout way I do. It's the babies that got me, though. The fact that I'll never have Aiden's babies—a couple of blue-eyed, cushiony-lipped smashers, with the kind of curls you spend half your life untangling—makes me want to burn the world and everyone in it.

"Oh right, so I royally fucked Maryanne over, which gives you the right to fuck her brother over, is that how it works?" He lets out a mean burst of laughter. "Don't come here playing the martyr, Catrina. I know you, remember? I know you're every bit as ruthless as I am. You want what you want, end of."

"What I *want* is for Frank Hickey to stay away from me."

He shrugs. "That's no problem, sweetheart. Consider it done."

My turn to laugh. "Oh, it's that easy, is it? You've got him on a leash these days?" It's what I want to hear. It's what I came to hear. It all seems too easy, though. "We are talking about the same thug, right? The animal who broke your cheekbone with a pool cue. Who signed off on the battering that put your own son in the hospital."

Another shrug. "Noel deserved a battering. You don't skim from Frank Hickey and not expect a few slaps."

"Maybe he thinks *I* deserve a few slaps. You said it yourself—me seeing Aiden affects him too."

He shakes his head, shaking out the thought. "He wouldn't. No way. He's not a—"

"Oh, spare me the Villains' Moral Charter, Dad. He does what he needs to do, and he was threatening me with something, I know he was. I just haven't figured out what yet. Oh, and he gave me money."

"Money?"

"Yeah, you know, the paper stuff. The thing you sold yourself down the river for."

The thing that landed us in this purgatory.

"What for?" He's standing up straight now, intrigued. "How much?"

"I don't know. I gave it back to him. But it was a fair bit. He said it was for my birthday, but it was *weird*. Is he trying to bribe me into finishing with Aiden or something? Is that it?"

Dad rubs at his temples, thinking and fretting and trying to channel Frank's mad mind. "Listen," he says eventually. "I don't know why he'd give you money but I do know that he's bored." I pull a face. Men like Frank Hickey don't get "bored." Not when they see everything as theirs for the taking. "Ah, you'd be surprised, Cat. There's not much criminality in the criminal world anymore. Every scam is run like a public company and, well, Frank's old-school, isn't he? His style is dying out a bit. I mean, he still gets respect—he'll *always* get respect—but he's not quite the force he once was." He takes me gently by the shoulders. I stiffen, then soften. "Do you know what I think, honestly? I think he's bored, and he's getting a kick out of winding you up, sweetheart. Nothing more. Honestly, I'd put the house on it."

Relief washes over me like warm foamy water.

Later, upstairs, we sprawl on opposite sofas, swigging Jameson from the bottle and reminiscing about Mum. The time she dressed me as a ham sandwich for a fancy-dress party. "A little fat kid in a pink leotard, Dad. What *was* she thinking?" The time she slipped on a banana on Charing Cross Road—not a banana skin, an *actual* banana.

There's tears, but they're happy tears and it takes a good hour, and nearly half the whiskey, before we're scratching at the door of maudlin.

"I feel guilty 'cos I can't remember certain things about her now." I'm staring at a cobweb on the ceiling, thinking how it would never be there if Mum were still here. She was ruthless with the feather duster. "Just stupid things, you know, like her shoe size and what she ordered from the Chinese."

Dad smiles. "Size six and sweet-and-sour chicken. Every. Bloody. Time. She never was the adventurous type."

"Is that why you cheated on her? She wasn't adventurous enough?"

Bye-bye maudlin, hello conflict.

He sighs, probably angry at himself for leaving such an open goal. "For the love of God, Catrina, change the record . . ."

I roll onto my side, propping my head on my hand. "OK, well, here's a new record—brand-new in at number one. Do you think Mum ever cheated on you? Gave you a taste of your own medicine? I mean, you were a shit and she was a good-looking woman, so why not?"

He turns, not to look at me, to look at Mum. The photo of her cradling Finn, the grandchild she only knew for a year. "I think your mum loved me," he says, simply. "That's all that matters. Who did what to who isn't important anymore." It's a bland nonanswer to an incendiary question and just a year ago, things would have gone nuclear. Pulling his gaze away from Mum, he adds, "But what made you ask?"

I probably shouldn't say but the whiskey purrs, "*what the hell.*" "Oh, it's this case I'm working on. Our suspect's a cheat—a cruel bastard, as well—but I think his wife might have been cheating on him, getting her own back."

"I was never cruel to your mum. Never."

Which is debatable but *probably* fair enough. He never rubbed her nose in it, not like Joseph Madden. He never told her she was stupid or ugly or lucky to have him. Dad did what he wanted and lived how he pleased, but his motivation was never to make Mum unhappy.

His happiness was simply worth more.

"Look, stay here tonight," he says, checking the time on his phone. "It's nearly two and we've put a good dent in this"—he wiggles the Jameson—"no way you're driving now."

"I didn't drive. I'd need a car to drive." I kick myself, hoping he doesn't take this as a hint. I don't want Frank's money and I haven't wanted Dad's for years either. "Good to see you're so law-abiding, though."

"I'm trying to be." He sits up, massaging knots in his neck. "Frank's always trying to tempt me back in, but I don't want the drama. Must be finally getting old, eh?" Right now, I wouldn't entirely disagree. While Dad could *never* look rough—he's got too much pride, too much pout, too many fortunate genes to look rough—at two a.m., under the glare of the living-room light, he looks exactly what he is. A fifty-five-year-old man at the end of a sixty-hour week. "'Course, you know the main reason I don't want back in?" He pauses. "It's the way you look at me. I'm sick of my baby being ashamed of who I am."

"Don't take it personally, Dad. I look at myself that way. I'm ashamed of who I am."

"Well, that makes me really, really sad." He looks it too, properly crestfallen. "Don't ever be ashamed of who you are, sweetheart. You're the one thing I'm proud of."

I give him the grin, *our* grin. "Jesus, don't let Jacqs hear you say that. You won't get your ironing done half as quick."

If I sound snippy, I don't mean to. Truth is, I envy Jacqui's relationship with Dad. The ironing. The nagging. The closeness that stems from not being close at all. Everything shiny on the surface, with all the bad bits stowed away.

He grins back. "I'm proud of Jacqs, you know I am. But anything she is, it's not down to me. Jacqui takes after your mum." His eyes laser mine. "You're me, through and through."

I'm not sure whether to be flattered or appalled.

"It's been OK tonight," I mumble—my roundabout apology for anything vicious I said earlier.

"OK enough to stay over? OK enough to come back? This used to be your home, Cat. I'd love to see you here more often." His face is full of hope, like he wants us to nail down dates, times, menus.

A long silence passes while I try to work out what to say. In the end I go with the truth. "It's just hard, Dad. I want to be a good person and you remind me that I'm not."

He nods, he understands. "So, this Aiden? Is he a good person?"

"The best." *Apart from going behind my back and coming here.* "Who knows, maybe he'll rub off on me? Maybe twenty-six years with him might cancel out twenty-six of you." I add a smile. A pointless attempt to disinfect the words, to make it all a joke.

But then, it *is* a joke, really. A sad, cruel joke. In twenty-six years from now, Aiden will be happy with someone who deserves him. Maybe Michelle Neary? She's got 542 Facebook friends. She must be doing something right.

"So you'll stay, then?" Dad says, not reacting to the dig. There's a desperation in his voice that isn't about the late hour or my personal safety. It's about loneliness. It's about the ties that bind. It's about one night pretending we're something we're not. Just an everyday dad making the spare bed up for his everyday daughter.

"Yeah, I guess so. Beats paying for a cab." I look toward the stairs. "So where am I sleeping?"

"Your old room, of course. I still call it 'Cat's room,' you know. There's a futon in there. Jacqui reckons it's comfy enough."

"What? You got rid of my princess cabin bed? How dare you!"

Suddenly, I realize *that's* why I love my sky bed. Magical memories of happier times. Sleeping six feet skyward with my mates Belle and Ariel.

He laughs. "Yeah, sorry about that. I haven't got any Frosted Cherry Pop-Tarts either."

He remembers. I can't remember Mum's shoe size and yet he remembers that, right down to the limited-edition flavor.

I stem tears with the heels of my hands, adding a yawn to make it look like tiredness. "Ah, I'm more savory these days, Dad. Give me a bacon sandwich and I'm happy. Still gutted about my cabin bed, though."

"I bet you are. You bloody loved that thing."

Another memory, this one not so magical. "Mmm, apart from that time Noel ran off with the ladder and I was stuck up there for hours until you saved me. Do you remember?"

"I do." A heated stare. "And I'll always save you, Cat. I might not make you feel good about yourself, but I'll always save you."

I'm six years old.

I'm back at the funfair.

And I can finally see his face.

19

Saturday

Lydia has a particular interest in cases that protect and promote the rights of women . . .

Next morning, I lie on the world's most uncomfortable futon, fangirling over Lydia Coe and avoiding the bacon sandwich love-in that Dad's preparing downstairs. Last night, under the cloak of whiskey, the idea of Dad frying the rashers while I buttered the toast seemed twee and benign and essentially *"Why not?"* but this morning it feels phoney. Our relationship's better suited to late-night confessionals than cozy chats over the breakfast table.

When I can't avoid it any longer, I get up, have a cold shower—because I can't figure out the temperature dial—and get dressed in yesterday's jeans and a smart cream blouse I find hanging on a clothes rail. Judging by the label, I'm assuming it's Jacqui's. At least, I hope it's Jacqui's. I can't go to work wearing one of Dad's conquest's clothes.

"Morning, sweetheart. You sleep all right?" Dad looks fresh, full of zing, at least ten years younger than he did last night.

"Yeah, not bad. I've, er . . . I've borrowed this," I say, tugging at the blouse as I look around the kitchen. There's red and brown sauce, enough bacon to feed a platoon, and the Jackson Five are ABCing on the radio at full volume.

It's all too chipper. I need to weasel away.

I walk straight to the sink and pour myself a pint of water, mainly because it means keeping my back to him while I make my excuses.

"Look, I'm not really hungry, Dad. Sorry. And I've got places to be . . . Don't worry, though, the bacon'll keep. Chuck it in a carbonara or something. Jacqui will know."

"I'll know what?"

My sister, the ninja.

I turn around. "Oh, hello, where did you spring from?" My nephew's trailing her in a green-and-blue football kit—an iPad in one hand, a packet of Skittles in the other.

"We've been here ages. Dad said to keep the noise down so we didn't wake Princess Catrina. Heard you had a rough night." For one crossed-wire second I think Dad's told her about Frank, but then I remember Dad doesn't tell Jacqui anything unpleasant and by rough she means boozy. "Hey, is that my Boden top, you cheeky cow? Well, I want it back, I'm not joking. And it's dry-clean only. Don't be throwing it in with your cheap-dye jeans."

It could be 2003 again. Kelis bragging about her "Milkshake" on the radio and me and Jacqui declaring war in this very kitchen over a top or a hairband while Mum tried to referee.

"Yeah, yeah, cool your jets. I *can* read a label." I peer past her. "Hey Finn-bo, don't I get a hug anymore?" Finn shuffles toward me, wafting his small body against mine—a seven-year-old boy's version of a hug, I suppose. "So what are you doing here? Have you got a game nearby?"

Finn makes a vaguely affirmative sound and sits at the table, blindly swiping at the iPad screen. Jacqui hovers behind him, picking the rind off a piece of bacon. "Yep, over in Islington. Same as every Saturday morning." *Which you'd know if you showed your face a bit more.* "You should come," she adds, before putting a hand up. "No, don't tell me. *Work.*"

"Girl's gotta make rent, Jacqs. We don't all have the privilege of part-time." It's childish and bitchy and I don't even mean it, but Jacqui has a way of winding me up as only big sisters can.

Dad pacifies the situation, giving Finn a playful shoulder-punch. "Last year of *Little Kickers*, eh, champ? Next stop West Ham under-eights."

Finn finally looks up, troubled. "Grandad, can't I support Chelsea instead? Alfie Keeler in my class says West Ham are shit." Jacqui howls, "*Finn!*" while Dad howls laughing. I try to look reproachful but I don't think he's convinced. Sensing he has two-thirds of his audience onside, Finn pushes his luck even further. "Actually, he said they're 'fucking shit.' Then Mrs. Benn put him on time-out and he called her another bad word."

I laugh. "Alfie Keeler sounds like a gem. I reckon I'll be nicking him in around ten years' time."

Jacqui picks up the iPad and issues a fate worse than death. "If I hear that word again, Finlay, you won't have this for a month and that's a promise."

Finlay. Catrina. Even names can be used as weapons. Aiden once told me Maryanne means "grace." To me it just means guilt.

Dad pretends to cover Finn's ears. "Which word do you mean though, Jacqs—'fucking' or 'shit'? I mean, be fair to the lad—there's an iPad at stake—you need to make yourself clearer." Jacqui rolls the bacon rind into a ball and fires it at Dad's head. It bounces off the extractor fan and lands in the middle of the floor. He crouches to retrieve it and comes eye level with Finn. "And no, you can't support bloody Chelsea. It's bad enough having a copper in the family, never mind a Chelsea fan. Some things are written in blood, I'm afraid, my boy. You're a Hammer by birth and you can't change who you are, not really." He stands up, turning to me. "We were talking about that last night, weren't we, sweetheart?"

There's patches of last night that are blurred and a little foggy, however one assertion from Dad remains crisp, clear and grave.

"You're me, through and through."

And the more time I spend with him, the more likely that'll come true.

"Right, I'm outta here." I push myself off the sink and plant a kiss on top of Finn's blond head. He giggles and squirms so I plant another then another, finishing with a great big wet smacker right on his left cheek.

"I can make you something else if you're not hungry enough for bacon?" Dad starts fussing in the fridge, shouting out random items. "I've got eggs, tomatoes, mushrooms, fruit salad, peanut butter, halloumi, yogurt, and beans." The wonder in his voice suggests he didn't do the food shop.

Good old Jacqui strikes again.

"Honestly, Dad, I'm fine. I've got to get to work." I waft my head toward his, a pseudo-kiss at best. "I'll see you soon, though, OK?" I blow a kiss to Jacqui. "And you. I'll see you all soon, I promise."

Soon. The ultimate get-out clause. Such a deliciously woolly word.

"Work" this morning consists of drinking cucumber water in the Connors' Instagram-friendly living room. The kind of achingly stylish space that makes you feel you're doing life all wrong. Clearly, while the kitchen only has half a roof and, according to Rachel, the bathroom resembles an air-raid shelter, no expense has been spared within these four walls. Parnell's sat on a rattan rocking chair that would give his £600 suits a run for their money, and I'm too scared to put my glass down in case I scratch the mosaic tiles.

Kirstie Connor's also scared. She's playing beautifully into our hands.

"For fuck's sake, I hardly even take drugs these days." An angry shade of crimson overlays her usual olive complexion—could be shame, could be anger, maybe both? "But the atmosphere was really strained, mainly because of Joseph and Rachel but also because of *you*"—a hot look toward Marcus—"and Rachel sulking with each other, and I knew some of my team were doing coke and I just cracked. They looked so young and carefree and I wanted to feel like that again, just for an afternoon. But I wasn't going to scavenge off them, no way."

"Why were you and Rachel sulking?" I ask Marcus, giving Kirstie a quick reprieve.

Marcus is sitting on the arm of a huge fuchsia sofa. His back is rigid, his neck long. I think he's aiming for stoic but it's coming off as staged. "Just sibling stuff. Stuff that pales into insignificance now." I give him *the* face. "Money stuff, OK. Joseph always leaves Rachel short, so I help out sometimes." Kirstie gives him *the* face. "I'd given her a few hundred quid a while back, but I found out last week she'd given it to *him* to buy a new five-iron. It's ridiculous. He's got her believing he could be the next Tiger Woods with all the right equipment. I honestly don't know who winds me up more, him or her."

"So what are you going to do?" says Kirstie, not interested in Rachel or Joseph, keen to get back to her own fate.

"They can't do anything about the drugs, Kirst. They didn't catch you with them." Marcus stares between me and Parnell. "And as for perverting the course of justice, can you prove there wasn't a window cleaner?"

It's a strong show of solidarity but his tone is far from impressed. Kirstie's well and truly in the doghouse. It's a different story in the photo directly behind his head: a younger Kirstie and Marcus, honeymooning at a guess, barefoot and flushed from either an afternoon in the sun or an afternoon of hot sex. Just the sea and a papaya tree for company.

And next to that, a photo of their wedding day. A handful of people arranged on the stone steps of a stately home. Rachel, willowy as ever, in a mint-green bridesmaid dress. Joseph in a three-piece suit and cravat, not the best man but definitely an usher.

Hard to imagine now.

Parnell rocks forward. "We knocked on every door in every surrounding street, Kirstie, looking for your mystery window cleaner. Numerous police hours wasted. That's old grannies being mugged, local shops getting robbed, *kids* getting stabbed."

Parnell went for the heart. I go for the jugular. "Look, Kirstie, we can make life very difficult if we want. For a start, we know there's some creative accounting going on in your business. It wouldn't take us too long to look into that." Marcus throws me a withering look. "Oh, I don't mean *us*," I add, waggling a finger between me and Parnell. "There's other departments who'd be *very* interested."

"Creative accounting? Who said that? I bet it was that shit-stirrer, Evie Whitlock." Kirstie takes a long, deep breath, trying to steady herself. "I got into a bit of a mess, OK. I told you, I'm not very organized. That's why I hired Naomi. She had finance qualifications. She was able to—"

"What do you want, detectives?" Marcus cuts to the chase, reading the situation perfectly.

"Just for you to talk to us," says Parnell, reasonably.

"We want info," I say, less inclined to pussyfoot around them. "We want to ask you questions about Joseph *and* Rachel—and if we think for a second that *anything* has got back to Rachel, we will charge you with perverting the course of justice, Kirstie, and then the drugs element will come out anyway."

She twists to face Marcus. I can't see her expression but I'd guess at abject horror.

When Marcus speaks, it's low, rushed, and agitated, as if we're not there. "You have to stop trying to protect her, Kirst. If *he* did this, you're not protecting her anyway. Protect yourself, for God's sake—protect me, protect Danny. You've got to tell them what happened." He looks up at me and Parnell. "I only found out about this last night, by the way."

Kirstie walks over to the window and stands with her back to us, gazing out at the garden, at Danny bouncing up and down again on the giant trampoline. "Look, there's something I didn't mention before. The reason I didn't mention it is that I was pretty wired by then and I can only remember fragments and I was embarrassed, I suppose. What I said, it doesn't exactly show me in a good light . . ."

This is priceless. The bigger the squirm, the bigger the payoff, generally.

"We were sitting in here, OK—me, Rachel, and Joseph—and Joseph had said something horrible to Rachel—it's all a bit hazy so I don't remember what, exactly, but it was something about her appearance, about how the years were showing. Anyway, I started goading him, saying I'd noticed he'd got a few gray hairs—he's *obsessed* with his black hair—and that to the girls in my team he's just an old man who they humor when they see him in Scarfes Bar." She turns back to us, pulling on a curl, probably a stress-reliever from childhood. "So, a few minutes later, Naomi walks past the door and Joseph says, *'Oh, so is she one of those who just humors me?'* and I said—and I'm not proud of this—*'Yeah, she might have the personality of a dead moth but even she'd draw the line at you.'"* The squirming intensifies. "And then that's when he said it. He said—and again, I can't remember word for word—but it was something like he could have her if he wanted, just like that." A click of her fingers.

We leave her hanging for a few seconds, waiting for her penance. Eventually Parnell says, "We could have really done with knowing this earlier, Kirstie."

"I swear, I actually forgot about it until yesterday. I get black spots, you see, when I mix booze and coke. And then when I did remember . . . well, I felt embarrassed about what I'd said about Naomi. It makes me sound like such a bitch, and she's dead . . ." She sits on the sofa, Marcus slightly elevated on the arm behind her. It reminds me of a school photo pose—Noel and I pretending we liked each other for just enough time for the camera to flash. "And anyway, it might not *mean* anything. Joseph—and I'm certainly not defending him here, but it's not like he singled Naomi out. She just happened to walk past. If it had been any of the others, he'd have said the exact same thing."

I jump in before Parnell can. I want to use this to go down a more interesting path. "So what you've actually just told us, Kirstie, is that Rachel's been holding back—because she never mentioned any of this and *she* can't blame black spots."

"She'd hardly mention it, would she? She knows it looks bad for him."

"Joseph claims she's trying to make things look bad for him. That she's lying about his alibi. That she got rid of his clothes to fuel suspicion. What do you say to that?"

"That's ludicrous." The Marcus we met a few days ago wouldn't have used the word "ludicrous." He'd have said "bullshit" or "bollocks." But that night, we were all still friends; we were just guests in his kitchen, getting context, chewing the fat. People have a habit of swallowing a thesaurus when they realize you're the enemy.

"Ludicrous is an understatement," agrees Kirstie. "She certainly hasn't been taking his crap quite as much lately, but the idea that she'd actively go against him?"

"So what's this personality change all about, then?"

"I didn't say she'd had a personality change. She's just seemed less jumpy. A bit better at ignoring Joseph, rather than getting upset every time he's a pig."

"Do you think she was considering divorce?"

Marcus moves to sit next to Kirstie. "Why are you asking about Rachel? You can't believe a word Joseph says."

I lie easily. "We're just trying to build a picture of Joseph's state of mind, and his relationship with his wife plays a big part."

"Well, you can forget about divorce," scoffs Marcus. "It's not like we haven't suggested it enough."

Parnell jumps in. "We know she called a solicitor a number of times—a firm that specializes in family law."

Their surprise seems genuine and it's hard to synchronize that kind of performance. One person can spin you a lie but it's hard for two to stay completely in step.

"How about an affair?" I suggest.

Kirstie laughs. "An affair! Rachel! With who?"

I keep it light, speculative. "Whoever, really. Someone in Portsmouth, maybe?"

"Portsmouth?" repeats Kirstie, flummoxed.

"We know she visited there a few times over the summer."

"Really?" She looks part-baffled, part-impressed by her sister-in-law's mystery trips. "Well whoever she was visiting, it wouldn't have been an affair. No. No way. She'd be too scared of him finding out."

"You said yourself, she'd toughened up lately."

"Not that tough. And look, whenever we've been out, Rachel's always got attention—she's six foot in heels and looks great when she makes the effort—and yet she's never once been tempted. Never. She doesn't even flirt. For reasons we all struggle to understand, she's completely loyal to Joseph."

Something occurs to Marcus. "Hold on," he says, nudging Kirstie. "Wasn't Clara looking at Portsmouth Uni? I know Rachel mentioned something about Portsmouth, I'm sure it was to do with Clara."

"*Everything's* to do with Clara. Wouldn't surprise me if Rachel was doing a security sweep or something."

"Portsmouth's a bit different from Leeds and York, league-table-wise," I say, casually.

Marcus shrugs. "I think she's got friends there in their first year and because of all the crap she's had at school, maybe the idea of a few friendly faces is appealing."

"Clara gives out as much crap as she gets, Marcus." There's an edge to Kirstie's voice that suggests they've done this discussion to death. "Although, actually, I blame Joseph. It's him that told Clara to hit that girl at college." She turns to us, explaining. "He kept saying she was weak for not retaliating. That violence is the only thing some people understand."

So it's not Clara's brains and beauty that other girls resent, it's her right hook. Interesting.

"Has Joseph ever been violent toward Rachel?" I ask, getting back to the Maddens' marriage, the reason we're here.

Kirstie looks away quickly. Marcus speaks. "Joseph can be quite . . . well, it's more emotional abuse than anything. Putting her down, flaunting his cheating, convincing her she's driven him to it. Convincing her she's nothing, really. And then there's the financial stuff. He controls her by leaving her short of money all the time."

"That's abuse in the eyes of the law." *Controlling and Coercive Behavior.* To think I'd once considered Joseph Madden might have been a victim of this.

"I saw him pull her hair once," Marcus goes on, miserably. "He kind of made it look playful but it wasn't playful. You could see he'd really hurt her."

Kirstie's voice is quiet, almost contrite. "I, um . . . well, I saw him grab her by the throat once. He didn't realize I was there. He'd come in and walked straight into the kitchen and just went for her. When he saw me, he stopped. She thought he was going to kill her, though." For a second, I think Marcus might kill *her.* Kirstie recoils to the other end of the sofa, raising her hand. "Just wait a minute, Marcus. Rachel *specifically* said she didn't want me telling you. She said it'd only make things worse."

"What kicked it off?" I ask, before a row ignites. They can tear each other to pieces later. Right now, we need to know Joseph Madden's trigger points. What switches him from his steady state of being an absolute bastard into a frenzied throat-grabber.

"I don't know, she wouldn't say. She was right about one thing, though"—she jabs a finger toward Marcus—"*he* would have made things worse." Marcus mutters "*bullshit*" into the ether. "Oh no? So what happened when you blew up at him about that sexual assault thing, back at his old job? We didn't see Rachel or Clara for months after that."

"Are you talking about TechMinds?" I say, synapses firing.

They both nod.

"So you knew about that—you knew what happened?"

Kirstie nods again. "Yeah. The woman didn't press charges but she tracked Rachel down, collared her one day. Told her a few home truths about the type of man she was married to. Rachel said she didn't believe it, of course, but she was still really upset."

So Rachel knew.

"Do you know what I can't work out?" Parnell's been largely quiet until now, happy for me to take the lead, like the ego-free mentor he is, but something's been brewing. I can tell in the cock of his head, the way he keeps pinching the creases in his trousers. "Why, when Joseph is such a terrible person, would you have after-work drinks with him and invite him here, to your employee party?"

"Well, that's a great question," says Marcus, dripping with sarcasm, eyeballing his wife. "Come on then, Kirst. We promised to tell them everything, so please, I'm dying to know too."

There's nothing contrite about Kirstie now. "Oh, like you didn't used to be best buddies with him. You're such a fucking hypocrite."

Marcus rolls his eyes. "We played squash once a week, until about three years ago. That's the 'best buddies' my wife's referring to. I stopped when I literally couldn't stand it anymore. Joseph's not competitive, he's cutthroat. 'Bad loser' doesn't quite cover it. I only kept going as long as I did for Rachel's sake, but in the end I had to give up. I used to dread Thursday nights coming around, and life's too short for that."

Kirstie's still on the attack, but now it's Parnell on the receiving end. "Firstly, I don't know where you got your information from"—a sharp glare at me—"but I don't have after-work drinks *with* him. He just happens to be in the same bar sometimes and I can hardly ignore him. Secondly, I invited him on Saturday because it makes it worse for Rachel if I don't—and I didn't think he'd actually come. And thirdly, whatever I think of him, Rachel's a grown woman and she chooses to stay with him. I have to respect that."

"Is that your stance as well, Marcus?" asks Parnell. "Bit different when it's your sister, surely?"

"It *was* my stance. I had no idea he'd half strangled her, though."

"And if you'd known?"

He thinks about this. "I'd like to say I'd have knocked seven shades of shit out of him. The old me definitely would. But I've worked really hard to make something of myself and I wouldn't let Joseph ruin that—because that's *exactly* what he'd want. So, I'd have told my sister to leave, no arguments. In fact, I'd have packed her things and carried the bags myself. Which is what my wife should have done, instead of drinking fucking mai tais with him in Scarfes Bar."

I give it ten seconds after we leave before a titanic row breaks out.

"The drugs," I say to Kirstie, moving things on, or dragging them back, I suppose.

"No!" she yelps. "No, that's not fair. I've answered all your questions. I've been as honest as I can, even though I feel like I'm betraying my sister-in-law . . ."

I put my fingers to my lips. "Sssh, keep your hair on. It's not about you. Did Joseph take drugs?"

An image of a seething Joseph—slighted by Kirstie, jacked up on coke and striding toward Naomi's house, hell-bent on proving there's life in the old dog yet—comes to mind.

Still surly, Kirstie says, "Joseph likes to be in control so he wouldn't take drugs, at least not as far as I know. He's got plenty of other vices to keep him busy."

But could murder be one of them?

Five days in and I'm still not 100 percent, ironclad certain that it could.

20

The incident room's a joy when we finally get back, everyone stomping around in a fog of frustration, paperwork stacked high, expectations set low. Even our news that Joseph attacked Rachel and made a cheap comment about Naomi doesn't lift the mood above neutral. Flowers and Cooke have given up on ever finding a scrap of our suspect's clothes—*"Every bin, every skip, every hedge, every-frigging-where"* is the general gist—and, to make matters worse, Flowers has ripped his trousers and doesn't have a spare pair. Emily's going through Naomi's personal emails and losing the will to live—*"No one uses email anymore, it's all spam and booking confirmations"*—and Seth's just confirmed that Forensics haven't recovered anything juicy from her work PC either, apart from the fact that she called Kirstie *"a miserable old bitch"* in an email to Evie Whitlock.

Meaning she had slightly more personality than the proverbial dead moth.

"And as if things weren't bad enough, the shrink's in residence," moans Flowers, gesturing toward Steele's door. "Pull up a pew, lads, it's psychobabble time."

The shrink. Dr. Allen. Dolores to her friends.

I thought I recognized her bag through the gap in Steele's blinds— the Italian suede tote, a gift from her niece on her sixtieth birthday. That one small detail was the only piece of personal information Dr. Allen ever disclosed over our twelve sessions together. Twelve long sessions where, in the course of trying to come to terms with a particularly grisly crime scene, I'd disclosed every fear, every doubt, every hope I'd ever had dashed. I'd even halfway disclosed some murky feelings about Dad.

It feels all kinds of weird having her here.

"Right, are you all ready?" shouts Steele, meaning you all better had be. Dr. Allen walks out of Steele's office and takes a seat at the front, although slightly to the side—she isn't the commandeering type. One by one we roll our chairs forward, bearing a mix of genuine and counterfeit smiles.

All of us apart from Renée, who can't seem to manage either.

I pull up beside her. "Hey Ren, what's up?"

"Oh, nothing." A pause and then, "Just suicides, I hate them." I'm momentarily confused. "Stacey Nash. We can't get the transcript of the inquest until early next week but I had a chat with the Coroner's Officer this morning, got a bit more detail. It's so bloody depressing. Give me a murder any day of the week."

Which tells me two things: Renée probably needs a holiday, and Steele didn't completely discount the idea of foul play if she's had Renée sniffing around.

"What's the scoop, then?"

"There isn't one, really. It's more or less what Swaines said. Hard to see how it could have been an accident as the balcony wall was over waist height, but there was absolutely no history of depression or any big worries, according to the family. Her ex-husband did say she got a touch of the baby blues after the first child but nothing major, and we all get a touch of them, Cat, it's normal. The ex isn't the father of the second child—*that* schmuck was being an arse about money and that was on her mind, so said the best mate, but she was more annoyed than anxious, apparently." She takes a quick look at Steele, keeps going. "Anyway, the upshot is the mum and the mate were convinced she'd never have taken her own life. *Convinced.* The mum said straightaway that she'd apply to the High Court for a judicial review if it came back as suicide. Thank God the open verdict spared them that, at least."

"Families never want to believe it."

"Yeah, I know, but she'd booked tickets for the theater a few days before, done a big food shop that afternoon."

"Happens. People bottle things up and then they just snap. It's sad."

"It's weird."

Steele's voice fills the room, shutting us up. "So I've asked Dolores to come in today to give us a steer on Joseph Madden, to help us know what buttons to press, given the clock is ticking and I want something airtight to hand the CPS. Dolores has watched Madden's interviews and she's read most of your reports, but bear in mind that what she says today is her broad opinion based on thirty years' experience. It is not—I repeat, *not*—a formal psych evaluation."

"Much as I'd love to do one," adds Dr. Allen with a touch of sparkle. "But as Joseph Madden doesn't trust doctors, he's hardly likely to talk to an old quack like me."

The quip goes some way to settling the naysayers, although, really, the only naysayer is Flowers. The rest of us are just simply too busy, and even a visit from Jesus Christ himself bearing pizza and a twelve-pack of Heineken would feel as welcome as root canal treatment.

Dr. Allen crosses her legs, assuming the position. "It is my strong gut feeling—although as Kate says, not my diagnostic opinion—that Joseph Madden suffers from a form of narcissistic personality disorder, NPD for short." I nudge Parnell who says, *"God, I'm good,"* under his breath—he called this days ago. "Firstly, I think it's worth mentioning that NPD is not as rare as you might think, especially at the milder end of the spectrum."

"Didn't think it was rare at all. It's the times we live in, right?" Oh, here we go—The World According to Pete Flowers. "I took Gill to Paris last year and she dragged me to the Louvre. Do you know what we saw there? People—and I'm not just talking kids, grownups too—taking photos of themselves in front of the *Mona Lisa.* The most famous bloody painting in the world and folk think they need to put their ugly mugs in front of it. If that's not narcissism, you tell me what is."

Because she's polite, Dr. Allen semi-agrees. "You may have a point. The difference is that lots of people 'liking' a photo on Facebook, or wherever, wouldn't satisfy a true narcissist. The admiration—or what we call the 'narcissistic supply'—is too remote. Let me explain . . ." I take a quick glance around the team: cocked heads, rapt faces— we're a fickle bunch, for sure. "Most narcissists are highly intelligent and highly ambitious people and yet they're also often underachievers, just like Joseph Madden, because their grandiose self-worth and sheer sense of entitlement makes it almost impossible for them to succeed at anything within normal society." A trickle of nods: so far we follow. "Therefore, the gap between their meager achievements and their inflated self-image can be quite staggering and it affects their grasp of reality. They start to truly believe in what we call their 'False Self'—the Self that is everything they are not: omniscient, omnipotent, charming, rich, well-connected, whatever it is—and so it becomes crucial for them to seek out people or things that reinforce that inflated image. We call these people or things their 'narcissistic supply.'"

"Things?" asks Parnell.

"Possessions." Her head dips as she scours her notes. "Ah yes, here it is. Joseph Madden has a classic old car, a fake Rolex, and a number of expensive clothing items were removed during the forensic search—leather gloves, designer jackets, high-end footwear, and so on." She looks up. "His earnings and the amount of debt he's in show that he can't really afford these things, but he *needs* them to feed his False Self so he'll *always* find a way of getting them: more credit cards, persuading others—rich lovers, for example—to purchase things for him. Or when all else fails, simply stealing from those around him."

"Marcus gave Rachel money when she was flat broke," I say.

"Joseph took it and spent it on golf clubs." Parnell finishes the story.

Dr. Allen's face says she'd expect nothing different. "Narcissists have no concept of other people's needs."

"Here, that's not narcissists, that's toddlers." Cooke gets the laugh.

"Christ, wait until they're teenagers, mate," adds Flowers.

Dr. Allen joins in, chuckling softly. I suppose, after thirty years of one-to-one pity-parties, you must long for bad jokes and camaraderie. "People, of course, are the primary source of narcissistic supply," she says, still smiling but bringing the class back to order. "Rachel, it appears, hangs off Joseph's every word and accepts his delusions of grandeur, despite being faced with quite overwhelming evidence to the contrary in terms of how they live. His wealthy lovers—Sadie Paulson and Siobhan Casey—are also a perfect form of supply. They provide him with the possessions he needs to reinforce his self-worth but they themselves reinforce it too—the crux of his thinking being,

'If someone highly intelligent and highly successful is interested in me, it must follow that I am highly intelligent and highly successful.' Although his choice of lovers does concern me slightly . . ." An uneasy look crosses her face.

Steele's brow furrows. "What's the problem?"

She pauses, gathering her thoughts. Dr. Allen does silence like most people do small talk—reflexive, automatic, no conscious thought required. "Well, it's not a problem as such, Kate, more an observation—Naomi Lockhart is a clear anomaly."

Naomi screams at me from the incident board, *"I am a daughter and a sister and a fund-raising Rihanna fan. I am NOT an anomaly."*

"Joseph Madden gets his narcissistic supply from women he deep down—*very* deep down—considers superior to him. A young PA with no real money, power, or standing clearly doesn't fit this profile."

I dive in. "You see, I've been thinking this." And I have. I'm not jumping on Dr. Allen's bandwagon, I'm simply mobilized by it; triggered to say the thing that's been flicking my ear from almost the very start. "Why won't Madden just admit to having a fling with Naomi? He's hardly been coy about all his other conquests. He practically drew us a map to Siobhan Casey's office on Harley Street."

"Er, because she's dead?" says Flowers in full-on dunce tone.

I don't bite. "But if he admitted their fling, he could explain away everything: the hairs, the photo, the CCTV, the gift box, the lot. He could say *'Yes. I was seeing her. Yes, I was in her bed that evening. No, I didn't kill her'* and that would put us in a weaker position. Lucas Stein must have explained this, surely? So why does he keep denying it? It doesn't make sense."

Dr. Allen raises a tentative, jeweled hand. "I may be able to help here, although again, I must stress this is theory, not science." Steele gives a wave of approval. "Ultimately, it doesn't suit Joseph Madden for you to think he was in a relationship with Naomi—and even in the face of overwhelming evidence, a narcissist will simply deny what doesn't suit them and then be genuinely outraged when you don't play along."

"But it *should* suit him," I insist. "It works in his favor."

"Applying your logic, yes, Cat." *Cat*—a note of familiarity I hope the others haven't picked up on. Only Steele and Parnell know about my trips to the psych chair last year, and I'd rather like to keep it that way. "But if I'm right about Joseph Madden, he isn't thinking about his legal standing—and in any case, he'll be convinced he can beat the legal system. No, he's far more concerned . . . well, obsessed, really, with his social standing. As I mentioned before, his lovers are rich, high-status women. They reflect well on him. They are trophies. Naomi Lockhart isn't a trophy—she's average in every way, certainly in the way that Joseph Madden views the world."

Parnell lifts his hands—*don't shoot*. "Look, I know I'm probably going to get hanged for this, but since when aren't twenty-two-year-old women trophies? Personally, I can't think of anything worse than dating someone who doesn't remember the original A-Team, but I've a feeling I'm in the minority."

Flowers opens his mouth. Mercifully, Dr. Allen gets there first. "You make a valid point, Lu. However, while I don't like saying this, I feel I have to make the distinction. Naomi was young—yes. Pretty—yes. But not beautiful. Not someone who would turn heads." She looks down at her notes again. "Erm . . . do we have DS Wakeman or DC Beck here?"

Seth and Emily raise their hands.

"Hello," she says, offering a quick smile. "You mention in one report that Joseph Madden's work colleagues assumed his daughter to be his girlfriend, and that he didn't do anything to dissuade them of this notion."

Emily nods. "Yep, that's right."

"I'm going to guess that his daughter is highly attractive. *Conventionally* attractive."

I've got this. "Tall, blond, legs up to my shoulders. Model material."

"I thought as much. *That's* why he played along with his colleagues' assumptions, then. A young, conventionally stunning woman enhances his self-image. Admitting she's his daughter means admitting she didn't *choose* him, so it suits him far more—it feeds his False Self—if people think this young, tall, hot blond singled him out. It's distasteful but perfectly logical when you consider his psyche."

Renée's troubled. "So you're saying it's inconceivable he'd have been attracted to 'average' Naomi, even though all our evidence suggests a relationship?"

Quick as a flash. "No, I'm saying it would pain him to *admit* being in that relationship. Naomi's 'ordinary.' She doesn't reflect well on him. He doesn't want to associate with 'ordinary.'"

"Even though he's in deep shit?" I say.

"Possibly even more so. There's significant public interest in this case. Newspapers, online speculation. He would hate—he would *detest*—the thought of his relationship with an 'ordinary' woman being outed. It would make him appear ordinary in the eyes of the world."

Parnell's eyes are closed, fingers pinching the bridge of his nose. "OK, so if he wasn't getting off on Naomi's beauty or brilliance or bank balance, what was he getting from her?" He opens his eyes, looks at Dr. Allen. "Subservience? Fear? The same 'supply' he gets from his wife?"

A brief ponder. "Mmm, it's a possibility. But as they couldn't have been together for very long, it's unlikely the relationship would have reached that stage yet. We're talking about a very specific form of abuse here that's insidious. It takes time for the roles to be set, and the abuser is often very charming to begin with. Narcissists can be obscenely charming, showering you with attention, praise, gifts—often quite over the top."

"Sending flowers and gifts to her work," says Renée.

Suggesting he whisk me off to Vienna. Presenting me with supposedly antique devil masks.

"I'd say it's more likely he recognized *potential* 'supply' in Naomi," concludes Dr. Allen. "He saw her youth, her vulnerability, her admiration of him."

" '*He runs his own business, he's got a flat in town, a swanky car.*' " Renée's impression of an awestruck young Naomi *could* be spot on. I don't know. I've never heard Naomi's voice, which suddenly feels wrong and remote and something I want to remedy.

Parnell puts his hand up. "So, just jumping back to what you said about Madden not wanting to associate with Naomi. We've been

STONE COLD HEART | 189

roughly assuming that whatever or however it happened, Madden must have attacked Naomi after an argument, *probably* because she rejected him that night, for whatever reason. But could we have it all arseways? Could it be that, far from wanting rid of him, she actually wanted *more* of him? Maybe she wanted to move their fling on, bring the relationship out in the open? Because based on what you've said, Dolores, he certainly wouldn't relish that prospect. That's motive right there."

Dr. Allen plonks both arse-cheeks firmly on the fence. "It's certainly a possibility, Lu, but they're both possibilities. If Madden felt he was being rejected *or* pressurized by someone he saw as inferior, *both* would be a catastrophic blow to his ego and that could certainly spark a violent reaction." She brings her hands together on her lap, settling in for another lesson. "Most people go through what we refer to as 'the seven levels of anger'—stress, anxiety, agitation, irritation, frustration, anger, rage. And at the lower end of that scale, a measure of self-control can usually be applied, which means the igniting issue often gets solved. The problem is, narcissists don't go through the seven levels like most people. The tiniest slight sends them straight to the top of the scale. To a narcissist, rage is a perfectly appropriate response to their ego being threatened, because channeling that rage restores their feelings of superiority."

"Well, I'm going with rejection," says Flowers, firmly, as though he's been asked to decree one way or the other. "We know he doesn't take rejection well. I mean, we're pretty sure he burgled his old boss's house after he had the cheek to fire him.

"So there you go then. She's protecting him. Which, whatever way you look at it, pisses on his claims that she's trying to make things difficult for him."

"But she's not protecting him," I insist. "*She's* the one who pointed me in the direction of TechMinds. *She* brought it up. Yeah, sure, she downplayed the whole thing, but she *must* have known we'd check it out. She's not stupid."

Parnell plays devil's advocate. "Perhaps she let it slip accidentally and then tried to make it sound like nothing when she realized what she'd done."

"Nah. Not having it, Sarge. She wouldn't just let that slip—not something that important." I'm glowing, warming to my own argument. "No, she can keep claiming he's innocent all she likes, she can carry on singing 'Stand By Your Man' until she's bloody hoarse, but in bringing up TechMinds she dumped him in it, good and proper."

"So you think there's something in this? She's deliberately trying to make trouble for him?" Flowers comes out with it in that forthright northern way I reluctantly admire.

"Well, if you do, you've changed your tune since yesterday," says Steele. "What happened to *'she'd never cause drama for Clara'*?"

"Speaking of," interrupts Parnell. "Someone needs to pay a visit to Clara's college on Monday. She was involved in a fight with some girl—I doubt there's much in it but we need to close it off."

"Do you know what I think?" says Flowers, clearly not finished with me. "You feel guilty that you sat across from Joseph Madden months ago and didn't clock anything dangerous, so now you're trying to look for ways to prove he might not be a killer." Dr. Allen watches me and Flowers, although with her inscrutable face she could be thinking anything from *"Get that girl back on my couch"* to *"God, that Flowers talks some shite."* "And you know me, Kinsella. I'm more than happy to say when I think someone's fucked up, but what were you supposed to clock, exactly? A big sign over his head saying 'Psycho'? You're not an FBI profiler. Give yourself a break."

He's wrong. He's wrong on just about every level, but credit where credit's due, it wasn't a bad angle to take. Flowers wasn't to know that I spent last night with Dad; the man I'd branded a monster for nearly twenty years until the truth taught me a lesson in always keeping a *slightly* open mind. Just like Steele wasn't to know that, while I am still struggling to believe Rachel would cause drama for Clara, I do believe in the muscular pull of revenge, of wanting someone to get their comeuppance so badly that your thoughts get cancerous, your intentions twisted.

I draw a deep breath and go for it. "Look, the fact that Rachel pointed me straight in the direction of that sexual assault . . . it's given me doubts. There, I've said it." I shrug. "Sorry, but it has. I think she's had a hell of a life with him and deep down she's enjoying watching him drown."

"Then take the scissors to his fancy clothes. Slash the tires on his classic car. Or here's a wild idea—divorce him." Flowers appeals to Steele. "Remind me why we're humoring this again?"

Steele stands up. "At the risk of sounding like your mother, Pete, because I said so."

Divorce. That reminds me.

"Oh, and that's another thing Rachel's lying about," I say. "She's claiming she called that Portsmouth family law firm to find work experience for Clara, but I went through her bank records last night and she actually visited Portsmouth four times in July. There's four transactions in a hotel—just little amounts, not like she was paying for a room or anything—but she must have been visiting someone. I mean, I *was* thinking an affair. It'd explain why she's lying—she wouldn't want it getting back to Joseph."

"Nothing on her phone suggests an affair," says Swaines. "And you'd think—"

"You said you *were* thinking an affair," Steele cuts in, tuned into every pulse, as usual, every slight shift in intonation.

"Well, I still am, maybe. But . . ."

And so I tell her. There's eight other people listening but I tell only her. The rest of them may as well go back to their bin searches and spam emails, because I'm only interested in the woman who can say yay or nay to what I think needs doing. So pouring forth on Lydia Coe, I tell her how she *"provides advice on domestic violence injunctions."* How she works with the *"End Violence Against Women Coalition."* How she has an interest in *"cases that protect and promote the rights of women."* How she often works pro bono. Which could explain why a financially strapped Rachel Madden might end up at her door, eighty miles from London.

"I didn't read too much into it to begin with," I say, closing my pitch and gauging Steele for positive signs—she's still listening, so that's good. "But now we know that Joseph is emotionally *and* physically abusive toward Rachel, it's got me thinking. What if she wanted help from this Lydia Coe woman? 'Cos if she did, Lydia might be able to tell us two things: one, just how bad things have been for Rachel, and therefore how badly she might want revenge, and two, how violent Joseph is."

"Lydia could be another of Madden's fancy women, have you considered that?" asks Parnell. "She fits the profile—good job, intelligent, presumably financially OK if she's a solicitor. So maybe Rachel's not as resigned to his affairs as she says. Maybe she was hassling this Lydia?"

"Lydia could be Rachel's fancy woman, have you considered that?" echoes Renée. "If she *was* having an affair."

I honestly hadn't considered either—props to Parnell and Renée, although I'm not entirely convinced. "I don't know, guys. From her company photo, she's . . . well, she's attractive in a regal, hearty sort of way, but . . ." I'm squirming, not wanting to discount it on the basis that she isn't cover girl material. "I just can't see it, that's all." I focus back on Steele. "I still think she's a conversation worth having."

Steele looks at me for a long second, lips pursed. "It's complete supposition, but it's a *phone call* worth having."

I shake my head, vehemently. "No, we need to go there, Boss. They've already confirmed Rachel's not listed as a client so I need to show them a photo in case she was using a false name."

She points to the far corner of the room. "There's a scanner over there, m'dear. I can barely switch it on, but they're a cracking way to send photos, I hear."

"Come on, you know how it is over the phone. It's easier to hide behind client privilege." She purses her lips again, thinking about it. I up the ante. "Look, Boss, something happened a few months ago to make Joseph Madden seek out police advice and Rachel Madden seek out legal advice, I'm *almost* sure of it. It's probably got nothing to do with Naomi directly but it could still strengthen our case."

"Our case against who? Joseph for potential murder or Rachel for potential lying?"

"Joseph," I say, double-quick. "Look, I still think he did this—there's plenty of evidence that says he did. I just can't work out whose team *she's* playing on, and that's bad news if we have to call her as a witness."

"Agreed," says Steele. "But you're not going to Portsmouth." She sits back down, coming eye level to soften the blow. "I take on board what you're saying and I applaud the lateral thinking, I really do. But we've got less than thirty-six hours to get Madden sewn up and I can't have officers swanning off to the coast when I need them here, doing the donkey work—the work that gets suspects charged." I nod. There's no point arguing. "Call this Lydia Coe by all means, but that's it for the moment. There's someone more important I need you to see, anyway."

I scream an internal *"Fuck off!"* as I envisage an afternoon spent interviewing some well-meaning dope who saw Naomi's photo in the paper and *"thinks"* they *"might"* have seen her somewhere or other at some time over the past few months.

"Alana Lockhart," Steele says, "Naomi's sister. She arrived last night and she wants to talk to someone."

"Ah, come on. Can't Family Liaison deal with her?"

"She doesn't want to be 'dealt with,' Kinsella, she wants to talk to someone." I feel two feet tall and I don't even deserve that height. "She's at the Soho Hotel. I've told her you'll be there by one thirty. Let reception know and they'll call her room."

In all honesty, this is probably what I need right now. To forget Rachel Madden and remember which team I play for.

The only team worth playing for.

The victim and their family.

21

Saturday lunchtime, and Soho is fully juiced; or as juicy as it gets these days, when you're just as likely to bump into a family with a double buggy on Frith Street as a drag queen or a sex worker. However, while it isn't quite the glorious den of iniquity it once was, Soho still remains the beating heart of London, and the Soho Hotel, set back on a quiet mews off Dean Street, is in overdrive this afternoon, full of high spirits and happiness. Some of it alcohol-induced, all of it noisy.

Alana Lockhart and I are sitting in a quieter nook to the side of the bar, but it's hard to zone out the revelry. The sheer evidence of shiny, happy people living shiny, happy lives. It's proving particularly hard to zone out the group of Naomi-age girls at the next table, downing Espresso Martini after Espresso Martini while debating whether to even bother with lunch.

"Fuck that, Liv!"

"Eating's cheating, right?"

Alana smiles at them; a sad, faraway smile.

"I know what you're thinking," she says, finally dragging her eyes away. "Odd choice of hotel, huh? Bit lively under the circumstances."

Her voice is low, deep, and soothing, her accent there but feather-soft; not the voice I'd imagined for Naomi. It's hard to say if they look alike when my two versions of Naomi—dead at the crime scene and glowing in photos—are almost impossible to compare with this jet-lagged, grief-stricken, but very much alive young woman. Alana's twine-thin where Naomi was curvy, and she has cropped boy-cut hair whereas everything about Naomi screamed GIRLZ! She's older too; quite a bit older, probably nearly thirty, but there's a definite *something* that links them. I'm thinking it's around the mouth, but I'm trying not to stare.

"Naz had a job interview here a week or two ago. She *loved* the place. Kept going on and on and on about that big cat sculpture in the foyer. She made me promise that when I came to visit I'd book in here so she could have a proper poke around." Her eyes well up. "Well, this is me keeping my promise, I guess."

The waiter's arrival stops me welling up too. I order tea. Alana orders champagne. "Another odd choice, huh? Naz wanted us to have afternoon tea here—a great big heap of cakes and bottomless bubbles. I said to her, *'Firstly, get you and your afternoon tea, you big Brit. And secondly, it probably won't be real champagne, you know?'* She said, *'Well then, we'll order the real stuff. 'Cos we're worth it.'"*

Naomi, swishing her lilac hair as she says this, preening herself, laughing out loud. Just this one image makes me realize I'm exactly where I need to be right now. Experiencing Naomi Lockhart through someone who knew her. Not someone who paid her wages or banked her rent for a matter of months.

"So you wanted to talk?" I say. "What can I tell you?"

She narrows her eyes, sizing me up, assessing if I'm up to the job. "This bloke you've arrested. You reckon Naz was seeing him?"

"Yes, we do." Her look says I'm an idiot, that I've failed the first test. "Why? What's on your mind?"

"Look, Naz told me everything. I'd have known if she was seeing someone." She offers it as fact, not opinion. "Like, sometimes it was a bit, 'Ew, too much information! You're my baby sister. I don't want to know *that*,' but we were really, really close, despite the age gap."

Jacqui. When I was little, I used to bore her with everything. Every insect I'd seen. Every Tamagotchi I'd killed. Every new step I'd learned at Irish dancing. Now she doesn't even know my current address.

I drag my mind back. "Everyone has secrets, Alana."

"Not Naz, not from me. And isn't he like forty or something, this bloke?"

"Forty-three."

Her face puckers. "See, even that doesn't make sense. Jono, her ex from back home, he was like, thirty, and that was too old. After they broke up she said she was sticking to guys her own age from now on."

"She changed her mind," I say with a weak smile. "It happens."

"Maybe. Maybe you're right. I dunno. The thing I can't get my head around, though . . ." She closes her eyes, massaging her temples. "The thing I literally can't compute is that this bloke's married."

"That's possibly why she didn't tell you."

She shakes her head. "No, listen, you don't understand. The reason I couldn't get here until now is because I've got a two-year-old daughter and I'm a single mum. Single in the sense that her dad's not involved at all—he didn't want to be, since he's married with three kids already." She looks down at the floor. "I'm not proud of it, but there we are."

"She probably thought you'd try and talk her out of it then, that's why she kept quiet."

"No," she snaps, pissed off that I'm not grasping their special relationship. "All she'd have thought was, *'Alana won't judge'* and I wouldn't have. She never judged me. She was brilliant." She looks up again, eyes blazing. "Mum and Pops are judging her, though. Oh, they don't mean to and they'd never say as much, but I swear I can hear them thinking it."

"Thinking what?"

"*'Didn't we raise them both better than this?'*"

And I dare say she's right. They probably are thinking that. The *only* thing worse than a dead child is a dead child with a tarnished reputation.

"So she'd have been scared of your parents finding out?"

The waiter comes back, lays my pot of tea on the table then hands a flute of champagne to Alana. She holds it lightly by the stem in the style of someone well accustomed to drinking it.

"To Naomi," she says, angling her glass toward me, battling back tears again.

I clink my teacup. "To Naomi."

She drains half the glass. "Naz knew the last people I'd tell would be Mum and Pops. I mean, they weren't exactly impressed with me, but the idea of St. Naomi following my lead . . ." She instantly regrets saying it. "Ah, look, she used to call herself that as a piss-take. She was sick when she was little and once a poorly baby, always a poorly baby. She couldn't do any wrong in Mum's and Pop's eyes. Nor mine. She was a good girl. A *really* good girl."

And good girls don't sleep with other people's husbands—capisce?

I pour my tea, wincing at the weak color. "Alana, I can't go into a lot of detail and I know that's frustrating, but there is strong evidence to suggest Naomi and our suspect were having some sort of relationship. She told people she was seeing someone. He sent her gifts. We think he sent her flowers a couple of weeks ago. We're still checking that out, but—"

"Flowers?" she breaks in. Her eyes are wet but she hauls a half smile out of somewhere. "I think you'll find those flowers were from Cedric."

Cedric? If this is a one-eighty U-turn with less than thirty-six hours to go, Steele will punch a hole in every wall of the building.

"Cedric was me," she says, the half smile turning full blast. "Naz felt uncomfortable living with that Kieran guy so she told him she was seeing someone so he didn't put any moves on her. Then, because he knew her boss, and she wasn't sure how well, she had to keep up the pretence at work too. We laughed about it heaps. We even gave the imaginary boyfriend a name—Cedric, after our first cat. Made up all this backstory. Said he had a flat around here, drove a fancy sports car, ran his own business. Anyway, one day she was feeling a bit bummed out—no big drama, she just didn't like working at that fashion place, that's why she had the job interview here—so I sent her some flowers the next day and when they asked me what message to put on the card, I thought for a joke I'd put 'Love Cedric.' She called me straightaway, laughing her head off."

My phone rings—Parnell. While I should probably take it, it seems wrong to interrupt Alana in the midst of a happy memory.

"Well, it's good that we know now," I say, muting the call. I can't wait to tell Swaines, who spent the best part of a day playing "Find-the-Florist." "But there's other evidence, Alana. Stuff I can't share yet."

She stares ahead, out of the window. A group of Chinese tourists are spilling out of a black cab, arguing over who's paying. "At least she was happy in her last few months." *As far as you know.* "That counts for something, right? I mean, she wasn't enjoying that job and her house situation wasn't great, but Naz didn't let stuff like that get her down for long. She was in London, seeing the sights, loving life. She was figuring out who she was, shaking off St. Naomi . . ." She points at her head. "I think that was what the hair was about. She wanted to *feel* different from the girl back home, so she wanted to *look* different. I thought it looked awesome. Mum didn't."

"How are your parents?" I say, uselessly.

"Besides not being too impressed that I'm staying here? Pops is bearing up, I guess. Well, he's pretending to, God knows when it'll hit him. Mum's . . ." The tears are back. I'm tempted to take her hand but that might set me off too and that helps no one. "Mum's not good. Do you know what she said last night? That there isn't any point to anything she does from now on. She said she knows, on an intellectual level, that she'll come out the other side. That she'll go to the supermarket again, mow the backyard, all those things you've gotta do in life, but she just can't see the point in any of it now. And now Pops is worried that she's gonna do something stupid, which *is* stupid—Mum's the biggest atheist going, it's not like she thinks dying will mean she sees Naz again. And anyway, she wouldn't do that to me and Pops. But it's as though she just wants life to pass quickly now, you know? How sad is that?"

"It's early days," I say, knowing this to be true but also knowing it to be the most half-arsed cliché going. "Look, take my number." I write it down on a napkin. "Call me if there's anything I can do, OK?"

"Early days? There's no more days for Naz, though, are there? She won't be mowing the backyard or going to the supermarket again." She reaches across the table and grabs my hand. Her anger courses through me; a kinetic energy to power me through the next thirty-six hours. "That's why I need you to be *sure* about Naz and this bloke. It's *gotta* be reported properly. I want people to know that the bastard did this out of hate, not some soap-opera love-affair-gone-wrong crap." My phone rings again. I look at her apologetically. "Take it, it's fine," she says, slumping back, suddenly drained of all energy.

I walk out into the foyer, my mind speeding in ten different directions. The tourists are taking photos of the bronze cat sculpture and one of the Espresso Martini girls is looking like she's definitely going to be sick.

I throw her a pitying smile. *We've all been there, honey.*

"Sarge."

"I called you a few minutes ago, why didn't you ans—"

"Hey, hold on a sec, listen to this—Naomi had a job interview at the Soho Hotel in the last couple of weeks. If her CV is on file, they'd have her address, right? So we've got to find out who interviewed her, check them out, rule them out, surely? Also, Naomi's sister isn't convinced—"

"Shut up, Kinsella. Sorry, but you need to get back here now. We've just hit the mother lode." I head for the stairs, away from the bustle. "You know Madden's fancy leather gloves, the ones Forensics took away?" He barely pauses but it feels like an eternity. "They've found blood in the stitching. Naomi's blood.

"We've got him, kiddo."

22

So he did it.

He unequivocally did it.

A lot of evidence can be explained away, dismissed by a good solicitor, rendered laughable by a showy barrister, but blood is king. In fact, it's higher than a king, it's the ace in the pack. It makes hairs in a bed look like the four of clubs at best. Blood means it doesn't matter, on any real level, whether Rachel lied to make things worse for Joseph or not. Blood means it's not important if she was divorcing him, cheating on him, planning to do a full John Wayne Bobbitt on him. All of that's mere side dressing now that we have blood.

As far as a jury's concerned, anyway. We know it's not infallible. Nothing ever is.

"Blood on a glove. It's all a bit OJ," I say, leaning against the wall in Steele's office.

She points at us all, frowning. "Yeah, and OJ walked, remember, so let's bear that in mind. Right this minute, Stein and Madden will be coming up with some sort of game plan and I can assure you lovely people that it won't include a full and frank confession."

"Why'd you tell them about the glove?" asks Parnell, gingerly. "Wouldn't the element of surprise have been better?"

Steele half shrugs. "Yes. No. Maybe. If we sprang it on them in the interview, they could still ask to break for consultation so it's much of a muchness, Lu. And anyway, I didn't want to waste anymore time. So you and Kinsella get fed, watered, and then piss off any loved ones who were hoping to see you tonight. I think this could be a long one."

Aiden's back tonight. I assume he's not hoping to see me, given the radio silence ever since he set foot in Dad's pub.

"So you don't need us, then," asks Renée, meaning her and Seth.

"No. No disrespect, you did a grand job, but he clams up too quickly with you pair. Those two got him chatting last time, and I want him chatting."

"Don't know why," says Flowers. "Just throw the book at him. He can deny everything if he wants, there's no way the CPS will knock it back now."

Steele shakes her head. "I want a confession, Pete. I want this nailed to the wall. Young girl comes to London and winds up dead within twelve weeks? Not good."

"The public like a motive," says Emily. "It makes them feel safer."

"True, but frankly, Ems, I couldn't give a toss about Joe Public. I care about Roger and Kath Lockhart." *"And Alana,"* I say, but I don't think she hears me. "I want to tell them what happened to their daughter." She checks her watch. "Which is why I'm meeting Dolores in the canteen in five minutes. I want to get her advice, see how we should approach this." A nod to me and Parnell. "You two, follow me."

Shame and flattery, that's what Dr. Allen advises. Make Joseph Madden the star of the show then the shit on our shoe. Confuse the hell out of the bastard.

We know this won't be easy.

Parnell's given Shame Cop on the basis that Madden's never liked him anyway. Madden doesn't crave approval from portly, fifty-something, low-ranking male coppers, no matter how snappy their new suits are. However, if Parnell can somehow make him feel small and insignificant, Madden's need to feel big and important *might* just get him talking, Dr. Allen reckons. And then if I, Flattery Cop, can make him feel clever and like a worthy opponent, he might just take his eye off the ball while he basks in my esteem.

The thought turns my stomach, as does the fug of testosterone that hits us as we walk into Interview Room One. Lucas Stein's standing, feet planted wide, thumbs in his belt loops like a sheriff in a spaghetti western. Joseph Madden's seated, legs equally splayed, chest puffed out so far his Armani shirt's threatening to split.

A tank ready for battle.

Although he smiles when he sees me. A tiny, shit-eating grin that makes me want to bring up my lunch.

We sit. I make a show of smoothing down my ponytail and fluffing up my blouse, while Parnell presses buttons and goes through the preliminaries. Joseph's clearly made the effort for us—there's not a custody-issue item of clothing in sight and his black hair's glistening with some sort of styling product.

Cool Hand Luke's underlings have been busy on Oxford Street.

Although, imagine that. A double first in law and you wind up shopping for killers' hair wax.

Parnell kicks things off, holding up an exhibit bag. "I am showing Joseph Madden Exhibit BS42. A pair of leather gloves—brand, Bonetta Venega." Madden sneers at Parnell's mispronunciation, not realizing it's intentional. It's sometimes good to make your suspect think you're a bit of a dope. "They are a deep navy color and have a distinctive weave pattern across the front. Can you confirm they belong to you, Joseph?"

He leans forward, peering, assessing. "Mmm, yes they do, actually. I haven't seen them in quite some time, though, I thought they were lost. Thank you so much for finding them."

"And can you tell us how Naomi Lockhart's blood came to be on both of these gloves?"

He sits back. "No, I cannot."

"OK." Parnell puts the bag down. "Well, how about I propose that Naomi Lockhart's blood came to be on these leather gloves because *you* are the person who attacked and killed Naomi Lockhart in the early hours of Sunday the 5th of November at number fifty Coronation Gardens?"

He doesn't move a muscle, not a tendon or a twitch. "I am not that person."

Stein opens a file, his manner as placid as ever. "Listen, irrespective of the fact that Joseph denies ever being at Coronation Gardens . . ." He slides a CCTV still across to Parnell. "You'll see his hands are deep in his pockets in this image and therefore you can't categorically prove he was wearing those gloves on the night in question. As he explained, he thought he'd mislaid them."

"Look, Joseph," I say, summoning Flattery Cop. "You're a clever guy, we know that. *I* certainly know that. You've run rings around us for days because you've known that most of what we had was circumstantial, or at least open to a little scrutiny, right?" I pick up the exhibit bag. "This isn't, though." I almost sound regretful, like it's a damn shame a good man has to be punished for one bad deed. "This changes things, Joseph. Come on, you know this. You know the score."

Stein goes to speak but Madden throws a hand across, holding him off while offering me the saddest of smiles. "Cat, I'm really sorry to have to bring this up—honestly, I am. You're at the start of your career, mistakes are only natural." Every mistake I've ever made comes screeching into the room, and yet none of them, not one, has Joseph Madden's name attached—yet. "You see, I understand from Lucas that you attended the crime scene, the place where this poor girl died, and that you've also been to my house on a number of occasions. Well, that's cross contamination, surely? A basic error." He winces. "Sorry."

I don't owe him an explanation, but it'll make him feel the Big Man if I offer one. "Yep, that's right, Joseph. However, I attended the crime scene on Tuesday afternoon in full protective clothing, and I first entered your flat on Wednesday evening wearing entirely different clothing and footwear—I can provide evidence of this if required." He glazes over, completely uninterested in anything but his own version of the truth. "I was not involved in the search of your flat—as is standard procedure—and I only became aware of the existence of these gloves roughly half an hour before you did."

Happy now?

Apparently not.

"The problem must be your lab then. Lucas was telling me about it just now—about all the mishandling of evidence that goes on. Even the Forensic Science Regulator has been critical of the quality of services since everything was privatized or brought in-house." He basks in his own knowledge before gifting us a gracious smile. "I'm sympathetic to the pressures—really, I am. But I won't be punished for them and I warn you now, I will sue." Parnell laughs, which draws Madden's eyes away from me. "Laugh away, but does the name Patricia

Hylands mean anything to you? No? Well, she is an eminent lawyer and a very dear friend of mine. She specializes in bringing civil action against the police."

"Good for her," says Parnell, folding his arms. "You know, your opinions, your conspiracy theories, they really don't matter now, Joseph. Things are looking very bad and as Mr. Stein will tell you, we're actually doing you a courtesy by being here, letting you tell your side of the story. But, you know, if you're not going to tell it, we can just walk out. We're in control here." Madden's face hardens, eyes burning with malice. "And if you want to sue—go ahead, sue. I can see why you'd be chasing a payout. You're not exactly a financial success, are you? Tell me, does it get embarrassing having all these rich women paying for you? We know Sadie Paulson is covering Mr. Stein here, so she essentially holds your freedom in her hands. You'd be screwed if she stopped the cash flow, wouldn't you? Doesn't that make you feel a bit . . . well, emasculated?"

"Sarge," I say, pretending to chastise.

Madden stares coldly. "Emasculated. That's a big word, Sergeant Parnell."

"Isn't it? So's asphyxiation. Do you want to tell us about that?"

Stein's hand flies across. "Do not say a word, Joseph. Now, what's all this about? There is *nothing* in the pathologist's report to suggest that Naomi Lockhart—"

"I'm not talking about Naomi," Parnell interrupts, keeping his focus on Madden. "I'm talking about your wife. About you strangling Rachel."

He yawns. *He actually fucking yawns.* "I've never laid a hand on Rachel. I keep telling you, she's a liar. You won't listen."

"Like you never laid a hand—or a knee—on Stacey Nash," I say.

"Poor, poor Stacey." An artist's impression of sadness—slanted eyes, downturned mouth, fist pressed tight against his chest. "She also lied, *yes* . . . but clearly she wasn't well so I forgive her, of course." The sadness lifts and in its place there's something like triumph. "So terrible what happened to her, don't you think, Cat? Such a brutal way to go. Those last few seconds . . ."

My guts swirl. I open my mouth but nothing comes out.

Parnell intervenes. "Rachel didn't tell us you strangled her, Joseph. Kirstie Connor did."

"That head case! And you believe her?" His laugh fills the room, slamming off the walls and scrabbling along the carpet. "I can see how you'd be taken in by Rachel—she's a lot smarter than people think—but Kirstie?"

I'm back, composure regained. "Kirstie also claims you said you could 'have' Naomi if you wanted."

Madden looks at us in turn—Stein included—as though we're speaking Swahili.

"So everyone's lying except you, is that it?" Parnell smirks, which is good; Madden won't like smirking. "Rachel, Kirstie, Stacey Nash, our lab assistants—oh, and me. I believe I'm in the frame for planting hairs in your car, despite never being within five miles of it."

I step in, the calm voice of reason with the nice swishy ponytail. "Help us understand, Joseph. Why would Kirstie lie? What possible reason would she have? Rachel would be furious with her and she obviously cares a lot about Rachel."

"Let me tell you how much Kirstie cares about Rachel." He hesitates for a moment; maybe for effect, maybe weighing up the wisdom of what he's about to say. I've really no idea anymore. I can't figure him out and I'm not sure I want to. Flowers was right, we should just throw the book at him. "Kirstie and I had a thing a few years ago." He waits for my reaction. I don't give him the satisfaction, although inside I'm reeling. "It meant a lot to her, it meant less than nothing to me. The sex wasn't even that good—all rather samey, a bit vanilla, you know? Anyway, she got quite clingy—well, she got *a lot* clingy— and when I finished it, she was furious. She still holds it against me. *That's* why she'd lie."

"Does Rachel know?" I ask, trying to sound barely interested.

"Of course. I thought it only fair she knew her sister-in-law wasn't exactly . . . well, very sisterly, shall we say."

Roughly translated as "I wanted to humiliate her. Make her realize she can't trust anyone."

"And Marcus?"

"Not that I'm aware. Marcus is too busy do-gooding to notice what's going on under his nose. And there's no way Rachel would tell him. She couldn't bear to hurt the poor lamb's feelings."

Parnell says, "You're jealous of Marcus, aren't you? That's why you had an affair with his wife." Madden cocks his head as if jealousy isn't a term he's familiar with. "Well, I mean, he's a success. You're a failure. Sleeping with his wife must have evened things up a bit."

I frown at Parnell for Madden's benefit, then pull things back a step. "So, wait a minute: Rachel knows and yet she's still friends with Kirstie? How does that work?"

At this point, it's hardly even relevant, but the dynamic intrigues me. Rachel and Kirstie are like oil and water as it is. Throw in something like this and how can they share the same city, never mind the same kitchen?

"It gives Rachel something to lord over her," Joseph says, oozing contempt. "Kirstie's so desperate to make it up to Rachel that she fawns over her and Rachel laps it up. Rachel's never been the type of woman to inspire fawning, you see, so she takes it where she can find it."

"So we hear." Parnell taps my foot under the table, signaling a gear change. "Have you ever thought that what's good for the goose might be good for the gander, Joseph?"

"What?" His tone says he's bored but there's a tightening in his shoulders, a pink flush creeping over his collar.

"An affair. Have you ever thought Rachel might be having one too?" Madden stares incredulously. "Oh, I can see it might come as a surprise because Rachel wouldn't rub your nose in it. She'd be far more discreet than you. She wouldn't do it on her own doorstep."

Madden forces a thin smile. "Rachel barely leaves her own doorstep, so unless she's been shagging the postman or the old man next door, I very much doubt it."

"Oh, but she does," says Parnell. "You don't know your wife as well as you think, Joseph. We've been looking into her, and let's just say we've found out she's been enjoying some sea air."

I'm not sure about this. For one, we don't know that Rachel *was* having an affair, but more importantly we're handing Stein information that could potentially discredit Rachel *and* we're handing Madden information that could put Rachel in the hospital if he somehow managed to get bail.

But we have blood. We have blood. And having blood means no bail. Joseph Madden isn't getting within a mile of Rachel, or any other woman for that matter, for a very, very long time.

And Parnell knows what he's doing.

There'll be a point to all this.

"See, I think Rachel was cheating on you, Joseph, and, deep down, I think you knew it. Or, who knows, maybe you knew it for sure. Maybe you followed her down south, caught her at it?" Madden's breathing through his nose now, anger rising with each sharp exhale. "And I think losing control of the women in your life made you livid. It made you violent, made you need to show, once and for all, what a big man you are, what power you have." Parnell pauses, leaving Madden space to respond. Nothing. "So what happened? Did Naomi reject you that night and it tipped you over the edge? Or have we got it the wrong way around? Was she starting to get too demanding, wanting more from you, like Kirstie Connor, only this time you thought you'd nip it in the bud properly?"

Madden pounds a palm down on the table. "For the final time, I was not in a relationship with Naomi Lockhart!" He jerks his head toward me. "If I'd wanted a younger woman to play with, I'd have gone for that over some chubby bean counter." *That.* "Oh, come on, Cat," he snarls. "You know you wanted me." My skin pricks at the thought of his hands on me, like being stung by a thousand nettles.

Parnell's voice is intense and low. "Oh, I think you wanted Naomi Lockhart. You wanted a shy, vulnerable girl, someone you could bully, torment, terrify. Not like your rich, successful women. Oh sure, they spoil you rotten but they won't be pushed around by you, will they? So you needed someone to take the place of Rachel and Clara, now that Rachel's getting her kicks in Portsmouth and Clara can't wait to put a few hundred miles between you."

"I beg your fucking pardon?" There's an ugly twist to Madden's mouth as his eyes scour around the room: a foaming, rabid dog looking for something, *anything*, to bite.

"Oh yeah, Clara's not staying in London," I say with a little too much spite for Flattery Cop, although, seriously, fuck her. I'm bored with her now. Her halo wears heavy after a while. "You won't be able to goad her or belittle her anymore, not when she's mixing with the privileged crowd in York or Exeter. See, they're quite middle-class, those universities: Daddy's in medicine, law, banking, that sort of thing. You'll be an embarrassment to her, Joseph. I doubt she'll bother with you again."

"Fuck you." He moves his hand to his throat, pulling at his skin, maybe miming what he'd like to do to me right now.

I tilt my head. "Is that why you did it? Did taking someone else's daughter make up for losing your own?"

His chair flies backward as he lunges forward, muscles straining against his shirt, veins straining against his skin.

And then I'm not sure what stuns me more.

His hot spit on my face or the sheer panic on Lucas Stein's.

Cool Hand Luke. Feathers ruffled at last.

An hour and a half later, after I've drunk three cups of sugary tea and endured a whole load of fussing, Parnell's still not happy. In fact, he's light-years from happy and he doesn't care who knows it. Even the mighty Kate Steele isn't exempt from his beetroot-faced wrath.

"Have you lost your mind?" he shouts, looming over Steele's desk, nostrils flaring and fists balled tight. If it was anyone else they'd be on a fast track to a disciplinary by now. "We should be in there, Kate, charging that bastard with Naomi Lockhart's murder *and* common assault on Kinsella."

Steele's quiet but assertive—the best way to calm an angry bull, Aiden once told me. "Look, I'm not mad about this either, Lu, but Stein's serious. He thinks Madden's about to confess but he'll only talk to Cat, that's the deal."

"Well then, no deal," booms Parnell. "It's not safe. You heard what Dolores said." He points at the video screen. "You saw it with your own eyes. He goes from nought to nutter in a matter of seconds. We don't need a confession that much, Kate. Charge him. Please."

"Er, hello!" I give a little wave from the corner of the room. "Since it was me who got spat on, surely it's up to me to decide whether I'm up for Round Two—and honestly, I am."

"Don't care," barks Parnell, not entertaining it.

I look behind him to Steele, who makes a tiny circling gesture with her finger. I think it means *"give him a few minutes, he'll come around."* I nod.

"Hey, Sarge, what do you reckon to what he said about Stacey Nash?"

"What?" He's growly, confused by the change of direction. "I don't know. I'm going to have to listen to the whole thing again. I can't remember much apart from those last few minutes."

"It wasn't what he said, exactly. It's not like he admitted anything, but it felt like he was taunting us."

Steele rolls her eyes. "You do realize that happens a lot more in Hollywood than it does in Holborn, Kinsella? You should listen to it again too before you start heading down that road."

"OK, but how did he know what happened to Stacey? Michael Redfern didn't even know—he told us to track her down through LinkedIn."

"She's got a point," says Parnell, his voice lower now, which almost certainly means he's thawing.

Steele's hands are open, placating. "Look, as soon as we get the inquest transcript, I will *personally* pick through every last word of it, OK? Make sure once and for all there's nothing that needs revisiting in light of all this." She points at me. "But for now, can you just concentrate on Naomi? And can *you* quit throwing your toys out of the pram and trust me on this Madden thing?" A pleading look to Parnell—she doesn't need his approval but she desperately wants his support. "Listen Lu, if Madden pleads not guilty, the Lockharts' nightmare goes on for months. Maybe even a year. Just one final go, OK? Stein honestly thinks he's ready to spill."

"Why doesn't he spill to Stein then?"

She fires back at him. "I don't frigging know! Maybe Madden hates him? Maybe he can only open up to women with long curly hair because of his first sexual experience? Maybe this is all one last game before he goes down for twenty years. We won't know until we try."

"Twenty years," grunts Parnell. "As far as we can tell he didn't bring a weapon to the scene, so he'll claim 'loss of control' and we'll be looking at voluntary manslaughter. Fifteen years, tops. And that's only if we get a judge in a foul mood."

I put my cup down on Steele's desk and perch on the edge, staring straight at Parnell. "We can't do anything about that, Sarge. All we can do is try to make the Lockharts' lives a bit more bearable." His face softens at this, his shoulders slacken slightly. "I want to at least try. I want to see what he has to say."

"And we'll be watching on the feed," assures Steele. "*If* he lays a finger on her, we'll be there in seconds."

"If he lays a finger on her, Kate, you might as well clear my desk because I'll be the one going down for twenty years. As long as that's understood."

My chin wobbles. *Swallow it down. Swallow it down.*

"It's understood. So are we agreed?"

"We're agreed."

Like Parnell ever had any real say. Steele's may be a benevolent dictatorship but it's a dictatorship nonetheless.

"I do have one stipulation," he adds.

Steele groans, throwing her head back. "What is it with men and their bloody stipulations today? Come on then, what is it?"

"That I stand outside with a radio. The room's soundproofed, Madden won't even know I'm there. Seriously, sod watching it on the feed, Kate. The viewing room's up the other end of the corridor. That's fifteen, twenty seconds away. At least if I'm outside, you can give me the say-so and I can be on him before he knows what's happening."

Steele nods. "Fine. But bring Swaines too, OK? Not being funny, Lu, but Madden's got more than ten years on you."

"No problem. I'm not bothered if you think I'm a useless old goat. All I care about is this one getting hurt. So bring Swaines, bring Flowers, bring a bloody army. I don't care."

It could be the visit from Frank. It could be because Madden spat on me. It's *probably* because I'm facing the mother of all conversations with Aiden in the very near future, but suddenly Parnell's action hero posturing seems like the safest, sweetest, kindest thing in all the world.

Safer than Dad's whiskey-tinged promises, that's for damn sure.

23

He apologizes. I accept. Insincerities out of the way, we begin.

"So you wanted to chat?" I say, giving a little shrug to convey that this is all in a day's work for me. Just another red mark through the to-do list. "Chat away. The floor's yours."

He says nothing, staring at the dirty gray oblivion of the back wall. He's staring so intently that, as I turn to follow his gaze, I half expect to see his thoughts splashed there: apparitions of Naomi, flashes of their time together.

Naomi cooing over his brilliance.

Later, begging for her life.

His eyes are hard, though, stony. Whatever he's seeing doesn't move him one bit.

"You know, my boss isn't happy about this." I force a small, conspiratorial smile, pitching my voice lower, semi-seductive. "I had to beg her to let us have this time alone together—if you don't talk, she'll use it as an excuse to pull me." The threat works. His eyes meet mine. "So what d'you say, then? Shall we just start at the beginning and see where we end up? There's no rush. Take all the time you need."

There's a dead-eyed husk of a man sitting here in place of Joseph Madden. The sinister sparkle is gone. His shoulders sag. His chin is dipped toward his chest.

The unmistakable posture of defeat.

So defeated, in fact, I barely hear him say it.

"I did not kill that girl. Someone has framed me."

You are absolutely kidding me. I slide my hands under my legs to stop myself punching him, or the wall, or even myself in blunt frustration.

His voice swells a little. "And I know who it is and I know why they've done it, but I'm never going to tell, so don't even ask. It's between us. Me and *them*." He spits the last word, the taste of it repugnant in his mouth; like a piece of cold fatty meat rind that's been stuck in his teeth for days.

I sigh deeply, summoning up every teacher, parent, colleague, friend who's ever expressed disappointment in me. "Really, Joseph? Is that it? *That's* what you got me back in here for? To say the same ridiculous thing you've been saying for the past three days?"

He shakes his head, equally disappointed. "No, you're not listening to me, Cat. This isn't about someone having fun at my expense. This is about someone purposefully framing me. So what I'm saying now is *entirely* different."

And I know it is, but I don't want to hear it. Because the hope of a swift ending, in the absence of a happy one, was the only reason I signed up for this toxic pantomime, and now it's clear that's not happening, I want to be a hundred miles from Joseph Madden. A thousand would be preferable. Although frankly, right now I'd settle for being twenty yards away in the viewing room, gawping and gasping and *"bloody hell!"*-ing with all the others at every new lie that slithers from his twisted, fucked-up mouth.

"So . . . Naomi's blood on your glove? Is that 'someone's' doing? Can I let our sloppy forensics team know they're in the clear?"

Silence.

"And if it was Rachel's doing—because I'm going to assume that 'someone' is Rachel, otherwise you'd have said, 'This isn't about Rachel having fun at my expense.'"

"Assume what you want," he says wearily, rubbing at one eye. "Who it is isn't important."

I make a noise somewhere between a laugh and a small scream. "Well, it's pretty damn important to us, Joseph. Because if 'someone' *has* framed you, then they must have killed Naomi—do you follow? I mean, how else would they have got hold of her blood?"

More silence. And the longer the silence, the more volatile the situation. Or at least that's how Parnell will read it. I picture him outside the door, pumped up and primed for the green light from Steele, wondering about the consequences if he steams in on amber.

"So if you're not going to give me a name, what is this all about? What is it you want?" No one can resist being asked what they want. It's a feeling cemented in childhood; the comfort of feeling valued, of having your needs considered.

"I want you to focus on me, OK. *Me*." He thumps his breastbone so hard the noise echoes around the room. "Whatever this person has done, there *has* to be other evidence out there that proves I didn't do it and it's your job to find it, Cat. *Do your job*."

I lean in, even though every sinew in my body longs to stretch in the opposite direction. "No, Joseph, it's my job to put killers in prison. And you're either a killer or you're shielding a killer. Guess where I'd put my money?"

A noise behind me. The door.

"Who the hell are you?" says Joseph, returning to form, his old high-and-mighty self.

There's no need for me to turn around; I know who it is. I can smell her perfume. I can sense her energy at ten paces. I can feel her small, formidable presence filling up the room and signaling the end is nigh for Joseph Madden.

"My name's DCI Kate Steele, Mr. Madden, and trust me, I'm the last person you want to see." She slips into the chair beside me, hands together, the picture of serenity. "Still, you like to be in the company of important people, I hear, so if it's any consolation I'm a *very* important person. Basically, if I'm in your interview room, you can bet something big is about to happen."

The room holds its breath.

"Joseph Madden, take notice that you are charged with the following offense. That on Sunday the 5th of November, in the London Borough of Haringey, you did murder Naomi Anne Lockhart, contrary to common law. You do not have to say anything, but it may harm your defense if you do not mention . . ."

I let her words wash over me. Madden does the same.

24

Sunday

A sharp poke to my left shoulder and the scent of something fruity wafting past.

"Well, it's Redfern's Rolex, all right. DNA came up trumps." Steele turns in her office doorway. "Anyway, lady, what are you doing in early? I told you to take it easy today."

I'm in early this morning because there was no celebrating last night. While Steele's not a big fan of celebrations, not when there's a family who'll never celebrate anything ever again, she usually gets the need for a collective exhale over a few pints. Not last night, though. Last night the mood was muted and cagey. Thin smiles and limp backslaps. Nothing even approaching party time. Parnell, as ever, had asked if I fancied a quick scoop, assuming I'd need it after the head-to-head with Madden, and usually that'd be *exactly* what I'd need—a few vinos and an hour of him whinging about the price of kids' uniforms.

Last night, I couldn't even face that. All I'd wanted was a shower, a pillow doused in lavender spray and a twelve-hour dreamless sleep.

I'd managed two out of the three.

"I am taking it easy," I tell Steele. "Parnell's making the tea."

"Make that three, Lu!" Steele hollers in the direction of what we call the kitchen—the single wonky shelf that houses a kettle, a mini-fridge and a microwave that hasn't worked for two years. "I don't suppose there's any point in ordering you to go home?" she says, turning back to me. "I'll only find you hiding out in the loos with a stack of witness statements."

Once. I did that *once*.

"Good news about the Rolex," I say, following her into her office. "Adds to bad character, at least." She's standing over her desk, frowning at a printout. "Hey, don't you think it's weird he didn't get rid of them? The gloves, I mean."

She looks up. "Don't worry, I asked Dolores about that. He's arrogant, for one, and they're expensive, for two. He probably couldn't afford to replace them so he'd be pained to get rid of them. Possessions fuel his self-esteem, remember?" She flops down, exhausted, holding up the printout. "I tell you something, we could do without this."

"What is it?"

"Bless you, Lu." Parnell walks in, just about managing three mugs. "The other day, after we found out about Kirstie Connor's little habit, I got in touch with a mate in the drugs squad. Asked him to dig a bit deeper into Kieran Drake's history. Now, there's nothing on his record because it was pre-2014, before they were made illegal, but his name did come up on several intelligence logs in relation to the production and distribution of 'legal highs'—meow meow, n-bombs, spice, that sort of thing." I sit down with a heavy feeling about where this is heading. "Well, that sort of thing doesn't show up in a routine tox screen, so just to be absolutely sure, I requested a second screen on Naomi—bang goes the Christmas drinks budget, but hey ho—and guess what?"

"Bang goes our 'perfect' victim," I finish.

"Correct. She had benzofuran compounds in her system. Benzo Fury as it's known. It was massive a while ago, not so much now, but it's still out there. Kieran Drake must have sold it to Kirstie Connor and she gave some to Naomi. Another thing she's neglected to tell us."

"Legal highs, designer drugs, aren't they more of a kids' thing?" Parnell poses the question. "I can't see Kirstie Connor going for that."

"They're more of a cheap thing, so my guess is Kieran Drake was after more than a fifty-quid profit and Kirstie was none the wiser. Benzo Fury mimics ecstasy and speed but looks like coke when it comes in powder form, to the untrained eye anyway. Kirstie probably didn't realize she'd been stung until she'd taken it. And then who was she going to complain to? Trading Standards?"

"So Naomi wasn't quite the 'square' everyone thought," I say.

"Apparently not."

"Peer pressure?"

"Could be," agrees Steele. "Or if the man you've been shagging is sitting in the next room with his wife, that's going to make you want to get wired, right?"

"Do you think that's Kirstie Connor's excuse?" Blank faces. "You know, what Madden said about him and Kirstie—their 'thing.'"

"Ah, but do we think that's true?" asks Steele. "He'll do and say anything when he's in a tight spot. Well, actually, he only ever says one thing—*they're lying because they're out to get me.*' That's his defense every time. Rachel the vengeful wife and now Kirstie the spurned lover."

"I'd believe it." I've said it before I've even properly formed an argument. *Shoot from the hip time.* "I hadn't thought about it before, but you've got to admit, she's a bit *too* animated when it comes to him. I mean, I loathed my sister's first fiancé—oh yeah, there've been three—but he didn't get to me in the way Joseph gets to Kirstie. And he certainly never sent me gifts." Parnell's nodding. "And all that stuff she said yesterday morning, her goading him about his gray hairs, saying that young girls think he's an old man? That's got a touch of romance-gone-bad about it, if you ask me."

"Only one way to find out," says Steele. "Ask Kirstie."

"Or Rachel," says Parnell. "He said Rachel knew."

I sit up straighter. "See, that's another reason why I'd be inclined to believe it. It kind of makes sense now, their relationship. Kirstie's all over Rachel, protective of her, keen to stress how close they are and Rachel's a bit . . . well, a tiny bit distant, I suppose. A bit sneery. It's subtle. I thought it was just an in-law thing—you know, 'no one's good enough for my brother,' but maybe there's more to it . . .'"

Emily Beck pops her perfectly contoured face around the door. "Sorry to interrupt, Boss. Cat, your phone kept ringing and it was annoying me so I answered it. It was Clara Madden. Her mum's been drinking heavily and she's in a bit of a state, apparently. She wants to talk to you."

"Oh goody." I glance back at Steele. "Not the best time to bring up the Kirstie 'thing' then."

"Or anything else. You're not going."

"Boss, I really should. She's vulnerable."

"Which is very lovely of you, Kinsella, and if I were in the business of handing out *Being Kind* stickers, you'd have a giant one just here." She taps the lapel of her suit jacket. "But I'm not, and you're not Rachel Madden's nursemaid. And anyway, I need you here."

"You were threatening to make me go home, earlier."

"Yes, because you need a rest. Christ, I know I'm no oil painting this morning, but you look awful."

"Thanks for that."

"I'm being serious. You've worked six days straight, Cat, and you were put through the mill more than most yesterday, so I either want you here on desk duty or at home watching *Columbo* repeats with Mr. X. There's your two options."

I wish. Oh, how I wish.

"Look, I'm not playing nursemaid," I say, standing my ground. "She's probably going to end up a prosecution witness, whether we have to compel her or not, so we need to look after her every step of the way. We need her onside."

"I agree," says Parnell, quietly.

Steele holds her hands up. "Oh, whatever! Fine, go. But I want you to go home afterward, OK? And don't think I've forgotten about tomorrow either." *My birthday.* "You've had it booked off for ages and you're bloody taking it. I mean it, I do not want to see you in this office tomorrow. Not unless you want the special Kate Steele version of the birthday bumps."

Maybe I do. It doesn't look like I'll be getting the sexy version of Aiden anytime soon.

He got back last night.

He still hasn't called.

The Pendown has visitors. A small coven of reporters, champing at the bit now that they've got a name and a sketchy narrative to construct.

Luckily, reputation keeps the numbers low. It takes a certain type of hack to brave an estate where even the bailiffs get a warmer welcome. Hell, even *we* get a warmer welcome than Those Bastard Journalists. But then, when your kids are called "feral" and everyone else is branded "pond life," you don't have a lot of time for the people who depict you as less-than-human for the rest of the country to see. Last year, two residents set up an initiative to support old folk on the estate, many of them completely isolated, too scared to venture out. The launch attracted one measly journalist. A guy who'd grown up here who understood that sometimes good things happen on the Pendown too.

Although, admittedly, not today.

Word's traveled fast, judging by the graffiti on the Maddens' front door. The not-altogether-accurate graffiti, I should add.

FUCK KILLER RAPIST SCUM

Marcus Connor stares at the handiwork, forlornly rubbing his scalp. "Little shits. I'll get some paint thinner from somewhere and get it scrubbed off. Although, of course, me standing outside attracts people toward the flat and I don't want that, not when Rachel's like this, so it'll have to wait. Hopefully she'll be calmer later."

I prepare myself. "It's bad, then?"

He gestures for me to go inside. "See for yourself. I can't get any sense out of her and I doubt you will either. I don't understand why Clara called you, to be honest."

"I think Rachel asked for me."

He laughs miserably. "She was asking for our mum earlier, so that tells you how far gone she is. Mum was never the cuddly, supportive type at the best of times, and she hasn't spoken to her in years, anyway. The last time she did she called her a malevolent old hag, although that was straight out of Joseph's mouth, no question."

I check my watch. Eleven seventeen. "She must have started early if she's *that* drunk. Is she usually a heavy drinker?"

My voice is flooded with concern. My head's flooded with *heavy drinker = bad witness*.

Marcus shrugs. "Depends what you mean by heavy. She uses it as a crutch but she's not usually drunk before midday, no. But then . . ."

He doesn't need to say it. *Her husband hasn't usually been charged with murder.*

"So what triggered it this morning?"

"God knows. She's had Clara's laptop all morning and she's been reading lots of articles, getting upset about Naomi's family."

"You should take it off her." I look back toward the door. "And you should try to get that graffiti scrubbed off as soon as possible. Seriously, it's journalist catnip. I can stick around for a bit, scare off the vultures while you're doing it."

"Don't worry, I'll be all right." He smiles. "Thanks for the offer, though. You've been really kind."

You deserve better than your wife, I think. *You might have once driven fifty in a thirty zone, and your hair's pretty much upped and left for good, but you seem like a good bloke. You deserve better than this.*

"Is Kirstie here?" I ask, wondering if I'll be able to grab a discreet word about her "thing" with Joseph.

Wondering if it even matters.

"No, not now. She was, but she wasn't really helping so I told her to go home. Me and Clara are letting Rachel burn herself out and that's *so* not Kirstie's forte. She's good at starting fires, not putting them out."

I smile at the understatement. "Well, I'm not sure how much help I'll be either, but I'm here now. I'll pop up."

I've never been upstairs in the Maddens' flat, but it's not difficult to work out which room is Rachel's—there's a soft keening noise coming from behind the second door on the right.

I knock gently, put my face around the door. Rachel's lying on her side with her back to me while Clara sits at the foot of the bed, staring at her mum like she's a piece of abstract art, something she can't begin to fathom. The room's dark, the only light coming from a thin gap in the curtains and the glare of a phone on a bedside table.

"Hi there."

Rachel jumps at my voice and turns quickly. She looks like something dredged from a lake, her face bloated and sodden. "Cat," she slurs, extending a thin, pale arm. "Come in, Cat, come in. I have to tell you something. I have to make you understand something."

I walk around the bed and crouch down beside her. Clara flicks her head to the side, a signal that she's going to leave us to it. I nod and wait for her to pull the door half-closed. "So what's this all about then, Rachel? Hmm?" She says nothing, staring through me. "I know things are awful right now but this, the drinking, it isn't fair on anyone. It isn't fair on Clara. She needs your support, Rachel, not this."

The strap of her nightdress has fallen down, completely exposing her left breast. I think about pulling it up, preserving whatever dignity she has left, but I feel hesitant to touch her. Her misery might be catching.

"*I* need support," she slurs, full of self-pity. "And he does. I know what he did was fucking terrible but he's not all bad." She pulls herself up to sitting, making long, hard work of it. "They're saying he's an animal, but he's not an animal, Cat. He's not. S'not fair to say that."

"Who's saying he's an animal?"

She lifts the duvet, fumbling around for Clara's laptop. "This! The internet. Fucking people. All of them idiots thinking they know what's what." Her head tilts as if it's an effort to hold it straight. "He loves me, you know, Cat. No one else ever loved me. Shouldn't have happened. Shouldn't."

"No, it shouldn't." I speak slowly and firmly, as though my clear diction can somehow compensate for the lack of hers. "But it *has* happened and Joseph has been charged. You need to start thinking about you and Clara, how you're going to get through this." I pick up a bottle of gin from the floor. "And this is never the answer, Rachel. Never."

Except for every single occasion when I've decided it is.

She's not listening. "It's her fault, y'know. Oh yeah, t'is. *Bitch*." She stops, head waggling slightly. "Oh, all right, OK, maybe s'not her fault but she shouldn't have done that, should she? He's *my* husband. *Mine*. Why can't women just leave *my* husband alone?"

I stand up. There's no reasoning with her. I wonder if we should call a doctor but there's no way they'd give her any medication in this state, so what would be the point? A bucket of cold water would probably work better.

"Naomi's got a niece," she whimpers, looking up at me with rheumy eyes that won't focus. "Paper says she's only a baby. There's a picture of them together—look, I'll show you." I quickly snatch the laptop off the bed. She scowls but doesn't try to snatch it back. "So sad . . . baby niece won't even remember her . . . Isn't that so sad? Be so sad if Danny forgot me. So sad."

Marcus appears in the doorway, shaking his head, urging me to give up.

I don't need much encouragement.

"Rachel, I'm going to go downstairs now, OK? I might pop back up in a minute."

She ignores me, scrabbling for her cigarettes on the floor. "And her poor mum . . . poor, lovely lady. She deserves to know the truth, doesn't she? But I deserved to know the truth too." She fires the cigarettes at the wall, raging. "And they all fucking lied to me. *All* of them. Everyone lies. He does. He's a fucking liar." She drops sideways onto the pillow, as if running out of steam. "He's not an animal, though. S'not fair. He's not."

"Come on," says Marcus, quietly. "Humoring her isn't helping. If we ignore her maybe she'll pass out, with any luck."

I leave Rachel gibbering about animals and nieces and the scarcity of truth in modern society, and follow Marcus back downstairs to the living room where Clara is curled on the sofa, staring at MTV with the sound down. Taylor Swift silently shaking it off.

"Guys," I say, eyes darting from one to the other. "You've *got* to keep her away from the media, do you hear me? I know she's drunk, but she's saying some pretty awful stuff about Naomi—blaming her, basically. If a journalist gets wind of that, they'll crucify her." I hand Clara her laptop. "And keep her off that."

"She blames everyone but Joseph when she's pissed." Marcus sounds resigned rather than resentful. " 'He's misunderstood, his mummy didn't love him, he never had a male role model growing up.'

It's all bollocks, of course. Neither did half the ex-cons I work with and, yeah, they might have broken the law a few times, but they're not cruel, heartless . . ."

Clara sits up. "Look, I saw them—Dad and that girl."

Her words come out of nowhere, like a jab punch to the jaw.

"Naomi?"

She nods. "That's why I called you. That's what I wanted to talk to you about."

OK. I'd assumed when Clara told Emily that *"she"* wanted to speak to me, she'd meant Rachel.

"What exactly did you see?" My head hammers with possibility.

"Oh God, I don't mean I saw Dad hurt her. I just mean I saw them together. It was at The Grindhouse, about a month ago. I needed money for a textbook. Mum didn't have any and I thought the only way to get it out of *him* was to ask in front of other people. Anyway, I saw them as I was walking up the street. They were standing outside talking—maybe arguing, I'm not 100 percent sure. It was definitely her, though. The hair's pretty distinctive."

Finally, someone who can put Joseph and Naomi together weeks before the Connors' party. We've got her hair in his car, of course, but fibers are the poor cousins of people. Your average jury trusts people over science, which is kind of sweet, if a little misguided.

"OK. We're going to need you to amend your formal statement ASAP. And I don't need to tell someone who wants to study criminal law that you really should have told us this before."

"Am I in trouble?" She looks wide-eyed at Marcus, then back to me. "Please, I can't get a record, I can't!" Her fear is good. It means we can keep her on a leash, just like Kirstie Connor, although I feel worse doing it to Clara. "Honestly, I swear I didn't put two and two together until a couple of days ago when there was that picture in the *Standard.* All the photos before that, she had blond hair and I honestly didn't twig. And then when I did . . . well, I was just looking out for Mum. She's *always* looked out for me and I wanted to protect her from more hurt." Her lip curls in disgust. "I mean, that girl's like half his age, it's disgusting."

I feel for her. She's seventeen. She should be dealing with hangovers, homework, and maybe the odd pregnancy scare. She shouldn't be dealing with this.

"So why are you telling us now?" I ask, my voice a little softer, less officious.

"Well, because he did it, obviously. I wasn't sure before. The fact that I'd seen them together didn't prove anything. But now . . . I mean, you wouldn't have charged him without good reason." Which is true, but you usually expect more denial from family members, especially at first. Unpleasant as it is, Rachel's blame-the-victim stance isn't completely unusual. "And anyway, I was wrong about Mum not needing to know. She does. She needs to stop making excuses for him. She needs to see him for what he really is. A bad person. A *really* bad person."

Bad people. Our jails are full of them. So are our schools, our boardrooms, our gyms, our buses, our nightclubs, our churches, our politics, our homes.

But the type of "bad" it takes to murder a young woman, deny you even know her, then claim a shadowy *"someone"* is framing you but you'll never, ever name who, is a quantum leap into "mad," which, knowing Lucas Stein, could be the line of defense we end up with.

It doesn't bear thinking about.

25

Later, in a rare burst of proactivity—when it comes to matters of the heart, anyway—I get the bus to Mile End.

Actually, I get three buses. The journey from mine to Aiden's is pretty symbolic of our relationship, in that it's complicated, taxing, and only undertaken by fools. I could have got the tube, of course, but I know, deep down, that I'm playing for time. And in any case, I'm in a top-deck, nose-pressed-to-the-window kind of mood, and there's no denying it's a more cheering mode of travel. There's a little kid up in the front pretending to be the bus driver while making the "choo-choo" sound of a steam train, and two gorgeous old biddies behind me moaning that they keep changing the timetable and why do the Christmas adverts keep getting earlier every year?

Just life. Normal chitchat. No craniocerebral traumas or narcissistic personality disorders. No benzofuran compounds or having to refer to the love of your life as Mr. X.

After nearly ninety minutes of soothing Bus Life, I'm standing on Mr. X's doorstep, prepared to tackle things head-on. Prepared to walk back down his path a newly single woman if that's how things are meant to be.

Or at least that's what I'm telling myself. Really, despite the ridiculously long journey, I'm hoping he won't be in. On most Sunday afternoons when we aren't together, Aiden's usually out kicking a ball somewhere or watching a ball being kicked in one of Mile End's many drinking establishments, and with any luck that's where he is now. With any luck, I'll be able to say, *"Ah well, at least I tried,"* as I trundle back to the bus stop, pretending to be disappointed but actually wilting with relief.

But he *is* in.

And he looks as conflicted as I feel.

"I suppose you've come to eat the head off me?" he says, instantly launching the first serve.

"I had. But now I just want a cup of tea and a hug. Can you sort me out with both?"

He tugs me into the flat where the warmth and the smell of burnt toast instantly restores something in me: a normality I haven't felt for the past forty-eight hours.

"'Fraid I'm all out of tea bags." He opens his arms out wide. "But I've got shitloads of hugs. Great big piles of them if you want."

I want.

"I know you went to my dad's place," I murmur into the crook of his neck, breathing him in, committing his scent to memory. "I know you met him."

"I did. And your uncle, but so what? I didn't say I was your boyfriend." He pulls away. "Don't worry, I'm still your dirty little secret."

"So you don't think you did anything wrong?"

"I think I did something you didn't want me to do. Whether it was wrong is debatable."

"You went behind my back."

A torrent of self-loathing floods me. *Dear God, the things I've kept from him . . .*

"Yeah, I know, and I'm sorry. But hey, at least I understand now why you're ashamed of them." My heart stops until I spot a tiny grin emerging. "Sure, I'd be ashamed too if my family were West Ham fans. I don't blame you for keeping your distance." He grabs me by the shoulders, frowning, mock serious. "But we can get past that, Cat, I know we can. Love conquers all, even god-awful football allegiances."

If only that were true.

I grin back and walk into the living room. There's a small carrier bag on the table, its contents spilled out to one side. "Hey, are those for me? Do you think that's all it takes to get back in my good books—a bottle of duty-free perfume and a giant Toblerone?"

He doesn't smile like he's supposed to. "Actually, I had fifty euro left and I couldn't be arsed changing it back. I wasn't aware I was in the bad books. I just thought we were giving each other a bit of space . . ."

I spin around. "Space? You could have at least called, sent a text."

"And so could you, so that makes us even-stevens, right?"

"Right." Suddenly, all my resolve, all my tackle-this-head-on bravado, dissipates. I don't want to argue with him right now. I just want to look at him, be with him, berate him for always managing to burn toast. I want to keep things light for a little while longer. "Anyway," I say, "some Irishman you are. You know, my gran had a saying about people who run out of tea bags. Something like *'He who has no tea bags has no soul,'* but it wasn't that exactly. That makes her sound like Socrates, not a little Irish woman in a tabard."

"Your gran—so would that be your dad's mum?" It's a pointed question.

"My mum's, actually, but I see what you did there."

"So not Granny *McBride*?" I look away, embarrassed. "Oh yeah, that was a shock all right, when I says to your dad, *'Nice to meet you, Mr. Kinsella'* and he says, *'The name's McBride,'* and I realize I don't even know my girlfriend's real surname."

"Kinsella's my real surname. I changed it a few years back. It's no big deal."

"The kind of thing you mention, though?"

"It didn't cross my mind, sorry. There were no male Kinsellas left, no one to carry on the family name, so it was a tribute to my mum." And a *go-fuck-yourself* to my dad, but I leave that bit out. I drop down onto the sofa, narrowly missing a plate of toast crusts. "So? What do you think then?"

"What do I think? It's a grand old place your dad has there. No decent beer on draft, but sure, if the hipsters are happy . . ."

"Don't be obtuse, Doyle. I meant, what do you think of him?"

He shrugs. "I liked him, inasmuch as you can like anyone after ten minutes. Frank's an awful gobshite, though. Funny, mind."

"He isn't my real uncle, by the way." I don't care that I sound petty. "So what now?"

There's football on the TV, a swarm of men arguing over a penalty.

Aiden switches it off—a huge, reverent gesture in this flat. "What do you mean, what now?"

"Well, are you going to visit again? Become bezzie mates?" It should be the stuff of dreams; your boyfriend and your dad bonding over a few jars, not a cruel nightmare, a purgatory of your own making.

"I don't want to be bezzie mates with him, you eejit. You really don't get it, do you?" He sits down beside me. Our thighs touch and I feel a stirring. "Look, it'd be one thing if you were completely estranged, Cat, but you speak to him. I've heard you speaking to him. So why's it so bad for me to speak to him too occasionally? *Very* occasionally." There's no answer. It shouldn't be. "I just wanted him to know I exist, OK? Because you hiding me away . . . well, it makes me wonder if we actually exist. In any proper fucking sense, anyway."

"Oh, we exist. I promise you, we exist." I take both his hands and shower his fists, his palms, his fingers, with small kisses. "Now, if you don't mind, can we go and exist in the bedroom? It's been over a week."

"In a minute. I want to ask you something first." He slides off the sofa and hunkers down in front of me, taking my hand. It's not quite bended knee, but it's sailing a bit bloody close.

"Ah, ask me later," I say, panicking, moving in for a kiss. "Enough talk . . ."

"No, I'm going to ask you now. I'll have lost my nerve later."

Oh God.

"And, look, it doesn't matter how you answer. Everything's still grand, OK?"

I nod, or at least I think I do. My whole skeleton feels fused.

"Are your family dodgy, Cat?"

I laugh. A wild hysterical roar, fueled mainly by relief and pure mental exhaustion.

Aiden starts laughing too. "Because, you know, I've watched enough gangster films to know a wiseguy when I see one. I'm not sure about your dad but Frank *definitely* is. He's more crooked than a corkscrew."

I wipe my eyes on my sleeve. "What makes you say that?"

"Er, maybe because when I mentioned I worked in Risk Analysis,

he said, '*I'm into a bit of that meself, Aiden, son. The riskier the better.*'"
His impression is spot on. It sets me off again. "So, well? Are you
going to confirm or deny? Am I going to wake up with a horse's head
on my pillow? Do I have to call your dad the Don? A guy needs to
know these things."

And for once I tell him the truth. A part-truth, anyhow.

"Look, he's not quite the Don, but he's not quite legit. Can we leave
it at that?"

He nods, pulling me to my feet. "OK, that'll do for me. Now, what
were you saying about bed?"

Much later, after several rounds of sex, sleep, and a lot of Toblerone,
we're woken by the sound of my phone ringing. Aiden murmurs
sleepy swear words, then turns over and slips straight back into the
land of Nod, while I scrabble in the dark, looking for the damn thing,
assuming it's work but also praying no one's dead.

Twelve thirty-three a.m. Dad.

A riptide yanks me from the safety of Aiden's bed to a choppy,
dangerous ocean.

"What's the matter?" I blurt in a whispered panic.

"Bloody hell, sweetheart, calm down. Nothing's the matter. You
were born at twelve thirty so I wanted to be the first person to wish
you happy birthday." I walk into the living room, feeling around for
the light switch. "Sorry, did I wake you? You were always a night owl,
like me, I thought you'd still be up."

The light comes on. Aiden must have snuck out earlier and left
my birthday presents on the sofa. There's four of them in total, all of
them terribly wrapped, none of them ring box–sized, which brings a
fresh wave of relief.

I sit down next to my haul. "Never mind happy birthday, have you
spoken to Frank yet?"

He hesitates. "Briefly."

"And?"

"And Cynthia's ill. The pair of them are getting all sentimental and
they wanted to give you a birthday card, that's all it was. You know
they always thought of you three as the kids they never had."

Did they?

Frank had my brother, Noel, beaten up.

He offered Jacqui a job in his strip club the night before she took her A-levels.

He attacked Dad with a pool cue while I cowered behind the fruit machine, then gave me twenty pounds afterward for being a "good girl" and not crying.

It's worrying that Dad thinks Frank's losing his edge when he's clearly the one who can't sense danger.

"Frank found out my address easy enough. Why didn't they post the card?" I lower my voice to a whisper again. "And all that stuff about Aiden?"

"I'm telling you, sweetheart, he's getting bored in his old age and he likes playing the wind-up merchant. Stop worrying. You might be twenty-seven now but you're still my baby and I won't let anything bad happen to you. Protection—that's what fathers do, OK?"

My mind flashes to Clara Madden. One parent in a custody cell, the other one flinging cigarettes around a darkened room that reeks of gin.

No wonder she wants to study a few hundred miles away.

Which reminds me.

I *"uh-huh"* and *"m-hm"* my way through the rest of the conversation while hunting for my bag and switching on Aiden's laptop. Aiden's snoring now, a sound as sweet as soft rain, while Dad rambles on about Finn's sporting triumphs and a new ale he's got on tap. Half listening, I take the case file out of my bag, sifting through documents until I find what I'm looking for: Clara Madden's internet history. Something I've been meaning to glance over but haven't quite made a priority.

I run my finger down the pages looking for Portsmouth University, figuring that if Clara even had half a notion of applying there, she'd have visited their website a number of times.

Nothing.

Plenty of Exeter Uni, York Uni, Durham Uni, Leeds.

Plenty of history that's "a bit on the dark side" too, as Ben Swaines put it.

"British serial killer Peter Sutcliffe linked to unsolved Swedish murders."

"St. Austell fire: Arson arrest while search for missing girl continues."

"Should gang violence be treated as a public health issue?"

And then, halfway down the nineteenth page, after Dad's long-said goodbye and Aiden's been in twice to moan about the light being on, I spot them.

A handful of Google searches:

drug dealer attack stabbing Portsmouth
drugs stabbing attack portsmouth
Portsmouth 2002 man attacked death killed

Followed by a couple of articles:

"Hundreds turn out for the funeral of Portsmouth teenager, Abby Slater."

"On the 15th anniversary of Abby Slater's death, Portsmouth remembers . . ."

"Murder of Portsmouth Teenager, Abby Slater. Lydia Slater speaks out."

My own Google search quickly confirms it, although I know it instinctively in my gut.

Lydia Slater is now Lydia Coe.

26

Monday

Happy Birthday to me.

Or *Lá Breithe Sona Duit*, according to Aiden.

I start the day how I start most days—wishing that I'd slept more and switching my phone on while having a wee. A flurry of texts greet me: Aiden—who went off to work at some ungodly hour—Dad, Parnell, Jacqui, an assortment of other folk making an assortment of "getting old" jokes, and a message from a pizza place offering me a free side dish on my "special day."

And Alana Lockhart, who's WhatsApped me a bunch of photos.

Recent snaps of Naz—all the photos you've got are old, apart from that one in the Standard. Alana L. 7:04

They're old. I'm old. I quickly scan a couple then go back to reading my messages. When I'm done feeling loved, I shower and dress and have a grope of the presents I've promised Aiden I won't open till later, then I poke about the kitchen, snacking on biscuits and buttered toast, while making promises to get healthier tomorrow.

So far, so familiar.

Which wouldn't please my grandad Pat.

Grandad Pat—Dad's dad—always maintained you should spend your birthday doing something out of the ordinary. Something you've never done before. Something that takes you out of your comfort zone. Granted, he first came up with this theory on my seventh birthday, when he wanted me to put my new Game Boy down for *"five fecking minutes"* and help him weed his allotment. But ulterior motives aside, it's always kind of stuck with me. What better way to mark the start of another birth year than to try something you've never tried, go somewhere you've never been?

And I've never been to Portsmouth.

So here's what I know about Lydia Coe, *née* Slater. You won't find it on Morgan Cripps's website where everybody—even poncho-wearing Lydia—looks kind of steam-cleaned and dependable.

Lydia Coe is a woman who's been to hell and back.

Lydia Coe tried to take her own life three months after the death of her daughter, Abby.

Lydia Coe once chained herself to a railing outside the offices of a certain newspaper to protest against their salacious depiction of murdered young women.

And here's what I know about Abby.

In 2002, eighteen-year-old Abby Slater, a 'happy-go-lucky' trainee dental nurse, was staying at a friend's in the Fratton area of Portsmouth. Unbeknownst to her mum, this "friend" wasn't childhood pal Viv Jenkins, but twenty-six-year-old Joel "Spider" Stevens, manager of the Jack of Hearts pub and general low-rent scoundrel-with-a-sexy-smile. Details are sketchy, as Stevens *claimed* to have slept through the whole thing, stating that when he came downstairs at seven a.m. the next morning, the pub had been broken into and Abby was on the floor, dead. As her phone was found behind the bar, with an incoming missed call logged at one forty-two a.m., Stevens put forward the theory that she must have heard it ringing and come downstairs to retrieve it, interrupting the burglary in progress.

She'd died from a single stab wound to the throat.

While, surprise surprise, Stevens maintained his innocence, he did later admit that he'd been involved in the theft of a large number of mobile phones, and that it wasn't exactly uncommon knowledge, within certain fraternities, that the phones were being stored at his pub until the heat died down. Abby's mates claimed that she knew about the phones and had rowed with Stevens about his involvement. On the night she died, they were seen arguing by several independent witnesses, one of whom said he heard Stevens call Abby "a stupid nosy bitch." *Whatta guy.* Abby's best friend, Viv Jenkins, also claimed that Abby suspected Stevens of cheating on her with numerous women and had often joked about making an anonymous tip-off call about the phone stash, although Jenkins insisted she'd never have gone through with it. She had, however, planned to break it off with all-around arse-wipe Stevens.

Stevens was the first and only real suspect. Hampshire Police believed that Stevens staged the break-in to cover up for the fact that he killed Abby during a row over the phones or his cheating, or maybe the one forty-two a.m. missed call from her male friend, Mike. Sadly, though, they couldn't find one piece of forensic evidence to back up this theory and Joel "Spider" Stevens scuttled away to New Zealand in mid-2003 and has never returned to the UK.

No other arrests were made in the murder of Abby Slater. Plenty of people "helped police with their inquiries." Plenty more bandied around names and lager-fueled theories. Not so many helped Lydia Slater pick up the pieces as she tried to make sense of how the only thing she'd ever been proud of had been taken from her so violently.

That was until one day in 2004 when she discovered the Open University.

And then a later day in 2008 when she graduated with a Bachelor of Laws with Honors (LLB).

Since then, she's twice been nominated for the Family Law Pro Bono Lawyer of the Year Award, and she's appeared on national and regional TV discussing Abby and her work. Last year, she completed the Machu Picchu trek in support of the charity Refuge, and according to a gorgeous article I've just read, she's also a passionate supporter of the Hedgehog Preservation Society—a cause close to Abby's heart and so, naturally, to hers too.

I can't deny I'm looking forward to meeting this thoroughly kick-ass woman.

And on my birthday too.

Grandad Pat would approve.

I call Lydia Coe when I'm halfway to Portsmouth, hoping that if I'm already en route she'll feel begrudgingly obliged to see me, and on the off-chance she's isn't there—well, like I say, I've never been to Portsmouth. They've got the HMS *Victory*, the Spinnaker Tower, Charles Dickens's birthplace, and a cathedral with a twelfth-century chapel.

And there's the sea. The Holy Land for an urbanite like me.

I needn't have worried, though. One mention of Abby and Lydia has her secretary performing diary gymnastics. I'm clear to point out that it isn't about Abby per se; that it's really quite tenuous and I won't be able to go into much detail, if any detail at all, but she's adamant I come and see her between one and two o'clock, as long as I don't mind her scoffing a sandwich while we talk.

Morgan Cripps's office spans the top floor of a listed Georgian terrace, on a double-parked street, a couple of blocks from the sea. I haven't picked the best day to be beside the seaside, even by November standards, and I arrive windswept and drizzled-on and dying for a cup of tea. Lydia meets me in reception, radiating warmth and hospitality, telling me she's ordered sandwiches for two and insisting I take her umbrella when I leave. She looks different from the website. A little older, a lot heavier, and infinitely more fun. There's a red streak at the front of her hair and a tiny dent in her nose where a stud used to be. Her hot-pink lipstick doesn't really suit her and yet somehow suits her perfectly, and her laugh isn't filthy, it's nigh on pornographic.

"Sorry I haven't got longer." She shows me into her office, a small snug made even smaller by her big, colorful presence. "And sorry you're not seeing the city at its best. You should come back in the summer—there's no better place."

She talks with the pride of someone who took her first steps here, had her first kiss, her first legal drink.

Her first and only child.

I lift some files off a chair, making myself at home. "Born and bred, are you?"

"One hundred percent Portsmouth—look, it says it on my mug." I smile. "I spent most of my life on the Paulsgrove Estate. I only moved away a few years ago and I'm still getting used to it. The whole social mobility thing makes me queasy, if I'm honest. I preach it but I still feel weird having an en suite. Ridiculous, huh?" Not really. I spent my first decade living above McAuley's Old Ale House and part of me will always be that untamed pub kid. "I've been offered a few jobs in London since I got myself a bit of a 'profile'—God, I hate that word—but I could never leave. All my friends and family are here. Abby's here." She pauses for a second, then straightens up behind her desk, fortifying herself. "Speaking of which, what brings you here?"

I take out my phone. "Does the name Clara Madden mean anything to you?"

Her mouth twists as she thinks. "No, I don't think so."

"Maybe you recognize her?" I pull up Clara's Instagram page. She only joined a few months ago, which makes her weirdly late to the party for a teenager, but she's clearly been making up for lost time. There's over fifty photos to choose from. Lydia pores over them carefully, tutting good-naturedly at the more risqué ones, smiling softly at the more natural shots—Clara blowing a kiss from a carousel, posing next to a llama God knows where.

"Beautiful girl." She looks up. "But no, I don't recognize her. Should I?"

I bring up her Facebook page, which is a little less self-absorbed. Two photos also feature Rachel. "What about her?"

"Oh God, yes, I remember her." She executes an eye-roll of epic proportions. "Helen Something—the so-called journalist."

My *"What the fuck?"* is curtailed by the arrival of Lydia's secretary with a tray of club sandwiches and a pot of tea. Lydia thanks her profusely, tells her to take some herself.

"Well, so she led me to believe," she says, carrying on. "I found her out quickly, though. She picked the wrong woman to lie to. Just ask my ex-husband." That gritty, throaty laugh again.

I feel like a stunned cartoon character; a halo of twittering birds circle my head. "Right, I'm totally confused here, Lydia. We need to go back a bit. I need to know everything."

Her eyes narrow, the curious lawyer stepping forward. "Why? What's she done?"

"Nothing. Nothing *directly* related to Abby's case, anyway. I just need some background on her." I pick up a sandwich, a sign that I don't expect to be speaking for a while. I'll eat the whole bloody plate if it means she keeps talking.

A journalist?

Lydia's happy to spill. "Well, she was booked in as a client at first. Diane—my secretary—had taken the basic details. She was looking to start divorce proceedings, all very standard. Anyway, within a minute or two of sitting down—right there, right where you are now—she suddenly announces she's actually a journalist and she wants to talk about Abby." She shrugs. "Well, apart from the fact that I'd never had a journalist con their way into my office before and I was livid, it was also a case of 'join the queue.' It'd been the fifteenth anniversary of Abby's murder in June, see, and *Crimewatch* had done a reconstruction."

"A reconstruction? But I thought Joel Stevens was pretty much—"

"I pushed for the reconstruction," she cuts in, squaring her broad shoulders. "I've never shied away from saying the Hampshire Police focused *too* obsessively on Joel Stevens. I'm not saying I think he didn't do it. On the balance of probability, there's a very good chance he did. Believe me, I know the stats inside out—in two-thirds of murdered women cases, it's the current or ex-partner—but I think the police gave up after Stevens left the country, and I wanted to remind the public that Abby's killer, whether it's Joel Stevens or someone else, is still out there."

"So she came to see you not long after the reconstruction?"

"I'd have to check with Diane, but early July, I'd say. I remember it was a scorching-hot day and she was wearing long sleeves and trousers, but sadly that's not entirely unusual with some of the women I see. A trip to my office often follows their final trip to the emergency room before they decide 'enough,' if you catch my drift."

I nod, grimly. "So what did she want to know? What was her pitch?"

"We didn't get any further than her name, Helen Something, and the online newspaper she worked for. Well, the minute I heard the word 'journalist' I gave her ten seconds to get out of my office before I called security." She makes a quick grab for a sandwich. "Not that we have security, but she wasn't to know."

She probably should have security. There's a certain type of Neanderthal—a minority of people, I should add—who doesn't take kindly to the Lydia Coes of this world.

"So anyway, after she left . . ." She's talking with her mouth full.

Steele's the exact same. Table manners be damned when everyone wants a piece of you and all you want is lunch. "I decided to check her out online and I couldn't find hide nor hair of her. The name of the newspaper was false too."

"What did you think?"

"I didn't really think too much about it, in all honesty. Obviously, it was a bit strange, but life is strange. You learn to stop sweating the small stuff when something big happens, trust me."

I do trust her. I think I know this to be true. Mum dying can't quite compare with the torture Lydia Coe went through, but I understand the concept of having a "Before" and an "After." "Before" is when things like weight and overdrafts and parking spaces seemed to matter. "After" is when you realize that simplicity is key. A life stripped bare to make the living of it more bearable.

"Did she come back here?" I ask. "We know she came to Portsmouth a few more times."

"Oh yeah, she sure did. Tea?"

"Always."

She pours. "So it must have been a week or two later, Diane puts a call through to me—someone wants to discuss fees and she'll only speak to me. Well, this puts my back up straightaway. Diane was working in the legal industry back when I was still pulling pints, but you always get the odd snooty one who insists on dealing direct. Anyway, I said put her through and, lo and behold, if it isn't Helen Something, asking if she can come and see me. So I tell her I don't believe that she's even a journalist, and basically to get lost, but immediately she starts apologizing, saying something about how she was only trying to help her daughter and she's sorry she lied and so on. She said she'd come all the way from London to explain, and that she was in the Highcliff and would I meet her for coffee."

My head's spinning, thoughts pivoting and swirling. *Helping Clara?* Maybe Joseph had hurt Clara and that was Rachel's "enough"? But then why the journalist ruse? The mention of Abby?

"So what did you say?"

"I said no. And I said it the next time and the next time and the next. Milk?"

"Just a drop, thanks. So you never actually met her again?"

She hands me a mug. "Oh, I did. You see, usually she'd call late morning, early afternoon, but she obviously got bored with me giving her short shrift because one day—well, one evening—I was leaving the office and she leapt on me. Not literally, of course, but not far off."

A far cry from the flimsy wisp I met at the Connors' house nearly a week ago. But then, I've seen with my own eyes that there's more to Poor Rachel than meets the eye.

"People underestimate her."

That's what Joseph Madden said three months ago.

"In the end, just to get rid of her, I say I'll hear her out. So we go over to the Highcliff. She insists on buying the coffee and then, well, she comes clean." A small eye-roll. "Helicopter parenting at its worst, if you ask me. Basically, her daughter's a bit of an academic highflier, by all accounts—I take it her daughter's this Clara Madden, the girl you were asking me about?" I try to look noncommittal, although there's very little point. "Anyway, they're keen to push for Cambridge, apparently, but they know it's going to be really tough. She starts throwing statistics at me about how many poor kids get Cambridge places compared with rich kids. Like I have some say in the matter."

"I'll be honest with you, Lydia—I'm completely lost here."

"So was I, to begin with." She takes a gulp of tea. "Her daughter wants to go into law, or criminology, or criminal law, I can't remember which, and she—Helen, I mean—feels that to have a chance at Cambridge, her daughter's going to have to do something really impressive to make herself stand out. Now, I'm not sure if it's part of the formal submissions process or just something for the CV, but her daughter decides that she wants to write a piece about Abby—specifically, a piece on how working-class female murder victims are portrayed in the media compared with their middle-class counterparts. Well, that stuff's my bread and butter and Helen thinks that if she can get some direct insights from me, it'll give the piece real clout. It'll show huge initiative on the part of the daughter."

"Just to be clear, she was still using the name 'Helen'?"

She cocks her head. "Yes. Why? Isn't that her name? Look, what the hell is this about?" It's her first show of anger, although I'm not sure who it's aimed at: me for stirring this up again or "Helen Something" for duping her twice.

I lean forward and put my mug on the table—I've drained it in two minutes flat. "I'm so sorry, Lydia. I honestly can't go into it in any detail at the moment, but I promise you, this is all really helpful."

Is it, though? Is it telling me anything about the murder of Naomi Lockhart? No. So what am I doing here?

"I understand," she says, her anger quickly extinguished. "You'll have your reasons, I'm sure. It'd be great if you could share them as soon as you're able, though?"

I nod emphatically, then, "So was she trying to set up a meeting with her daughter, or was she wanting the information herself?"

"The latter."

"Bit odd?"

"Maybe." She thinks about it briefly. "Like I said, helicopter parenting gone mad. I got the impression the daughter didn't even know her mum was asking, actually. She seemed really excited at the thought of going *'ta-dah!'* and bringing her all this information from the horse's mouth, so to speak."

"I'm always proactive when it comes to Clara's education . . ."

"And the journalist thing?"

"She thought I'd respond better to a journalist. Me, of all people!"

"So you did talk to her, then—gave her an interview, or whatever it was she was after?"

She nods. "A bit. Once I knew she was just a pushy mum, I was happy to chat for a while. Don't get me wrong, I think you can be *too* involved in your child's life, and it doesn't always help them, but I understood where she was coming from. I understand the desire to give your child a leg up. Especially when the odds are stacked high enough against them."

"So what did you talk about?"

"How the media portrayed Abby. How they'd made so much of the fact that she'd grown up on the Paulsgrove, that she'd been dating this older petty criminal, staying at his pub overnight—*'Girls love a bad boy,'* all that nonsense. It was as though they were saying she somehow deserved it, or should have expected it. It makes me sick to my stomach." Her dazzling rage hasn't dimmed one watt in fifteen years. "Anyway, then we ended up having a much broader chat about how hard it is bringing up daughters on 'problematic' estates. Her daughter's more or less the same age as Abby was when she died, so we had a lot in common, really. I think she'd wanted more for her life and she was living vicariously through her daughter—and I'd felt like that too. I knew I was a good mum, despite what the papers wrote, but I'd thought that's all I was. Of course, I'd give anything for those days now, but it can be stifling."

"It was good of you to give her the time."

I glance at the clock behind her desk. If I'm out of here by two, I can see the sights for a few hours and still be back in London by teatime.

"I'd have probably given her more time, but then the conversation started to go down a path I didn't feel comfortable with so I decided against it, made my excuses."

"What path?"

"Oh, just more about the investigation: how it was going, new leads following the reconstruction, did the police do their job, that sort of thing." She pauses. "You see, I might not have always seen eye to eye with your employers, Cat, and God knows they have their own failings when it comes to handling working-class murders, male and female." I'm not even going to try to argue. "But I've always tried to work *with* the police. They're the ones who are going to find out what happened to Abby one day, not me. And I wouldn't want anything I say about them twisted, even if it is just in a student essay."

"Did she respect this?"

"Oh, definitely. She apologized and said she wasn't asking for her daughter's college work. She just wanted justice for Abby, like any mother would. I said 'fair enough' and that was that, really. We said goodbye." She turns to the clock and pulls an "eek" face—it's one fifty-five. As we stand, she keeps talking. "You know, I fully expected her to be in contact again, but I heard nothing after that.

A little note or a card or something to say thanks for my time—that would have been good manners, don't you think?"

"They're in short supply these days, my boss reckons."

"Well, I hope the daughter's got better manners because you don't go far in life without them, Cambridge or no Cambridge."

She walks me back to reception where, true to her word, she produces a ginormous ladybird-print umbrella.

I hope I never need the services of a family law solicitor, but if I do, I'm definitely choosing Lydia Coe.

"So *did* the reconstruction throw up anything new?" I ask as we hover at the top of the stairs.

"Yes and no. Lots of calls—only half of them crank. The problem's the lack of forensics, always has been. There's various sets of prints on file but it's a pub—well, it was back then. It's closed now, converted into flats." She stops, drawing in a deep, pained breath. "Stevens has got two kids now, you know? Two daughters." I open my mouth. "Oh, I have my ways, Cat. I might think the police were unwise to make him their only suspect, but I keep tabs on that man, don't you worry about that."

Remembering the other searches on Clara Madden's laptop—"*drug dealer attack stabbing Portsmouth*"—I steel myself to ask Lydia a final thorny question.

"Was Abby involved in drugs at all?"

"No." She's not offended, just resolute. "She lost an uncle and cousin to smack. There's no way."

"Did she know anyone who'd been stabbed, or attacked?"

"She grew up on the Paulsgrove, she'd seen violence." She blows out her cheeks. "As for whether she was friends with anyone . . . not to the best of my knowledge, but she was eighteen, she clearly didn't tell me everything.

"She told me she loved me a lot, though. That's all that matters now."

Between tourist attractions and delayed trains, it's gone six by the time I'm back in Dear Old London Town, straight into the onslaught of the peak-hour exodus. Slipping outside Waterloo Station, I dial Steele's number, gazing across at the London Eye and feeling like a tourist in my own town for one sentimental second.

Steele answers, singing a tuneless "Happy Birthday" with an equally tone-deaf Parnell in the background.

I laugh. "Thanks for that. Hey, are you still in the office?"

I'm keen to do this face-to-face. I always find phone bollockings *so* awkward.

"I'm not, as it happens. Where are you? Painting the town red somewhere? Well listen, don't go too mad. Big day ahead tomorrow— we have issues, although when don't we?"

"So do I, Boss. I need to talk to you—tonight preferably, if we've got other shit to deal with tomorrow. I want to try a theory out on you."

She mutters, *"She wants to try a theory out on me,"* to Parnell, who mutters something inaudible in return.

"That's fine. Lu says if you can get to his in the next forty minutes, you can try his Sin-free Creamy Tomato Courgetti as well. Isn't that a temptation?"

"You're at Parnell's?"

I don't know why this surprises me, they've known each other over two decades. Steele buys his kids Christmas presents, and there's a rumor Parnell once ran out to buy Steele tampons when she got caught short in an all-day meeting.

And anyway, I'm glad she's with someone. With Parnell as a witness, she can't actually kill me when I fess up to where I've been and what I've found out.

Although the question I keep returning to is, *What exactly have I found out?*

27

I'm turning the corner onto Parnell's leafy street when my phone rings: Rachel Madden.

My finger hovers. Answer. Reject. Answer. Reject. In the end, I do my duty.

"I'm so sorry," she says, instantly.

My body's in Finsbury Park but my head's still in Portsmouth, and for a split second I think she's apologizing for that. For lying to Lydia. For lying to me. For embarrassing Clara—there's no way on earth I'd have wanted my mum snooping around, playing fantasy journalists on my behalf. That's not pushy parenting, that's obsession.

"Honestly, I can hardly remember anything past waking up yesterday," she goes on. "Marcus said I was in a total state, Kirstie's hardly talking to me, and Clara's gone into a shell. I'm so, so sorry, Cat. You must think I'm terrible."

No, but I know you're a liar, I want to say. *I know you're hardier and wilier than the Poor Rachel you like to portray.* However, I can't say that, of course. We need her batting for our side, and if I think Steele's going to be pissed off with my off-the-record Portsmouth jaunt, Rachel Madden would burst a blood vessel.

"It's fine," I say—not clipped, not warm, just icily professional. "People say things they don't mean when they're drunk, although you said some pretty awful things about Naomi. You can't be saying those things, Rachel."

"Oh God, what did I say?"

"That what happened was her fault."

A long pause. "I'm sorry. I'm honestly mortified. I poured every bit of alcohol down the sink this morning, I promise. I need a clear head from now on, for Clara."

I'm outside Parnell's now, leaning on his gate, admiring his salmon-pink begonias. "Has Clara explained what she told me yesterday?"

"That she saw Joseph with that girl?"

"Naomi, Rachel. Her name was Naomi."

"I know, I know . . . it's just . . . I can't even say it . . . not after what my husband did." A noise—half cry, half gasp. "I just can't believe he *actually* did it, Cat. I can't wrap my head around it. Maybe I should have known, but I never thought he'd harm anyone but me. It's only ever me he wants to hurt."

I. Me. My. Mine. I haven't got the patience for her today. "Did Clara make an amended statement?"

She hesitates. "Somebody came around but she wasn't up to it. She'd been sick all morning—the stress, you know? Maybe if it had been you . . . Can't you take it, Cat? We know you. We feel comfortable with you." I don't say anything. She reads the silence perfectly. "OK, whoever then. She'll do it tomorrow, I promise. We always go to Marcus's for dinner on a Tuesday and I want to keep that as normal— Clara needs *some* normality—but apart from that she'll be in all day." She sighs. "I don't know when she's going to get back to college. She's falling behind already."

Back when Steele told me to play the *"You're the victim too"* card, I hadn't actually thought I was playing anything—I'd believed Rachel was a victim. The truth is the suspect's family often are. They're the ones left with the jibes and the judgment. They're the ones scrubbing graffiti off front doors, while the real villain's being asked if the temperature's OK in their cell and if they'd prefer the chicken or the fish for lunch.

It's hard to see her as a victim now, though. Naomi's family have had their lives rerouted in the worst way possible and Rachel Madden's focused on normality, on tomorrow night's dinner.

I say a quick, curt goodbye and trot down the path to Parnell's garish front door. He and Maggie let the boys choose the color a few weeks ago, sweet trusting fools that they are, and they chose bright green.

And I mean *bright* green—sunglasses-bright.

STONE COLD HEART | 245

I ring the bell. Steele opens the door.

"Nice umbrella," she says. "Was that a birthday present from Mr. X? I'd give him the push, if I were you."

Parnell comes into the hall, carrying a ridiculously large bunch of peach roses and white lilies, maybe fifty in total.

"Sarge, you really shouldn't . . ."

"Bloody hell, they're not from me." His voice is muffled by the gargantuan display. "Looks like Mr. X hasn't done too badly, after all. Although he shouldn't have sent them to work. They'd die a death with our central heating so I thought I'd save them for you."

"He hasn't done that well—aren't lilies funeral flowers?"

"Can be. They're a symbol of purity too."

A bark from Steele. I relieve Parnell and walk into the kitchen, quickly putting the bouquet down on the side. "God, I'll have to carry these all the way home now. I wish he hadn't bothered."

"That's gratitude for you." Parnell's turning up the heat on dinner—it smells as good as tomato courgetti's ever going to smell.

I join Steele at the table; only three places laid. "Maggie and the boys not dining with us? Or have they seen sense, gone up the chippy?"

He's doing something with basil leaves now—a sure sign he's trying to mask the taste of the main event. "Maggie's at her book club and the boys"—he points upstairs—"are watching *Danger Mouse*."

"And the puppy?" I ask, looking around.

"The kids' playroom. It's like Armageddon in there anyway, so if he destroys it, we'd barely notice." He puts a glass of white wine in front of me—it's dark, probably Chardonnay, but I'd drink anything right now. "Anyway, forget about me, how's your day been? What were you doing at Waterloo? Champagne on the Eye? Lunch at the Oxo Tower?"

"Mmm." I pick up my fork, the only artillery at hand. "Boss," I say, looking nervously at Steele. "I know you're going to shout at me, but I went to Portsmouth, OK?"

She folds her arms. "Well, it might be OK. Depends what you went for."

I throw her a sheepish glance. "Can we say I fancied a bit of sea air, and while I was there I *just happened* to bump into Lydia Coe? As it's my birthday, can we just say that? No shouting?"

"Fine by me," says Parnell over the spiralizer.

As I wait for the verdict, I lean back and prize the small card from my bouquet. I slip it from the envelope expecting to see Aiden's name.

Happy Birthday, Catrina. Hope you like the flowers—especially the roses. It's called a "Marianne" rose.
Uncle Frank x

Marianne. *Maryanne.* The merciless prick.

I can't even begin to think what this means right now.

"We can postpone the shouting, that's the best I can do." Steele's voice is tinny and remote as I try to stamp down the shock of seeing Frank's name. Maryanne's too. *"As it's your birthday,* I'll ignore the fact you completely ignored my instructions. Tomorrow, we'll do battle—how's that sound?"

It sounds as good as I'm going to get so I summarize. I'm actually glad of the opportunity to talk myself calm and by the time I've got to the end, got through the various arcs of Lydia and Abby's story, my head has stopped hammering and my pulse is a little steadier.

The tomato courgetti is also ready. We all hesitantly tuck in.

"So what's this theory you wanted to run by me?" Steele's chewing her food slowly, painfully.

"Oh, it's not really a theory, I suppose. I just think what Rachel did was bizarre—Lydia Coe called it 'helicopter parenting gone mad'—so I wanted to get your view, that's all. I mean, I know she's dedicated to Clara. I know she's focused on her education. But still . . . it was a bit extreme, don't you think?"

"Definitely, but then I don't have kids. To me, the Connors sound extreme. Mortgaging yourself to the hilt in an area you can't afford, just so your kid can play in a better class of sandpit? Sod that."

Parnell adds, "Rachel sounds more of a mix of tiger and helicopter mum to me." Steele grins at me—*get him.* "She wants Clara to excel, like the tiger mum, but she's happy to take on a lot of the pressure herself, like the helicopter mum. She'll go to extreme lengths to make her child's life easier."

Steele points her knife in my direction. "Come on then, out with it—what's bugging you? So what if Rachel's a solid ten on the pushy parent scale? It's got to be better than the alternative. Look at Joseph Madden—his mum didn't give a shit and that turned out well, didn't it?"

"So why lie when I asked about Portsmouth? Why all that guff about Clara going to uni there? Why not admit the real reason she'd gone?" I put my cutlery down, wincing at Parnell. "By the way, Sarge, this is disgusting. Sorry."

Steele bursts out laughing. "Fair play to you, Kinsella. I might just let you off a bollocking for that." She leans over, patting Parnell on the hand. "It's not your cooking, Lu, honestly."

"Gordon Ramsay couldn't make that shite taste nice," I add, supportively.

Parnell pretends to look hurt but it doesn't last long. He's chuckling by the time he opens the fridge door. "Cheese and crackers?"

"Now you're talking." I flick my head back. "Oh, and while you're up, bin that bouquet, would you? They're not from Mr. X, they're from an old flame. It's awkward."

Parnell whips around, frowning. "I will *not* bin them. There's £100 worth of flowers there! I'll keep them if you don't want them."

This is worse. The idea of Frank contaminating Parnell's snuggly family home.

He comes back to the table with not just cheese and crackers but crisps, cashew nuts, mini-samosas, and grapes, quickly picking up where we left off.

"I'd say she lied about Portsmouth because, like you say, it was a bit extreme. That journalist crap. It doesn't exactly show her in a great light."

"But she could have left that bit out," I insist. "Yeah, I'd still have thought she was a bit much but that would have been the end of it. It was the fact she was almost certainly lying that made me pursue it." I stuff a samosa in my mouth, chewing and thinking. "Look,

I just think we need to be mindful that she's not above deception when it suits her. And I know I'm jumping the gun here, Boss, but I'd be wary of putting her on the stand if it goes to trial. God, can you imagine if Stein got wind of that journalist stunt? He'd have a field day."

"He's having a field day anyway." A worried look passes between Steele and Parnell. "I told you, we have issues. We're in an 'evidential pickle' according to that smarmy wanker."

"How? Her blood's on his gloves. What's he saying? That Naomi had a nosebleed on him?" I give a derisive snort. "He'd have to admit to knowing her first to make that one work."

"Don't joke," says Parnell. "He *could* claim something like that yet. And without firm evidence he was in her house that night . . ."

"Er, his lovely black hair in her lovely clean bed?"

"Transference," chorus Steele and Parnell, infinitely more tuneful than their attempt at "Happy Birthday."

"OK, well, have we got the bedsheets back yet? If they were clean on that morning and his DNA's on them?"

"No, there's a backlog at the lab," says Steele. "Bedsheets take a while at the best of times—and you don't even want to know the estimate on the mattress. You think we're understaffed—they're chronic."

"So what's giving Stein his stiffy then?"

"The gift box." She spears a chunk of Stilton, eats it directly off the knife.

I'd forgotten about the gift box. In the pantheon of evidence, it's a fairly low-score Top Trump. "What's wrong with the bloody gift box?"

"Naomi's prints aren't anywhere on it. Joseph's *are* but only on the gift tag. And it's a shiny, glossy cardboard box—lab says it should be perfect for lifting prints, but nada."

"It *could* be an anomaly, just one of those things," mumbles Parnell with a worrying lack of conviction. "It's not the end of the world."

He's right, it isn't. Every case has that *thing*, sometimes more than one thing, that doesn't quite fit the narrative. The perfect murder might exist but the perfect solve sure as hell doesn't.

So this isn't seismic, just annoying. A tiny tugged thread in the tapestry of guilt.

Steele's not so sure. "It's not a major piece of evidence, no. But do you know what it is? It's the *first* piece of evidence that pointed us toward Joseph Madden, and *that* makes it major. Sure, Kirstie showed us that photo of the two of them talking, but would we really have got our knickers in a twist about that on its own? Madden said it himself, a photo just captures a fleeting moment. The gift box was far more damning." She stares at me as if to say, *"Thoughts?"*

I gather them quickly. "Well, there's two—no, actually, three options. First: both of them were wearing gloves when the gift was exchanged."

"And when he bought it? And when she put it in the drawer?" Parnell shoots that theory down as quickly as it deserves.

"Agreed. So the second option is it's been wiped."

Steele groans, which isn't a good sign. She should be hopping up and down, asking me if I'm stark raving mad.

"The third option," I say, so reticently I'm practically hiding under the table. "And I'm *not* saying it's what happened, I'm just covering all bases, OK? Someone wearing gloves planted the box in Naomi's drawer."

Silence. Just the theme from *Danger Mouse* drifting from upstairs.

Steele nods, gravely. "That's pretty much what the lab said. A complete lack of prints *suggests* a deliberate wipe or a plant by someone wearing gloves. Which *could* mean, of course, that Madden's telling the truth. He's being framed."

"It's a huge leap, Kate," says Parnell, trying to soothe the tension. "We need to think it through properly. We've dealt with trickier pieces of evidence in the past."

I jump in. "Yeah, but we haven't dealt with a framing defense before. You're right, Sarge, we need to think this through. So listen, Naomi and Joseph wearing gloves for the *entire* time the box was in both their possessions, that's the only explanation that *isn't* dodgy, right? And we all agree that's pretty unlikely?" Nods. "As for the box being wiped—why would anyone do that? If you're the guilty party and you somehow got access to Naomi's drawer, surely you'd just take the box. You wouldn't wipe it and put it back. So that leaves us with it being planted. It's the most horrific option, but it's the most plausible, you've got to admit that."

They admit nothing. They say nothing. Parnell pops a grape in his mouth and stares off into the middle distance.

In the gap, an atomic theory forms.

I say it super-quick before I think better of it. Before I know whether I even believe it. "Maybe Kirstie Connor's framing Joseph?"

Again, I'd love a hissy fit from Steele, but worryingly, she's all ears.

I keep going, my brain working overtime to keep one step ahead of my mouth. "It was Kirstie Connor who showed us the photo. It's Kirstie Connor who's got easy access to Naomi's drawer. Joseph Madden admitted he'd sent Kirstie gifts in the past so maybe she'd kept hold of a few gift tags. Memento-hoarding, that's typical of unrequited love, right? And Madden did say she was gutted when he finished their affair." I pause. "Although, has anyone confirmed that definitely happened?"

"We have, would you believe." Steele's voice is sing-song, loaded with sarcasm. "Imagine that, eh, Lu? Work still getting done when the super-sleuth's out of the office." I stick my tongue out: *point taken*. "Renée paid Kirstie Connor a visit earlier. She tells a very different story from him, though. It meant nothing to her. It was just a cheap thrill while she and Marcus were going through a bad patch. And she says *she* finished it. The guilt over Rachel was killing her, poor love."

"I'd nearly believe Madden over her," says Parnell.

"Exactly." I'm still picking up pace, ideas forming faster than I can share them. "So is there any way of dating the gift tag? Can we tell by how ingrained the ink is whether it was written recently or years ago?"

"This isn't *CSI*," says Steele with a heavy dose of side-eye.

I ignore her, still on my roll. "And, you know, Madden said he hadn't seen those leather gloves in a long time. Maybe Kirstie had them? Maybe she was the one who bought them for him and she thought 'sod you' and pinched them back when he ended it."

Parnell, skeptical but always open-minded, adds, "She's also the one who told us about Joseph strangling Rachel."

"Has Rachel confirmed that?" asks Steele.

I shake my head. "Not yet. I'd have asked her yesterday, but she was hammered, there was no point." I could have asked her just now, of course, but it's not really a phone question. I'd want to see the whites of her eyes, the set of her jaw. I look from Steele to Parnell, gauging if they're on board at all with my shot in the dark. "Hey, look, it's just a theory, that's all. The scorned woman framing her ex-lover."

"The old hell hath no fury?" Steele sounds dubious. "What you seem to be forgetting is that if your theory plays, it means Kirstie killed Naomi. Why?"

"Why not?" I say, more brazen than I feel. "If she still has it bad for Madden, she wouldn't take kindly to him shagging her meek little PA, would she? And we said right at the beginning, it *could* be a woman, remember—when Vickery said Naomi's face had been slapped?" Steele nods quietly, taking it all in. "It's a bit weaker but it could even be a financial thing. Evie Whitlock, remember her? She implied Kirstie's finances were more than a bit lax. She was invoicing clients with her own bank details, that sort of thing. If Naomi found that out, threatened to report her?"

"Or an argument over drugs?" suggests Parnell. "Now we know what we know."

I take a deep breath. "Look, I'm really stirring the pot here, but we know there was a phone call between Rachel and Kirstie around one a.m. that night. What if they're in it together?"

Parnell rubs his chin. "What, Kirstie kills Naomi and calls Rachel to help? Why would Rachel help her? It'd work better the other way around—*Rachel* kills Naomi and gets Kirstie to help *her* by planting the gift box. We know Kirstie's desperate to make it up to Rachel after the affair with Joseph."

"What's Rachel's motive?" asks Steele.

"Jealous rage," says Parnell. "Same as Kirstie. I know Naomi's not the first, but everyone has a tipping point."

Steele's jiggling a fistful of cashews. "But Rachel Madden's been adamant all along that he didn't do it—well, she was until he was charged. Why defend him if she's involved? Surely she'd be trying to stir the pot, to quote the birthday girl."

The birthday girl's got this. "If she defends him, it makes Joseph's claims that she's lying about his alibi seem ridiculous. And actually, the more I think about it, why wouldn't she just alibi Joseph if she honestly believed he was innocent? Wives lie for their husbands all the time, especially wives of abusive men."

Steele's straight back at me. "Yes, but the problem with it being Rachel is that Joseph Madden puts her at home that night. He *claims* she threw a photo frame at him when he got back, remember? And if she wasn't there, I can't see him making that up to cover for her, can you? Not when the finger's being pointed at him."

"He only puts her at home when he *supposedly* gets back at twelve fifteen. And if he did end up sleeping downstairs, he wouldn't know for sure whether she'd gone out again, especially if he'd taken a Temazepam."

Parnell points a finger at me. "'Course, the problem with Kirstie being involved is that Marcus Connor *definitely* puts Kirstie at home all night—wasted, comatose."

"Marcus might be covering for Kirstie," I say. "He's definitely no fan of Joseph. Maybe he's known about their affair all along and he's happy to see him go down."

"I dare say he is. But covering for a murder? That's a big ask."

"You wouldn't cover for Maggie, no?"

Parnell's chest goes out. "I'm a police officer, Cat. And anyway, you promise to love, honor, and obey, you don't promise to help bury the body." He's quiet for a second, pondering his scruples. "Maybe— *maybe*—I'd bend the rules for my kids, but Maggie?" He shakes his head. "No way. She'd have to face the consequences, I'm afraid."

"Hold on—you're saying you'd break the law to protect your kids?" Something throws my breath out of sync, a sudden drop in air pressure.

"I said I *might*."

And there it is, clear as day.

So might Rachel Madden.

She proved with that Portsmouth stunt just how committed she is to making Clara's life easier. There's no way she'd mess up her life, her education, her prospects, by framing her dad for murder—not for as lame a reason as marital revenge.

She might do it to cover up her crime, though.

"Clara," whispers Parnell, reading my mind.

"Clara?" says Steele, not half as quiet. "Bloody hell, what is this? A game of Happy Families? Well, Unhappy Families."

I stand up; movement always gets my brain working faster. "Think about it. Maybe Madden's refusing to say who's framing him because he knows his daughter killed Naomi. He's afraid of it coming out. Seriously, watch the video again—he says, *'Who it is isn't important,'* and *'I want you to focus on me.'* He's basically saying he wants us to find the evidence that exonerates him, but not to bother looking too closely at who the real culprit is—as if that was ever going to wash. But that *could* be what he's doing—he could be protecting his daughter."

". . . you're still my baby and I won't let anything bad happen to you. Protection—that's what fathers do . . ."

"Would he protect her, though?" says Steele, her face scrunched into a tight ball. "Would he care enough? Not according to Rachel. Not according to Dolores's assessment either. And stop bloody pacing, would you?"

I stop but I still need movement. I pluck an apple from a fruit bowl, throw it from hand to hand. "Well, I think we know we can't trust Rachel, and Dr. Allen's wasn't a formal assessment. Sure, a lot of what she said fit his profile, but it wasn't a clinical diagnosis."

Parnell backs me up. "There's plenty of terrible men who still care about their kids, Kate, in their own warped way. Don't you remember Timmy Grey, back in the nineties? Raped six young women but still cried like a baby when he was told his youngest had to have her appendix out. Other people's kids aren't their kids, that's the way those bastards see it."

I sit back down again, leaning in, mainly toward Steele. "Just hear me out, OK? We said it before—a woman *could* have done it. Also, Clara's got a temper. I've seen it firsthand, and we know she hit a girl at college."

"Renée went there this morning," says Parnell. "Head of Year reckons there wasn't much in it, and he had harsher words for the girl Clara hit, apparently. Clara's been the target of bullying for a while."

"OK, so that means she's been under a lot of pressure, maybe nearing breaking point? We also know there's no love lost between her and her dad, and I thought at the time that she seemed to accept his guilt a bit too easily. *'You wouldn't have charged him without good reason.'* Come on, Boss—you usually expect more kickback from the family than that."

"Motive?" says Steele, staring me down.

This is what I need more time with. Protecting Clara is the *only* way I can make sense of Rachel's and Joseph's actions, but why would Clara harm Naomi? If she'd been mad about their relationship, surely she'd have reacted weeks ago, when she first saw them outside The Grindhouse.

If she did see them outside The Grindhouse.

"I'm not sure," I admit, also not sure Steele will take much more hypothesizing. "We know she was at the Connors' house and left early on. She says Naomi hadn't arrived by then, but we don't know that for definite and if all the adults are covering for her . . . We need to go back to Kirstie's employees, see if they can put Clara and Naomi at the party at the same time. It'd be something, at least. I don't know, maybe she cornered Naomi at the party, told her to back off her dad and Naomi told her to get lost?"

Steele leans in, arms folded. "Clara's grown up with it. She knows what he's like. Why flip over this one? And how would she know where Naomi lived?"

"Can't answer that one. But as for why she'd flip—Naomi being so young could have triggered something." Parnell doesn't look convinced. "I'm telling you, Sarge—dads and daughters, it's complicated. Be grateful you have boys."

What I don't share is that about a year after Mum died, Dad dated a twenty-eight-year-old nail technician with scarlet red hair and an aversion to bras. Let's just say it didn't end well for any of us. It's hard to explain, but when they're only a few years older than you, it somehow stings a lot more.

Parnell's still uneasy. "Look, I get where you're going with this, Cat, and I'm not saying it's without merit, but what I still don't understand is, why frame Joseph? If Kirstie killed Naomi, or Rachel did, or Clara did and Rachel's covering for her, why not just walk away from the situation as quietly as you can? Framing Joseph brings the spotlight back on them and surely that's the last thing they'd want?"

I don't have a great answer right now, so instead I offer the best I can manage at short notice. "To be honest, Sarge, I'm struggling a bit with Kirstie. But Rachel—maybe she sees it as a way to get him out of her life, once and for all? I mean, he's an abusive pig—we know that—and abusive pigs don't just let you walk away. He'd never give her a divorce, and he'd make her life hell if she went ahead and got one. Getting him sent away for murder gives her fifteen to twenty years' peace, at least."

Parnell doesn't disagree, although maybe he doesn't have the energy. All this hypothesizing saps your strength after a while.

Right on cue, Steele yawns. "Remind me, what do we know about Clara's movements on Saturday night to Sunday morning?"

"She was in her room listening to music then asleep. But we've only got her and Rachel's word for that. We don't know anything for sure."

She brings a hand down on the table.

"And that's precisely it. We don't *know* anything. This is all conjecture. We're letting one piece of problematic evidence make us go shooting off in ten different directions." She stops for a minute, thinking, breathing heavily. "OK, so tomorrow morning, go back and interview Kirstie's employees about what time Clara left, but be damn subtle about it. Find something else to talk to them about and throw it in casually. Then, after I've had my morning catch-up with Blake"—sarcastic jazz-hands at the thought—"*I'll* request cell site analysis on the three women's phones and ANPR traces on Rachel's and Kirstie's cars, but—and this is a career-ending *but*, by the way—this is completely hush-hush: not a living soul outside the immediate team, OK? Because if Stein gets the slightest wind of us contemplating alternative theories, we're fucked, *mes amis*. Fucked. Naomi's blood won't mean a thing if he can prove all three women *could* have had access to his gloves, and if that happens, shame on us, because I still believe Madden's our man. I really do."

I can hear it in her voice, though. I can smell it in the air: sour, like off milk. It's in the acrid taste that coats the back of my throat, slowly drip, drip, dripping into the lining of my gut.

Doubt.

Two hours later. Aiden's flat. Bed. A wonderfully low-key end to a high-stress birthday and without a sliver of a doubt, no place on earth I'd rather be. My presents are scattered at the foot of the bed—boots, books, a sky-blue slip dress that makes me feel all grown-up and chic, and a receipt for a washing machine to be fitted next week.

They're perfect. *He's* perfect.

Mr. Perfect himself is dozing in front of a documentary about sharks while I catch up on messages, mainly the barrage from my sister.

Jacqui's not happy, but then again, what's new?

> *"U got a b'day card from Frank & Cynth?? WTF?? Last card I had was my 18th. Bet there was £ in it too!?!?"*   22:58

I daren't tell her about the flowers. I daren't tell anyone except Dad. I won't tell him tonight, though. I can't face the facade of him playing it down when we both know Frank's circling for a reason.

> *"There was ££££. I gave it back"*   22:59

A few minutes' reprieve before my phone pings again, stirring Aiden.

> *"Oh to be that rich! U could have given to me ☺ Car on last legs. Might have to tap Dad up."*   23:03

> *"Your car's been on its last legs since 1972. Can't tap Dad up, he spent all his money on my b'day ☺ ☺ ☺"*   23:05

> *"Wouldn't surprise me. Maybe I should start ignoring him. Works for you."*   23:06

"You don't do too badly. How's that lovely loft conversion that Dad COMPLETELY FINANCED."   23:09

"That's a loan."   23:09

"Yeah right."   23:10

"Whatevs. When am I seeing you?? You're gonna love your present."   23:11

"Is it Sparkle Beach Barbie? You promised that in 1999, still waiting . . ."   23:13

"☺ ☺ ☺ you didn't answer my question—when?"   23:13

"When? When? When? Soon."   23:14

"S'cuse me for wanting to see my baby sister. Anyway bed time. Happy b'day again. Love u xxxxx"   23:16

And now I feel bad.

Aiden rolls onto his belly, looking up at me with drowsy blue eyes. "You know, you shouldn't stare at your screen before sleep. It stops your brain releasing melatonin."

"Does it really? And what's that, clever-clogs?"

"The hormone that tells your body it's nighttime."

I point at the TV, the small flat-screen mounted on the wall. "Does that not count, then? Does watching programs about killer sharks guarantee a good night's sleep?"

He prods me in the hip. "Actually, smart-arse, sharks only kill four humans a year, whereas humans kill twenty-five million sharks."

"That's some seriously sexy bedtime chat. Tell me more."

He comes up onto his elbows. "OK, how about this: some species of shark are carnivorous in the womb. The first pup to hatch eats all its other siblings. Pretty gross, huh?"

Or expedient. Saves all the heartache that having siblings inevitably brings.

Take Aiden. His heart ripped out by Maryanne, twice. First when she disappeared and eighteen years later, when she was found murdered.

Take me and my brother, Noel, the unashamed leech. I'd have cheerfully eaten him. I hope he rots in that Spanish jail.

And take Marcus Connor. Charity-owner. MBE. But still dragged into the gutter, largely due to his sister's taste in men.

But then there's siblings like Jacqui, I suppose, clucky and naggy but loving and safe. And Alana Lockhart. She and Naomi were best friends, really. Confidantes. Swapping secrets and in-jokes and photos every day.

Photos.

I kiss the top of Aiden's head. "I'm just going to check one more thing, OK? Then I'll release the melatonin, or whatever I'm supposed to do."

He goes back to his sharks and I swipe up to find the message Alana Lockhart sent me this morning. I feel bad that I just glanced at it. I feel worse that I only replied *"Thanks."*

Recent snaps of Naz—all the photos you've got are old, apart from that one in the Standard. *Alana L. 7:04*

I scroll through slowly, determined to find something meaningful to say. That's why Alana sent them to me, after all, to remind me that Naomi was a *recent* human being. Not just the dead girl in the morgue or the blond chick back in Oz.

She's the tourist by Big Ben the night before she died.

She's the thrift-freak hunting for biker jackets at Portobello last Sunday morning.

She's the girl at the Soho Hotel, grinning madly beside the cat sculpture. *27 October—11:42.*

I stare at the last photo, or rather the date and time header, feeling the rumblings of something crucial. Something that isn't conjecture, but simple hard fact. My mind whirs, tracing timelines, wondering if this might be the piece of the jigsaw that makes everything else fall into place.

Because Steele was right. We didn't *know* anything earlier. Everything about Rachel, Kirstie, Clara, that *was* all conjecture, even if it felt like we were sailing tantalizingly close to the truth at times.

But *I* do know something now.

I know that on the 27th of October 2017, Naomi Lockhart still had honey-blond hair.

Which means I won't be interviewing any of Kirstie's employees tomorrow morning.

There's somewhere far more important I need to be.

28

Tuesday

I'm back at Finsbury Park again by seven thirty the next morning. A long, early schlep for a defected south Londoner like me.

"You should have stayed at mine," says Parnell as I plonk into his passenger seat. "It'd have saved you all that faffing about on tubes."

"And if I could see the future, I probably would have done." I buckle myself in. "Anyway, I'm good at faffing about on tubes. You get good at it when you don't have your own car and your sergeant hardly ever lets you drive."

"Yeah, yeah." He pulls away, only managing twenty meters before we have to stop again. "So did you get hold of her then, Alana Lockhart? Because you know, those date and time things aren't foolproof. We've got to be 100 percent sure before we take this to the top."

The top being Chief Superintendent Blake. The repercussions of this go way above even Steele's important head.

"I did, and I'm sure. Naomi dyed her hair lilac on Sunday the 29th, a whole four days *after* Madden's car was booked into Shelby's garage."

"Where it stayed until our guys removed it last week." A fretful side-glance. "So how the hell did those hairs wind up in Madden's car?"

"Either he broke into the garage and had a bunk-up with Naomi in his car for some mad reason, or someone else got access and planted them."

"Shit."

"Quite."

We drive the five miles to Arnos Grove in virtual silence. We don't battle for supremacy of the radio, or even chat about the theories we cast into the wind last night. I actually manage to switch off entirely from the journey, losing myself in my own reflection and thoughts of Joseph Madden imploring me to do my job; to find the evidence that exonerates him.

Well, I'm doing my job now, Joseph, although I can't promise you'll like what I find.

"This is it," says Parnell, pulling up the hand brake somewhere between fifteen and fifty minutes later.

"It" is a repair garage, tucked away at the end of a quiet residential street off the North Circular. To me, it looks like every other garage I've ever been to. Tires. Dust. Debris. Men. The steel gates are open, and even though it's still early, there's already one guy hard at work on the front wheel of a Ford Focus and another wearing an eye mask, blasting rust off an old Jag.

And a third guy drinking tea, of course.

"Marc Shelby," I shout, just as the sound of the rust contraption cuts out.

"Who's asking?" says the tea-drinker.

I wave my warrant card. "We need to talk to you about a car you recently worked on. A Mazda convertible, registration SB52 VDX."

"Oh right, *him.* I wasn't here when your lot came to take his car away but tell them cheers, would you? I was sick of looking at it. They did me a favor." A long slurp of tea. "Yeah, Joseph Madden, cocky little wanker—never had him down as a murderer, though."

Which probably isn't what he tells his mates down the pub.

"He had these cold, staring eyes, bruv. I always said he looked evil."

"Cocky wanker?" repeats Parnell, shaking Shelby's hand. "We were under the impression that you were friends. His wife said you gave him mates' rates."

The mug stops halfway to his mouth. "Mates? Me and Joseph? Jesus! He talks to me like I'm brain-dead most of the time. Doesn't strike me as the kind of bloke who's got many mates. I used to try and talk to him about the football but he wasn't interested. He likes golf, he said. So next time he comes in, I try to talk to him about the golf. Didn't get very far. Up himself kinda bloke, you know what I mean?"

"So no mates' rates?"

"Well, kind of, but it's not out of mateyness. How it works is, I give him a good discount on the understanding that when it comes to his motor, I'll get around to it when I get around to it. He doesn't actually *need* a car, see, so he's always been happy with the arrangement. Same when my dad had the place. He's been coming here for years." He eyes us warily. "Here, why are you asking about my rates, anyway? It's all aboveboard here, no cash in hand."

"Relax," I say. "We're not here about your rates, or even the car, as such." Parnell's taking in a panoramic view of Shelby's oil-and-grease empire. "Have you had any break-ins recently? I mean, *very* recently. Perhaps nothing was even taken but you got a sense that something wasn't right?"

"You'd have a job breaking in here, love. My old man, he was *super* security-conscious. You have to be when you're on a quiet side street and there's no council cameras backing you up. Thieves think you're easy pickings, see." He starts pointing off in different directions. "But you can see for yourself, besides the camera on the main forecourt, we've got spikes on the fence and the same on the main gate—you'd have to be desperate *and* a pole-vaulter to get over either of them. And then we've got the roller shutter on the main garage and office. Good luck trying to take my livelihood, I say."

Good on him. "To go back to the car for a minute—you checked it in on the 25th of October, is that right?" He nods. "Do you want to go and check? It's important, we need to be sure."

"I can, but I know it was the 25th. It was my old man's anniversary—two years gone. I checked Madden's car in then nipped up the cemetery."

"OK." I decide against sending him off—he's unlikely to have got the date wrong and anyway, Forensics would have checked the docket. "And our forensics team took the car away on the morning of Thursday the 9th of November. So in those . . ." I tot it up quickly, ". . . fifteen days, did Joseph ever come back here, maybe ask to take it out for a quick spin? Could he do that if you hadn't started work on it?"

"He could. He didn't, though. And if he spoke to one of the other lads, they'd have checked with me first, no question."

"Are you closed Sundays?" asks Parnell.

"Too right I am."

"OK, so between Monday the 6th of November and Thursday the 9th of November, did anyone come to look at Madden's car?"

He laughs, confused more than amused. "Look at it? It's not a Lamborghini."

I explain. "We mean his wife, maybe his daughter . . ." I'm being so casual and airy here, I'm in danger of floating off above the nasty spiked gates. "Did either of them stop by, pick anything up? Surely people leave things in their car all the time and only realize when they need them?"

"Happens now and again," he says, nodding. "But I didn't see them and I'd recognize his wife, at least, I've done work on her car in the past too. And look, I might not be one of the branded big boys, but I run a tight business here, and if someone did come in wanting access to the car, someone who wasn't the registered owner, the lads would send them to me to authorize it, even if it was a family member. I don't take risks with my customers' motors, even tosser customers like Joseph Madden."

Parnell and I look at each other, out of ideas, close to stumped.

"So where was Madden's car parked?" asks Parnell.

"Last bay over there."

Parnell ambles over. I dutifully traipse behind, slightly bewildered by what he's hoping to find. A trapdoor? A tunnel? A *Mission Impossible*–style cable wire?

"Oi, wait up," calls Shelby, trailing us across the tarmac. "I always play a straight bat with the police so I should probably tell you, I had Joseph's car back at mine that weekend—the fireworks weekend."

We spin around so fast, it's practically a synchronized pirouette.

Shelby's defensive. "What? Nothing wrong with that. Sometimes the only time I can get around to those 'mates' rates' jobs is over the weekend, and I'm damned if I'm spending my weekends here too."

Parnell speaks slowly. "So Madden's car was parked *where* from Saturday the 4th of November until Monday morning, I presume?"

"Yeah, I drove it in myself. It was parked on my drive."

"Bit risky, surely? I thought you didn't take risks with customers' motors?"

"I've got business insurance, mate, don't you worry about that. And there's no one more security-conscious than me, not after I got burgled twice in as many years. Trust me, no one sets foot near my house without me knowing about it."

Hope rises.

"How do you mean?" I almost fall over the words.

"Got myself a top-of-the-range pan-tilt-zoom jobbie, thank you very much. I didn't have a summer holiday this year to pay for it, but it's worth every penny."

Accurately translated: he's got home CCTV.

Roughly translated as: this could crack open our case.

"Well, I never thought I'd say this, but God bless the lowlifes who ransacked his house. I'd buy them a drink if they were here now. I'd buy them several."

Steele does a little dance, sweeping Swaines into a waltz, which he's neither familiar with nor prepared for. I love her when she's like this. Twinkly and bullish, with total trust in the murder gods to deliver. It's hard not to get swept along.

Although it could be premature. Two hours in and still nothing.

Swaines has a bunch of comrades this afternoon. Usually he's MIT4's sole CCTV desk jockey, but with over thirty hours of footage from the front of Marc Shelby's house, the team are pulling together like never before—seven of us in total, taking five-hour chunks each. I'm on the Sunday four a.m. to nine a.m. slot. So far just a paperboy and a pensioner on a slow jog are the only people to have gone anywhere near Joseph Madden's car.

Parnell's dodged the CCTV drudgery by offering to cover all other side jobs, and, amusingly, Steele's taken responsibility for making the tea so that none of us have to leave our screens, other than to go to the toilet.

It's like working in a call center, and the pay's probably not much better.

"Do you know what this hair business also means," announces Steele at one point, marching between desks. "It means Clara Madden lied about seeing her dad with Naomi a month ago. I went through her statement again and she insists Naomi had long lilac hair. She's adamant about it. She says it's why she remembers her."

"Boss, what do we do about Madden, you know . . ." I leave the "if" part unsaid. It still feels unreal saying it out loud and, bizarrely, it feels like a betrayal of Naomi. An admission that we've failed her.

"We leave him where he is for now. He isn't going anywhere until we've got beyond-doubt proof that he didn't do this, and right now, a gift box without prints and The Curious Case of the Lilac Hairs isn't enough for me to go groveling to Stein." She pretends to vomit at the thought. "*But*, if we have got it wrong—and I'll argue long and loud to the powers-that-be that we didn't get it 'wrong,' we just followed the evidence—then we need to make sure we get it right this time. No room for doubt. No anomalies."

A shout from the corner: Emily Beck. "Got it! Over here, Boss."

Emily's on the Sunday ten p.m. to two a.m. slot. The fever in her voice has us swarming around her desk in seconds, nudging each other out of the way, jostling for prime position. Emily winds back the footage, reveling in the glory. Steele gnaws at a knuckle. Renée whispers, *"Please God."*

"It's not perfect, it's a bit fuzzy, but it's definitely female." She stops the footage a few seconds before the shape comes into view. "Tall, slim build. You can only see the side of her face, though, and then only for a few seconds. And you can't see what she's doing once she gets in."

I don't need to see her face. I know her by the way she walks. By the way she opens the car door and slides effortlessly into the passenger seat. Quick. Graceful. As fluid a movement as you'll ever see.

You never lose that ballerina gait.

It's definitely Rachel Madden.

And we can definitely take a guess at what she's doing. Planting Naomi's hair in Joseph's car, either to cover for herself or to cover for Clara. My money's on Clara.

"Bingo!" shouts Steele. "That'll do me, we've worked with fuzzier."

"Er, not wanting to kill the mood." Parnell's arrived into the throng. "But the ANPR trace on Rachel's car—and Kirstie's, for that matter—hasn't thrown up anything for Saturday-night-stroke-Sunday-morning. I'll put in another request now to trace Rachel's car on Sunday night. If it puts her near Shelby's house, at least we don't need to worry about fuzzy footage."

Renée pipes up, "You know, from the Pendown to where Naomi lives off Turnpike Lane—someone needs to check, of course—but it's *possible* you could make that drive through the backstreets without hitting any main roads. Without hitting ANPR, I mean."

Swaines doesn't need to be told; he trots off like a good boy.

"Or you could walk to Naomi's from the Maddens' place," I say. "It's only around a mile, and that's what we initially assumed Joseph was doing when we picked him up on CCTV."

Steele's commands come thick and fast. "Right, pull Rachel Madden in. And Clara Madden—we need to find out why she lied about seeing her dad with Naomi. I'll sort out an appropriate adult for her now. And while we're at it, pick up Kirstie Connor. She's the one who could have planted the gift box the easiest. She hates Madden and she's lied to us in the past—she could be helping Rachel." She raises her voice another notch. "I want those three women under this roof within the hour, OK? And they aren't leaving until we know exactly who's been lying about what, and why."

There's a fair chance one or more of them won't be leaving here at all.

29

Rachel and Clara are having dinner at Kirstie's. All our suspects in one place, completely unsuspecting.

You could work your full thirty years and never get that luck.

So, exactly one whole week since we first stood in the Connors' unfinished kitchen, Parnell's leaning against the fridge again, doling out even worse news.

"My God, are they under arrest?" asks Marcus, scarcely believing the answer could be yes.

Clara's clutching Rachel. Kirstie's holding Danny in front of her, her button-nosed battle shield. Their faces are the color of dried glue.

"Not at present," I reply. "We'd like all three of you to accompany us to the station for a voluntary interview under caution. You can refuse, of course, but then we can consider exercising our powers of arrest."

I don't sound like me. I sound too formal and austere, like I've got a *"rod up my backside"* as Parnell sometimes says. I'm doing it for Rachel, though. I want her to know that we can all have two sides. We can all pretend to be something we're not.

"But why? What do you think we've done?" Rachel's hand flutters against her chest, the other clamped to her cheek. An acting master class in *"How to look shocked."* I can't believe I didn't see it before.

"I'm not going to divulge that now, Rachel. We'll explain in detail at the station." I sweep an arm, ushering them out of the kitchen. "Now, if you could make your way outside, please? I'd recommend bringing something warm."

"Do they need solicitors?" asks Marcus, still reeling. "And Christ, what am I going to do with Danny? I'll have to call Kirstie's sister . . ."

"They are entitled to legal representation but it isn't compulsory and it can slow things down." I look to Clara. "We'll arrange for an appropriate adult to be present throughout your interview."

Clara's frozen solid, still clutching her mum like it's her first day at school.

"Can Uncle Marcus be my appropriate adult?" she says, just an octave above a whisper. "I don't want to talk in front of a stranger."

Rachel's hunched in the chair, a knitted white cardigan draped loosely over her shoulders. She looks brittle, insubstantial. As if two harsh words could crumble her to dust.

Which is probably the look she's aiming for. The "Poor Rachel" prototype.

"Was Joseph here, in this room?"

That's the first thing she asks us after we've gone through the formalities. "Us" being me and Renée. "Poor Rachel" doesn't respond all that well to men.

"It's just . . . I swear I can smell him. That sweet minty cologne he wears. I've never been able to stand it, but then, he doesn't wear it for me."

"Rachel, we're not here to talk about Joseph. We're here to talk about you."

"Me?" she says, as if no one's ever shown an interest before.

"Yes, you. Specifically this." I spin my laptop around and click play. "For the benefit of the tape, I am showing Rachel CCTV footage taken from outside the house of Marc Shelby. The location is 34 Kingsbrook Lane, Arnos Grove, London, and the date is Monday the 6th of November: the time is precisely 1:05 a.m. Can you confirm this is you, Rachel?"

She leans forward; the cardigan slips off her shoulders. After a long, vague stare, "Yes, that's me."

"Can you explain to us what you were doing there?"

She dips down to retrieve the cardigan, wiping dust off the arm. When she looks up again, there's a new expression on her face: defiance. "Look, I needed a cigarette. I was dying for one and I knew there were some in his car." She points at the laptop. "That's what I'm doing there, getting them out of the armrest."

Renée peers over the rim of her glasses. "You were that desperate you drove a six-mile round trip in the early hours of the morning?"

"There's a twenty-four-hour garage across from the estate," I point out.

"I had no money. Nothing. Joseph had left for Barcelona . . ." A shrill bark of laughter. "Sorry, Joseph had gone to *Croydon* and he didn't leave me any money, not even enough to get milk. It was a punishment. He'd been in a foul mood all day, jumping down my throat, even more than usual." She lifts a hand, drumming her fingers on the base of her throat. "Of course, now I know why."

A subtle reminder—*he did this*.

Renée picks up Rachel's statement. "You previously stated that Joseph was entirely normal the next day."

I join in. "Cooked roast lamb for lunch, didn't he? With proper roasties?"

She gives me a thin, irritated smile—*traitor*. "Yes, he did. And then later on he was foul. That's how he is. Changeable. Volatile."

"You should have told us that. We asked about his state of mind that day."

"I didn't want to show him in a bad light. I knew it would make things worse for him and I honestly didn't think he'd done it."

The pure, unadulterated front of her. I'll admit, I'm borderline impressed.

"So, that night." I point at the laptop again. "You got the craving for a cigarette and you had no money to buy them. Couldn't you have asked a neighbor?"

"At that time? You must have good neighbors, Cat. Besides, I fancied a drive. It helps me clear my head."

"Of what?"

"I had things on my mind—Joseph, Clara's issues, her uni applications. The fact that I was going to have to ask Marcus for more money and it was already a sore spot."

"Why were there cigarettes in Joseph's car?" asks Renée, abruptly.

"I left them in there a few weeks ago."

I tilt my head. "Really? That surprises me. Joseph loathes you smoking, thought you'd given it up, in fact, but you casually stash cigarettes in the armrest of his car?"

She shrugs.

"Oh, you'll have to do better than that, Rachel."

Problem is, she doesn't. Her explanation's laughable but it's just about plausible.

And she knows this; there's a clear confidence in her voice. "Look, why don't you just tell me what you think I was doing? Maybe then we'll get this cleared up and I can go to my daughter."

"Fair enough," I say, brightly, shifting in my seat, sitting upright. "We have reason to believe that hairs found in Joseph's car—hairs belonging to the victim, Naomi Lockhart—were planted. We also suspect that a gift box, found in Naomi's drawer and supposedly from Joseph, could also have been planted. Naturally, there's a strong possibility that whoever planted these also killed Naomi Lockhart, or at least knows who did." *Clear enough for you?*

She looks stunned but not stunned enough. Her shoulders aren't tense. The rise and fall of her chest stays the same. "Look, I'm sorry, I'm still a bit dazed by all this, and I can't remember what was said back at the house. Am I under arrest?"

"No, you can leave at any time. But it won't look good, let's put it that way."

"I don't care about looking good," she storms, humming with indignance. "I've done nothing wrong. Nor has Clara." *No defense of Kirstie.* "We're victims, me and Clara. You said so yourself."

I channel my Mean Girl. "I only said that to make you trust me, Rachel. Although I probably shouldn't have bothered because all you've told me is a pack of lies."

"I am *not* a liar."

"Lydia Coe would disagree."

Fuck it. We don't need her onside anymore.

Rachel doesn't flinch. Her eyes stay locked on mine. I leave space for her to say something, to ask me why the hell I've been talking to

Lydia Coe, but she says nothing. Complete and utter shutdown. After about fifteen to twenty seconds, even I start to find the silence a bit awkward.

Time to get to the crux.

"Do you know who else is a liar? Your daughter."

Straight back with us. "You leave Clara out of this."

"No can do," I say, feigning sorrow. "You see, it might be a little tricky disproving that you went on a one a.m. cigarette hunt, but we *can* prove that Clara lied about seeing Joseph with Naomi, and that means that after we've finished up here, I'm going to go a few doors up and charge your daughter with perverting the course of justice." I turn to Renée. "What do you reckon? Somewhere between one and three years?"

Rachel grips the table. "You wouldn't! No you wouldn't . . . how can you prove it?"

"That's really not your concern, and it's not a case of whether I would or I wouldn't. I have to. It's the law."

She reaches across the table, makes a futile grab for my hand. "Clara's not involved in all this. Please."

I pounce. "Not involved in all *what*, Rachel?" Her mouth opens then closes. She might have been about to tell us everything, or she might have been about to tell me to fuck off; we'll never know now. "Did you tell Clara to say she saw them together? Because if you did, and you admit that—and you admit your involvement in '*all this*'— maybe we can go a bit easier on her."

That look again: defiance. "I didn't tell her to do anything."

"Wow." I shake my head in a kind of appalled wonder. "You're *actually* sacrificing Clara to save yourself? At the very, very least, you're sacrificing her career. She'll never work in the criminal justice system now, you realize that? Not with that charge hanging over her."

In a flash, Poor Rachel's back, beaten, shaky. "*Please* leave her alone, I'm begging you. She must have been mistaken, that's all."

"Mistaken? No, that won't wash. Duress might, though. Being asked to lie by a much-loved parent, the only parent who's ever given a toss—*that's* quite a strong defense. Maybe even a mitigating circumstance. Don't you want to help your daughter?"

Nothing, although she's crying now. Not the *poor me* wailing of that drunken Sunday morning, just two fat tears followed by two more, then two more. A steady trickling fountain of regret.

I drive the nail in harder. "I thought you'd do anything for Clara? I thought you cared about her future?"

More nothing.

I sit back and watch her for a moment. A tragic sculpture, barely moving. Renée gives me a look that says *"this is pointless, let's wrap things up"* but I'm not quite finished yet.

"Do you know what I think, Rachel?" I fold my hands on the table, happy for her to make another grab. Happy to bond this time. "I think you *would* do anything for Clara. I think if it was as simple as you killing Naomi and framing Joseph, and Clara really did have nothing to do with it, apart from telling a lie for you, then you'd be spilling the beans right about now in exchange for giving Clara a free pass." She turns her head slightly—not quite looking at me, just a signal that she's listening. "And so I think the only reason you'd sit back and let Clara be charged with perverting the course of justice is because you know she's guilty of something far worse. And you also know that if you admit framing Joseph, we're going to want to know why, and we're not going to accept that it was over something so mundane as payback for being an utter pig. Basically, what I'm saying is: I think you'd only frame Joseph to protect someone else. The same person Joseph's trying to protect."

She stands up suddenly, hands opening and closing at her side. "You said I can leave if I want? I can walk out of this room right now?"

I look at Renée, who shrugs, presumably thinking the same as me: there's no harm in letting her leave—she won't go anywhere while Clara's still here.

I insist on seeing her out—a farcically civil gesture given I've effectively just accused her daughter of murder. When we get to reception, as expected, she doesn't head for the door but sits down. Chin high, back straight, challenging the world to even dare look at her.

————

Steele's buzzing around me as soon as I come back upstairs.

"Good work, lady. I reckon she'll crack as soon as she knows we mean business. I'm not sure she actually believes we'll charge Clara yet." She throws a finger in the direction of Interview Room Three. "Speaking of Clara, there's a delay."

"What's the problem?"

The flattest of stares. "She felt faint, apparently. Low blood sugar. She hasn't eaten since breakfast."

"Join the club, unless you count that meal-replacement shake I nicked off Parnell."

"No, I bloody don't. Pull up a chair in the viewing room with Seth and Cookey and I'll grab you a Mars Bar. If there's anything left in the vending machine, that is. For someone who weighs less than my handbag, Clara Madden's got one hell of an appetite."

As instructed, I head for the viewing room where Seth and Cooke have their feet up on the table. On the screen, Parnell's having fun with Kirstie Connor.

Fun in the sticking-your-head-in-a-wasp's-nest-while-someone-sandpapers-the-soles-of-your-feet sense.

"Look, I'm not sure how else I can put this. Seriously, you need to get a hearing test. I did not plant any gift box. I did not see anyone planting any gift box." She lets out a manic laugh. "And I certainly didn't pluck Naomi's hair off the floor of my office and give it to Rachel to plant in Joseph's car!"

Top marks to Parnell. I hadn't thought of that. Long dyed hair always sheds heavily—I should know—so it could just as easily have been taken from Kirstie's office as the crime scene.

Cooke fills me in. "It's been like this for the past half an hour—'No I didn't,' 'Yes you did,' 'No I didn't,' 'Yes you did.' It's like locking horns with my four-year-old."

Steele comes back with my Mars Bar—king-size, no less.

On the screen, Kirstie's still spluttering. "I mean, why would I even do that? What possible reason would I have? I'm hardly Joseph's greatest fan, but Jesus!"

Parnell plays it calm, a counterpoint to her fury. "Because Rachel's not your greatest fan, is she? Not since you slept with her husband."

A pause to let her bloat with shame. "Maybe helping Rachel was pay-back? A ticket back into her good books?"

"Oh, for God's sake!"

"So I'll ask you again, Kirstie, did you plant that gift box?"

"And I'll tell you again—no. And that thing with Joseph? It was just a stupid, stupid mistake. And Rachel knows what Joseph's like. She knows that when he sets his sights on you, that's it, *it happens.* She was angry for a while, of course she was, but we moved on from it ages ago."

God, she really is quite dumb. Astonishingly so.

A longer pause this time. "Well, somebody planted it, Kirstie. It's more or less a given. And as you've lied to us before, and you had easy access to Naomi's drawer, that makes you top of the pops, I'm afraid. Unless you're going to tell me that Rachel or Clara just happened to drop by your office sometime last week."

"No. But Clara knows the code to get in. She's done work for me in the past." Her hand flies to her mouth, trying to stuff the words back in. "Of course, not that Clara would . . . I wasn't saying . . . I didn't mean . . ."

Parnell cuts her off. "So Clara knows the code? And is that all she'd need to get in?"

"No." Her voice is full of hope, maybe she can repair this. "Some-one would have to buzz her into the main building, and she'd need the alarm code too, not just the door code."

Steele pokes Cooke. "First thing tomorrow, Craig. Every office in that building, OK?"

Parnell's dubious. "And you always set the alarm, do you? Every evening without fail?"

"Well no, *I* don't. It's my PA's responsibility. They're usually the last to leave."

I almost laugh. She's making this way too easy.

"But as your PA was Naomi, who, what with her lying in the morgue, wasn't in a position to be setting alarms last week, are you therefore saying that the alarm probably wasn't set at all?"

"Probably." Her face pulls into a tight scowl. "Look, maybe I should be more like Rachel with all her locks and bolts, but I'm not. I'm not scared of the world like she is."

"Good for you, but I don't think your insurers would be too happy to hear that. You might want to check your policy, Kirstie. I'd say setting the alarm's a prerequisite for a payout."

Steele and I exchange a smirk at Parnell's inherent dad-ness.

"Fine, I will." She sits forward. "So is that it? Can I go now? I need to get back to Danny."

Parnell's searching through a file. "You can go, not a problem." He doesn't even bother to look up. "But I've still got a few questions, so it'd look better if you stay."

"This really is beyond ridiculous."

She stays, though.

Parnell finds what he's looking for, places the document on the table. "Now, I've been going back over your various statements, Kirstie, and you really can't remember a lot about Saturday the 4th of November, can you? Lots of black spots, you say."

She bristles. "Yes? So? I've admitted I was out of my tree."

"You didn't admit to giving Naomi drugs, though."

"Oh, so I gave her some coke, or whatever that awful stuff was. I didn't force it down her! I just caught her yawning, made a little joke about having something for tiredness, and she *leapt* on it. She wasn't squeaky-clean, you know? She said that while she was away she might as well try everything—that's what traveling was for. I mean, I was trying to be *nice*, friendly." Suddenly, she freezes. "Anyway, hold on, why are you bringing that up again? You said you couldn't charge me with anything to do with that?"

Parnell smiles, but it's not the smile he does when Arsenal wins or someone's picked up Yum Yums. It's false. Predatory.

"We can't, and I'm not. But I just wanted to remind you how much you've lied to us, or neglected to tell us, throughout the course of this investigation, so that you're not *too* offended when I suggest you might be lying about something else."

"Oh, for the millionth time, I did not plant any—"

Parnell puts a hand up. "I want to understand how, when you have so many 'black spots' about that day, do you recall *so* clearly what Joseph said about Naomi?" He reads from the statement.

"A few minutes later, Naomi walks past the door and Joseph says, 'Oh, so is she one of those who just humors me?' and I said—and I'm not proud of this—'Yeah, she might have the personality of a dead moth but even she'd draw the line at you.' And then that's when he said it. He said—and again, I can't remember word for word—but it was something like he could have her if he wanted . . ."

Parnell looks up again. "That's well remembered. Especially for someone whose recollection of everything else is sketchy. You can see how that's got me wondering, can't you?"

And just like that, she saves herself.

"Look, I didn't hear him say it, OK? Rachel did." Steele grabs my forearm. "She told me about it at the end of last week. She wanted to tell you herself, she *really* did, but she's so scared of Joseph, she didn't want it coming from her." Her head juts forward. "I'm not scared of him, though, and I think Rachel guessed I'd tell you. So, you know, she has been helping in a roundabout way, despite what you think."

Steele whispers, "Is Kirstie Connor the biggest mug in history or is she cleverly throwing Rachel under a bus? I can't decide."

Parnell raises his voice a little. "So, to clarify, for the tape, you never actually heard Joseph saying he could 'have' Naomi."

"I was in the room, apparently," she says, hoping this will carry weight. "But, well, no. I don't remember hearing him say it. But, it's exactly like something he would say. He's said it about other women."

"I vote mug," I reply, in answer to Steele's question. "I think Rachel's been manipulating Kirstie all along. Getting her to drop Joseph in it so she doesn't have to. That way she can keep doing her Tammy Wynette routine and that makes us find Joseph's claims less plausible."

Steele nods. "Maybe. Although, if Kirstie's that gullible, I reckon she could be persuaded to help cover up a murder, don't you?"

Parnell's on the same page, the same paragraph, the same sentence.

"Picking up on what you said about Rachel being scared of Joseph, can you remind me why that is?"

"I'm sorry?"

"Well," explains Parnell, "you told us you saw Joseph grabbing Rachel by the throat, throttling her. Do you still stand by that?"

Her chin's up but it's wobbling slightly. "Yes, I still stand by it."

"And is that because you saw it happen? Remember you're under caution, Kirstie."

She says nothing, leaning forward onto the table, propping her head up with her fingers.

"Or is it because Rachel told you he did?"

She pulls her hands through her hair, corkscrew curls sticking out at mad, jaunty angles.

"Can you answer the question please, Kirstie."

"She's gonna *'no comment,'*" mutters Cooke. "Bet you she *'no comments.'*"

"No. I didn't see Joseph do it." Her voice is loud, clear as a bell, a death knell sounding for Rachel's innocence.

"So you admit you made a false statement?"

"It wasn't false. I believe what Rachel told me. He did it—it doesn't matter whether I saw it or not."

"When did this supposedly happen? Remind me."

A hysterical huff. "God, I don't know. A couple of years ago."

"And when did Rachel tell you about it? Was it at the time?"

She shrinks in on herself, shoulders hunching in defeat as the penny starts to drop. "No. She told me last week, after they arrested Joseph."

"And do you think she'd have guessed you'd tell us that too?"

Silence. Just a sulky pout masking the devastation of being played for a fool by someone you thought cared. By someone you thought inferior.

Parnell stares at her for what probably seems like an eternity, although it can't be more than a few seconds. Eventually, he says, "You'd do a lot for Rachel, wouldn't you? She means a lot to you."

"Yes, of course." Her voice is barely a cracked whisper. "She's family."

But not your blood, I think. And when it comes to two things—

forensic evidence *and* steadfast loyalty—*nothing* compares to blood. Blood always wins.

I should know.

"So I'll ask you again, Kirstie. Did you plant that gift box in Naomi's drawer?"

"No," she croaks. "How many times do I have to tell you!"

And off they go again.

I take my Mars Bar and leave.

30

Another delay. Steele's spooked about Marcus. He's not the most appropriate of appropriate adults, even I'll admit that.

Although not out loud.

"Look, he's not a suspect or a witness, in any real sense," I argue, knowing I'm on the shakiest of ground. "I completely get we're pushing the boundaries here, but he's the only adult she'll talk in front of, and above all we want her talking."

Renée backs me up. "I had a chat with them both while you were in watching Kirstie. They seem close. He seems to calm her down, loosen her up, which is what we need. I'd say he's been more of a father figure to her than bloody Joseph Madden."

"He's the first one she called when Rachel lost the plot the other morning," I say.

"And he's done the appropriate adult thing a few times through his charity work," adds Renée. "He understands the drill, what he should and shouldn't say."

In the end, we go with it.

Steele says to leave all questioning about the gift box—the fact that it was found in Kirstie's office is obviously too linked to Marcus—and in any case, we'll be better armed tomorrow if someone from the building recalls buzzing Clara in.

Oh, and she wants to sit in. She wants me focusing on Clara while she hawk-eyes Marcus.

Me and Steele interviewing together.

Like duetting with your favorite pop star and them insisting you sing the lead.

As we get ourselves settled, Clara Madden tries to style it out, emitting sharp little huffs and dispensing over-the-top eye rolls, all designed to make us forget that she nearly wet her pants in Mummy's arms just two hours ago.

Marcus Connor's looking tired. Tired but appropriate. Sitting close enough to Clara to offer his support and encouragement, not so close that she can smell his primal fear.

"So are you feeling better now?" I ask, fingers laced, smiling warmly. I haven't decided how I'm going to pitch things yet. Will it be soft-play or hardball?

"S'pose." Clara even shrugs just like Rachel. *So like her mother.*

I offer another smile. "Clara, for the benefit of the tape, could you confirm a little more clearly that you feel better."

"Yeah, whatever. I feel better, all right? Although, don't you have any healthy food in this place?" She gives me a pitying look. "I mean, no wonder . . ." She doesn't finish.

And a lot like her father.

Hardball it is.

I pick up my pen. "OK, so before we get to the main thing we want to talk about . . ." Unsettle her and keep her hanging; that's all I'm doing. "We're going to hop back to Saturday the 4th of November briefly. We're just trying to establish a more solid timeline for everyone, you see. You say you left before Naomi arrived? What time was that again?"

Another shrug; it seems to be her natural reflex on hearing my voice. "Can't remember. Maybe two, two thirty?"

"That was early. Not your thing, right?"

"What, a load of try-hards creaming themselves over handbags? Not really."

"Hey, I get it. You didn't fit in."

She scoffs. "I wouldn't *want* to fit in. Actually, I left because I had a stack of reading to do and that's far more important than any fireworks party. See, I want a proper career. One that makes a difference, not one that mythologizes shoes."

Marcus arches an eyebrow. He might not be holding his wife in particularly high esteem these days, but that's her livelihood Clara's insulting—and I'd say it puts more of a dent in a Muswell Hill mortgage than his charity kickabouts. Steele and I look duly impressed by her use of vocabulary while she preens herself for a second, effortlessly redoing her bun.

My cue to bring her back down to earth.

"Clara, tell us again about seeing your dad with Naomi."

She's impatient, inconvenienced. "I amended my statement this morning. Someone came around, I didn't catch the guy's name." A little smirk. "I wish I had, though."

Which means it was boy-bander Swaines or posh-totty Seth. If it was Flowers or Cooke, she's even more messed up than I think.

"Yeah, I know you did—and thank you. There's just a few points we need to go over."

Marcus's head is lowered, studying me warily. He's done this before and knows an ambush could be imminent.

"What points?" She glances quickly at Marcus, who gives her a little nod to say it's all fine, nothing to worry about.

"Well, you don't seem to be able to give many specifics. How close were you to them, for example?"

She pulls a face. "I don't really understand all that yards and meters stuff."

"That's fine. Just tell us where they were and where you were."

"Oh, right." She's more comfortable with this. "Well, they were outside The Grindhouse and I was—do you know where the HSBC cashpoint is, next to the bookshop?"

"I do." I write it down, nodding. "OK, so that's quite far away, maybe twenty or thirty yards. I suppose if you've got good vision . . ."

"I have. Perfect twenty-twenty." Another little preen. "I had an eye test last month, you can check."

"So you're 100 percent sure it was Naomi?" I say, tightening the noose. "I mean, your dad does talk to a lot of girls."

A little cruelty can set a suspect beautifully on edge. Marcus looks at me as though I've stamped on a puppy's paw.

"It was her, definitely. That awful hair stands out a mile." Marcus frowns at her. She mouths a tiny *"sorry."*

"Fab. That's all fab," I say, clapping my hands together like a complete sap. It does the job, though—Marcus visibly relaxes and Clara has a small stretch. I launch straight back in for the kill. "So now we just need to figure out *when* you saw them. I know you said it was about a month ago, and that you couldn't be more specific, but it's really, really important, Clara. You'd be the star of this station if you could narrow it down a bit more."

I need her to commit to a date we can prove wrong. A wily barrister could argue that time doesn't fly for your average seventeen-year-old in the way it does for *"some of the more vintage members of our jury, ha, ha!"* With their whole lives ahead of them, he or she could argue, days can seem like years, and two weeks could certainly seem like a month to a preoccupied teenager, wrestling A-level stress and university applications.

I need a date, an anecdote, a *lie* she can't back out of.

Her face is scrunched, a good actress like her mother. "Well, I was going to The Grindhouse to ask for money for a textbook, and I needed that particular textbook for an essay that had to be in by Friday the 27th, so it was definitely before then. Probably the week before as I'd have needed time to do the work."

I do a quick calculation. "So the week beginning the 15th of October?"

She does the calculation herself, clearly not trusting my math. "Yes. Later in the week, though, Thursday or Friday. I'm at college all day from Monday to Wednesday."

"So the 19th or 20th?"

"Yes." So ten whole days before Naomi dyed her hair. Steele gives a tiny sniff in place of a huge *"Yahooo."* "Sorry, I suppose I could have worked that out before, but the cute guy who took my statement seemed a bit rushed. You're a lot more thorough."

I am honored.

I take out a printed screenshot, rotating it toward Clara. It's a message and a photo that Naomi sent to her sister on Sunday the 29th.

"Whaddya reckon to the new color? Mum will go ape ☺"

I tap the printout. "So, I'm going to share something with you now, Clara. We know this was taken the day Naomi dyed her hair lilac. Can you tell us what the date says?"

She peers forward, color draining from her face. "Sunday the 29th of October."

"How do you know that," says Marcus, his voice hot and crabby. "She could have dyed it days before and only got around to sending the photo on the 29th."

Steele swoops. "Er, you're not Clara's lawyer, Mr. Connor. You're here to ensure her welfare, not her freedom." A pause. "Although, not a bad observation."

Freedom. The word smacks them both square from behind.

"Well, let's clear that up, shall we?" I place two more photos on the table, side by side. "This one was taken at the Soho Hotel on Friday the 27th—Naomi's blond, as you can see. And this one . . ." Naomi, posing with a Beefeater outside the Tower of London this time. ". . . on the 19th of October, around the time Clara claims she saw her with Joseph—blond again."

"I must have got the dates muddled," Clara stutters. Gone is the preening brainiac of two minutes ago, and in its place is a shit-scared teenager whose life just took a sharp turn.

"Oh Clara, you're a sharp tack. I don't think you get muddled too often."

Marcus can't help himself. "She's had her life turned upside down, she's going to get things mixed up. Cut her some slack, will you?"

Steele again. "That's twice now, Mr. Connor. You're here to support her, not speak for her."

"I would cut her some slack," I say to Marcus. "One or two days' slack. Not nearly two weeks." Clara's staring at the table. I dip my head to meet her eyes. "Look, it's a given that you've lied, Clara. That's not really up for discussion. The only thing we want to know is why."

No response, but I plow on regardless.

"Do you remember the other day when I was at your flat—you said you wanted to look out for your mum like she's looked out for you? Is that what you were doing? Trying to protect her, trying to help her?" I dip my head a little lower, lean in close. "Or is she protecting you, Clara? Either way, I think it was your mum who told you to lie, to say you saw your dad and Naomi together."

She looks up, eyes inches from mine. "No. No it wasn't."

There's something in her shaky, righteous tone that wants me to believe that, if I believe nothing else. I can't, though. Whoever killed Naomi, Rachel Madden's burrowed at the heart of it, I know it.

I try another tactic.

"You know, if you think your mum's protecting you, you're wrong."

"Clara, remember you can leave any time," says Marcus, shooting an angry glance at Steele. "And before you say anything, I'm allowed to remind her of her rights."

"Actually, Clara won't be allowed to leave," I reply levelly. "I'm going to be charging her shortly with perverting the course of justice."

Her head dips again. Under her breath she's muttering, *"This isn't happening, this isn't happening . . ."* I slap my hand hard on the table to get her focus back.

It works.

"Do you know what that means, Clara?" She's still muttering, straight in my face now. "It *can* carry a life term, although I won't insult you by threatening that—you know your criminal justice, you know that rarely happens. But you'll be looking at a couple of years. Obviously, you'll still be young enough to pick up the pieces once you've served your time, but you can wave goodbye to any hope of that 'proper career' in law or criminology."

Marcus's eyes prick with tears. "Please don't do this," he says, just about keeping it together, holding back the river. "This isn't fair . . ."

I nod. "And that's what I told your mum, Clara. Oh yeah, I gave her the chance to save you. I said, 'Admit you killed Naomi, and got Clara to help frame Joseph, and we can probably look at a "duress" defense for Clara, she probably won't even serve time.' She wouldn't admit it, though. And do you know why I think that is? I think that's because *she* didn't kill Naomi but she knows *you* did. And your dad knows it too. That's why he won't reveal who's framing him. Sweet, really. And you thought he didn't care."

Clara looks like she's landed on Mars without oxygen. Marcus looks even worse.

"What happened?" I say, keeping the pace and pressure high. "Did you see them talking at the party? Did you think Naomi was like all the other try-hards? It must have really stung that a try-hard rich kid was getting attention from your dad when you couldn't get any. Thing is, Clara—Naomi wasn't like them. She was just a normal, nice, sweet girl."

"This is crazy," she finally gasps, barely able to breathe and speak at the same time. "I didn't kill anyone."

Marcus's hands are up. "Really, stop this. You have to stop this now. It's not fair."

I turn the screw again. "And, well, you know what it's going to be like, Clara. You know exactly how girls like you get treated in the media. Working-class girls—they get a much rougher ride, don't they? They'll call you council-estate scum. I mean, look at poor Abby Slater, and she was the victim!"

"What are you on about?" There's strength back in her voice. "You lot are insane . . ."

I open my mouth, but a knock at the door interrupts me.

Parnell.

"Boss, can I have a quick word."

Steele announces her exit for the tape and steps outside. Clara, Marcus, and I sit in disharmonious silence while voices murmur in the hallway. After what can only be thirty seconds, a minute tops, Steele strides back into the interview room, heading straight for the tape.

"Interview terminated at eight twenty-two p.m."

There's a competition to see who can look the most baffled. I reckon I win hands down.

Steele stays standing. "Mr. Connor, I've just been informed that cell site analysis has located your wife's phone operating in the Turnpike Lane area in the early hours of Sunday the 5th of November, not long before she made a call to your sister, Rachel, at one a.m."

Just three words from Marcus—*"Oh God, no"*—before his head disappears into his hands.

"This obviously casts doubt on your wife's claim that she was at home that night, chatting to Rachel before sleeping off a hangover. A claim you supported. If you could follow me now, we can start to get to the bottom of this. Clearly, your wife is facing very serious charges." She looks to Clara, then to me. "Charge Miss Madden with perverting the course of justice, and then I think we all need a short break."

Marcus's head comes up, a heavy ton weight. "No. No, this has gone far enough. This has to end now." The tears in his eyes are still stubbornly refusing to fall. "It was me, OK.

"I killed her. I killed Naomi."

31

In the great British tradition, we take a break and have a cup of tea. None of us needs it more than Marcus Connor, who isn't so much distressed as obliterated, so much so that Steele insists on suicide watch and then agrees to him having five monitored minutes with his sister, the person he's asked to speak to repeatedly.

As it goes, their meeting yields very little. Just lots of tears and hand-squeezing and solemn insistences from Marcus that it's time to tell the truth. For what it's worth—and Marcus Connor won't be worth spitting on in the eyes of the world any day now—I think his remorse is genuine. While anyone can grunt *"I'm sorry"* or conjure up a few fat tears if required, even the best actors can't fake the unmistakable pallor of guilt. It's just not possible to drain your own skin of all hope, unless you truly know how it feels to wish you could start life over again.

It's the end of the road now, for me and Marcus Connor. Steele's decided I look totally whacked and not fit to run a cake stall, never mind another interview, so Parnell and Renée get the call-up, and I don't mind admitting that, for once, I'm glad.

Glad to have my feet up in the viewing room.

Glad to have my headphones on and my head right back.

Glad to have my eyes closed so I don't have to look at him.

Because after seven days and several witnesses, countless interviews and an avalanche of lies, all I'm interested in now is what happened to Naomi Lockhart.

Metropolitan Police
RECORD OF INTERVIEW

PARNELL: This interview is being audiovisually recorded and will be given in evidence when your case is brought to trial. We are in Interview Room Two at Holborn police station. The date is Tuesday the 14th of November and the time is 22:09. I am Detective Sergeant Luigi Parnell. Also present is Detective Constable Renée Akwa. Please state your full name and date of birth.

CONNOR: Marcus Robert Connor (COUGHS), the 16th of August 1982.

PARNELL: Also present is Philippa Grayswood, your solicitor. Do you agree that there are no other persons present?

CONNOR: (INAUDIBLE).

PARNELL: Could you repeat that please, a little louder.

CONNOR: Yes.

PARNELL: Thank you. I'm now going to formally caution you that you do not have to say anything. But it may harm your defense if you do not mention when questioned something which you later rely on in court. Anything you do say may be given in evidence. Also, while you obviously have your own legal representation present, I'm obligated to remind you that you are entitled to *free* and independent legal advice, either in person or by telephone at any stage. Do you understand?

CONNOR: Yes.

PARNELL: At the conclusion of the interview, I will give you a notice explaining what will happen to this recording and how you and/or your solicitor can get access to it. (PAUSE) Now Marcus, you were quite upset earlier. I believe your solicitor has explained that we're happy to delay this interview until tomorrow morning, as we understand it's been a very distressing few hours and it's important you feel comfortable and rested.

CONNOR: A distressing few hours? Rested? Do you think I've actually slept in the past ten days?

PARNELL: Which is why we want to be sure you feel fit enough to be interviewed.

CONNOR: I feel as fit as I'm ever going to feel. I just want to get it over with. I want to tell the truth. (PAUSE) What's going to happen to Clara?

PARNELL: That's still to be decided, and not what we're here to discuss. I understand from your solicitor that you wish to make a full and frank confession to the murder of Naomi Lockhart.

CONNOR: It wasn't murder. It was an accident. (SUSPECT CAN BE HEARD CRYING)

PARNELL: Well, now is the time to explain your version of events, Marcus. And can I just point out that we—me, Detective Constable Akwa, and your solicitor Mrs. Grayswood— are not here to judge you or to antagonize you. We just want to know what happened. We may ask some questions along the way, and we'd appreciate it if you could answer those to the best of your ability. (PAUSE) So start where you think you need to start. Perhaps with how you came to know Naomi.

CONNOR: I didn't know her. A lot of what I said in my first statement was true. She worked for Kirstie and she was invited to the fireworks thing we were having. She arrived sometime in the afternoon. I answered the door to her and she was smiley and friendly. She'd made a huge potato salad that she'd carted all the way on the bus and I just thought that was nice of her. It was more than any of the others had done. (SUSPECT CAN BE HEARD CRYING)

PARNELL: Marcus, we're still trying to establish an accurate timeline of Naomi's last day. I know we asked you this before, but now that you're talking more openly, can you shed any light on what time Naomi arrived at your house?

It could be important for any inquest. It's important to Naomi's family.

CONNOR: (SUSPECT BLOWS HIS NOSE) All I can say is that it hadn't got dark but it was quite a while after two o'clock when the first guests arrived, because I remember her looking a bit lost when she saw that everyone was well on their way to being pissed. I don't think she knew anyone that well, despite working with them, and, well, walking into a room full of drunk people is hard for anyone, never mind someone who's a bit shy.

PARNELL: How did you know she was shy? You said you'd never met her before, or had you, Marcus? You know, if there's something you're not telling us, we really can't help you.

CONNOR: (AGITATED) I'm telling the truth. Kirstie had mentioned her in passing, that's all. Just how her new PA didn't talk much. How she kept herself to herself.

PARNELL: So when did you come to speak with Naomi again?

CONNOR: I didn't really. I smiled when I walked past her a few times. I might have asked her if she was OK for a drink, that sort of thing, I don't really remember. I honestly didn't pay that much attention to her.

PARNELL: So tell me about the afternoon.

CONNOR: It started off OK—just pointless small talk and a load of rich kids giving me advice on house renovation. But, as always, it started to get lairy. I never wanted the party in the first place. We'd had one earlier in the year and I'd walked in on two people cutting up coke on this little blue desk in my baby boy's bedroom. Do you know what they said when I asked them what the fuck they were doing? *"Oh sorry, the bathroom was busy."* I swore after that, never again, but Kirstie has a way of grinding you down. And she promised there'd be none of that this time. *"Just a big fuck-off chili and a few fireworks,"* she said.

PARNELL: You said it "got lairy"—what do you mean, "lairy"?

CONNOR: You see, Kirstie's problem is that she wants to be twenty-one again. She wants the family and the nice house and the business cards and all that, but deep down, she doesn't like responsibility. It's funny, because when we met, I was the wild one—petty crime, nicking cars, drugs—*ha*. She says that's what attracted her to me and then I got boring. But I didn't get boring, I just grew up. I wanted to do something good with my life. I wanted other people to get the second chances I'd been given. That's why I started Be a Good Sport, I suppose. (SUSPECT PAUSES. EVENTUALLY PROMPTED BY SOLICITOR TO CONTINUE) Kirstie, though, she doesn't want to go forward, she wants to go back. Back to when we double-dropped pills three or four times a night and danced till dawn. I think she saw the rest of her team—young, carefree—taking drugs and she wanted to join in, plain and simple.

AKWA: Did you see Naomi taking drugs with your wife, Marcus? We believe they both took the same substance, purchased from—

CONNOR: (SUSPECT INTERRUPTS) Kieran-fucking-Drake. That was a blast from the past. Normally when a BAGS ex-con goes off the radar, it's because they've either gone back to crime or to prison. Kieran stopped coming but I could see on Facebook that he was still around, still doing his personal training thing, so I thought maybe he just didn't feel the need anymore, didn't want the reminder of who he used to be. (SUSPECT LAUGHS) How wrong was I? And how wrong was Kirstie, or how drunk was Kirstie, more like. Idiot told him to meet her in the alley by the side of our house, like she was some drug baron doing a big deal. She totally didn't realize the fence wasn't high enough and I could see the tops of their heads the whole time. I should have gone out there and stopped it—God, if only I had—

but I was just so mad at her. I was like, *"Go on then, buy two grams, buy ten grams. Have an overdose, see if I care."* Sorry, I know that sounds bad but I was raging. After last time, after having to wipe coke off the little desk where my son draws his dinosaur pictures. I just couldn't look at her.

AKWA: Thanks for sharing that with us, Marcus. That's all really helpful in terms of context. Can I just ask again if you saw Naomi taking drugs with Kirstie?

CONNOR: Yeah, I caught them. Well, I say "caught them"—they weren't exactly being discreet. Kirstie was racking up lines of whatever that shit was on our bedside table and Naomi was trying on Kirstie's shoes like she was this cool big sister. I closed the door and went downstairs.

PARNELL: What time was this?

CONNOR: Around eight, I think.

PARNELL: OK, thank you. And then what happened?

CONNOR: Nothing, for a while. I certainly didn't see Naomi again after that. I was mainly in the living room, arguing with Joseph about Brexit. *That's* how bad it was with Kirstie—I'd rather sit in a room with my brother-in-law than have to look at her. (PAUSE) Anyway, the last of Kirstie's lot left around ten. Rachel and Joseph left about half an hour later, and when I went up to bed, Kirstie was flat out on the bed. She'd been sick on the floor, and in the bed, and she was just, well, *lying in it*. My heart nearly stopped. I thought she might be dead, and I couldn't stop thinking about what I'd thought earlier—you know, about her having an overdose. Obviously, she wasn't dead. She wasn't even passed out, she was just . . . I don't know, sort of spaced out. Not happy spaced out, though. She looked frightened. She kept slurring, *"No way was that coke. No way was that coke."* I said she needed fresh air but she said she was scared to go outside and would I just lie with her? Well, I wanted to absolutely fucking kill her, but at the same time, the thought that she'd been upstairs on her own, out of it, *frightened*, while I'd been downstairs arguing about trade deals . . . So I made her be sick—in the toilet, this time—and then I cleaned the bedroom up as best I could and I put her in the spare room. I lay there with her for a while but then suddenly Naomi occurred to me. Kirstie had fallen sound asleep by then. Dead to the world.

PARNELL: You were worried about Naomi?

CONNOR: Yeah, I was. Kirstie—well, she doesn't take drugs that often anymore but she did back in the day, we both did. What I'm saying is that *she's* used to drugs and she'd still had a bad reaction. I got the impression Naomi wasn't so experienced, so yeah, I was worried. Anyway, I lay there thinking about it, and after a while, I decided I wasn't taking the risk.

PARNELL: So you went to Naomi's place?

CONNOR: Yeah. I wasn't pissed, but I'd have definitely been over the limit, so I took my bike. It's only a couple of miles from ours to hers and I know all the shortcuts, all the quiet backstreets.

AKWA: How did you know where she lived? Did Kirstie tell you?

CONNOR: Kirstie? She was in no fit state to remember that. I doubt she'd have known it off the top of her head anyway, even if she was straight. No, I played five-a-side with Kieran a few years ago and I used to pick him up and drop him off most weeks.

PARNELL: Marcus, it was explained earlier that cell site analysis had located Kirstie's phone in Naomi's area. Why did you take Kirstie's phone?

CONNOR: At first, I couldn't find mine. The house was a bomb site and I was starting to worry that one of Kirstie's little leeches had nicked it. It's an iPhone X, it only came out the Friday before last. So I was thinking I was going to have to take Kirstie's anyway, but then when I picked it up and saw a message from Joseph on the screen, that sealed it. I stopped looking for mine and I took it and left. The idea was I'd check on Naomi, and then I'd find some late-night bar on the way back and drink myself stupid while going through Kirstie's phone, sad fuck that I am.

PARNELL: What did the message say?

CONNOR: (PAUSE) Do you know, I can't even remember now. Something about what she was wearing that day. How she always looked good in red, whatever. I always knew something had gone on there. It wasn't actually a great shock. (PAUSE) Anyway, it all became a bit insignificant after what followed.

PARNELL: Just talk us through it, Marcus. You're doing great. You're doing the right thing.

CONNOR: Actually, can I just say, even though it was her—her complete *idiocy*—that led to all this, I want to make it clear that Kirstie played no real part. I know she . . . she hasn't always been entirely truthful but, well, what I'm getting at is, she didn't lie about calling Rachel that night. She honestly thought she had. She was so out of it, so confused, she believed me when I told her she'd phoned Rachel. She put it down to another black spot.

AKWA: The same as she believed Rachel when she told her that Joseph had made comments about Naomi in front of her? She thought she was so drunk or so high she'd forgotten?

CONNOR: (SILENCE) (CONFERS WITH PHILIPPA GRAYS-WOOD)

AKWA: That's OK, Marcus. We can go back to Rachel later. Just carry on. You're doing great. So you get to Naomi's?

CONNOR: (PAUSE) The thing is, I know this is the bit where you'll want detail and I want to give it to you, I swear I do, but on Danny's life, some of it's a blur. It just happened so quickly. One minute I was the good guy, checking on someone, making sure they're OK, the next I was ... I was ... the next I ... (SUSPECT BREAKS DOWN)

PARNELL: Marcus, do you want to take a short break? We understand this is very distressing.

CONNOR: No. No. I want this to end. I want it to go away. (SUSPECT BREAKS DOWN AGAIN)

PARNELL: I think we should take a short break. Interview suspended at ten forty-nine p.m. Detective Sergeant Luigi Parnell and Detective Constable Renée Akwa will leave the room briefly. Marcus, can we get you anything? More water? A cup of tea, perhaps?

CONNOR: (INAUDIBLE)

GRAYSWOOD: Water, please.

I head back to the incident room, joining Renée and Parnell in Steele's office, where she's been on the phone to the Crown Prosecution Service for the past hour, trying to work out charges. Marcus is the easy one, the *fait accompli*. Rachel's a little complex and Clara Madden, as a juvenile, is trickier still. Kirstie Connor might be shown some leniency on the basis she truly believed what she was being told by Rachel, and her kid needs one parent, at least.

And then there's the Joseph Madden nightmare, of course.

"He won't be out for a few days," says Steele, currently on hold. "He'll be informed in the morning and the paperwork will take a day or two."

"What does that mean for Clara?" I ask, pointing out that there's another child that needs protecting. "In all likelihood, she'll get bail—and she can't be in that flat after he's released. She dropped him in it, for God's sake, and while he might not have done *this*, I still think he's dangerous—Stacey Nash, the spitting at me. And we don't know for sure that he didn't try to strangle Rachel. Just 'cos she chose to reveal it at a mightily convenient time doesn't mean it didn't happen."

"Could she stay with Kirstie?" suggests Renée. Amazing how Kirstie with her *"complete lack of responsibility"* is coming out of this wretched mess the most responsible of them all.

"Joseph might be gunning for Kirstie too," I argue. "He knows it was her who told us he tried to strangle Rachel. Whether it's true or not, I can see him being out for revenge."

Steele looks troubled, but she's got no choice but to tell it like it is. "He didn't do this, Cat. We can't keep him locked up because we're scared of what he *might* do. We'll have a chat with Kirstie and Clara—after she's bailed—about keeping themselves safe, calling us if they're concerned. That's all we can do. We don't need to worry about Rachel. There's no way *she's* getting bail, so she's safe in that respect."

Seth sticks his head around the door. "Boss, Rachel Madden's insisting she speaks to Cat tonight. She's got a lot to say, apparently, and she wants to say it now."

An eyebrow comes up. "Does she now? Tell her . . . what was that thing your mum used to say? Tell her, *'I want never gets.'* Tell her Cat needs her beauty sleep."

I laugh—for the first time all day, I think—and then we all head back to where we were stationed before. Steele being put on hold by the CPS for the seven-hundred-and-fifty-second time. Me with my eyes closed and headphones on in the viewing room.

And Parnell and Renée watching a man destroy himself, right in front of their very eyes.

PARNELL: The time is now 11:07 p.m. Present again in Interview Room Two are Detective Sergeant Luigi Parnell, Detective Constable Renée Akwa, Marcus Connor, and Philippa Grayswood, Mr. Connor's solicitor. Are you agreed that there are no other persons present, Marcus?

CONNOR: Yes.

PARNELL: Can you just confirm for the purposes of the recording that you're happy to continue with this interview, and that you've been made aware that you can stop at any time if you're feeling tired or overly distressed?

CONNOR: Yes.

PARNELL: Good. So you were telling us how you arrived at Naomi Lockhart's home. What time was that?

CONNOR: I honestly don't know. It couldn't have taken me more than fifteen minutes to cycle there but I don't know what time I left ours. I was angry about that text from Joseph. I wasn't really paying attention.

PARNELL: Well, let me help you out. You called your sister, Rachel, at 1:03 a.m. from Naomi's home, we're presuming to tell her what had happened. So was it long before then that you arrived at Naomi's?

CONNOR: (SILENCE)

AKWA: What DS Parnell's getting at, Marcus, is did you kill Naomi instantly on arrival and then call Rachel? Or were you in her home for some time before?

CONNOR: (CONFERS WITH SOLICITOR) It was probably around twelve fifteen a.m. when I got there.

PARNELL: And was Naomi dead when you called Rachel?

CONNOR: (CONFERS WITH SOLICITOR) She died about half an hour after I got there. (SUSPECT'S BREATHING IS AUDIBLE)

PARNELL: Can you take us through what happened—in as much detail as you can?

CONNOR: It was an accident. I was trying to help her. (LAUGHS) Fucking hell, that's where being the good guy gets you. I should have stayed bad . . . I should have stayed with my old life. At least then it'd be my fault . . . I mean, I know *this* is my fault, but . . . (LONG PAUSE) So, um, all the lights were off when I got there. I hoped that meant she hadn't gone home. That she was somewhere else with other people—at least then she wouldn't be on her own if she felt unwell.

AKWA: How did you know Kieran wasn't home?

CONNOR: I didn't. But if he was in, I'd be killing two birds with one stone, I figured—checking Naomi was OK and telling him that if he ever supplied drugs to my wife again, he'd be doing personal training in prison.

AKWA: OK, carry on.

CONNOR: I rang the bell a couple of times. I was just about to go when a light came on at the back of the house. I could sort of tell by the time it was taking her to get to the door that something was up. She said *"Who is it?"* and her voice didn't sound right. I mean, I didn't really know her voice well, but I know a scared voice when I hear one. I spoke to her through the letterbox for a minute, told her who it was, asked her if she was OK. She was sort of whimpering. I asked her if Kieran was there—it crossed my mind that maybe he'd hurt her, or something—but she said he wasn't there, he'd gone away for a few days and that she was all alone and "they" were going to hurt her. I thought about calling the police, honestly I did . . . but you know, what with Kirstie . . . I couldn't . . . it'd have all come out and . . . oh God, there's no excuse, I know that. I should have called for help. Why the fuck didn't I?

PARNELL: Don't think about what you should have done, Marcus, just tell us what happened. It's the best way, honestly.

CONNOR: She wouldn't let me in. I could hear her on the other side of the door saying, *"She's sent you. She hates me. She wants me dead."* It was dark—she hadn't even switched the kitchen light on. I didn't know what to do. I couldn't call the police but I couldn't just leave her, so I got a bit . . . well, I suppose I got a bit forceful with her. I told her if she didn't let me in so we could see about making her feel better—'cos she was obviously having a bad trip or something—then I was coming in anyway. I'd pick the lock, break the window. Basically, I was coming in and that was that. I thought she might start screaming and I kind of regretted saying it, but she went completely quiet. After a minute, she opened the door and walked away. I went in and switched the light on and she was standing there, just a couple of feet from me with a fucking kitchen knife in her hand. She looked . . . gone. Not there at all. She was sweating and her eyes were like saucers. Kirstie had been bad, but at least she'd been sick—she was wasted but she was "there," you know. Naomi wasn't.

PARNELL: So to clarify, you believed Naomi was having a reaction to the drugs she'd taken with your wife?

CONNOR: Yeah, and I didn't know what they'd taken. I assumed it was coke, that's what it looked like when Kirstie had been chopping it up in our bedroom, but then later Kirstie had kept saying, *"No way was that coke,"* so I didn't know what I was dealing with. I mean, you read about people gouging their own eyes out on crystal meth and here I was, in this tiny kitchen with this wired-to-the-eyeballs girl pointing a knife at me. (SUSPECT CAN BE HEARD CRYING) I should have called the police then, I know I should have . . . but I couldn't risk it all coming out—my charity could lose its funding—and anyway, I thought I could talk her down. I've dealt with people on bad trips before, and I don't mean back in my youth, I mean through my work. The kids I work with, the ex-cons. I honestly thought I could manage the situation.

AKWA: Marcus, quite early on in this investigation, we took a statement from the owner of an off-license just up the road from Naomi. He stated that she came into the shop just before half past nine that evening and she seemed fine. (PAUSE) Um, here it is—*"She might have been a bit pissed because she was chattier than usual. She called me 'hon' when I gave her the change, but apart from that she seemed fine."*

CONNOR: So?

AKWA: Well, you yourself have claimed that you saw Naomi taking drugs around eight p.m. so it's strange this shop-keeper thought she seemed normal.

CONNOR: Actually, I didn't say I saw her taking them. I said I saw her in the room while Kirstie was cutting it up and then Kirstie told me afterward that Naomi had taken some. And anyway, depending on what it was, it can take time to kick in. Hours, sometimes, if it's cheap stuff. Kirstie really should have realized that something was up, though—a line of coke should have you buzzing in five to ten minutes, depending on the size, but she was really drunk by then and maybe she just assumed it was shit quality—it would be if it was off Drake—and so that makes you take more and more, waiting to feel the buzz. God knows what they were shoveling.

PARNELL: Benzo Fury—a nasty little substance; what we used to call a "legal high" until the courts saw sense a few years back. It looks like cocaine in powder form but mimics ecstasy and other amphetamines, so it's no wonder they reacted badly. I mean, if you're expecting one sensation and get another, that's going to mess you up . . . It's not a hallucinogen, typically, so Naomi wouldn't have been having a "bad trip" in the truest sense, but anxiety, panic attacks, extreme paranoia—they're not uncommon. There's a reason we banned it.

CONNOR: (PAUSE) Fucking hell. That's *exactly* what she was like. She kept asking if Kirstie had sent me. She thought Kirstie was trying to kill her! (RAISES VOICE) Are you going to charge that bastard that sold it to them? This is all his fault. All this fucking mess just so that Kieran Drake could make a bit of pocket money.

PARNELL: That's not your concern, Marcus. Keep going, what happened?

CONNOR: (PAUSE) Um, so I did talk her down a bit, to begin with. She put the knife down, anyway. Like I said, I've been around people with drug-induced anxiety before so I knew the best things to do—talk to her, get her to copy my breathing, keep telling her *"It'll pass, it's just the drugs,"* and then I started telling her stupid little stories about Kirstie, just to try and chill her out, you know. She'd got it into her head that Kirstie was this monster, so I thought if I took the piss out of her a bit, it'd help. I told her about Kirstie getting in the shower with her jeans on and I told her she was feeling pretty rough too. It seemed to be working, as well. She was still wired but she looked less . . . well, less terrified, I suppose. (SUSPECT TAKES SEVERAL DEEP BREATHS) But then as soon as I stopped all the constant chat and there was a bit of silence, she'd get all jumpy again.

PARNELL: What do you mean, jumpy? Did she pick the knife up again?

CONNOR: No, but she kept looking at it.

PARNELL: OK, carry on.

CONNOR: Um, well, the light in the kitchen was mega-bright and flickery—it must have needed a new bulb—so I thought she could do with being somewhere calmer. I remembered someone once telling me that a good thing to do with someone on a bad trip is to change their environment—get them somewhere they feel safer. (PAUSE) So I said she should lie down. I asked her where her bedroom was. It never occurred to me she'd think I was trying something on because nothing was further from my mind, but when I moved toward her and put my hands on her shoulders, just to kind of steer her down the hall—she wasn't great on her feet, you see—she went absolutely mental. Like, *mental*. She started trying to claw at me but I had the top of her arms almost pinned from trying to hold her up, so I didn't think she could do that much damage. But then suddenly, she just lunged forward, headbutting me in the chest, knocking me back against the sink. I couldn't believe the strength of her.

PARNELL: OK, so she attacked you first?

CONNOR: Yeah, but the thing is, she started screaming then and I panicked and slapped her. I didn't mean to hurt her, I was trying to shut her up, that's all. And it did shut her up for a minute, she was that stunned. It didn't last, though. She lunged at me again, headfirst, so I pushed her backward and she went flying into the corner of that glass cabinet and split her head. Oh God . . . and then when she saw the blood on her fingers . . . She actually didn't scream or shout at all but she started talking in this really weird low voice, saying me and Kirstie were evil, we were probably like Fred and Rose West. She said she was going to tell the police that I came to her house, that I'd tried to force her into her bedroom, that I'd tried to rape her. I mean, *rape* her? I didn't do anything but try and *help* her. (SILENCE)

PARNELL: Keep going, Marcus. (SUSPECT CAN BE HEARD CRYING) You're nearly there. You're doing well.

CONNOR: (CRYING) This is where it all gets blurry. I just remember feeling this pure, hot rage. This . . . this fucking *injustice* that I'd gone there to help her and now she was threatening all this. And it was all going to come out . . . *everything*. I didn't have a choice, see. So I grabbed her here (SUSPECT GRABS TOP OF THROAT/CHIN) and I . . . pushed her head back . . .

PARNELL: What do you mean you "pushed" her head back?

CONNOR: I . . . (SUSPECT MAKES A FORCEFUL PUSHING MOTION) I slammed it. I slammed it back into the corner of the glass cabinet. And then I slammed it again and again. Harder and harder. (LONG PAUSE) And then she was . . . dead. (SUSPECT CAN BE HEARD CRYING)

PARNELL: So that wasn't an accident. The first time was, that was arguably self-defense—but you're a lot bigger than her, you could have restrained her and called us.

CONNOR: You don't understand, I couldn't.

PARNELL: I understand that it would have been a difficult call to make, but it'd have been the right call. Instead, you lost your rag and you repeatedly—*purposefully*—slammed her skull into that sharp edge, and that's murder, Marcus. (SUSPECT CAN BE HEARD CRYING)

PARNELL: So then you called Rachel? What for? To get your big sister to help clear up your mess?

CONNOR: (VERY QUIET) Naomi was just mental. There was no reasoning with her. It would all come out. I had to stop her.

PARNELL: (LOUDER) Rachel, I said. What part did she play?

CONNOR: Rachel can speak for herself. I'm trying to tell you why I had to do what I did. Naomi was a madwoman, she was going to . . .

PARNELL: (INTERRUPTS) No, she wasn't a madwoman. She was a nice, normal, twenty-two-year-old girl who naively— and probably just to fit in—took drugs at a party and then ended up bleeding out on a tatty kitchen floor, nearly ten thousand miles away from the friends and family who loved her. At one point in that kitchen, you had a choice and you made the wrong one, Marcus. And you're going to have a long time to think about that. A very long time.

CONNOR: (SUSPECT BLOWS HIS NOSE) You don't under- stand. I didn't have . . .

PARNELL: You did. You could have called us and told us what hap- pened, exactly the way you just told it now, and I think there's every chance we'd have believed your version of events and Naomi would still be alive.

CONNOR: I couldn't . . . I couldn't risk it.

PARNELL: Risk what? That we wouldn't have believed you?

CONNOR: After she split her head the first time, I knew I was fucked. You see, I was wearing gloves the whole time I was in her house—I needed them for the cycle and her house was so cold I didn't take them off inside—but I knew if I called you, even if you believed it was self- defense, you'd probably still have to arrest me. And if I was arrested you'd take my prints.

PARNELL: And why would that have been a problem, Marcus?

CONNOR: Has Rachel said anything yet?

PARNELL: Why wouldn't you want us taking your prints?

CONNOR: Tell me what Rachel's said and I'll answer your question.

PARNELL: Well, not that it works like that, Marcus, but because of your candor here today, I'll tell you that Rachel hasn't said anything yet in relation to this crime. Now I did as you asked, so answer my question.

CONNOR: (LONG PAUSE) Guess it's up to me, then. He can't get away with everything. He has to be punished too. I mean, he's the problem, he's the *poison.*

PARNELL: Who is "*he*"? What are you talking about? Why didn't you want us taking your prints?

CONNOR: (LAUGHS) God, who was it that said lightning can never strike twice? It was exactly the same with the other one. Joseph always said she'd still be alive if she'd only calmed the fuck down.

The other one.

Naomi Lockhart and Abby Slater. The girl from the sunshine state of Adelaide and the girl from the Paulsgrove Estate in Portsmouth.

I should be sitting bolt upright now. I should be racing back to the incident room, bursting through Steele's door and shouting, "*I knew it. I bloody knew it.*"

But then I didn't know it. I think for one nanosecond on the train back from Portsmouth, I might have suspected it on some vague, itchy level. I might have dwelled a beat longer on one of the many things Lydia Coe had said—mainly the fact that Rachel had started asking "more about the investigation: how it was going, new leads following the reconstruction, did the police do their job, that sort of thing."

But we have Madden's prints and they haven't flagged—that's what my subconscious whispered. That's why I'd discounted it before it'd even had the chance to plant, never mind swell. It honestly hadn't occurred to me—or anyone else, in fairness—that there might have been two of them. Two of them robbing the Jack of Hearts pub that night in 2002. Only one of them unfortunate enough to leave his print behind.

So Joseph wasn't protecting Clara. He was protecting Marcus to protect himself. He knew that Marcus, and probably Rachel, were framing him for Naomi's murder, but he knew that if Marcus was ever arrested, it'd be life imprisonment anyway, because there's no way on earth Marcus wouldn't take him down too.

And that's exactly what he's about to do.

CONNOR: I want to report Joseph Madden for the murder of Abby Slater. I know he did it because I was there too. I played no part in her murder, though, that was all Joseph. I wish we'd never been there that night. I wish he hadn't done it. To be honest with you right now, I wish I'd never been born. (SUSPECT CAN BE HEARD CRYING)

32

Wednesday

"So you needed someone to take the place of Rachel and Clara, now that Rachel's getting her kicks in Portsmouth and Clara can't wait to put a few hundred miles between you."

I should have seen it. It doesn't matter how many times Parnell tells me to take off the hair shirt, I should have seen it.

When we watch the interview back, as we have done four times already this morning, it's hard to see anything else now. It's just so damn obvious that it was Portsmouth that set him off, not Clara. Portsmouth that changed the rules.

Portsmouth that launched his hot spit on my face.

We should have seen it, Parnell eventually concedes. He was in the interview too. He let me keep pushing Madden, prodding him about Clara, laughing that he'd be an embarrassment to her soon, goading him that he wouldn't see her for dust once she got herself some nice middle-class uni mates.

Joseph Madden couldn't have cared less.

There isn't one cursory mention of Clara in any of his interviews. Not a request to see her. Nor an inquiry about how she's coping. I should have seen *that*, at least, surely? I should have realized that his daughter had barely even entered his head.

But hey, hindsight's a bitch and foresight's a rarity in this job. We can't analyze risk like my lovely Aiden. We can't predict how people will act. What they'll slip us and what they'll hold back.

But still.

I *probably* should have seen it.

However, I do see something in the Stacey Nash inquest file. Despite Steele promising that she'd be the one to personally read it word for word, it's actually me who ends up trawling through it. Partly because Steele hasn't got the time now, not with the shit hitting the fan and spraying itself over every surface of her beloved station, and partly because she knows I'll do a good job.

It's a show of trust and I'm grateful for it.

It pays dividends too. Well, it provides food for thought, at the very least.

I find it among the reams of paper: the statements, the notes, the testimonies, the reports. It's a letter from Stacey's mum to the coroner, something the deceased's family has every right to do. Four handwritten pages giving examples of her daughter's resilience—examples of all the many, many times Stacey Nash simply refused to let life grind her down.

Three pages in, one example catches my eye.

"... *Stacey never let life get on top of her . . . Her car was vandalized AND her flat was broken into in the six months prior to her death, and she joked that whoever keyed her car had done her a favor as she'd gone off the color and had been thinking about getting it resprayed! The break-in—well, she had a few choice words for the burglar—but typical Stacey, her first thought was for the safety of others and she started a neighborhood watch group the very next day.*"

Resilience isn't evidence she wouldn't kill herself, of course.

And a vandalized car and a break-in isn't evidence that Joseph Madden killed her. Far from it.

As I say, though, food for thought . . .

Rachel's in the exercise yard, ambling around in lazy, hazy circles, smoking a cigarette and looking up at the sky, a pure, uninterrupted blue on a perfect November day. She seems lighter and freer than I've seen her before, but then confession does that to some people. It can take years off them, weight off them—it puts the pounds back on some people as appetites spring back in line with their newfound peace. Rachel ate well this morning, I'm told.

It hasn't worked for Marcus Connor, who cried all night, refuses all food and only speaks to repeat one statement—that it'd be a blessed relief to die.

I hope he doesn't die. Abby Slater's justice has been a long time coming, but Naomi Lockhart won't get any at all if Marcus Connor takes the easy way out. It wouldn't be fair on Kirstie or Danny either, or his parents—despite both their offspring branding them "cold" and "unsupportive," Harry and Sue Connor have barely left the station since the news broke. Of course, that could be because our reception area provides sanctuary from the flashing lights and the media scrum, or it could be because they care, in their own buttoned-up, understated way.

Rachel doesn't know Marcus is suicidal. We need her focused and relaxed and so, as I join her outside, I stick to idle chitchat about the beauty of the day and the blandness of the food. Eventually she asks where Clara spent last night, but she doesn't like the answer.

"Where else can she stay?" I ask, genuinely open to suggestion. "She barely knows your family and Joseph's are dead, so it's either Kirstie or care, they're the two options. You said it yourself, Rachel, Clara needs stability right now, and at least Kirstie's been a constant for nearly her whole life."

"*Marcus* has," she says quickly. "Marcus has always been there for Clara. Kirstie's never been interested. I meant what I said, I admire her get-up-and-go and I hope Clara mirrors that in whatever she does, but when it comes to Kirstie's heart, her values . . . she's not the kind of influence I want for my child."

But a man involved in two murders is.

Figure that one out.

An hour later, we're in Interview Room One. The preliminaries are done and the broad blue sky is a distant memory.

"Typical Joseph. Always one step ahead of me." Rachel's in a stoic mood. As resigned to a long prison stretch as she is to the pointlessness of trying to get over on Joseph. "If he hadn't spoken to you about me months ago, you'd have probably written him off, wouldn't you? You wouldn't have believed a word he was saying."

She's right. While it's not altogether unusual for suspects to claim they're being framed, it *is* unusual for them to halfway predict it.

"But then, he's always been good at the preemptive strike. Sensing trouble. Hurt them before they hurt you, that's what he lives by. I found that really attractive when I first met him—he was just so ruthless. He didn't take anyone's crap, and when you've been brought up to be good and meek and polite to the point of sniveling, that kind of confidence is powerful." She takes a small sip of water. "Well, it is when you're only twenty and he's talking about how he's going to rule the world one day with you right beside him. That's what men like Joseph do, see. They shower you with praise and promises and then when you're hooked—and I don't use that word lightly, Cat, I was *obsessed* with him—they start to withdraw from you. Then you end up feeling so starved of their affection, you'll do anything to get it back. *Anything.* You do more and more to try to please them. I can see it so clearly now. I couldn't back then."

What she's describing sounds like pure mental torment. I'm not sure if she's telling me as a defense or just an anecdote, or maybe a stern warning: be careful who you fall for.

She doesn't need to tell me that.

"What happened in Portsmouth, Rachel? Were you there?"

She nods. "We were living in Shepherd's Bush at the time. God, we've lived all over. Clara was two and we were in this poky one-bedroom flat. There was nowhere for her to run about and I lived in fear of her getting onto the balcony and . . ." She shudders at the thought, as do I. "Anyway, money was tight. Joseph hadn't started ruling the world yet—it was always just around the corner. But it was coming up to my birthday and because, back in those days, he still used to be nice sometimes, he suggested a trip to the seaside—to Portsmouth. Well, Marcus was living in Fareham back then, about ten miles from Portsmouth, working in a bar and getting up to God knows what, so I thought it was the best idea ever. Chips on the pier and a chance to see my baby brother. What I didn't realize was that Joseph didn't give a stuff about my birthday—he'd arranged to rob a pub down there with Marcus. So we go down, check in to a B&B, but when it gets to the evening, he tells me point-blank that he and Marcus have got some 'business' they need to take care of and he's got to go out. So that was my twenty-third birthday—sitting in this crummy B&B that wasn't even near the sea, with a cranky toddler and just a bag of chips between us for dinner."

"Quit with the violins, Rachel. Naomi didn't make it to twenty-three. Abby only made it to eighteen."

A slap of red across both cheeks. "I know that, Cat. I probably know more about them than you do. Did you know Naomi was learning Mandarin, or that Abby led a campaign to save a local playground?"

"Are you trying to show me you care? Because there's really no need, I'm sure you do. It doesn't change a thing, though."

She takes a long, appraising look at me, as if she's only just realized that I'm a police officer, not a priest. That I'm not hearing her confession, I'm committing it to memory, making a record of it. While she's looking for absolution, I'm just looking for a way to spin things to make sure she gets the maximum possible sentence. The realization sets in her jaw and stiffens her shoulders.

Thankfully she keeps talking.

"You know, when I look back now, those last few hours in that crummy B&B were the last time I ever felt . . ." She pauses, struggling for the word. " 'Happy' wouldn't be the right word, because I was furious, but I felt sort of content, safe. That all changed when Joseph came back hours later, his bomber jacket all covered in blood. I said, *What the hell happened?*' and he said something had gone badly wrong and we needed to get out of Portsmouth straightaway."

"So he told you about robbing the pub?"

She laughs. It's loud, but there's no energy behind it. "Don't be ridiculous, of course he didn't. You're talking about *Joseph*, of course he had to lie. He had to make things sound grander than they were. No, he tells me that the real reason we'd come down here is because he and Marcus were part of some consortium involved in the shipping of coke from Costa Rica into the UK, via Portsmouth Docks." She shrugs. "He sounded convincing. He said it was supposed to be the making of him—enough money to set up his own luxury car business and no more market-stall shopping for me. Oh yeah, it was all for me and Clara. He used to pretend that, back then." Her voice is getting hoarse. She takes another sip of water. "But the deal went wrong, he says. There was some sort of bust-up and he ended up stabbing one of the other dealers—self-defense, *of course*. So we have to leave now. The other people in the consortium, they're going to come after him, come after *all of us*. But he says we can't go back to London straightaway because they might know where to find us, so he's going to drive us to this little caravan park on the Kent Downs, near where he grew up. We'll be safe there, he reckons, for a few weeks, while he sorts out a new place back in London. And so that's what we did. We lay low, the four of us—me, Joseph, Marcus, and Clara. Joseph and Marcus would go off occasionally, but me and Clara never left the site. There was no TV, no internet on our phones back then, no contact with the outside world. Of course, now I know he was trying to keep me away from the news about Abby. That's what it was all about." She shakes her head, marveling at Joseph's arrogance, *her* ignorance.

"How long were you there?"

"Two, three weeks. Then Joseph says that the flat he was trying to get had fallen through and we had to go back to Shepherd's Bush as we'd run out of money. I was out of my mind. I said we should go to my mum and dad's in Uxbridge—we were still speaking back then—but he says that's putting them in danger too, and the best thing to do is go home and be on our guard. So that's what we did. But I never felt safe, even after we moved."

The locks, bolts, and latches. "That's what all the security's for?"

Her eyes are on the floor. "He's evil. Pure evil. He had me believing that these people—these *completely made-up people*—could find us at any time. That they could harm Clara. He said they'd harmed other people's kids before and they'd never stop looking for us. That revenge was everything in their world, so we could never relax. It was like being in witness protection except there was no protection, only Joseph. But he wasn't protecting me, he was tormenting me, I just didn't realize. He used to say people were following him. Or, when we were out, he'd claim someone had been looking at us funny. Keeping me terrified kept me small, you see. It kept me reliant on him. And it rubbed off on Clara. I stifled her growing up, I was so overprotective. I barely even let her use social media until . . . well, until I found out that my life had been one big lie."

Her voice is really cracking now. I refill her water and she looks at me fondly, like it's the greatest act of kindness she's ever been shown.

"How did you find out?"

"A complete and utter fluke . . ." She pauses, head tilting. "Although is anything ever a fluke? Don't you think life sometimes conspires to right certain wrongs? I do. Clara usually works on Thursday nights, see, but because it was my birthday, she'd got the night off and we were having takeaway in front of the telly. I'd made her watch some rom-com, which really wasn't her thing, and the deal was she got to see *Crimewatch*—she's mad about that sort of show. Anyway, Abby Slater's fifteenth anniversary appeal was first up. I wasn't really paying attention at first but the word 'Portsmouth' always jumps out, so the minute I heard that, I started watching. And then when they said the 15th of June 2002 . . . my birthday . . ." She stops, calling up the memory, taking a moment to massage the center of her forehead. "Well, I got out of the chair and I went upstairs and I threw up every last thing in my stomach. I mean, what were the chances? Joseph covered in blood the same night a girl is murdered less than a mile from where we were staying?"

"And you didn't confront Joseph?"

A tiny, mirthless laugh. "Like I said, funny how life conspires. I think if he'd been home that night, I probably would have done. I think I might have actually killed him. But he was gone somewhere. Off on one of his 'work trips.' And then, by the time he got back, I'd had time to think about the implications."

"Marcus?"

"Marcus." She thumps the pit of her stomach. "I knew, right here in my gut, that *he* wouldn't have hurt that girl, but I knew he'd been with Joseph. I couldn't ignore that."

"So did you confront Marcus?"

She nods. "Eventually, not straightaway. If I was going to accuse him of being involved in something so . . . so awful, I had to be completely sure I was right."

Me hounding Dad about his alibi for the night Maryanne died.
The look on his face.
The scar tissue that still remains, red, raw, and ripe for picking.

"So I started reading everything I could on the Abby Slater case, try-ing to find something that would convince me once and for all that it was Joseph behind it, but there wasn't anything conclusive. They didn't have solid leads. I tried keeping an open mind too—the police seemed sure that her boyfriend had done it, so I held onto that. I spent ages searching for information on other attacks in Portsmouth that night, anything to do with drug dealers, men admitted to hospitals with stab wounds, that sort of thing. And I knew that just because I couldn't find anything, didn't mean it didn't happen. I mean, drug dealers—real criminals—don't just walk into emergency like the rest of us."

She's clinging to that ownership. The right to still belong to "Us" instead of "Them." I fight the urge to ask her what she thinks a "real" criminal is. Is it a gangster with a gold tooth, maybe? A souped-up BMW and an attack dog on a leash? Or is it just anyone who thinks the law doesn't apply to them? Like willowy blond housewives who pluck the hair from dead girls' heads.

And focus.

"In the end, I confronted Marcus because I was driving myself mad. He didn't even try to deny it. I think he was relieved to be able to talk about it. Joseph had written it off like it was nothing, just a minor incident, not worth going over."

"So what did Marcus say happened?"

"Basically, the two of them were robbing that pub and when Abby came down, Joseph killed her because she saw his face. Marcus didn't do anything, but he wasn't wearing gloves, Joseph was—so Joseph always threatened that Marcus would be the one who went down, as his prints must have been somewhere."

The sheer pointlessness of it boots me in the stomach. "If Joseph had left her alone, he'd have got twelve months max. It really wasn't worth killing for. She was only eighteen."

"Marcus reckons he did it for fun. He tormented me for fun too. That's what me and Marcus fell out about, not money—the fact he'd stood by and watched me live in fear of this so-called 'consortium' for years, knowing there was no such thing, knowing I was completely safe, in that sense, anyway. I was so angry I thought about report-ing them both, I swear I did, but . . . he's got Danny, he turned his life around after what happened." A tiny flicker of pride shores her up, despite everything. "That's what all the charity stuff is about—atonement for Abby Slater's death."

"And what was going to see Lydia Coe about?"

She hesitates. "I don't expect you to understand, but I'd spent fifteen years waiting for a knock at the door, for 'those people' to have found us. Now that I knew it was all lies, I couldn't spend another day not knowing how life was going to pan out. I needed peace—I *deserved* some peace. I needed to know what Abby's case being back in the spotlight meant for Marcus. Obviously, I couldn't just waltz into Portsmouth police station and ask them how they were getting on, so after reading up on her, I engineered a meeting with Abby's mum. I'm not proud of it. I talked myself out of it half a dozen times. But she seemed the type of woman who'd be all over their investigation—and she was. She was the one who told me they had prints on file. Well, when I heard that . . ." Her stare is challenging, provocative. "Marcus is a good man, Cat. At least he tried to be. And he's family—you always protect family."

You do. I did.

"Even if that meant protecting Joseph? You let him get away with murder."

"Oh, I was determined Joseph would pay one way or the other. And I told him that too, although I never told him why or what I knew." A smile laced with venom. "His confusion—it was brilliant. It was retribution. He'd made me live my life in fear of something vague and terrifying, and now he was getting a tiny taste of the same. I just never thought he was so *weak* that he'd go running to the police saying I was threatening him." She thinks again. "But then it wasn't weakness, I suppose. It was a way of getting back control. That's what Joseph lives for—control."

I'm leaning in now, so close I can smell her; stale cigarette smoke and three-day-old hair. "So what was the endgame, Rachel? How were you going to make him pay?"

"I didn't know. I didn't have an endgame. I just liked knowing I had one up on him, and I'll be honest, once the initial shock had worn off, I was relieved that I could breathe for the first time in fifteen years. I could ease up on Clara too, give her more freedom. Don't get me wrong, I was in a fresh kind of hell knowing what Joseph had done to that girl, but at least I wasn't scared anymore." Her eyes are on the ceiling briefly, lost in the memory of the few months' "peace" she had before life screwed her over once more. "And then Marcus calls that Saturday night, hysterical, inconsolable. He said there'd been an accident—a girl from the party had banged her head and she was dead. I thought he meant at their house at first, like she'd fallen over drunk or something, but then . . ." She gives a long, low sigh. "Then he told me."

"You should have told him to call the police."

Her eyes flare. "Should I? It all was Kirstie's fault anyway, giving her those drugs. Not content with screwing my husband, she'd now got my brother involved in all this. No way. Joseph and Kirstie were to blame for everything that had gone wrong in Marcus's life. It wasn't fair."

"It's her fault, y'know. Oh yeah, t'is . . . OK, maybe s'not her fault but she shouldn't have done that, should she? He's my *husband . . . fucking bitch."*

She'd been railing at Kirstie, not Naomi.

"I told Marcus to stay put and wait for me. Joseph was already fast asleep on the sofa and I knew he'd taken a Tammie, which meant he'd be out for ages, so I left. I was going to walk at first. I thought it was less risky than driving. But then I needed to hurry and I knew the backstreets well—well enough to avoid the cameras. By the time I got there, Marcus was talking about confessing, saying it was self-defense, an accident. I had to slap him, make him see sense, remind him that there was every chance his prints were at the scene of Abby Slater's murder. I told him, '*This* was an accident, and *you* didn't touch Abby, and yet you could end up in prison for both.'"

Do I tell her it wasn't an accident? Do I pop her sad, deluded bubble? The place where bad things happen to Marcus and it's always Somebody Else to blame?

I might . . . once she's told me everything.

"Eventually, he calmed down a bit," she carries on. "So we wiped the place down—we weren't taking any chances, even if he was wearing gloves—and then we . . . well, we talked, I suppose. We'd hardly spoken since I found out about Portsmouth, other than to keep up appearances."

"And you were due a catch-up. How nice. You should have checked the fridge, Rachel—there might have been a bottle of wine you could have cracked open."

It's crass and it's catty and if Steele's listening, I'm on the naughty step for a week. But, seriously? *"We wiped the place down and then we talked."* Like the Sunday lunch clear-up, but oops, mind the dead girl.

"What else were we going to do?" she cries, wounded. "We couldn't bring her back, and we needed to work out what to do."

"And whose idea was it to frame Joseph?"

"Whose idea?" she whispers to herself, hopelessly. "It wasn't like that. It wasn't a light-bulb moment. It just happened. I was ranting about Kirstie, how she was tucked up in bed like some poorly little princess, while me and Marcus were dealing with the fallout from her shit. And then Marcus, out of nowhere—just like the worst thing possible had happened so he might as well get everything off his chest—says that he thinks Danny is Joseph's. Joseph had been hinting at it for ages, apparently, but after I started looking after Danny, it got worse. Joseph started taunting Marcus that he was paying me to look after *his* child. Well, when I heard that, I just . . . I *hated* him." She slaps the table hard. "I hated him and I hated him and I hated him. What with all the lies he'd told me, what he'd done to Abby Slater, and now *this*. It honestly felt like my body couldn't contain all the anger. Like if I didn't hurt him somehow—if I didn't *finish* him—it would finish me."

The non–police officer in me wants to ask, *"Didn't you ever think about killing him?"* Because, let's be honest, if you can cover up someone else's crime, you can sure as shit cover up your own.

The police officer says, "Hate isn't a defense, Rachel. What you did wasn't fair on Naomi, on her family."

Her face sours. "But I'll tell you what is fair—Joseph being punished for *something*. I couldn't shop him for Abby or else he'd take Marcus down too, but this was a chance to watch him squirm. And if we managed to pull it off, much, much more. God, he had to be punished for *something*—don't you understand that?"

I nod to keep her talking, but also because on some fucked-up, way-down spiritual level, I do understand.

"Marcus wasn't convinced at first. He didn't think it could be done without us leaving the house and coming back later, and there's no way either of us could face that. Once we walked out that door, that was it. But I told him not to panic, we could work with what we had."

"Which was what?"

Her voice takes on a tone, somewhere between bland and borderline gossipy, like she's relaying a vaguely interesting tale she once heard, not something she produced and starred in.

"There was a pair of Joseph's gloves in my car. They'd been there for ages—months. I don't think he even realized. So I crept out to the car to get those, and while I was there I thought I'd check the boot. Joseph had been driving my car while his was at Shelby's, and I knew he'd been to the driving range a few times and, well, there it was—a bag of stuff: a bottle of water, a towel, a packet of tees and this stupid woolly hat he wears for winter golf. I couldn't really see properly in the dark, but I brought it inside and under the kitchen light you could see there were hairs trapped in the hat. We could use them."

On her body. In her bed.

"But then Marcus pointed out that if the police weren't looking at Joseph in the first place—and why would you be—none of those things would help anyway. You'd only test his hair, search our house, find the glove, if something pointed you toward him."

"The gift box?"

A nod. "I had this box of stuff, little mementos from times when Joseph was nice to me." There's actually a yearning in her voice, a wish for just one last time. "Poems he'd written, ticket stubs for places we'd been, birthday cards, and a few old gift tags. Marcus got a silver box from somewhere—it was fairly standard, not hard to match—and he planted it in Naomi's drawer the next evening." I open my mouth. "He knew the alarm. *He's* the one who trudged in on a weekend to let the alarm fitters in. Kirstie forgot about that, yeah? Doesn't surprise me. She's always taken him for granted."

"And planting Naomi's hair?" I say, driving my nails into my palms under the table. The fact that they took one hair from her head feels like the worst kind of robbery—a violation. "How did you know Joseph's car would be outside Marc Shelby's house?"

"I didn't. But he'd fixed my car a few years ago and I'd picked it up from there, so I thought it was worth a shot—and it was, it paid off." An almost dreamy smile. "It felt like the stars were aligning. This was meant to happen. Joseph was meant to be punished."

I fix her with my fiercest *don't-lie-to-me* stare. "So Clara? Did you tell her to say she'd seen Joseph with Naomi?"

She out-fierces me. "No, I didn't. I've no idea why she lied, but she knew nothing about what we'd done. I didn't tell her *anything*. I wouldn't drag my child into all this."

For the very first time since I met this curious changeling of a woman, I think I believe her, entirely and without question.

Which is probably a good time to finish.

As we walk back to her cell, I say, "You do realize it's not going to be straightforward, linking Joseph to Abby. There's only yours and Marcus's word for it, and your word won't count for much now, not after this."

She sits down on the bed and gives me one last dizzying flash of those dove-gray eyes. "Our words might not count for much, but Joseph's bomber jacket will. I was supposed to get rid of it, you see. One day at the caravan, when Joseph and Marcus had gone off somewhere, I was supposed to set fire to it in the back field." She lowers herself down, staring straight up at the ceiling. "But I've always been wary of fires, and even back then I was wary of Joseph. I think I always knew I might need an ace up my sleeve someday." She turns to me, her face the picture of serenity. "It's at my parents' place in Uxbridge—stuffed in a bag, in a crate, at the back of the loft they never use. It's all yours now. There's nothing to protect Marcus from anymore."

Rachel Madden. In many ways the perfect ballerina.

Fragile on the outside, rock solid at her core.

33

Naomi's photo comes down a respectful few days later. Abby Slater's, on the other hand, never goes up. *"Not our patch, not our problem"* is rumored to be Chief Superintendent Blake's stock response, although he also sees no problem with MIT4 taking the credit for bringing Abby's killers to justice.

And yes—*killers*, plural. For, as predictable as death, taxes, and Parnell falling off the health wagon, Joseph Madden doesn't go down without a showy, wrathful fight. The robbery was Marcus's idea, apparently. It was Marcus who brought the knife. Marcus who stabbed Abby. And it was Joseph, of course, who tried to help—frantically stemming Abby's wound with his bomber jacket until Marcus threatened to stab him too.

And he's never forgiven himself for leaving her to die.

She's in his dreams every night.

He can still smell the blood.

DI Martin Pike of the Hampshire Major Crime Unit tries to reassure us that he didn't come down in the last shower. "This ain't my first rodeo," he claims on his first visit to Steele HQ. "Don't worry, folks, I sniff bullshit at ten paces."

Unfortunately, there's a difference between sniffing it and *proving* it, and as I warned Rachel Madden, it's not going to be straightforward sorting out who Abby's killer was and who was the "mere" accomplice, not with Madden fighting back for all he's worth.

Although, he doesn't have Lucas Stein onside anymore. Nor his cash cow, Sadie Paulson. You don't make a living providing PR advice on sticky situations without knowing a thing or two about the best time to desert a sinking ship, and while charges still need to be decided on and sentences are a far-off worry, it's fair to say that both Joseph's and Marcus's ships have well and truly sunk, and will stay sunk for the next couple of decades, with any luck.

Lydia Coe sends me a thank-you note; an unnecessarily sweet gesture that has me weeping silently in the ladies with my fist pressed to my mouth, even though I'm generally not a big weeper and I'm not even sure what I'm being thanked for.

"You took an interest," she says, later, on the phone. "Even if we were both duped by Rachel Madden, she told *you* the truth eventually. She gave *you* the piece of evidence that will nail those bastards."

I tell her she should be thanking Alana Lockhart, really. If it hadn't been so important to Alana for me to have lots of recent photos of Naomi—to get to know her as a person as well as a "case"—I might have never realized, or it would have taken a lot longer to realize, that Naomi's hairs must have been planted, and then the chain reaction might never have been set in motion. Abby's murder may have remained unsolved.

Lydia says she will thank Alana Lockhart.

I know it's a promise she'll definitely keep.

About a week later, by request, I meet up with Clara Madden. It's a bright November day, clear and crisp with not a cloud in the sky, Christmas on the horizon but the swivel-eyed panic still at bay.

We're standing in a kids' playground where she's pushing Danny, her cousin or could-be half brother, way too high on a rubber-tire swing. She knows it's making me nervous, which only makes her push him harder. This might be how Joseph started out—reveling in watching other people squirm.

"Oh, chill out, he likes it," she says, and to be fair he's shouting, "*Me higher! Me higher!*" "Do you know how good it is to hear someone actually laugh? All Auntie Kirst does is cry and call Uncle Marcus a psycho."

I make a grab for the swing chains, convinced Danny's going to fly off and not entirely convinced that's not what Clara's aiming for. Danny scowls at me for ruining his fun and then he's off, scampering in the direction of a playhouse without a care in the world or a clue about how tough his life's going to be as the son of a killer.

Clara's clued-up, though. Her eyes are sharp and cautious, her stare a great big "*fuck off*" to the world. It's only been a week and she's already become quite the hot property, all kinds of media vying for her story once all the legal stuff's been done. I can see it now:

Wife Who Framed Husband—DAUGHTER TELLS ALL!

"You're not seriously thinking about it?" I ask, with more than a hint of warning. "You'll have no control over how they portray you. You'll regret it, I promise."

"Can you regret £10,000?" *Oh, to be seventeen again.* "It's one less student loan I'd have to take out. Oh yeah, I'm definitely still starting my degree, even if I go away. You can do it by distance learning, I've read up on it." She makes a tiny, shrill noise, an attempt at a laugh. "And anyway, law and criminology—where better to study than in prison?"

I doubt she's going to prison. My guess is a suspended sentence. But I'm not about to tell her that; she deserves to sweat a bit at least.

"Hey, is it true that you can't send Christmas presents to prison? That sucks, because I wanted to send a few gifts—to Mum, not to Dad. Dad slagged off every present I ever gave him. Even the cute little things I made at school. I drew him a Father's Day card once—just this stupid stick drawing of him playing golf. Do you know what he said to me—and I was only eight at the time? *'Other fathers get actual golf clubs, all I get is this piece of shit.'*"

Jesus. I think of Danny's three-letter words proudly displayed on the Connors' fridge. I think of my nephew, Finn, making cakes that taste like bricks but score a ten. I think of Parnell's lovely boys—champions of the field, scholars of the highest order, at least in their doting father's biased eyes.

And then I think of a little girl finding her Father's Day card screwed up in the bin.

Joseph Madden deserves a life sentence just for that, if you ask me.

"So why did you want to see me?" I cast a glance toward Danny, because Clara doesn't seem to be bothering. "Apart from to ask if you can send Christmas presents—and no, you can't, by the way."

She sits on the swing, swaying gently from side to side. "I've been thinking about court, about my defense. I wanted to ask your opinion on something."

"That's really for your solicitor, Clara. For one, I'm not qualified, and two—"

"My solicitor's useless," she cuts in. "Seriously, I'd be better off representing myself. And two, yeah, *I know*—you're the one prosecuting me, so you're hardly likely to help. But I also know you feel sorry for me. I'm good at reading people, you see. Just like my dad."

She's wrong, actually. I don't feel sorry for her. I don't feel sorry for anyone, myself included, who tries to obstruct or derail a murder investigation. But I do feel empathy. *So* much empathy. I know what growing up feeling scared can do to an adult psyche. You'll do anything—and I mean, anything—to get to a position where you feel safe.

"Go on then, ask me," I say. I won't answer but I'm intrigued.

"OK. Do you think love or hate is a stronger mitigating factor?"

I frown. "I think that sounds like a thesis, Clara. Or a philosophical conundrum. What exactly are you asking me?"

"Will it make me look spiteful if I say I lied to get back at him for being a shit dad? Will they view that badly?"

"Hate isn't a defense, Clara—I told your mum the exact same thing. But if it's the truth, then that's what you tell them. They'll view lying a lot worse, trust me."

She considers this. "It's partly true, but I do want to tell the whole truth. I just don't like the thought of Mum knowing."

"Knowing what?"

"That I thought she did it. I thought *she* killed Naomi. I was protecting her, see—that's why I lied."

Another quick glance to Danny. "What made you think that?"

"That morning she was really drunk . . . she'd been reading stuff about Naomi online, about how she'd been born sick and survived a car accident, and she just kind of lost it. I listened at the door and I heard her on the phone to Uncle Marcus saying that she couldn't cope, she couldn't live with the guilt, stuff like that. I asked Uncle Marcus straight out and he said Mum was just being Mum—beating herself up, feeling guilty because she was married to Dad, she should have known, blah blah. But I *knew* it was more than that. I told you, I'm good at sussing people and I could hear it in her voice. I could see it on her face after that too." She stops the swing, swelling with teacher's pet pride. "And I was almost right, wasn't I?"

"But your dad had been charged by then," I say, slightly confused. "There was no need to protect her."

"That bloke, Dad's solicitor—Luke or something? When he called to tell us about Dad, he was giving it all this blag about 'inconsistencies' and 'losing the battle, not the war.'"

"So you hammered another nail in the coffin."

A proud, defiant nod. "And I'd have hammered ten more in if it meant losing Dad, not Mum."

"I'd probably leave that bit out of your testimony if I were you, Clara. Get punished for what you did, not what you were prepared to do."

But she's not listening anymore. She's looking past me, squinting into the distance. "Oh, this is getting beyond a joke now. Not another bloody one."

"Another what?" I twist around, following her line of sight.

"That guy watching us, the one leaning against his car. You wait, the cameras will be out in a minute. Fuck, it was bad enough them loitering outside the house, but now they're following me."

But there are no cameras. She hasn't been followed. The man's here for me, not for Clara.

Frank Hickey.

I reach into my bag and pull out a fiver. I'm shaking as I hand it over but she doesn't seem to notice. "Look, that café over there does a mean hot chocolate. Why don't you and Danny go and get one while I get rid of this idiot? It'll only take a minute. Don't worry, I'll sort him."

She gives a little shrug and saunters off to fetch Danny. I march toward the gate where Frank's now standing, as relaxed and immovable as a centuries-old oak.

Conscious that Clara may be watching, I stop myself from getting right up in his face and stay two paces back. "What is this, Frank? Following me home, giving me money, sending me flowers, and now this?" I laugh scornfully. "Is it a late-life crisis, or something? Because if it is, it's fucking creepy—and I can promise you, you're not my type."

He smiles. I shiver. "Ah, don't flatter yourself, Catrina. I've turned down better than you, you can be mighty sure of that. Now get in the car."

I look at the car, then back to him, trying to process what he's just said. "What do you mean, 'get in the car'? What planet are you on? Of course I'm not getting in your fucking car."

I turn to go. Even slightly screw-loose Clara Madden is better company than this.

"Get in the car or you'll regret it, Catrina. Seeing as we go way back, I'll give you that bit of advice for free."

I take two steps forward. His face is so close, it's just a blur of broken veins.

"And what are you going to do? Put me in the hospital like my dad and my brother? There'd only be Jacqui, then, and you'd have the full set."

"Sure, what would I do that for? I can do way more damage to you with a quick phone call to your boss or over a pint with that lovely fella of yours. How is he, by the way? Did he have a great old time back yonder?" A sad face. "Ah, but sure, weddings, they're never easy when there's someone missing. Maryanne'd have loved a good wedding, I'd say. She loved a party, I remember that well enough."

Somewhere in the playground a child starts crying, wailing out in torment over a dropped biscuit or a cut knee. I could cry for the time when life used to be that uncomplicated. It feels like all I've ever done is fear and hustle and lie.

And I'm tired of it. So tired.

"What do you want?" I say, resigned to the fact that it might just be easier to give it to him.

He frowns, then shrugs. "Ah fine, we'll do this on the street, then. I thought a spin out somewhere would be more civilized, maybe a bit of lunch if we spotted somewhere nice. But fine, have it your way." He takes a step back from me. "I need information on a man called Damian Malik—previous convictions, known associates. A current address would make you my new favorite person, and given what I know about you, darling, that's not a bad person to be."

"You are actually serious." I'm somehow laughing through the horror.

"Oh, I'm serious, yeah. Deadly serious. But sure, I don't expect you to say yes right now. God, even I'm not that unreasonable." He chucks me under the chin, gives my shoulder a soft playful punch. "Of course you're going to need to think about it, I understand that. You're going to need time to think about how much your fella and your career mean to you, but when you've made up your mind, give me a call."

"Fuck you."

There's only one call I'll be making. I'm scrolling for his number as I walk back through the gate.

"Don't leave it too long, though," Frank calls after me. "I'll see you again soon. Real soon."

I'm back by the playground when he answers. Clara and Danny are still in the queue.

"Hey, sweetheart." There's music in the background.

"Dad, I need you to listen. Can you go somewhere quiet?"

He laughs at something, says, *"You all right, mate?"* to someone. "It's not a great time, angel. I've got two staff off sick and there's a massive lunch crowd in."

"Frank Hickey just blackmailed me."

He says nothing, but within seconds the sound of footsteps echo in an empty hall.

"What the fuck did you just say?"

"Frank—he wants me to pass him information or he'll make sure my boss and Aiden find out about . . . well, you know what about."

"Information on who, for Christ's sake?"

Rage soars through me as I give Danny a little wave. "You're missing the point here, Dad. *Who* doesn't matter. What he's asking me to do does. He wants me in his pocket and I can't be. I just can't . . ." I swallow hard. "Look, you said the other night that protection is what dads do—so protect me, OK? I need you to make this go away."

A hopeless pause. "OK, look, I'll have a chat with him, I'll tell him this isn't on. I'm sorry, sweetheart. I honestly thought he was messing with you. I didn't think—"

"Shut up, Dad, I don't think you're quite understanding me. No chats. No messing.

"I need you to make him go away."

Acknowledgments

So if you've got this far, it probably means you've finished the book—and so my first thanks is to you, wonderful reader. Life is so hectic these days; it truly blows me away that you've taken the time to immerse yourself in Cat's world. She's grateful. I'm grateful.

Being asked to write a second novel is both the greatest privilege and a scary prospect. An army of people kept me sane, laughing, supported, and regularly replenished with tea and wine throughout the process.

Eugenie Furniss, your faith in my writing and your patience with my *I was just thinking . . .* emails is hugely appreciated. The same goes for the fabulous Katherine Armstrong and Emily Griffin, editor extraordinaires at Bonnier Zaffre and Harper US, respectively. For every insight, every cheerlead, every push in the right direction—thank you. You made this book better.

Huge fist bumps also go to Jennie Rothwell, Clare Kelly, Felice McKeown, Nico Poilblanc, Alex Allden (LOVE my covers!), Ruth Logan, Ilaria Tarasconi, and Kate Parkin. Another round going to Heather Drucker, Katie O'Callaghan, Amber Oliver, Caitlin Hurst, Jen Murphy, and Kim Racon.

To Alan Howarth, who continues to field my (many) procedural questions. Authenticity is so important to me—thanks so much for keeping me on the straight and narrow, time and time again.

One of the best rewards for writing a crime novel is the amount of new friends you make. The crime writing community really is the most supportive in the world and I could fill another book listing the numerous people who've provided advice, made me laugh, bought me a drink, or politely told me to get a grip when I needed it. You all know who you are. You all rock.

To old friends—thanks for continuing to listen to me bang on about imaginary people. That's you, Helen Powell, Cat Sweatman, Carla Todd, Fiona Kirrane (cousin, and therefore the first friend I ever made), and many, many others. Friendship is everything.

As, of course, is family. Mum, Dad, Garry, Alison (plus the awesome foursome!), and the entire Frear family. I couldn't have been born or married into a more supportive bunch. I hope you're proud of me. I'm so proud of you all for a myriad of different reasons.

And to Neil, who else, who lived with the horror of a "Writer on Deadline" with grace, patience, and humor. There are no words, baby. OK, maybe just three—love you forever.

READ ON

FOR AN EXCERPT FROM

SHED NO TEARS

BY CAZ FREAR.

AVAILABLE IN HARDCOVER,

E-BOOK, AND AUDIO

IN DECEMBER 2020 FROM

HARPERCOLLINS PUBLISHERS.

When the first blow lands, it's almost a relief.

A karmic debt paid.

A manoeuvre, at least.

She battles at first, of course; kicking and clawing and begging and bargaining all the way from the cold kitchen floor, where they first bounce her skull, through the hall, across the driveway, and into the boot of the waiting car.

A car she knows well.

A car she's sat in maybe ten, fifteen times – always the passenger, but always firmly in the driving seat. Queen of the world. Top of her game.

Tonight, the gun glinting in the midnight light signals that, for her, the game's now up.

She had this coming. She accepts this. She knows she created this whole sordid mess herself. And yet she'd prayed that they'd stop at a beating – because a beating she could take; bruises fade, fractures heal, even the worst scars can be covered with make-up. And God knows she'd taken enough beatings in her life and still lived to tell the sorry tale.

She won't live to tell this one.

She doesn't deserve to. Even by her standards, this one was cruel.

And she is sorry. She knows they don't believe her, but maybe if there's a God upstairs, He will.

Maybe next time around, she'll come back as a better person.

This time around, there was only ever one way this mess was going to end.

1

We'd prayed for rain for weeks. Or maybe it was months? It's hard to remember a time when griping about the heat wasn't a national fetish. When days weren't spent sighing and swearing and spraying yourself with Magicool, and nights weren't spent tossing and turning, wondering if sleep was now a pleasure of the past.

And then there were the arguments. *Christ, there were the arguments.* Civil war over air-con settings. Men carping at women, jealous at the sight of us drifting around in lightweight dresses while they sweated buckets in the same suits that saw them through winter. Old versus young: Steele and Parnell crowing that *this* was no way near as brutal as the summer of '76, when the rivers ran dry and the tarmac melted, and using your hosepipe was a crime routinely punishable by social death.

Of course, we – 'The Young' – stated long and loud that, as *we* weren't even twinkles in our parents' eyes in 1976, 'The Olds' point was entirely moot and, frankly, not helping. *You can only play the hand you're dealt,* we'd endlessly argue, and we'd been dealt *this* cursed summer. The paralysing heatwave of 2018. We were living through it, sweltering through it, surviving it – *just* – with the aid of desk fans and ice-packs, and the constant yet sagging hope that it might one day rain again on England's green and pleasant lands.

And now here, on a grassy dirt track, running alongside a remote field in the molten heart of Cambridgeshire, our prayers are finally answered.

'Fucking rain,' I say, scowling at the sky. All our sweaty, parched misery forgotten in an instant.

'You don't get rain in London, no?' DC Ed Navarro – our crime scene guide, *and boy, does he resent it* – is smirking in a way that makes me want to to flick his pale, waxy face, like a boiled potato with a goatee. 'Because seriously, you're looking a little frazzled there. Do you want to go and sit in the car for a bit?'

'Why, is it acid rain?' I bite back.

He rummages in his pocket, retrieves an opened packet of Polo mints. 'Not that I'm aware.'

'Well then, I reckon I'll survive.'

'Ah, come on, Kinsella, this is bliss,' DS Luigi Parnell raises his hands, letting the rain patter off his palms: pennies from heaven. 'It's not even that heavy. And remember what the boss says, "It's good for the garden."'

'I don't have a garden.' I lift my plastic file of crime scene photos above my head, a macabre makeshift umbrella. 'I do have frizzy hair, though.'

Immediately, I regret saying it. Holly Kemp doesn't have to worry about frizzy hair anymore. Or the fact that her cheap cotton work shirt is getting more see-through by the minute.

Holly Kemp hasn't worried about anything in a long time. 'So, yeah, this is where we found her.'

Navarro nods towards the deep ditch at the side of the track, then leads us to a gap in the covering hedgerow, presumably cut away to give Forensics easier access. Just yesterday, a crime scene tent would have stood here, preserving evidence and privacy for the army of white suits going about their crucial black art, but we're quick to get them down these days. It's not 'resource efficient' – to use the term *à la mode* – to keep them under guard for a second longer than necessary.

Money. Budgets. PR. Stats.

The four horsemen of modern policing.

'Well, of course, *we* didn't find her. Lady Persephone III did – that's a dog, before you ask.' Navarro pops two mints in his mouth, not bothering to offer them round. 'Honestly, I don't know what planet some people are on. What's wrong with Patch or Rex or Rover all of a sudden? Proper dog names.'

'I like it,' I say, just to agitate him. In my defence, we're under strict instructions from DCI Kate Steele to play the agitators today. The standard 'up from London' arseholes who think the rest of the force are an *el cheapo* version of the mighty Metropolitan Police. Steele's hoping a blast of belligerence might put a rocket up their backsides.

'So, any danger of a post-mortem?' asks Parnell, casualness spliced with scorn. 'It's been over forty-eight hours – *well* over forty-eight hours.'

Navarro widens his stance. 'Hey, hang on a minute. It's been over forty-eight hours since we contacted you about the locket, but we only got her back to the morgue last night. You can't rush forensic archaeology – it's a fiddly business.' Parnell pulls an unimpressed face. I opt for *majorly* unimpressed. 'And, look, we've got a backlog, OK? Our pathologist's run off her feet.'

I fold my arms, giving up on my file-cum-umbrella. 'Whereas ours just sits around sharpening her rib-cutters, waiting for a body to roll in.'

'Bodies, actually.' Navarro looks more sad than defensive. 'There was a pile-up on the M11 a few hours before this. Two cars, five teens, four dead – two from the same family.' He raps a knuckle on his forehead, knocking out the thought. 'I knew one of them – not well, mind. I used to coach him at Soccertots. But I'd see him in the pub sometimes, acting the big guy, getting the pints in. They grow up so quickly and then bang . . . gone.'

And then *bang*, the 'up from London' arseholes feel like bona fide lousy arseholes. We offer quick but sincere condolences, Parnell catching my eye to convey that Operation Arsehole is being immediately stood down.

I bring the conversation back to safer ground – the dog with the dumb name. 'You know, we really should be shaking Lady Persephone III by the paw. She did what we failed to do. She found Holly Kemp. Poor soul's been missing for years.'

Nearly six years, to be precise. Six birthdays. Six Christmases. Six anniversaries spent wondering if this is the year you get 'closure' – that storybook notion they talk about on TV.

'Er, *we*? What your lot failed to do, you mean?' Navarro can't stop himself – the pissing contest between forces is as predictable as it is puerile.

I let the dig pass, mainly because I feel heartsick about Navarro's ex-Soccertot, but partly because it's fair enough. This is on the mighty Metropolitan Police, no question.

'So, how in God's name did she lie here for so long, unnoticed?' I ask of no one in particular.

'All this,' says Navarro, drawing a semi-circle on the drizzly horizon, 'belonged to an old farmer, Johnny Heath. He died a while back, but he'd let the field lie fallow for years; more to do with bad health than good crop rotation, I think.' The reference is lost on me but I nod sagely. 'His son lived in America. Didn't even bother coming home for the funeral, so they say. And he never got round to selling the place when the old man passed because he was making a king's ransom on Wall Street and didn't need the money. So after Johnny died in 2015, the whole estate just sat here. The son paid a local to cut the grass a few times a year, but that's about it.'

'And the tractor wouldn't go anywhere near the ditch,' says Parnell.

I pull a photo from my file. 'And even if it did, she was well hidden.'

Twigs and branches and bracken and logs. It was the logs that were the chilling detail; the logs that proved this wasn't some tramp looking for shelter who'd died of hypothermia in the night, or a binge-drinking casualty, staggering home across the field. The logs were placed on top of the body, no doubt about it. They'd covered it, cocooned it, made sure that a grieving family didn't get closure any time soon.

'So, to finish the story . . .' Another mint in his mouth. 'The son's luck ran out in the US of A a few months back – redundancy, he says – and lo and behold, suddenly he's Old MacDonald. Over here like a shot, talking about organic farming, setting up a shop for fools with deep pockets.'

'So is the dog his?' I ask, giving up on Lady P's full title.

Navarro nods. 'She'd been scrabbling around the same spot for days. He didn't think much of it until a few days ago when she wouldn't come when he called. And then when she wouldn't respond to the whistle either, he knew something was up. The whistle always works, apparently.'

'A whistle? So she's a puppy. He's training her.' Parnell fancies himself as a bit of an expert, having walked his kids' dog twice in the last year.

'Got it in one.' Navarro wipes the rain from his face with his shirt-cuff. I'm past the point of caring about my halo of fuzz. 'He thought he'd mastered it, too. But, you know, give a dog a bone . . .'

Not *a* bone, it turned out. *Bones.* One hundred and eighty-nine of them which, according to my GCSE B in biology, means seventeen are missing. Lost to foxes or scattered by starlings, we'll assume. An almost entire female skeleton left to decompose in a ditch, miles from where she was last seen.

6 Valentine Street, Clapham, South-West London.

Six years ago, the press dubbed it the ultimate 'House of Horrors'. More recently, an estate agent called it a *stunning, characterful mid-terrace home, with a newly extended kitchen and a real oasis of a garden. Seldom do properties such as this make it onto the market.*

Which is true, if a little sugar-coated.

'So why here?' I ask in place of *Why do we do this job when it's all dead Soccertots and bones and standing in fields in the bloody rain?* 'And I don't mean, why not Valentine Street? I mean, why here – Caxton? Why this spot, specifically?' I do a slow 360, taking in our surroundings, which to be frank aren't much. Apart from the three of us standing here like peasants in a Constable painting and a rusted tractor in the next field, there isn't a single point of interest as far as the eye can see. Just a vista of bleached land and a temporarily sullen sky. 'OK, sure, you're off the beaten track a bit, but you aren't exactly sheltered. Even at night, you'd have to feel slightly exposed.'

Navarro shrugs, as though the methods of a killer aren't his to judge.

'Ah, come on, Ed, help us out,' says Parnell, all chummy now. 'You know the area. If you were going to bury a body, would you really do it here?'

'Maybe. We aren't exactly spoiled for choice around these parts. There aren't too many wooded areas, and The Fens, just north of here, is a completely flat landscape.' The smirk is back. 'Do you know what my guv'nor says? He says FENS stands for Fucking Enormous Nothing.'

I smile. Parnell laughs generously. 'Fucking Enormous Nothing, that's a good one.' He's back to business quickly. 'But seriously though, there must be somewhere safer than this? Somewhere more secluded?'

He considers it this time, rubbing at his goatee. 'Me, personally, if I'd killed my sister-in-law – which would be an honour and a privilege, I tell you – I wouldn't bury her at all. I'd weigh her down and throw her in the Ramsey Forty Foot – it's a big drainage dyke about twenty miles north of here.'

Dragging him from his daydream, I say, 'You know, you both keep using the word "buried", but she wasn't buried, not really.'

'Well, she wasn't under the ground, no,' Navarro concedes. 'But he did a thorough job of hiding her.'

I step closer to the ditch, peering at the space left, the nothingness. 'Hiding is different to burying, though. Hiding's quicker. This person was in a rush.'

'Hold on, "this person"?' Navarro's eyes narrow, piqued and suspicious. 'Look, I know we're skirting around this until we get dental records back, but this *is* Holly Kemp. The locket, it's engraved "HOLLY". It's got photos of her parents inside. It's *hers*. And she's one of his, isn't she?' We say nothing. 'Well, my guv'nor spoke to the DCI who headed things up back then and they're still convinced. He admitted it, right?'

He, Christopher Dean Masters, did indeed admit it. And then he denied it, then admitted it, denied it, then admitted it, and so on and so on, until the original investigators stopped giving him the airtime and the warped satisfaction.

'Believe me, I wish she was one of ours. Our clear-up stats aren't great at the moment.' This should rattle my cage but depressingly, I hear him. Too many cases and a major drop in the number of murder detectives makes you clinical – brain-fried and clinical. 'I thought she *was* one of ours, actually. The minute the call came through, I said, *That's Ania Duvac, that is.* I had a £10 bet with Jonesy, our exhibits officer.' He clocks my expression and his face flushes – boiled potato to raw beetroot with one misjudged admission. 'Look, it wasn't my idea. Jonesy'd bet on two flies crawling up a wall. He's got a real problem, that one. Anyway, I knew I'd lost my tenner the second I got here. Ania only went missing last September, see. You'd expect to see a bit of muscle tissue still attached.' He smiles to himself. 'The lads think it's weird, but I've got a real interest in this type of stuff. I know a thing or two about decay.'

Fair play to him. It's more than I do. You see, policing is generally a conveyer belt of firsts. You walk your first beat, make your first arrest. You brace yourself for the first time you shatter a heart with the words, 'I'm so sorry to have to tell you . . .' And despite what the old guard say – the know-it-alls, the thirty-year-service brigade, the retired peacocks propping up the bar at so-and-so's leaving do, regaling anyone naïve enough to listen about the time they met the Kray twins – you never *ever* stop learning. There's no finite number of head-fucks this job can serve up. Today, for example, despite it being four years since I first joined Murder, since I crouched over my very first corpse at my very first crime scene, *this* – Holly Kemp – is my first set of bones.

No blood. No wounds. No gag reflex smell.

No small but poignant detail to connect you to your victim.

I admit it. I'm finding it hard to connect with just bones. With a skeleton laid out like a science project, or a cheap thrill on the ghost train. Holly Kemp's photo is all I've got to gauge the essence of who she was. The 'famous' photo. The classic news feed fodder. The one of the bottle-job blonde with the duck-pout lips. Tan straight out of a bottle. Teeth straight out of a Colgate advert.

And 'tits straight out of a catalogue', according to Navarro. They found implants among the bones. Silicone's a hardy bugger to break down.

As are rubber soles.

'Did I see something about footwear?' I rifle through my file, looking for the relevant print-out.

'You did,' confirms Navarro. 'There was a trainer – pretty distinctive, actually. Possibly custom-made. A photo's been sent to her mates – they should be able to ID it, hopefully.' There's a spark in his eyes; morbid curiosity. 'Odd though, isn't it? The trainer.'

'Yeah. No. Maybe.' I let him read what he wants into my airy non-answer.

'Thing is,' he goes on, the mints click-clacking against his teeth, 'there were a few scraps of fabric too, sticky patches melded with the bone. Jeans, probably, as they found copper rivets – you know, the tiny bits of metal you get on the pockets?'

I shoot a fidgety glance towards Parnell, who quickly looks away.

Navarro spots it. 'Oh, I know what you're thinking. You're thinking the same as me. I mean, it's hard *not* to think it.' He pauses, and for a moment there's only the dripping-tap trickle of the weakening summer rain and the soft, tidal rush of motorway, God knows how far away. 'The others . . . they were naked.'

The others.

Strangers in life, bound together in death.

Names on a Wikipedia page.

The Victims.

ALSO BY CAZ FREAR

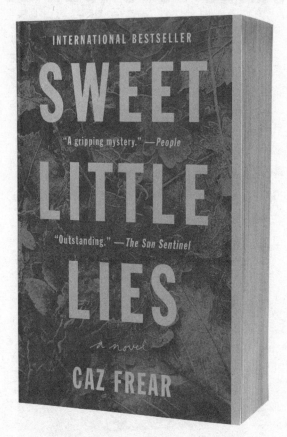

SWEET LITTLE LIES
A NOVEL

"A dark and smart page-turner." —*The New York Times*

Your father is a liar. But is he a killer?
Even liars tell the truth . . . sometimes.

In this gripping debut procedural, a young London policewoman must probe dark secrets buried deep in her own family's past to solve a murder and a long-ago disappearance.

COMING DECEMBER 2020

SHED NO TEARS
A NOVEL

Four victims. Killer caught. Case closed . . . or is it?

Acclaimed and internationally bestselling crime novelist Caz Frear returns with her third superb novel featuring Cat Kinsella, a cop "on par with Susie Steiner's and Tana French's female detectives" (*Kirkus Reviews*)